Sing Me the Anger

Edward Keebler

ISBN: 0615988067
ISBN-13: 9780615988061

Dedication

This book is dedicated to my dad, without whom this book
would not have been possible. His life is a testimony to
humanity's ability to choose change and become
a better person in the process.

Acknowledgements

Constanze Rayhrer, M.D., F.A.C.S., muse, friend, encourager, critic and ardent supporter.
Patrick Spreco, El Cajon Chief-of-Police (Ret.), friend, fact checker and encourager.
Gus Iwasiuk, M.D., F.A.C.S., mentor at-large and generous guide to anyone in need.
George Berger, a great neighbor, supporter and friend.
Robin Sweet-Ransom, author, Monzungo friend and fellow traveler.
Brian Owen, mortician.
Cathy Coburn, author, guide and friend.
Judith Gill, patient editor, teacher and friend.
Jordon Trimas, photographer, artist and generous friend.
Chris Braden, marketing professional and long-term friend.
Bill Hayes, generous heart, nurturing soul and great friend.

Table of Contents

Part I

Fanfare

Goddess, sing me the anger of Achilles, Peleus's son, that fatal anger that brought countless sorrows on the Greeks and sent many valiant souls of warriors down to Hades, leaving their bodies as spoil for dogs and carrion birds: for thus was the will of Zeus brought to fulfilment.

Homer's Iliad

I

The Old Bridge

With arms outstretched, clutching a wine bottle in one hand and a scribbled note in the other, Justin Manus taunts an oncoming pair of headlights passing on the highway below. Barefoot and dressed in tattered jeans and a faded T-shirt, he precariously leans over the bridge's edge, standing on the slippery middle rung of an antiquated pedestrian fence. He sways in the darkness, aimlessly peering into the damp summer night; only the slick top rail pressing against his knees prevents him plummeting over the bridge's edge. The structure is an older and seldom used two-lane overpass that diverts local traffic from the new highway that passes below. Southern California maps identify it as the Virgil Overpass. Locals simply refer to it as "The Virgil" or the "Old Bridge."

In his mind Justin entertains himself with the comedic notion of being a matador, challenging the approaching automobile on the underpass as though it were a fearless beast. The oblivious driver disappears and passes beneath him, completely unaware of being animated as a raging bull. Turning quickly, Justin sees the red taillights reemerge under him on the other side of the bridge and speed away. The mere rotating motion is more than his inebriated equilibrium can bear. With his mind swirling, he staggers to a sitting position on the bridge's narrow walkway. Slightly slumped over and backed against the railing, his legs extend the length of the sidewalk while his bare feet dangle over the edge. He is nearly content to sleep on the bridge. If it weren't for the constant drizzle, which has now saturated his jeans and formed droplets on his face, he would likely be in a drunken slumber. His thoughts fade in and out of better times, a time when he felt loved and life made more sense.

"Hello Mr. Toes!" Justin, in a conscious moment, feels almost surprised to see the appendages attached to his feet. In his current state of mind they have become a group of friends. With an additional degree of clarity, he may have been able to provide each with a name. For now, he refers to the collective entourage as simply, "Mr. Toes."

"Do you remember the good ol' days Mr. Toes? I had a good career, a beautiful wife who loved me and money in the bank."

Mr. Toes wiggles with enthusiasm, apparently eager to hear the story. "I guess I messed that up pretty good. Do you remember how we met in college? She was so pretty and I was so stupid. We were sitting in the school cafeteria with a bunch of my friends and it all started over a piece of apple pie."

"Do you remember the pie Mr. Toes? Wiggle if you're listening." All of Justin's digits wiggle with excitement and he celebrates by taking another swig from his bottle of bargain wine. "My roommate was going to toss away a perfectly good piece of pie but did he give it to me? No, I had to earn it, didn't I?" Justin glances at his toes as they nod in agreement with him.

"On a dare, with all the guys at the table watching, I had to walk across the cafeteria to the table with all the pretty girls and whisper in her ear, 'You're so hot!' and then kiss her. At first they wanted me to kiss her on the lips but I wouldn't do it so they agreed that a kiss on the cheek would be okay. When I stood, they started drumming on the table, soft at first, then louder as I got nearer to her. By the time I got to where the girls were sitting, I think everyone in the place knew what was going on except for the pretty blonde and her friends. I paused once but when the guys started yelling at me, I knew it was either do or die. I turned toward them, gave them a quick salute and went into action. Do you remember what happened then, Mr. Toes? I put my hands on the pretty blonde's shoulders and when she looked up, I bent down to whisper in her ear. She leaned her head into me but by the time I gave her the message, the whole room went silent. My whisper thundered like I was making an announcement over a loudspeaker." Justin laughs at the memory.

"Everyone in the cafeteria heard the message! After I kissed her on the cheek, all the people started cheering and the pretty blonde turned several shades of red. A couple of the other girls responded with wide-eyed gasps and dropped jaws. Another one put her hands over her mouth. I was embarrassed at first, but when I realized everyone was rooting for me, I raised my hands over my head like a victorious boxer. What do you think of that Mr. Toes?" Justin holds up his bottle as a salute to his wiggly friends and slushes down another drink.

"I didn't see the pretty blonde for a couple of weeks after that. I looked for her, but not for reasons you might think. I wasn't so eager to see her again as I was to avoid seeing her at all. Then, just about the time I was beginning to feel at ease, the pretty blonde got me back. She waited until I was sitting in the cafeteria with a group of my friends and she snuck up on me from behind. Before I knew what was going on, she planted a big red kiss on my cheek. And while she was still leaning over and holding onto my shoulders, she announced to the table and onlookers, 'You're so pretty!' I didn't even have to look around to see who it was. I just nodded and smiled as everyone applauded her. It didn't take long after that for us to start talking, which led to a first date and several dates after that. Within a few weeks we were a couple, and by the middle of the following year, we became engaged. What do you think of that Mr. Toes? It all started with a piece of forbidden fruit and a kiss on the cheek."

Justin's disposition suddenly becomes more somber as he continues to tell the story to his new group of friends. "Today would have been our twelfth anniversary, Mr. Toes. I miss her a lot. I shouldn't have made work such a high priority, but I convinced myself I was doing it for her. Remember the cubical I began my career in? I practically lived in that drab, grey 'office coffin' for the first few years! But I was good at my job, worked hard and moved up the ranks... remember that? I was in an executive office after only a decade with the company. I think everybody liked me except for my wife. We had a nice house, drove nice cars–even had a good retirement account! She wanted kids but I wanted the financial security first. Then, when the economy tanked and I lost my job... it had all been for nothing. I'd made her put off having kids until we could afford it, and then we were broke. She resented me for that. I can't give that back to her… I can't fix it Mr. Toes."

Oblivious to the car parked at the end of the bridge, Justin continues with his walk down memory lane until the driver of the older model Japanese car moves his vehicle onto the bridge and stops immediately in front of him. The driver rolls his tinted window down and calls out, "Hey, are you okay?"

Justin's head takes a shaky path upward and after a brief attempt to focus he responds, "I'm a great matador!"

"You look wet. Can I give you a ride somewhere?" offers the voice from inside the car. After a brief silence and lack of response, the driver exits the vehicle, walks over to Justin and offers him his hand.

"Do you need help?"

"Sure, why not? You can be my new best friend. I can even teach you to become a great matador."

"I gave up wanting to be a great matador a long time ago," Travis Kilborn explains as he helps lift and guide Justin into the front passenger seat. By all appearances, Kilborn is the collective image of the middle or high school math teacher everyone can visualize in their mind but can't remember by name. He's a dozen years older than Justin, wearing slim-fit khaki pants with a short sleeve dress shirt. His reddish brown hair is cut short to the scalp and his narrow head is accented with eyeglasses too large for his face. Justin is too drunk to notice the drops of blood on his new acquaintance's shoes.

"Comfortable?" asks Kilborn while examining his new passenger who is now seated with his wine bottle between his legs and the car door still open. There's no response as Justin Manus rests his head on the dashboard and seems to have faded from consciousness. Kilborn takes a lingering look at the slumbering man, and then surveys his immediate surroundings. It's nearly 3:00 a.m. and there hasn't been traffic on the old bridge since his arrival several minutes ago. Although an occasional car passes underneath on the highway below, their driver's view is obscured from any activity on the murky overpass. It's a damp, dark, and near soundless night.

Kilborn opens the rear passenger door and reaches under a blanket to grab a pair of handcuffs and cable ties that are hidden from view. He cautiously approaches the open passenger door where the younger and stronger Justin Manus remains in a drunken stupor. Kilborn leans in, wraps one loop of the handcuff around his left wrist, and then gently squeezes it tight without alerting his victim. Realizing he can't overpower Justin, Kilborn nudges him, "Hey buddy, this old car doesn't have an airbag on that side so let me make sure you're safe."

"Safe? Okay, I'll be safe. Sure, safe is good," his nearly incoherent passenger mumbles.

With Justin's cooperation, Kilborn pulls his left arm into position behind him and joins it with the other wrist, successfully securing both of his hands behind his back. As the cuffs click into place, Kilborn asks with false compassion, "You doing okay? Comfortable?"

"'M' okay," slurs Justin.

"Let me get your feet and we'll be ready to go."

There's no resistance as Kilborn slips the thick plastic cable ties around his ankles and knees, completing the bondage of his athletically built passenger. With his victim secure, Kilborn gropes Justin's muscular physique in search of a weapon and his wallet. Finding no weapons, he removes his wallet, dumps the few remaining drops of wine from his bottle and tosses the empty container in the back seat. After closing the passenger door, he carefully scans his surroundings before entering the car and beginning his trek back toward a barn located in a more rural part of the county.

A different Kilborn emerges as he takes his place behind the wheel and drives away from the old bridge. His look is more intense. He seems invigorated by the successful capture of Justin Manus. His steely blue eyes display a surge of life, not as one experiencing joy but satisfying a hunger. Reaching across the front seat, Kilborn roughly pushes his drunken passenger's limp head away from the glove box as he gains possession of a voice recorder. Looking down at it, he carefully sets it to saved position five and leaves the device on pause until he needs it.

Kilborn drives in silence for a moment then violently shakes his hapless victim, "Wake up, dumb ass!"

"What! What? What are we doing?" Justin partially emerges from the fog of his intoxication.

"I'm going to introduce you to my pets." Kilborn's voice holds menace.

"You have pets? Cool. I like pets."

"You may not like these as much as you may think." Kilborn smirks. "What you're going to get is chopped up into pieces and eaten by three hogs and my dog, Stink."

"You named your dog 'Stink'?" Justin lets out a robust laugh. "How cool is that? I wanted a dog with a cool name… a dog named Stink, but my wife has a little foo-foo dog named Princh—Princh—Princess."

An increasingly agitated Kilborn pulls out a knife and places the tip near the end of Justin's nose. "Do you think this is a big joke? Do you have any idea how many people I've killed and how I killed them? I gutted one and another was—"

"No sir… no sir," Justin interrupts. He shakes his head in a wide and exaggerated side-to-side motion, "I don't want to appear ungrateful."

"Ungrateful? Ungrateful?" Astonished, Kilborn slams on the breaks and skids to a halt on the side of the isolated rural road. "You do understand that I plan on cutting your body up into small pieces, don't you?"

"You keep saying that… but I'm starting to think you're not that sincere." Justin attempts to refrain from laughing.

A moment of silence ensues as Kilborn studies his passenger. Justin is slightly more coherent but his eyes are closed and he's resting his head on the side window.

Clearly agitated, Kilborn inquires, "What exactly were you doing on the bridge tonight?"

With a slight slur to his speech and a languid smile, Justin explains, "I wash gonna get drunk n' hang myself… but I couldn't find any rope. I was already drunk so I thought I'd jump off the bridge."

"You know that bridge is only fifteen feet high and has a grassy median below it, right?"

"I forgot… I didn't remember about it until I got there."

"If you jumped, you'd be lucky to break a leg. I suppose after the failed attempt you may manage to hobble onto the road and get in front of a car to finish yourself off. With broken bones, you wouldn't be very nimble so you probably wouldn't have succeeded at that either. As drunk as you are, you'd have a better chance of dying of exposure. Let me guess," Kilborn continues in a sarcastic tone. "Your life is like the lyrics to a country song; the wife left you and your dog died so you have to kill yourself to end your miserable existence."

"Yeah, something like that," responds Justin with a smile and low volume chuckle. "We were married for ten years… she left me for a wannabe rock star who still lived with his mother."

"Why is that funny?"

"A friend told me that a week after my ex and the wannabe rock star were married, my ex walked into the bathroom while her new hubby was in the shower. His long, rock-star hair was draped across the chair! He was just a little bald guy who dressed up like a rock star! But… just sayin'… that makes me pretty pathetic if she chose him over me."

"I agree you're pathetic but it has nothing to do with your wife. Chances are she left you because of her issues as much as your own. What did you do to him for sleeping with your wife, or to her for betraying you?"

"What did I do? What could I do? I left."

Enraged, Kilborn screams, "You just left? Don't you have any fight in you?"

"I had nothing left to fight for. She didn't love me. I lost my job. Our house was in foreclosure and I couldn't find work…"

Justin drifts into a semiconscious swirl of flashbacks as his mind skims over the recent years of his life. He was a faithful and loving husband but after six years and three promotions, he seemed to stop listening. She consistently complained that he always had time for work related causes. Justin seemed to have an extra minute for practically anyone at the office but not for her. The final straw was when their social circles became dominated by company events and activities with other employees…

"Hey! Dumb ass… wake up! People get divorced every day."

"Is not… it's not just the divorce." Justin slurs as he attempts to regain his thought process. "It's the betrayal… I was betrayed by my wife, my employer, my friends… even the legal system failed me."

In a surprisingly calm reversal of his rage, Kilborn cocks his head to the side, nudging his helpless passenger. "Go on. I want to hear this."

"I was never perfect... no, no, no... but I was a good provider and I was really good at my job. Maybe I worked too many hours and left her alone too much, but I did it with her in mind."

Kilborn's voice is filled with accusation and doubt. "Is that when you started sleeping with the boss's secretary, or got caught skimming company funds?"

Justin, with his chin touching his chest and head swaying, says, "You're not paying attention, Mr. Three Pigs. I said I was a good husband and I was really good at my job. I was one of the youngest persons... youngest people... earliest guy, ever to be promoted... to an executive position. Companies all over the country tried to recruit me but I stayed loyal... I was committed to those who hired me. I was fired after the economy slumped... the CEO's son wanted my job. The company was losing money so they wanted me to go bye-bye. I tried to fight back but without income, my only option was to file a complaint with a perfunctory government agency... I like the word perfunctory. You should say it with me... perfunctory. Say it in a deep voice... perfunctory. You feel your tongue bounce around in your mouth? Cool, huh?"

Kilborn studies his victim for a moment, then nudges him, "As an executive, you must have had some type of severance package and unemployment—"

"No, no, no..." Justin interrupts. "During the good times they agreed to a really nice benefit package so they could keep good people. But during the downsizing, they intimidated most into resigning or accepting a settlement. Those who refused were eliminated for manufactured causes... totally made up. I stood my ground on principle but lost my severance package and unemployment benefits in the process. Many of us did."

With a scowl on his face and eyebrows tightly perched over the bridge of his nose, Kilborn speaks in a tone of disgust. "Did you fight it? Did you do anything to retaliate... anything?"

"I stood loyal to my convictions... I did what I thought was right. I was naïve. I was great at my job but once I was targeted everything...

everything became subject to criticism, formal review, disciplinary actions and eventual dismissal. I didn't realize... afterwards the company saved tens of millions of dollars and only had to fight off a handful of complaints and lawsuits in the process. The worst part..." Justin slumps.

"The worst part is what, you idiot? Wake up!" Kilborn demands.

"Oh, yeah... yeah... the worst part was trying to find another job. After you're terminated, the longer you're unemployed, the worse it is. Even the companies that had once tried to recruit me didn't want me. My credit bombed. Everyone turned me down. I couldn't even get a low paying job unless I lied. They said my credit was bad and that I was overqualified. I was losing my house and willing to do anything, yet I was too much of a risk."

"Is that when your wife left you?" Kilborn sounds more curious and less condemning.

"Our savings were gone and credit card balances started climbing. We were in a financial death spiral... being without money was something she had never experienced before. After a year of unemployment, she met some guy on a girl's night out. He presented himself as a rock star but he was just some guy who lived at home with his mother and played in a minimally talented garage band."

"So, she left you and moved in with him?"

"No, that's the hard part. She had money stashed away from an inheritance so she kept the house and he moved in with her. I didn't even know she was having an affair until I came home from a job interview in Florida. She'd had the locks on the house changed, and served me with a copy of a Restraining Order. I tried to get into the house to get some clothes. She called the police and had me arrested for domestic violence. Today would have been our twelfth anniversary."

"And you did what?" Kilborn yelled in renewed rage. "You did nothing!"

Slightly more coherent but with eyes dripping of exhaustion, Justin turns, looking into the soulless eyes of his captor, "It wasn't all her fault. I know now, how much she resented me for not paying attention to her needs. I built the life I wanted. I convinced her it was the life we both needed... and it all fell apart. She invested nearly all of her healthy child-bearing years with me and I took that away from her. I feel like I deserve the hell I've created for myself. I wrote a poem. That's what I did... I wrote a poem."

"You wrote a poem?" Kilborn sneers. "Is that what you have crumpled up in your hand?"

With little resistance, Kilborn retrieves the moist and wadded paper from Justin's loose grasp. Without asking for approval, he unfolds and straightens the document, pulling it over the edge of the steering wheel to smooth out the wrinkles. He glances at Justin with a snide expression, then, nearly annoyed with himself for making the effort, he reads it aloud with surprising skill.

"Sing to me.
Let your voice drape my tormented soul
and quench the fire that smolders in my wounded heart.
Play me a melody that entices my upward glance;
tempt me to look up from my place of desolation.
Fill my mind with intrigue; bait me with a promise of hope.
Sing to me.
I will succumb to the delusion of peace
grasping the air for each fading note.
Hope, even false hope, is a distraction from my despair.

I can no longer tell day from night.
Time swirls around my head,
a confusing rhyme and offbeat melody.
I want to end the confusion,
bury myself in the comforting arms of solitude and quiet.
But there is none.
My unrested mind is captured in a whirlpool of despair,
dragging me deeper and deeper into its grasp.
In the distance I hear the alluring note of sweet death,
no longer a fearsome, gruesome adversary
but an ally and liberator.

Come to me sweet song of death.
Sit in my lap, rest your head on my shoul-
der and sing your song to me.
Bring me peace.

Her dance is slow and deliberately seductive;
her embrace has captured the essence of my will.
I am snared in a rhythmic motion I know will be my last.
As I release my hand from the edge of despair,
I feel myself falling.
All the voices of confusion
and the myriad notes of distractions fade
as I firmly hold to her.
She is beautiful.
Her succulent red lips grow closer,
enticing me to make the final surge and meet my lips with hers.
This is my final kiss, the final act of my will.
She is death; beautiful death."

"That's it?" Irritated, Kilborn scans the final lines of the poem for a second time. "You want to give up and die? All I have is an eighty-one-year-old grandmother who lives in an apartment in Torrance. Her neighbors are all Koreans and because of the onset of Alzheimer's, half the time she can't tell me apart from them. I lost my wife, kids, retirement and my career. But I fought back and made the bastards pay for what they did. I didn't sit around drinking, writing poetry and feeling sorry for myself."

"I'm not like you," Justin murmurs in a soft voice.

"You're damn right, you're not like me you spineless bitch! I've killed four people in three years and have never even been a suspect. I correct myself, you'll increase the total to five."

"So, if you've already killed everyone who wronged you, why do you want to kill again?"

Kilborn pauses for a reflective moment. "Because I've found I like it now." He exits the vehicle and hurries to the passenger side. Opening the door he grabs Justin by the legs and yanks his limp body from the seat. As Justin lies shoulder down in the damp soil, Kilborn reaches into the car to retrieve his voice recorder and sets it on the edge of the seat of the opened passenger door.

Activating the play button, Kilborn kneels beside his helpless victim and harshly slaps him across the face. "Let me see your eyes!" he orders.

"I'm too tired now, dude. Can't you do this while I sleep?"

"Beg for your life!" Kilborn demands as he places his knife at Justin's throat.

"Beg for what? Dude, what is that smell? Are we in Chino?"

Furious, Kilborn screams into Justin's face, "Haven't you listened to a thing I've told you? Do you not have a thread of intelligence and pride?"

Kilborn continues his lecture for another minute and at the end of his tirade, he looks for terror in the eyes of his new victim but hears only his light snoring. He rolls Justin onto his stomach, raises his knife, and then plunges it into the hardened plastic cable ties, freeing his legs. In another quick motion he removes the handcuffs, darts back to the car and drives away. Kilborn watches the motionless man from his rearview mirror as he speeds into the darkness, muttering to himself, "We're a lot more alike than you know, my drunken friend."

The cold and discomfort of the muddy soil causes Justin to stir. A few hours have passed and the first signs of dawn are beginning to appear on the horizon. Still very groggy, he attempts to sit up but decides in favor of staying on his back a few more minutes. The light mist has stopped but the ground remains wet.

"Oh my god, where am I? Damn! Did I jump off that bridge?" Justin asks himself as he pats himself down, checking for broken bones. Cautiously, he opens one eye to survey his surroundings and seeing no bridge, he sits up and opens both eyes. There's a rural road, fences, and looking behind him, he sees two eyes staring back at him. "Moo!" is the cow's response to being discovered. Justin jerks a little in surprise at the volume of the cow's low. "I'm in Chino? How the hell did I get to Chino?"

II

Kilborn Rises

Three years earlier...

Travis Kilborn does not exist. He officially died a few years ago in a boating accident when the small fishing vessel he rented overturned in rough seas off the California coast. There was no claim for the payout of a life insurance policy, no suspicious circumstances and no criminal record. He had no family to speak of except for a grandmother who was experiencing the onset of Alzheimer's. Besides that, no one really cared. Had it not been for the boat's owner who reported his vessel missing, Kilborn could have dropped off the planet and aside from a few creditors, no one would have noticed.

His brush with death and the subsequent twenty-four hours adrift at sea that followed was a revelation of sorts for Kilborn. It was a catalyst in transforming the former middle school 'teacher of the year' into a new person. After he washed ashore he realized that his former life was virtually devoid of purpose and meaning. All the values he held to in his earlier days were simply eradicated by his divorce. The woman he loved betrayed him, his children forgot about him, the school district turned its back on him and the legal system utterly failed him. His life was shattered and lay in ruins, not so much from poor choices and bad decisions but from the destruction of his ideals.

Kilborn's life and personal principles were established with the mindset that marriage was sacred and every American was guaranteed certain civil rights and protections afforded by the Constitution and Bill of Rights. To his dismay, Kilborn discovered the fragility of his most intimate relationships and how easily his civil rights could be stolen from him by people with power and influence. The person that emerged from the sea was no longer the civic minded volunteer, loving family man and decorated educator; Kilborn had transformed into a monster, determined to make others pay a toll for the loss of his soul.

Kilborn wanted more than revenge. Revenge seemed too petty a word to describe what he wanted to extract from those who defiled him. Kilborn wanted to bring the individuals responsible for his anguish to the same place of utter despair and helplessness he experienced himself. In essence, Kilborn wanted to look into the eyes of his victims and devour the soul of their dying flesh. In the process, by recording their screams, he felt as though he was able to trap them in a state of eternal agony from which there was no escape. These recordings became the audible trophies of his success and his power over them.

Kilborn's first victim was as much an accident as it was by design. The court appointed psychologist that Kilborn was required to meet with during the onset of his divorce and subsequent custody issues was an Eastern European man by the name of Dr. Klaudios. His role in the process was to provide the court with psychological evaluations in order to determine the mental fitness of each parent. Dr. Klaudios appeared to be in his early sixties, was slightly shorter than the average man, and walked with a moderate hunch as though he was carrying a sack of apples on his shoulders. He was not a big man but his extra girth made him appear bigger than he was. His heavy, growling accent not only made him difficult to comprehend, but his soft voice made it nearly impossible to hear or decipher his words. Most often when he spoke to someone, his head was cocked to one side and at the end of his statement, he lifted his head in a pronounced gesture and looked at the listener as though he expected a response. It was an intimidating process that left the listener feeling inadequate and often stupid. It was exactly the effect he desired, not so much as a psychological ploy but to cover for his own inadequacies.

The appointment with Dr. Klaudios was a relatively simple process but his office was designed for utility without regard for ambience or comfort. There was no receptionist, or any staff for that matter, just an entry door into a small waiting area that felt like a holding cell. The near colorless room lacked visual stimulation or even so much as a few dated magazines. Pictures and photos were replaced by a security camera and small plaques with instructions as to how to fill out forms. Another set of instructions reminded one to wait until the light on the panel near the door changed from red to green before attempting entry. It had all the comfort of a human slaughter house.

Once inside, Dr. Klaudios seemed to avoid eye contact as his attention was almost exclusively focused on the completed forms in the client's hands. There was no need for him to display superficial concern or kindness toward his patients because there would be no therapy, and he would not have a need to merit one's return business or referrals. The county provided him with a steady stream of evaluations to complete, all of which were prepaid by the client. Few complained of his rude, coarse behavior, because his evaluation of them as parents and the ensuing custody issues of their children, lay in his hands. Any complaints made "after the fact" were easily dismissed as being made by disgruntled individuals whose test results did not conclude in their favor. County officials approved of Dr. Klaudios's work simply because the alternative was a pool of master degree level counselors who either lacked experience or competence.

The appointment was for two hours. The first ninety minutes involved a personality inventory test that Kilborn completed a few minutes early. Dr. Klaudios sat across the room behind his computer monitor, his unkempt bushy but balding head peering out every so often to check Kilborn's progress. The interior office was not as Spartan as the holding area he had just come from. Although lacking family photos, the room possessed a nautical motif, displaying several mounted fish and paintings of the sea. One personal photo, perhaps the only personal photo in the room, was of a beautiful forty-five-foot cabin cruiser with the name, *Bonhoeffer* on its stern. As a fishing enthusiast himself, Kilborn recognized the surroundings as being Marina del Rey.

With the written test completed, Dr. Klaudios arranged a series of shapes on a table. Holding a clipboard and stopwatch in hand, he displayed a picture while timing Kilborn's response in duplicating the same object. The results were carefully recorded and followed with a series of general knowledge questions that one might expect to hear on a television game show. With this, the testing was concluded and the data obtained was to be utilized to inform the court as to a person's worthiness as a parent. To Kilborn, the process was a sham. When a summation of the test results were released to the court, Kilborn was described by Dr. Klaudios as a man of average intelligence with a proclivity for violence. This report, along with the recommendation of the Guardian *ad Litem* (an attorney appointed to represent the children's best interest), was instrumental in the court's decision for custody. Add to the mix the manufactured child abuse charges conjured up by his estranged wife and her attorney, Richard Bantam, and it was all the court needed to grant full custody of the children to Kilborn's wife.

Kilborn fought the process for a year. He appealed the court's verdict; displaying letters from a noted psychologist that his personality inventory test results were all within normal ranges and there was nothing negative that could be substantiated from either the test results or his personal history that reflected anything but the model citizen he was. His academic achievements clearly displayed superior intelligence and the child abuse charges were all proven to be unfounded. By this time the children were living out of state, and no one was willing to budge on their decisions. He never saw his daughters again.

For nearly a year, Kilborn attempted to adjust to his new life. But on that fateful day, when he escaped from the sunken tomb and clawed his way out of the sea, he had determined to radically change his life or die in the process. Wearing only a life preserver and armed with a floating seat cushion, Kilborn successfully navigated the summer tides and currents to make his way back to shore. When his weakened limbs reached the beach in the early evening, he knew he had to act then or relegate himself to a life of despair. He needed a plan but had none. He couldn't return to his apartment or automobile, and had only the cash in his pocket to live on. The only thought that came to his mind was the photo in Dr. Klaudios's office, which proudly displayed his boat, *Bonhoeffer*.

Marina del Rey was not far from where Kilborn had come ashore. While resting, he discovered a broken piece of glass and was careful to cut away the name of the sunken vessel from the life preserver before destroying and discarding it. Aside from this act of deception, the first crime of his adult life occurred moments later when he discovered an unattended bike and rode away on it. Although the marina was only about six miles away, it felt more like three times that distance to Kilborn. He stopped to eat once and frequently to rest.

Finding Dr. Klaudios's boat and gaining access to the dock that Sunday evening was relatively easy. The real task was to get inside the boat in order to access the living quarters. On a hunch and out of desperation, Kilborn devised a plan to convince the teenage marina desk attendant that he was Dr. Klaudios. "Young man," said Kilborn with his head down and using his best impersonation of Dr. Klaudios's accent and voice, "I fell in the damn vater and I need my spare key..."

The very accommodating young man responds, "Yes sir. I just need your name, account number and to check your photo identification."

"Photo identification!" growls Kilborn. "If I had my key and identification I vouldn't need to come in here, vould I?" Utilizing Dr. Klaudios's mannerism, he snaps his head up after making the statement, immediately putting the young man on the defensive.

"That's just our—policy." The young man is wide eyed and almost stammering.

"You come vith me then!" Kilborn demands. "You dive into eighteen feet of vater and get my vallet and key for me...come on!"

"What is your name and berth number again?" asks the defeated young man.

"My name is Dr. Klaudios, berth number 716," states Kilborn as he jerks his head up and stares at the teen.

The young man disappears momentarily behind a wall, and then upon his return, slides the key onto the counter. Kilborn grabs the key and without expressing gratitude, turns to walk away. "Now open the security door for me so I can get on the dock!" he orders.

Only a few steps from the entrance, Kilborn hears the familiar buzz of a security gate unlocking, and only moments later he's onboard the *Bonhoeffer*. Before bothering to check any details of the boat's interior, Kilborn dives onto the nearest bed and instantly falls asleep.

The following morning Kilborn wakes up invigorated and possessing a sense of excitement for the first time in what seems like years. He feels powerful and in control of his life again. Oddly, he has done nothing but steal an unattended bicycle, bully his way past a teenage boy, and stow away on someone's boat. Although far from being notable crimes, the rejuvenated Kilborn is like an adolescent teen moving away from home for the first time. All the rules have changed and opportunities abound. Kilborn knows what he must do.

The following week Kilborn maintains a low profile, leaving the boat only once for the food and supplies he would need to carry out his plan. He remembers that Dr. Klaudios did not wear a wedding ring and displayed no pictures of family in his office. Kilborn is betting on the fact that Dr. Klaudios is single and lives alone. If his assumption is true, the boat is his true love and he cannot stay away from her long. Chances are the doctor will be at the docks to see his beloved *Bonhoeffer* by the upcoming holiday weekend.

By Thursday afternoon Kilborn has rearranged one of the storage holds on the large craft to provide himself with the perfect hiding place. Even if it were opened, Kilborn could expect to have a reasonable chance of avoiding discovery. All traces of his presence on the boat during the week were cleaned and now it comes down to waiting for Dr. Klaudios to arrive. The unsociable doctor is not likely to have contact with anyone at the marina office, therefore there is little chance his missing spare key will become an issue. As a precaution, Kilborn sleeps in the storage hold for the evening and wakes at dawn on Friday morning. He eats little, cleans up immediately, and then positions himself to be able to view anyone accessing the dock.

Kilborn's wait is brief as he observes a familiar, slightly hunched profile approaching the dock with a wheeled cooler in tow. He intensely scrutinizes the doctor's every move as he slowly trudges along the dock. As a precaution, Kilborn lingers in his sentry position for a few extra moments to insure the doctor is alone, and then quickly buries himself in the interior storage unit. Once onboard, Dr. Klaudios wastes little time getting underway and within a brief time, has the beautiful *Bonhoeffer* headed toward the open sea.

When the purr of the boat's engine comes to a rest ninety minutes later, Kilborn wakes from his unintended nap. He does not risk opening the hatch until it becomes obvious that the doctor is fully engrossed in fishing. Knowing he is within minutes of actions that will change his life forever, Kilborn continues to mutter to himself, "What is the plan?" He knows what he intended to do, knows what he wants to do but doesn't know if he can actually do it.

Can I kill a man? Am I able to plunge a knife into this man's heart and watch him die? Is there another way out of this without having to take a life?

Kilborn looks down, squeezing the objects which are now slightly shaking in his hands. In one hand is a small bait knife, the other a voice recorder. Both objects were found onboard the boat. The voice recorder was relatively new and seems to have only been slightly used, if at all. The knife is old and rusted.

Maybe I can scare him and force him to confess to being a fraud. Maybe that will work. Kilborn makes a last ditch effort to find justification not to go through with it. *But if I don't kill him, I still face years in jail for planning to commit murder. Even if a miracle happened and I was able to plea bargain to misdemeanor charges, I'd still have to return to my meaningless and torturous existence.* Finally, in a moment of stark reality, Kilborn concedes to what has always been a repulsive thought. He must kill Dr. Klaudios.

It's a mild day at sea as the *Bonhoeffer* bobs side-to-side with the motion of the waves. No other vessels are in view, only a few gulls diligently watching from above, hoping to be treated with an easy meal as a reward for their persistence. There are the normal creeks and groans every boat makes and then there's the muffled click as Kilborn gently pushes open the hatch to his hiding place. Stepping out of the storage unit, Kilborn freezes, waits, and intently listens. He hears the doctor's heavy steps on the rear deck where he expects the man to be. By this time he should have made all of his initial preparations and be only minutes away from sitting in his favorite chair; completely absorbed in fishing at the stern of the boat. Kilborn waits in the carpeted area within the hull interior and during a moment of silence, risks a quick peek around the corner. As Kilborn's head squirts out from behind the bulkhead, his view is immediately obscured by a wall of plaid as he inadvertently places his face within inches of the back of Dr. Klaudios's shirt.

Violently jerking his head back behind the small space separating him from his intended victim, he trembles while breathing through an open mouth in a desperate effort not to make a sound. Although the boat appears large from the exterior, inside there is little room to maneuver and now, no place to hide. If the doctor makes even a single step farther into the cabin, Kilborn will be discovered. With his back pasted to the thin veneer that separates the two men and his forehead beading in sweat, Kilborn concedes to himself he must kill the doctor, and soon. There is no other way out.

After several moments, feeling as though time had stopped, Kilborn hears the whine of a fishing reel and realizes the doctor is once again out on the deck. He cautiously peaks from behind the bulkhead to see his victim with his back turned. Kilborn is too anxious and too afraid to back down now. He nervously activates the voice recorder and sets it on the floor, maintaining an unrealistic and obscure hope that he can still force a confession. He steps into the open and cautiously walks toward the doctor's position at the stern.

Only a few feet away from his mark, Kilborn raises his arm and taking another step, begins the downward motion to plunge the knife into the middle of Dr. Klaudios's back. He intends to drive the blade deeply into his flesh and kill him quickly but his lack of experience and skill thwart the effort. His flimsy fishing knife was designed for slicing and gutting fish, not for making deep, penetrating and mortal wounds into human flesh. Kilborn thrusts the feeble knife into the doctor's back but achieves only shallow penetration as the frail tip deflects off of a rib. The impact of thin steel on the blunt and boney surface forces Kilborn's hand over the cutting edge of the blade, carving a gaping wound on the palm of his hand.

Dr. Klaudios screams in surprise and anguish, wheeling around to face his attacker. In the process, Kilborn is knocked backward into a sitting position on the deck, still holding onto his bloodied weapon.

In a desperate effort to fend off his attacker, the doctor grabs his deep sea fishing pole and whirls the loose line with the attached three-inch hook in a circular motion. Kilborn rises to his feet and lunges at the doctor, not perceiving the spinning hook to be a significant threat. To Kilborn's horror, the hook catches under his jaw and with a quick jerk on the line, the doctor begins to reel in the slack while swinging Kilborn from side to side.

Kilborn thrashes about on the deck, resembling a large fish that had just been hooked and landed onboard. Unable to free himself, Kilborn's agony grows with each second as the barbed hook works itself more deeply under his jawbone and into his mouth. He is pulled back and forth, side-to-side while attempting to hold the painful barb long enough to slice the line. Out of habit, the doctor tugs the line more tightly by leaning back and pulling the fishing rod toward him, drawing his catch closer. This proves to be a fatal error as the motion allows Kilborn the opportunity to spring to his feet and cut the fishing line with his knife. Falling to the deck with the large hook still firmly in his jaw, Kilborn latches on to the doctor's leg and slices into his left Achilles tendon. The detached tendon balls up in the doctor's upper calf, immediately slamming him into a prostrate position on the deck. Kilborn gropes along the surface of the stern and up to the mid-section of the helpless, screaming Dr. Klaudios. Placing his knee in his back, Kilborn encircles several lengths of the deep sea fishing rod's thick line around his waist. After removing his keys and wallet, he secures the doctor's life preserver, cutting away at his flesh with any move of resistance, and then rolls the chubby man off the open stern of the boat. With the doctor in the water, unable to climb out and clinging to the boat's outer deck, Kilborn retrieves the voice recorder and places it nearby.

The doctor howls in pain as much as fear. As an avid fisherman, he knows this part of the ocean as well as the deadly scent he is leaving in the water. His screams for mercy are not for release as much as to die quickly before the dorsal fins of sharks begin to appear around him.

The enraged Kilborn will have nothing to do with it. He yells back his accusations and obscenities to Dr. Klaudios, blaming him for the loss of his children and this being his fitting demise. The blood from the wounds of both men drip from the deck and into the sea as the first dorsal fin emerges only a short distance away.

"Kill me now!" begs Dr. Klaudios. "Please don't let me die like this!"

Kilborn chuckles, then responds, "Turns out you were right Dr. Klaudios. I suppose I do have a proclivity for violence after all."

Kilborn's heart has transformed and become icy cold. He takes the fishing rod with the line attached to the doctor and pulls him away from the stern, making it easier for the growing number of sharks to encircle him. Suddenly, Dr. Klaudios's screams take on a higher pitch but there's no evidence of a bite, only a bump. It's a shark's way of determining if an object is something it wants to bite into or eat. Kilborn can see three dorsal fins now. He watches from the rocking deck as they circle closer and faster. Another scream! The red cloud in the water makes it clear that the doctor has been hit. Continuous high-pitched screams radiate from the helpless hunk of human flesh as one of the saw-toothed creatures rips into his leg. The screams cease as the body is dragged underwater. By the time the doctor pops to the surface, he is out of breath and likely dead. Kilborn pulls the hunk of flesh closer to the boat, removes the life preserver and adjusts the fishing line from Dr. Klaudios's waist to his neck, and then continues to let the sharks finish their meal.

Kilborn watches for nearly thirty minutes as the creatures consume enough of the corpse so as to allow his line to go limp in the water. Whatever remains of Dr. Klaudios will be picked apart by smaller fish or left to decay at the bottom of the ocean.

Kilborn reaches for the voice recorder and erases the section after the doctor's screams cease. He sits in silence with the large fishing hook still protruding from his jaw, looking out to sea and laughing. "What a marvelous day!" he proclaims. The throbbing pain emanating from his mouth is nearly neutralized by the adrenaline rush of his struggle. As he reviews the event in his mind, his body begins to quiver with both fear and excitement. He knows that if things had not gone his way, he could have been the one on the other end of the fishing line. His brush with death, the ensuing fight and watching the doctor scream to his last breath… it was more than anything he could imagine. Kilborn lies face up on the deck, quivering in an ecstatic state over his accomplishment.

After cutting off the barbed tip and sliding out the shaft of the hook from his mouth, the resurrected Dr. Klaudios bandages his hand and washes down the deck. The ninety-minute trip back to the dock allows ample time for him to examine his new driver's license and familiarize himself with the details contained within his wallet. Once in port, the doctor cleans his boat, locates his new car and sets the GPS to the home position. He has the remainder of the day to sooth his wounds and when he wakes in the morning, he will be a new man. He will be Dr. Klaudios.

III

Two Detectives

Present day...

Mindless and near futile days pass into weeks; Justin Manus has nearly forgotten about his drunken episode on the bridge. The only reminders of his brush with death are the partially consumed wine bottles clinking together on the opposite end of an uneven table. A folded piece of cardboard placed under the uneven leg and used as a leveling device has become flat and worn. The table teeters with each shift of his weight, resulting in an annoying clink of glass. A stack of bills and unopened mail sit before him begging for attention but his dreadful bank balance nearly dissuades him from examining them. Only a single envelope appears to be different from the others. It lacks the bright colors of a late notice, the return address of a law firm or the threatening appearance of a collection agency. It's a statement from his retirement account; the only asset that survived his termination of employment and the scrutiny of his divorce. After examining the letter, Justin hurriedly calls the broker. An overly cheerful young woman answers the call and transfers him to another, more listless voice who places him on hold for several minutes. When the individual returns, Justin is quick to interject his inquiry before losing contact again, "Charles Anderson, please. He's no longer there? Will you connect me to the financial advisor who now handles my account?"

"Please hold," moans the voice on the line. A few minutes of generic music plays in the background, compounding the wait time and evolving into what feels like dog years. Eventually a young voice comes on the line and with his most reassuring salesperson's voice, "Hello, Mr. Manus? This is Mark Swansong, your financial advisor. How may I help you today?"

After a few pleasantries are exchanged, Justin gets to the heart of the matter. His request to cash out his account is rebuffed by a series of rehearsed replies, some of which are notably read from a cheat sheet. The advisor, determined to complete his litany of bullet points, only allows Justin brief moments to interrupt his sales pitch.

"Yes, I know I will have to pay a 10% penalty to the IRS but I need the money now."

"I know I have to report it as regular income."

"Yes, I'm aware that most Americans face retirement with a net worth of under $180,000... does that include divorced people who have thrown over half of that amount away to their lawyers?"

"If you have such a dynamic plan to offer now, why wasn't my account reallocated before I lost 30% of the value?"

"No, I do not want to roll the funds over into an interest only account... no, no, I just want..."

Exasperated now, Justin cuts into his advisor's string of product pitches and asserts, "Dude, just send me the money!"

His raised voice displays his determination as he finally obtains a degree of cooperation and disconnects from the call. It's not a lot of money but it's enough to buy some time, maybe a year or two. Justin realizes that even though he has yet to join the ranks of the middle aged, he may not ever be able to retire. Judging from the condition of the country's financial affairs, he assumes he may have to work well into his senior years.

Pulling into a parking space outside of the apartment complex is an unmarked police car. Inside sits two seasoned Orange County Detectives, a male and female; partners for only a few weeks. The female is a mixed-race, Black and Caucasian woman named Veronica. Only her mother addresses her as Veronica. Everyone else knows her as Roni, or if they want to be more formal, Detective Barnes. Barnes wears no makeup and pulls her thick, dark hair back into ponytail. Although her divorce was over a dozen years ago, she still considers most men to be a pain in the ass. She does date on occasion and enjoys a man's company on a social basis but doesn't make an effort to meet anyone. She's fit and attractive but her priorities are focused on dividing time between her twelve year-old daughter and her job.

Across the seat from Barnes sits Alex Emilio Rodriguez Fuentes from Miami, who with his Cuban accent, pronounces the name of the city "*Mijami.*" In his official capacity, he is Detective Fuentes. In his personal life, he rarely shortens his name. He is always, as he says with a colorful distinction and a sway of his head, "Alex Emilio Rodriguez Fuentes, *Mijami* born and raised, no, not for nothing." His proud family originates from Cuba, having come to America via a large raft which he often refers to as the Cuban Mayflower. Fuentes is slightly shorter than average but his petite size and choir boy face hide a tenacious fighter when challenged.

As Barnes turns off the automobile's engine, Fuentes looks over at his new partner and inquires, "So, Barnes, how did you end up in the police business?"

Barnes looks toward Fuentes with her head down, peering at him over the top of her sunglasses. With a restrained smile she retorts, "Is this one of those special moments where we get into one another's personal business?"

In an almost apologetic tone, Fuentes responds with a slight shrug. "Yes, of course guy… it's bound to happen sometime, don't you think? We can only talk business so much before we get to know a little about one another."

"I suppose," responds Barnes with some degree of reluctance and a reflective pause. "I was married to a guy that I met in my junior year of college. He was initially charming but being a party animal while majoring in alcohol consumption and juvenile antics did little to contribute to the longevity of the marriage. I come from a deeply religious family with a history of long-term marriages. I was determined to stay with him but it didn't work out. I got pregnant and when the marriage failed, I moved my baby and me in with my family. I finished school, joined the force and have been here since. That's it."

"That's it?" Fuentes, face riddled with frustration rolls his eyes in disappointment. "So, what you're saying is that you really don't care to discuss the details of your personal life with me? Alright, I get it." Fuentes reaches for the door handle, preparing to exit the vehicle.

Barnes gently grabs the upper part of his arm, "You want the dirt? Is that what you want?"

"No, not for nothing. I want you to trust me. I'm a good cop and can be a good friend but it all starts with a little trust. We've been working together for three weeks and I hardly know anything about you but your name."

Barnes slides her back to the door while removing her sunglasses, "Fine… that's fine then. Okay, here it is in a nutshell. I married a guy my family didn't approve of. They saw qualities and characteristics in him I was blinded to. I tolerated his drunkenness and verbal abuse but after I got pregnant, he started hitting me. One night I had enough, I grabbed a baseball bat and nearly beat him to death. He left without ever filing a police report. The feeling of empowerment from that experience resulted in a shift in my world view. I changed my major from advertising to criminal justice and I've never felt more suited for anything in my life. I know people perceive me as straight-laced and even rigid at times, but under the gruff exterior is a person who genuinely cares for people. Once I make a friend, they are usually my friend for life. It's a quality I hide well because I know a lot of people are afraid of me, and I don't mind that they are. Having said that, I still have the baseball bat and if I hear any of this from anyone else, I will not hesitate to use it on you."

Fuentes laughs out loud, "I'm Cuban so you can trust me on this one guy, I do know the power of a baseball bat! I hope I can earn your friendship, Barnes." He reaches for the door handle a second time but again, Barnes grabs his arm.

"Where you off to? I'm not going to tell you my story without hearing yours. All I know about you is that your family came here on a raft."

"You know about the raft? I guess word gets around," Fuentes replies as he eases back into his seat.

"I'm from *Mijami*. You know *Mijami*, right? My mother was six months pregnant with me when my family arrived on the Florida coastline."

With raised eyebrows and an extended index finger he continues, "I was the first of my family to have been born in America. We experienced a lot of discrimination and had few opportunities, but during my adolescence I refused to do drugs or go into crime. I was picked on a lot for my race, for being poor and because I possess a certain 'flair' if you know what I mean."

Barnes was well aware of what he meant but chose to remain silent. She had heard several remarks regarding Fuentes and what one might describe as his occasional feminine qualities.

"In Cuba my family was part of an underground communist Catholic Church. We were baptized and confirmed but didn't go to church. Now, as an American Catholic, I feel like I have the freedom not to go to church... but I still go... mostly special occasions. Whether influenced by my family, the church or a combination of the two, even as a kid, I always tried to do the right thing. Between you and me guy, I know the rumors floating around about me so let me just say this. I married my high school sweetheart, have three kids, and my family means everything to me. If I have to give up some things to have other things more important, so be it. That's how we do it in *Mijami*. How's that for an intro?"

"It's a good start," responds Barnes as she transitions the conversation back to the business they are there for. "Do you have the file on Justin Manus, the person of interest we're interviewing?"

—◊◊◊—

The two detectives approach Justin Manus's door and knock with a degree of authority. Justin, not expecting anyone, quickly opens the door and before the detectives have an opportunity to speak, he blurts out, "If you want money, I'm broke. If you're religious, I respect your beliefs but I'm not interested. If you're..."

The female cop interrupts him, flashing a police badge and declaring, "Mr. Manus, we're with the Orange County Sheriff's Department. I'm Detective Barnes and this is Detective Fuentes. We're investigating a crime and need to ask you some questions."

"I was hoping for one of the first two choices," quips Justin.

"What was the third option?" interjects Fuentes, indifferent to the apparent disgust of Barnes.

"Oh, the third one is, 'if you're a cop, I have an alibi,'" he responds with a smirk.

Fuentes chuckles while Barnes rolls her eyes and seems perturbed at her partner for asking the obvious. Justin invites the officers to come out of the hallway and to take seats in the living room. He sits on a padded folding chair while the two detectives deeply sink into a very old, garage-sale quality sofa. Barnes is a detail person and instinctively looks about the room, soaking in as many clues about Justin's lifestyle as she's able to gather. His Department of Motor Vehicles records indicate he's 5'11", 195 lbs., dark brown hair and eyes. Seeing him for the first time, Barnes notes his athletic build and the fact that he certainly has the physical ability to inflict harm on someone. He's an attractive man, not the pretty boy, magazine cover type, but someone who could make a woman blush by unexpectedly approaching her and asking her for directions. He initially impresses someone as being friendly and charming, but that could be part of his criminal allure.

Fuentes is much more focused on observing Justin's responses and behavior. He likes pushing buttons and making people squirm a little. His observation is that suspects often divulge much more information when they are asked odd and unexpected questions. "Actually, Mr. Manus," states Detective Fuentes in more of a business tone, "We're hoping you do have an alibi so we can eliminate you as a person of interest."

"A person of interest for what?" proclaims Justin in a more excited voice while sitting farther back in his seat. His eyes dart between the two detectives trying to determine how serious they're being with him.

"Do you recall where you were a couple of weekend afternoons ago?" queries Fuentes.

"That long ago? I don't know. It's not like I have a life since my divorce. I live alone. I look for work, go to the gym, grocery shop… that's about it."

"You left out community service," interjects Barnes.

Justin is visually agitated by the comment, feeling as though he's being accused or perceived as a liar. "Okay, yeah. I have a few hours left of community service to complete but I'm current on that… what's your point?"

Barnes presses for a stronger reaction and response. "I thought it was interesting that the one thing you're required to do, you eliminated from the list."

Justin becomes defensive in the tone his response. "Let's just say it's not my proudest moment. It's the one thing I'm a little ashamed, maybe even a little perturbed about."

Barnes feels she has hit a nerve and continues to add pressure. "You were charged with domestic violence. Did you physically assault your wife?"

"Are you asking me if I hit my wife?"

Visibly annoyed by the inference, Justin shrugs his shoulders and responds with the sincerity of an altar boy. "I've never committed a crime or hit a woman in my life. I understand why she did what she did but she went about it the wrong way. I know I was selfish and that I hurt her, but she didn't have to resort to lashing out at me like that. She claimed she was afraid of me and that I threatened her life. She lied her butt off as a ploy to get me out of the house and to give her control of the home. After a weekend in jail I was forced to either pay an attorney twelve thousand dollars to fight the charges or accept a plea bargain. I hadn't worked in over a year at the time so I had no choice but take the deal."

Fuentes, looking for a reaction, contributes a question that reeks of suspicion. "So, you had nothing to do with Art Conner's death either?"

Justin raises his hands like he's begging on a street corner and responds in an excitable voice. "Who the hell is Art Conner? How am I supposed to be tied to this?"

Barnes advises Justin to remain calm. "He's your ex-wife's divorce attorney, the one you threatened to beat the hell out of during one of your court appearances."

Justin returns to the edge of his seat, hands now flat on top of his knees and in a much more controlled voice, "I can't be the only one that threatened that guy. I went into court thinking the truth would prevail and all her lawyer did was lie. I never seriously threatened to hurt him or kill him. I have no knowledge of the circumstances behind his death or how he died. I'm not going to lie and say I have remorse over his death but I had nothing to do with it. Just out of curiosity, how did he die?"

Barnes refuses to appease Justin's curiosity and continues to maintain control of the conversation. "Do you have any guns or weapons in the home?"

Justin shakes his head slightly and looking a little dejected responds, "I've never owned a gun. Aside from that, I only have a few steak knives... I haven't been in a fight since middle school."

Barnes presses him further. "So you don't have an alibi for two weekends ago?"

"No, I've been going through a divorce, haven't worked in a couple of years and I was sick for a few days about then."

Barnes pauses, and then looks at Justin with a penetrating stare. "Are you a big drinker?"

"No, I really don't drink much at all," Justin proclaims in a matter-of-fact manner and a facial expression reeking of sincerity.

The observant female detective's eyes widen and her eyebrows rise in disbelief. "You have an awful lot of bottles of wine sitting on your kitchen table for someone that doesn't drink much."

Justin, having temporarily forgotten about the bottles, glances into the kitchen, then back at Barnes. "Okay, okay... I see your point but the truth is, I don't drink much, but I did drink a lot a couple of weeks ago. I haven't had a drop of alcohol since then. I was really depressed... it would have been my twelfth anniversary and for some reason, I thought it might help."

Barnes shakes her head in the affirmative to acknowledge Justin's statement but her facial expression displays obvious doubt. "Did you have any contact with Art Conner during that time?" presses Barnes.

"No! Absolutely not!" proclaims Justin with certainty. "You can check my phone records. I stayed right around here. It's not like I can afford to do much."

Barnes cocks her head slightly to the side and looks down at her nose at the suspect, "So, you're saying you never left your apartment that entire week?"

"Aside from my normal routine, the night of my anniversary I walked over to the Virgil Overpass, but that was in the middle of the week. That's about it."

"That's nearly a half mile away," interjects Fuentes with a smile. "Let me get this straight. You get drunk and just casually stroll over to the Virgil Overpass because it's the happening place in town?"

"I had a lot on my mind and needed to clear my head."

Fuentes sinks back into the overstuffed sofa. "I'm not buying that Mr. Manus. What was at the bridge that you needed to get to?"

Justin pauses, reaching for a plausible answer but his eyes dart around the room and his delayed response leads both detectives to the same conclusion. They patiently wait in silence for his explanation.

Justin's delayed response is much less assertive, even meek. It's as though he's been broken and is now confessing to the crime of the century. "Oh god... okay. I lost my wife, my job and most of what I owned. Life seemed pretty meaningless, I was depressed, feeling sorry for myself and felt like my life was over. I was really drunk and wasn't thinking clearly so when I couldn't find a rope, I walked over to the bridge with a bottle of wine and was thinking about jumping off."

Barnes, convinced of the sincerity of Justin's response, continues her questioning with a softer and more compassionate tone to her voice. "How long were you at the bridge?"

Justin looks at her with a bewildered expression. "I can't remember. I must have passed out. I woke up near dawn all wet and dirty."

"You woke up on the bridge?" Barnes continues.

"Not exactly. I woke up on the side of a road next to a cow."

Both heads turn toward Fuentes as he interjects a hearty laugh. "You woke up next to a cow? I personally have never woken up next to anything that wasn't human, but that's just me."

Barnes discretely bumps her elbow into Fuentes's ribcage and gives him a look to remind him to maintain his professionalism. She returns her attention back to Justin. "Did you have any blood or unusual marks on your body when you woke up?"

Justin gestures as though he's attempting to duplicate the imprint on his face with his own hand. "No blood, just a swollen eye and hand print like someone slapped me."

"You sure that was a hand print, not a hoof mark" remarks Fuentes with a chuckle while avoiding eye contact with Barnes who was giving him the evil eye.

Barnes responds to Justin in a more consoling voice. "So, are you in a better place now?"

Justin drops his head down and glances at the floor. "Yeah, like I said, I'm not much of a drinker and I was hung over for a couple of days so I don't think I'll be drinking again anytime soon."

The female detective stands to her feet and Justin follows her lead by walking toward the door. With Justin's back to the detectives, Barnes reaches over and pinches Fuentes, grabbing the soft spot under his arm.

"Oww! We best be going now but thank you so much for your time," Fuentes winces in slight pain but chuckles at Barnes.

The officers hand Justin their business cards and both leave with smiles on their faces. He tosses their cards on the table, still slightly miffed by their questions and the intrusion into his life.

Once safely in their car and out of visual range, the two officers begin to laugh aloud. Fuentes chuckles. "You have to love this job. Did you see his expression? Between you and me, guy, he would sooner confess to killing Conner than tell us about jumping off the bridge."

Barnes nods in agreement. "He was definitely out of his comfort zone... couldn't tell a lie to save his life. Every time we challenged his response, he looked around the room like he expected a good answer to pop up on the wall. Did you see his body language when I asked him if he hit his wife? I doubt this guy ever touched his wife and I'm positive he's not a murderer."

Fuentes laughs. "I almost lost it when he said he woke up next to a cow. You can't make that stuff up. Where the hell do they have cows around here anyway?"

Barnes looks sternly toward her partner with a wry smile and a soft spoken warning. "After what you did in there, you're lucky I don't chain your ass to a cow for a few days. I will get you back for that."

—∭—

Slightly over thirty minutes pass. Justin paces the apartment, still perturbed over the police visit when the phone rings. Caller ID indicates the call originates from the Rosewood Hotel but the number isn't familiar. He answers the phone and is greeted by a sneering, Grinch-like voice, "Well, do you want to thank me?"

With a crinkled expression on his face, Justin responds, "Who is this? Thank you for what?"

"I did a good job on your ex-wife's attorney, Art Conner, for you. That scum lawyer screamed like a small child!"

In a softer, more sincere manner, the voice continues, "I told him it was a gift from you. I told him he was a lying, deceitful man and he died with terror in his eyes... I almost had an orgasm! I saved the recording for you. Are you grateful?" said the caller with an eagerness in his voice.

Within seconds, flashes of memories began to reappear in Justin's mind; thoughts of events he assumed were only a drunken nightmare.

"Are you grateful?" the caller softly repeats.

Justin stutters in response, "Who... who is this? How did you know about... why did you? No, I didn't ask you to kill anyone!"

An uncomfortable silence follows before the killer speaks again in an almost consoling tone. "I understand where you're coming from. I was that way before my first one too. Your wallet is in a paper bag outside your door. I put it there after the detectives left."

Justin rushes to the door of the apartment, quickly swings it open and retrieves the bag. "You know where I live?"

"I know a lot about you now Justin... do you mind if I call you Justin?"

Kilborn waits for a response but there's only silence. "It appears the only thing you have left of your life is a driver's license and eighteen dollars in cash. Don't worry, I left it all there," he says with sarcasm in his voice. "I felt so bad I added a few hundred dollars of my own money as an apology for slapping you."

Justin's mouth is gaped open and he's completely astonished by the words of the caller. "What could you possibly want from me?"

"I think we share some common interests. We've both been beaten down and betrayed by people we trusted and loved. We could work together on common goals. I can give you control of your life again... provide you with a regular source of income and a new identity."

"Do you mean kill people like Art Conner? How did you know even know about him?" Justin demands.

"It's all public information. All I needed was your last name and an internet connection. I looked up your case and his name online."

"Stay the hell away from me you crazy bastard or I'll call the police!"

In a raised voice Kilborn snarls. "You can work with me or die in prison, Mr. Manus! You're the only suspect in his murder and all the evidence leads straight to you! There's absolutely no connection between me and Art Conner. If you go to the police, you'll seal your own fate and spend the rest of your life in prison!"

Justin holds onto the phone, not willing to concede to his demand but unable to provide an adequate response. A lengthy silence follows until Kilborn speaks again in a soft and alluring voice. "I'll give you another chance."

The phone clicks and it's apparent that Kilborn has disconnected.

IV

A Fellow Soldier

It is nearly an hour's drive before Justin arrives at the address he had hurriedly scribbled on the backside of a piece of junk mail. His tension is high as he sits parked in under a canopy of mature trees in an older Torrance neighborhood. Before he steps out of the car he reviews his situation, wresting with his options. There really isn't much of a choice. Art Conner is dead and it's apparent who's going to get blamed for it. Justin doesn't have money for a team of defense attorneys so the crazy caller is right... he's likely to face a long-term prison sentence for a crime he did not commit.

It's madness! he thinks to himself. *I haven't been in a fight since middle school but two appearances in family law court have somehow turned me into a hardened criminal.*

Justin wades through a few obscure memories of his captor and his drunken episode on the bridge. He can only recall the man's lifeless, steel blue eyes and a statement about his grandmother living in an apartment in Torrance... and something to do with Koreans. It's not a lot to go on but he has to do something besides sit around and wait for the police to arrest him. Judging from the insanity in his tormentor's voice, without agreeing to become his partner in crime, it's only a matter of time before the steely-eyed killer murders another victim, drawing increased suspicion and likely consequences to himself. He needs a place to live; somewhere off the grid where he can hide while searching for this killer he knows nearly nothing about. The police are already asking questions and Justin knows he has to quickly make arrangements to find this man or become the hapless patsy for his crimes. The room he hopes to rent here will keep him out of view from the police and give him a base from which to search for his tormentor's grandmother. If he can locate her, he may be able to direct the police to the true killer.

In preparation of his move, Justin provided notice at his former apartment complex and most of his furniture was donated to the nearby dumpster. He closed out his bank accounts, cancelled his credit cards, cell phone, and stuffed the cash from his retirement account into his socks; probably not the safest place but one that would suffice for now. Much of his clothing and several personal items are stuffed into his vehicle. Once settled, he'll return to pick up what remains at the storage facility and dispose of his car. He has an arrangement for the sale of his car to one of the dealerships that offer cash, but only pay a fraction of the car's value. It doesn't matter. It's not about the money now.

After filtering through several websites and online possibilities, Justin has narrowed his housing search to a single promising ad. Although he's only had written communication with the owner, the situation seems ideal. The landlord seems understanding of his divorce and the financial consequences that comes with it. He'll accept his poor credit with a higher deposit and proof of a steady income or financial reserves.

The narrow road leading through the neighborhood is lined with full grown trees and small homes, likely built in the 1950's. If they have a garage at all, it's detached and designed to accommodate only a single car. The houses were definitely built during a different era; two or three bedrooms, one bathroom, big back yards, fruit trees and slightly more privacy. It's a lot different than most of the suburban tracts that have grown up around the area.

Not knowing what to expect, he exits his vehicle and approaches the house looking for someone he only knows as Hugh. *Hugh*, Manus thinks, *who has a name like that? I don't know anyone under ninety with the name Hugh. It has to be some guy with wrinkles to his knees...*

"Hey! You can walk on the grass if you want," bellows a young sounding voice coming from behind the screen door. "Come on in!"

Justin reaches the door and cautiously opens it, uncertain as to what he may discover. "I'm looking for Hugh," he informs a mid-twenty-something Asian man sitting in a wheelchair.

"You found him. Come in and have a seat," says the trim and fit looking man as he gracefully spins his wheelchair around, doing a wheelie on the hardwood floor and darting into the living room.

If nothing else, Justin's first impression of the baby-faced Asian is one of entertainment and curiosity. Although both of Hugh's legs are amputated below the knee, his bold and engaging personality captures the entirety of one's attention. One almost immediately forgets about his missing limbs. After seeing Hugh's effortless mastery of his wheelchair, Justin amuses himself with the thought of him being a legless gymnast performing in a world-class production in Las Vegas. Before Justin sits, he walks over to the younger man and reaches out to shake his hand, "I'm Justin Manus. Nice to meet you."

"Justin?" replies the younger man. "I thought only teenagers had the name Justin." Both men laugh. While shaking his guest's hand, the young man states with a smile, "I'm Hugh."

Justin is perplexed and his confused expression reveals as much. "I thought a man named Hugh would be... uh..."

"You don't have to say it, you were expecting someone a little older, maybe by sixty years, with two legs and Caucasian," says Huge, still smiling.

"Yeah, you got me on all counts. I was worried you might be some guy that smells like dirty clothes and carries around an oxygen tank."

"Well not yet anyway," Hugh says. "Let me give you the breakdown and answer some of your questions. First, the house has only two-bed-rooms, one bath and I need all the space for myself. But," he adds, pointing to the rear of the house, "I have a nearly new recreational vehicle in the back and I can rent that out to you. I originally planned to tour the country with it but my buddy canceled on me."

"Seriously?" responds Justin with surprise. "Why would he do that?"

For the first time since meeting him, Hugh stops smiling and says with an emotionless tone, "Because he's dead. We served in Iraq together. I came back missing my legs and he came back missing a part of his mind.

He was severely depressed, became addicted to drugs and I couldn't get him off the stuff. I'm not going to lie to you; he died on the floor of the RV. If that's not a problem, I'll rent it to you."

Manus nods and responds, "I served in the Army for a few years. It was before the war so I was never in battle and I didn't have to go through the same things you did, but I do understand some of it. I won't have a problem sharing the space with a fallen soldier."

Hugh, with his smile restored, shoots his hand toward Manus. "Well, look it over and if you like it, we have a deal!"

"Just one question Hugh," says Justin in a sheepish manner, "are you Korean, Chinese, Japanese or what?"

"I'm glad you asked that, Justin, because I was thinking the same thing myself. I can't tell if you're German, British or French."

Both men laugh at one another, and then Hugh speaks up, "I'm Japanese, my friend. My family came here to the South Bay in the 1970's during what many Caucasians refer to as the Asian Invasion. About thirty percent of the population of Torrance is Asian."

Justin laughs at himself, "At least you know what you are. I'm a mix of German, British, and French." Hugh joins in the laughter.

It doesn't take long for Justin to move his belongings into the RV, after which he and Hugh hang out in the house and talk for a couple of hours. Hugh enjoys Justin's company but begins to think there's a missing piece to the puzzle. He decides to press him for the information. "Okay, Justin, I understand the divorce, cashing out your retirement account and being unemployed... but what am I missing? You seem like the kind of guy who would take his nest egg and start a new business, go back to school or take on a new job in another state. Instead, you move to the South Bay where it seems you want to disappear. Am I wrong?"

Justin is conflicted. He wants to tell Hugh all the details but at what risk? After a brief pause, he looks up at Hugh, takes a deep breath and divulges the details of his situation. He tells him about the night at the bridge, the visit by the detectives and the killer's phone call. Most importantly, he tells Hugh about the killer's grandmother and why he needs to find her. "Right now," explains Justin, "I've never committed a crime and I'm not wanted by the police but it's only a matter of time before he kills again and when he does, I know the detectives will be coming after me. I have to become invisible for a while."

"Dude, I got your back," says Hugh with child-like enthusiasm. "No one knows you're here, the utilities are all in my name and one more thing, I've got something for you." Hugh wheels around quickly and retrieves something from the bedroom and tosses it on the sofa next to Justin. "It's my roomie's cell phone. I know he'd want to help if he were here, so keep it."

Justin drops his head and looks away from Hugh, almost speechless in response to Hugh's support. "I don't know what to say. I was afraid to tell you."

"I'm glad you did. Us Marines have to stick together. *Semper Fi!*" Hugh beams with pride.

Justin looks up with a challenging smirk and responds, "I was Army."

"That's okay, soldier," says Hugh with a grin, "Not everyone can be a Marine." Both men laugh.

When the laughter subsides, Justin looks at Hugh's legs for the first time since their initial handshake. It was easy to forget Hugh had a disability. Largely due to Hugh's gregarious personality and the fact that he doesn't see himself as being handicapped in any way, it's easy to ignore. He refuses to let others make an issue of it. One quickly becomes oblivious to the absence of his limbs and can only see the depth and quality of his character. "So, tell me your story," says Justin.

"Which part do you want to hear? The part where my shiny butt comes out of the womb or just the recent stuff?"

Justin is agreeable. "Whatever you want."

"In a nutshell, my dad worked for a major Japanese company and my family moved to California in the mid-seventies. I was born here in Torrance about a decade later, grew up in a house on the hill in Palos Verdes, then set out to college. I was on track to become an electrical engineer but when I saw the Twin Towers fall in New York on 9-11, I felt compelled to join the Marine Corps. I was on patrol in Fallujah, Iraq in 2004, walked near an improvised explosive device which took out my legs. I was lying out in the open under heavy fire and my buddy, Eskel, saved my life. I was fully conscious and saw my legs dangling under me. As Eskel lifted me over his shoulder, I remember seeing rounds hitting all around us, almost in slow motion. I passed out right after that; woke up in a hospital. I was discharged and went through rehab. Now I'm back in school."

Justin looks at Hugh with admiration and respect. "Wow, that's quite a story. Thank you for your sacrifice and for serving."

"Hey, you served too, my friend!"

Hugh's supportive comment was deeply appreciated by Justin. "I didn't serve in battle like you."

"Were you combat trained and prepared for war?"

"Yes," said Justin.

"Would you have gone if you were sent into battle?"

"Yes, of course."

"That's all anyone can do—prepare and wait. The rest is fate. I've heard it said that when you join the military, it's like signing a blank check to Uncle Sam that is secured by your life. No one knows when or if that check will be cashed. Only about 1% of American citizens have served in the military so you're among an elite group. Dog, dude, you're out here trying to find a killer on your own. I'd go into battle with you."

There's a pause in the conversation and Justin notes the hour. "Hey, I've enjoyed the time but I'd better get my things organized and then get some sleep. Thanks for everything."

"One more thing," says Hugh as he rushes once again to the spare room to retrieve something. "Do you know how to use this?" as he hands a 9mm Glock pistol to Justin. "It belonged to Eskel. I'm sure he won't mind if you borrow it for a while. You Army boys know how to use these, right?" Hugh says smiling.

"Oh, sure," responds Manus, "Where do the bullets go again?" He drops the sarcastic tone and says, "Goodnight Hugh. Thanks."

"You're welcome, Justin. Hey, there's a nice park only a block away. You may want to check it out sometime."

—◊◊◊—

Justin wakes early the next morning. He would have slept longer had it not been for the ruckus caused by an invasive species of wild parrots fighting for domination of the fruit trees. Everything in the RV is set up pretty well. The bed is actually more comfortable than the second-hand one he was sleeping on in the apartment and there's a space that easily converts into a make-shift office. Justin spends a couple of hours on the phone and online with the City Planner's Office, uncovering key information from the city's demographics and census reports. He discovers that of the 426 apartment complexes in Torrance, there are less than 30 that have a large number of occupants with a majority of Asian names. Armed with the new data, Justin eagerly seeks out his new friend.

"He pounds on the front door. Hugh! You awake?"

"Yeah, what's up? Do I need my gun?"

"No, save your bullets for now," says Justin smiling as he enters the house. "I narrowed my search down to about thirty possible apartment complexes, and then cross-referenced the names, but I'm struggling to eliminate more."

Hugh studies the map and data for a few minutes, and then explains, "Well, if you were looking for Japanese, this would be really easy."

"How so?" says Justin, taking the bait.

"Because, we're the smartest and prettiest race on earth!" Hugh says, laughing aloud. "Okay, seriously, Japanese names are usually multi-syllable and Korean names are only one syllable, plus about half of all Koreans have the last name of Kim. In addition to that, you say the grandmother is elderly and lives in an apartment so she's probably in a lower-income, one bedroom unit. Make sense?"

Justin nods.

Hugh points to the map and continues, "The lower priced units are in this area and in one of these three zip codes. So, if you cross-reference the corresponding names with the zip code... there. You have a few strong possibilities. I would look for a bottom one-bedroom unit in a complex with a beige stucco exterior."

Justin gapes. "Beige stucco?"

Hugh laughs. "Nah, I'm just messin' with you now. But seriously, if you hadn't noticed, this is one of the older neighborhoods in Torrance and we're in one of the three target zip codes, so you're within a mile of all of these apartment buildings. It's a good start. Let me know if there are any other profound riddles I can solve for you," he says as he does a quick turn and begins to wheel away.

"Yeah, wait. Just one more question. The comment about the smartest and prettiest only refers to Japanese women, right?"

"Eat your heart out Justin!" responds Hugh as continues his retreat while laughing.

Exiting the house, Justin opts for a break from his research in order to explore the neighborhood. He envisions becoming a cave dweller once the police make formal charges and his picture is plastered in every local newspaper. He exchanges the demographic data in the RV for a baseball hat and sunglasses, and then heads off to the neighborhood park Hugh had spoken to him about the previous evening.

Today is nice, sunny, and a break in the normal pattern of what the locals refer to as "June gloom." The gloom is an early summer weather pattern that often keeps the South Bay covered in a low-level cloud layer. On gloomy days it can be overcast along the coast of the South Bay while being bright and sunny less than a half mile away. Today, however, it's comfortably warm. There's a nice breeze, kites are flying, birds are softly singing and the feeling it produces is one of tranquility. Justin finds a slightly elevated grassy spot in an open area on a rolling hill to sit and enjoy the surroundings. The midweek afternoon is serene. Workers gather at the parking spaces near the park's perimeter to eat their lunch and toward the bottom of the grassy hill is a basketball court that's presently not being used. School is out for summer break but it's apparent the students are opting for the nearby beaches today. To Justin's right, a comfortable distance away, a mother and her two children. The toddler is being allowed to explore the immediate grassy area, bereft of clothing except a simple diaper. A slightly older brother is face down in the grass, obviously inspecting some unknown crawling creature that his mother has no desire to explore. Behind Justin is a meandering concrete walkway that invites one to explore the rolling hills and valleys of the deeper portions of the park's interior. Benches accent the walkway at regular intervals.

On the nearest bench, situated near the crest of the small knoll, almost directly behind Justin and within conversational range, sits a woman. As Justin rolls to his side, he observes her leaning her head back, eyes closed, allowing the sun to glaze her face. Because her eyes are shut, Justin indulges himself with an extended glance. She's very attractive but dresses in a way that doesn't scream, "Look at me!" She's elegant looking without making a noted effort to present herself that way. Her shoulder-length brown hair is pulled back and allowed to drape off the backrest of the bench, exposing her delicate facial features in a manner resembling a sleeping beauty. With her head tilted and her full lips on display, Justin quickly finds himself engulfed in a fantasy that requires his services to wake her with a kiss. Before becoming too engrossed in his thoughts, he looks away, lest his stare is discovered. He turns onto his back and not long thereafter, drifts off to sleep.

"Do you know what this is? Hey, mister! I have a bug. Do you know what kind it is?"

Justin wakes up to a cherub-faced three-year-old boy with curly blonde hair poking him in the chest. The child is insistent on displaying his latest captured creature directly at the end of Justin's nose.

"Whoa! What is that?" asks Justin, jolting into a sitting position. Within moments, the fog of his nap lifts and in a more composed frame of mind he responds, "What have you got there big guy?"

"It's a bug!" announces the proud little voice as someone giggles in the background.

"Wow!" Justin says in an animated voice. "Let's see it!"

A chubby little hand unfolds once again and is brought almost to the end of Justin's nose for him to examine. "Yep, you sure have a bug."

"What kind is it?" questions the little voice.

"Well, it's a dead bug." Justin's face reflects both his amusement and sympathy as he continues to hear a light chuckling in the background.

After carefully examining the insect, but now with a frown the child sighs with obvious regret, "Maybe I mushed it."

"Yes, sorry, you definitely mushed it." As a consolation, he adds, "But there are lots of bugs."

"I know where they are so I can get another one for you!" proclaims the suddenly rejuvenated little warrior as he wipes his hands clean on his pants.

Justin smiles at the excitement in the little boy's eyes, but caution prevails, "I'll tell you what. Let's go find your mommy and if she says it's okay, I'll help you find another bug."

Without hesitation, his little feet scamper off toward the location of his mother and baby sister. Justin trails a minute behind but before he's able to utter a word to the mother, she grabs her two children and huffs off in another direction. Somewhat dejected, he retreats to his original position but before he occupies his former place on the grass, the woman on the bench says dryly, "That went well."

"Was that you laughing at me," says Justin with a smile in his voice. "I thought she was going to call the police. All I was going to do was help her son catch a nice, safe bug."

"I thought it was very sweet of you, even if you are afraid of bugs," said the woman with a smile.

"Afraid of bugs? I ain't afraid of no bug, lady! I was going to mush it!" Justin jokingly brags.

"Stop it!" Her smile widens. "You were not. You should have known better than talk to a child whose parents don't know you anyway."

"I do know better. That's why I said we'd have to ask his mommy." He sighs. "I grew up a different way. Not every adult who talked to me when I was a kid was evil. Do you mind if I sit on your bench or will you scream and call the police?"

The woman's smile disappears and is replaced with an expression of doubt. "That depends on how close you sit to me. As long as you give me three feet of space, it should be okay."

"It's only a four foot bench," states a puzzled Justin.

"Well, I'll move down to the end."

"You're not very good at math, are you?" laughs Justin.

"I'm sure I'm better at math than you are with kids," she responds with a smirk.

He sits as far away on the bench as space allows, taking note of the collapsible white and red-tipped cane near her feet, then states, "I'm Justin."

The woman sticks out her hand for him to shake and replies, "I'm Lucy. I'm blind."

"I know you are," responds Justin. "That's why I waited until now to tell you how super good looking I am."

The two laugh together.

V

A New Doctor in Town

Three years ago...

The Sunday morning sun trickles through the window, illuminating Kilborn's face as he lie in the bed of Dr. Klaudios. The intense spring light flickers through outside branches and into the room, causing him to stir. Rolling to the other side of the plush mattress, he is greeted by an unfamiliar scent. In panic, he violently jerks to a sitting position, waiting for the fog of sleep to dissipate. After quickly scanning the room, he cautiously reminds himself where he is—in the bed of Dr. Klaudios—the man he had recently murdered.

He had meticulously checked Dr. Klaudios's home upon his arrival Friday afternoon, but again Kilborn diligently rifles through every nook and cranny for signs of another occupant or occasional visitor. Finding none, he pulls the drapes closed in each room and continues to methodically examine all the details of the doctor's life. Dr. Klaudios's house is an older, moderately sized ranch-style home located in a Laguna Beach neighborhood that reeks of money. From the exterior, the dwelling is not an impressive or elaborate residence. Once inside, the architecture opens up to reveal a stunning ocean view. The doctor was obviously very comfortable without drawing a noticeable amount of attention to that end. The walls are adorned with original works of art, shelves filled with collectibles and the furnishings straight out of a high end magazine. It becomes apparent the doctor lives alone but Kilborn scours the home looking for records of family, housekeepers, gardeners or anyone else that may come poking around. He realizes that his best tactic is to maintain as low a profile as possible until he can literally and comfortably fill the doctor's shoes.

It seems as though the doctor maintained something of a clandestine existence. There is no cell phone and all incoming calls are directed to an answering machine. Playing back the recorded message Kilborn hears the accented voice stating, "This is Dr. Klaudios. Please leave a message." Kilborn practices the vocal inflections for several minutes until he feels he has an elementary grasp of it. For now, finding money and gaining access to bank accounts is of greater concern than his impersonation of Dr. Klaudios's voice and accent.

A cursory view of the doctor's home office displays a highly systematic mind. All the books are arranged by subject, files color coded and alphabetized; correspondence and bills neatly stacked. Everything in the room is categorized and organized, even passwords. Surprisingly, his passwords are neatly printed and listed on a sticky note which is conspicuously attached to the desk clock in plain view. Apparently the older doctor was a computer novice and losing his password posed a greater threat to him than a burglar. Perhaps he felt as though the average thief would not take time to rummage through his computer. If his computer was the objective, the criminal would certainly possess the skill to circumvent his password. Whatever the late doctor's reasoning, Kilborn is relieved to have crossed that hurdle. After entering the appropriate data, he wastes no time in discovering Dr. Klaudios's financial records. With jaw dropped, Kilborn exclaims aloud, "Oh my god! The crazy bastard has $1.2 Million in the bank! Further investigation reveals another $300,000 in gold coins and $30,000 in cash in his office filing cabinet. The doctor is earning approximately $480,000 each year. His home, boat, automobile and office are completely paid off."

Kilborn has an epifany of sorts. His initial scheme to take over Dr. Klaudios's life was concocted out of desperation and revenge. Deep in his heart, he never thought his plan was realistic or that it would really work. At best the doctor's home represented a brief respite from being chased by the police; a place to recuperate and possibly gain access to money while plotting his next steps. But with the deterioration of the American family unit and a growing cutlural obsession with gadgetry, his gut feeling is that society is fundamentally changing into a nation of individuals. His mind begins to contemplate the issue and the possiblities. Amid the throng of public gatherings, most rush from one appointment to another, scarcely making note of the human beings they pass. Many have their noses burried in electronic devices, exchanging meaningless drivel with people they only know by their manufactured names. The obcession with electronic devices is such that it is often not newsworthy when a person is killed while texting or tweeting. Pedestrains are run over as they cross the street; their final tweet sometimes revealing the very street they are crossing. Automobiles rear end one another as drivers attempt to navigate both the vehicle and their texts. Those that survive the crash face the quandry of who to communicate with first; emergency responders or their cyberspace following. Restaurants are filled with one or more people sitting at the same table, abandoning the company of those in their presence in order to carry on communication with others on mobile devoices. In urban America, an occasional exchange of obligatory waves while waiting for our gargage doors to open serves as the modern definition of being neighborly. Yes, Kilborn thinks, people have become so individualized and separated from family units that they can be replaced like old batteries. He relaizes his best option is to actually become Dr. Klaudios.

With all of the doctor's personal information at his disposal, Kilborn is able to establish an online banking account and order a debit card to access the funds. He has access to more money now than ever before in his lifetime. Kilborn's new life is coming together. He has a new identity, a place to live, a job and most importantly, he has the position and resources to strike back at his enemies.

A major hurdle still remains. Dr. Klaudios was slightly shorter, about thirty pounds heavier and eighteen years older than Kilborn. To Kilborn's advantage, the doctor lived a somewhat isolated lifestyle and worked alone. There is no indication the doctor spent a lot of time socializing with anyone but in order for Kilborn to pull off the deception, he would have to at least match a physical resemblance of the doctor.

Fortunately the internet is replete with products and services. To his pleasure and surprise, not only are there make-up artists for hire but products and videos available that display how to apply and enhance certain appearances. After making a few calls, Kilborn schedules a mid-day appointment for the next day with a woman who claims to possess extensive experience in the entertainment industry as a make-up artist. Until he is able to secure a disguise Kilborn has to get by on what he has, hoping his only contacts are with people who have never seen Dr. Klaudios before. Kilborn would also have to buy new clothes but for his first day at the office, he selects a pair of cuffed slacks from a business suit hanging in the closet. By cutting the hem and releasing the fold for the cuffs, he adds a couple of inches to the length of the trousers. There is little Kilborn can do to with the extra girth but pull the belt in tightly so as to prevent the pants from falling to his ankles. Adding a baggy short-sleeved shirt and sweater vest to the ensemble produces a very unremarkable rendition of the doctor. It would have to do for the first day.

Kilborn walks into Dr. Klaudios's office at 6:00 a.m. on Monday morning and within an hour, feels comfortable enough to manage the office and assume nearly all the doctor's responsibilities. Kilborn has been though the process before and already knows the routine. A client walks into the waiting area, reads the signs, fills out the forms and waits for the green light to come on. Patients are monitored by camera so there are no surprise visits and no one can enter the locked interior office beforehand. Once inside, they are given a written test to complete which is then followed up with a few puzzles and about twenty-four general knowledge questions. That's the easy part. The difficult matter is finding out what to do with the test once it's completed and processing the paperwork so as not to raise suspicion.

Fortunately, Dr. Klaudios was almost anal in processing his files. He had prepared a stack of preaddressed overnight envelops which were to be delivered to a psychological test scoring facility in Chicago. After reviewing the client files, it was evident that he kept one copy of the test while sending the original to the scoring facility, along with a processing fee. It seems that after a period of time, the results were returned from Chicago along with a detailed interpretation of the results. Dr. Klaudios used the language contained within the test results to compose several variations of a psychological profile that he in turn submitted to the court. There was a checklist with each file so the entire process was nearly on autopilot. Hardly a single component of the procedure required original thought or specialized training. The County referred a couple of requests for psychological assessments each week for which Dr. Klaudios received a prepaid amount of $2,400 from each individual. He was making nearly a half million dollars each year while investing no more than fifteen hours each week into the process. After examining several of the client files it becomes evident to Kilborn that the doctor's true talent is generating a very generic profile that reads like a daily fortune. He simply lines up the client's profile to the nearest matching report while changing the name and personal information. He's careful to add an original line or two into the introduction so as to make it appear more original than it is.

Kilborn's 9:00 a.m. appointment is with a tall, lanky middle-aged man. The gregarious gentleman attempts to engage him in personal chit-chat on a couple of occasions but Kilborn anticipates this and rebuffs him each time with the phrase, "Ve are here for you!" Each time he speaks to the client, he utilizes a harsh, guttural accent, jerking his head up at the end of the statement while staring him down with an intimidating scowl. The client's response is to immediately back down and comply with instructions. Although Kilborn uses what he thinks is his best imitation of the doctor's accent, he knows that it is a miserable rendition. It will never pass the scrutiny of someone more educated and worldly. By the end of the appointment, it is easy to see that the client is as relieved to have completed the exam as Kilborn is to be rid of him. Kilborn knows he will have to immediately do better.

With his client out the door, Kilborn quickly returns his focus to securing loose ends in the office. He checks the status of errands, bills, client's files, and reviews all entries on Dr. Klaudios's calendar for upcoming appointments. The last thing he wants is to bring attention to himself by making a clumsy error. His next psychological evaluation, with the wife of the man he just met, is not until the middle of the week. He has some time but needs to move quickly before he unexpectedly runs into a contact for which he isn't prepared.

Satisfied that matters pertaining to the administration of the office are secure, Kilborn sets out for his midday appointment with the Hollywood make-up artist he discovered on the internet. With his pockets stuffed with part of the cash uncovered in Dr. Klaudios's office, Kilborn drives to an older commercial building in Culver City to meet with a woman that goes by the name of Zeta. The lovely Zeta has been creating looks for screen and stage for over two decades and for $96 per hour, she can turn an ape into a beauty queen or visa-versa. Kilborn's story line is simple. He tells Zeta that he's a high school teacher who has agreed to do a part in a school play. He displays a photo and describes his character as a banker who, coincidently, looks exactly like Dr. Klaudios. According to Kilborn's ploy, this banker character will not only perform on stage but teach in his classroom for a week. As such, it's imperative his final look is convincing and natural, even close up.

Zeta is a tall, heavy set woman but in spite of her intimidating size, her wide and frequent smiles create a comfortable first meeting. "So, honey, if I understand you right, you want something simple enough to put together in less than an hour and natural enough to fool someone close up?"

"Yes, that's pretty much it. Is that a reasonable request?"

"That depends. If you want to be bald on top with frizzy hair sticking out on the sides, that can be done in one of two ways. The first is a skull cap and a wig. That's going to take more time and energy than you realize. The second option is easier but requires a lot more courage on your part."

Kilborn's facial expression in response to Zeta's comment induces one of her enormous grins. "Yeah, I think you're getting' me—you're gonna have to shave the top and use hair products to get the sides the way you want them. The end result will be the answer you're looking for. It'll be easy to keep up and it will look natural. I can show you some make-up techniques that will age your appearance and we can add 30 lbs. to your frame just by me telling you the name of my favorite ice cream."

Kilborn looks back at Zeta with a wide-eyed, serious expression, "As much as I love ice cream, I'd rather keep my original physique intact."

"I kinda had a feelin' you were going to say that. I'm startin' to think I'm the only one in California that actually eats ice cream." Zeta places her hand on Kilborn's shoulder and begins to spin him around. "Here, turn around darlin' and let me check you out a bit. You're a little on the trim side. You want somthin' to pad that ass with too?"

"No... no." responds Kilborn, slightly surprised and amused by the comment. "Just give me enough girth to fill out the pants I'm wearing."

"That's not going to be a problem at all but your face is a little too narrow for the body we're making so we're going to have to do something with that. I can add facial hair for you or you can grow your own, whatever works for you. Whatever you need, I can hook you up in no time... but we definitely need to do something with that hair."

Kilborn asks in a sheepish, nearly meek tone of voice, "Are you going to cut my hair right now?"

Zeta flashes another radiant smile in response, "Well honey, unless you can command those locks to jump off your head, I don't see any way around it."

"No, I just thought..."

"There ain't no thinking to it," Zeta says with a chuckle. We better get on to that part first before you run out on me."

Within the next few hours, Zeta cuts, shaves, pads, ages and dresses Kilborn, transforming him into nearly a perfect image of what he asked to be. As Kilborn looks into the mirror at the finished product, he experiences a surreal moment; a murderer looking back into the face of his victim. His new found look is convincing enough to deceive anyone who isn't a relative or close friend. Apparently that's an unnecessary concern. The socially isolated Dr. Klaudios has no close friends and there is no indication of a family nearby.

Kilborn admires the appearance in the mirror with satisfaction. "I think it's perfect for what I need."

"I sure as hell didn't make you better lookin' but that's what you said you wanted."

Kilborn manufactures a slight smile while continuing to stare at his reflection with a combination of amusement and disgust. "Yes, it's exactly what I wanted." And again, in a nearly inaudible voice that tappers off at the end, "Exactly what I wanted."

"How often do you do these plays? 'Cause I can provide all the materials and supplies you need. I even teach a class two nights a week on how to do this. Are you interested?"

"Absolutely!" interjects Kilborn, almost before Zeta finishes her question. "I can see this becoming a wonderful hobby. Maybe I can learn how to develop other characters… even take acting classes. I have a great interest in learning all I can."

"Well, you came to the right place. I have a class this Wednesday night. See you then?"

"Yes, I look forward to being there. Thank you… thank you for providing me with all I asked for."

Kilborn pays Zeta in cash for the services and the large bag of materials she provided, turning just before exiting the door to wave goodbye to her. Once in his car he takes out Dr. Klaudios's driver's license and examines it while looking into the rearview mirror at his new image. Marveling at the comparison of the photo on the license with his new appearance, Kilborn stares at his reflection and after a moment, begins to quietly sob. Putting his head down and slightly moving it from side-to-side he mutters, "I was a good man. I was an honored teacher, a faithful husband and loving father. They took everything that was important to me. I grew up believing in the goodness of our country and had confidence in the legal process. 'We the People' was supposed to include me… supposed to insure my basic freedoms. They stripped me of all my rights! They violated me to the core of my being!"

After a few moments of silence, Kilborn wipes his tears, raises his head and glares at the image in the rearview mirror, "This is Dr. Klaudios, please leave a message. This is Dr. Klaudios, please leave a message! *This is Dr. Klaudios, please leave a message!*

VI

The Long Line

Disguised as Dr. Klaudios, wearing a new suit and sporting a beret-styled cap, Kilborn approaches the courtyard of a castle-like edifice referred to as the Orange County Family Law Court. This is where his nightmare began. Being here stirs a pot of hellish memories that now resurface in his mind. This is where he was forced to stand in front of a crowded courtroom, only to be falsely accused of criminal acts and stripped of his dignity. The words, tossed out publically: "child abuse, domestic violence, sexual abuse and embezzlement" had hit him like knockout punches to the face. Within the space of this tomb-like building is where he lost his children, marriage, distinguished career, and nearly every possession he owned. The walls of this structure house a trillion lies, millions of shattered dreams and a sea of tears. If there is a location on the face of the earth that screams out as a reminder and symbol of Kilborn's pain, this is it.

There are two lines that lead to a security entrance into the courthouse. The long line on the right wraps around the building while the short line to the left is only a small fraction as long. The lines remind Kilborn of something comparable to a grand social affair. The invited dignitaries arrive at the front entrance with their glorious outfits and displays of finery while everyone else is relegated to the service entrance. Oddly, a ticket to the short line is not attained by business success, academic achievement, wealth or even competence for that matter. There is only one requirement to get into the short line. Excluding the hourly employees who arrive earlier in the morning, one has to be an "officer of the court" or more specifically, a judge or an attorney. The deeper someone penetrates the structure, the more aware one becomes of this privileged class. Kilborn is old enough to realize that there was a time in America when being an officer of the court was a highly esteemed position of trust. It was a time when legal professionals were mindful of their roles as public servants. As a group, they seemed more committed to correcting societal wrongs and representing those without a voice. That was a long time ago.

The divorce industry is huge source of income to the legal community and those who make the rules and benefit from the process are entirely resistant to change. To Kilborn, the American mindset has been overtly conditioned to expect to be fleeced of their lifetime earnings and possessions during a divorce. Like sheep, couples willfully plod through the long line, obediently filing past the American flag and the nationally recognized symbols of justice, only to forfeit the very rights for which they stand. In Kilborn's mind, above the entrance to the courthouse, a more fitting embellishment would be Dante's inscription above the entrance to Hell, "Abandon hope all ye who enter here."

Kilborn's disguise passes the scrutiny of security without incident. Aside from being watched while removing his glasses, notepad, keys and cap, he is hardly given a second glance. But why would anyone be suspicious? With the exception of the padding to his waistline, his appearance is completely natural. He quickly mixes in with the minions entering from the long line and blends into the throng, simply becoming another pair of legs within the crowd. Directions to Judge Raven's courtroom are unnecessary. He has walked this path on so many occasions that his feet almost guide him there on autopilot.

Kilborn enters the courtroom and takes a seat near the back and close to the wall. He's close enough to be able to be able to glean any information that benefits his future schemes but remains as inconspicuous as one can be in a small, confined area. The front row of the small, eighteen-row courtroom is reserved for attorneys, partitioned from commoners by a swinging, saloon-styled gate. The chiseled-looking bailiff dutifully protects access to the gate, even placing a hand on his

Taser weapon when a non-attorney gets too close to it. Kilborn is very familiar with the routine. Before the judge's grand entrance, only the privileged class is allowed passage into the sacred space beyond the swinging entry. Hot coffee is prepared for them and they gather there, joking with one another and conversing with the courtroom staff on a first-name basis.

In this emotionally charged atmosphere a slightly built, middle-aged woman approaches the bailiff while Kilborn looks on. The courtroom has filled, becoming very crowded and busy with activity. Overhearing an attorney address the Bailiff by his first name, the woman makes the mistake of addressing the deputy casually as "Frank". The Bailiff is so befuddled his face fills with disgust and he's nearly unable to respond. An attorney quickly intervenes, emphasizing the Bailiff's correct title and instructing the woman, *Deputy Grimm* is not the person to handle this matter. You should speak to your attorney about this because *Deputy Grimm* is unable to provide you with legal advice."

As several attorneys begin to reach in their pockets for business cards, the woman retorts, "I can't afford an attorney and I wasn't asking for legal advice. I only wanted to know if I'm supposed to sign each page of this declaration or once on the last page."

"I can't help you with legal advice," responds the Bailiff. "Please take your seat and keep this area clear."

The woman continues to stand her ground while asserting, "I'm representing myself so I'll sign every page just to be sure. And since I'm my own attorney, shouldn't I be allowed access to the legal forms and the pot of coffee on the other side of the swinging gate?"

The room becomes nearly silent as the crowd is drawn into the drama of their conversation. The Bailiff, becoming increasingly annoyed with the woman, sneers. "You can obtain forms at the self-help window on the sixth floor and coffee at the cafeteria on the third floor. Being *pro per* doesn't mean that you meet the educational and professional standards to be an attorney."

The woman's chin lifts as anger heightens the color in her cheeks. "Do you assume everyone on this side of the gate or those forced to stand in the long line are idiots? Do you even know what *'pro per'* means?

I'm a language arts teacher and I teach Latin. *Pro per* is not even a proper Latin word or phrase. A more correct term is *propria persona*. *Pro per* is comparable to replacing 'what's up' with the truncated slang expression, 'sup.' I don't know a single attorney who is able to parse a Latin verb yet a bastardized form of Latin 'shop talk' is bandied about in courtrooms across America…"

"Ma'am, you need to take a seat or go outside the courtroom!"

The woman retreats but continues her lecture, "…Our laws are written in such an obscure form of doubletalk and gibberish, Latin is only sprinkled in to give it the illusion of intelligent thought."

The woman takes a seat near the back but with the courtroom still silent and all eyes on her, she pops up from her seat, "And another thing… it takes five years to become a teacher and I invested another two years for my master's degree. Some attorneys have never graduated from college or law school. I have every bit as much time invested in my education as those pompous asses who did."

The courtroom erupts with laughter; some even offer a somewhat subdued applause in support of her fearlessness.

"Ma'am, I'm not going to warn you again!"

The outspoken educator sits, but only for a moment. The attention of all present is on her as she stands without saying a word, walks to the front of the courtroom and offers her completed paperwork to the Bailiff. Deputy Grimm politely accepts the documents but doesn't take his eyes off of her until she is seated again. Once she's settled, a slight chuckle rumbles from the crowd, almost as a display of relief in that the drama appears to have ended.

As a former educator himself, Kilborn resists the temptation to display support of the language teacher's courage. Although amused and wholeheartedly in agreement with her, he has a greater purpose and goal in mind. Richard Bantam's name is on the docket and he is scheduled to appear on behalf of a client with a child custody issue. If all goes according to Kilborn's plan, he will not only be in proximity with Bantam but the case will likely include the involvement of Ms. Strix, the same incompetent Guardian *ad litem* utilized to represent his children's interests in his own case.

Only a minute before Judge Raven is scheduled to appear, Bantam parades through the door with his chin up and smiling. He glides down the aisle with the style of a pageant queen and immediately nestles within the circle of his cohorts. His perpetually tanned face is accented by his silver-grey hair and overly white teeth. The price of his suit alone exceeds the value of the automobiles driven by many of those who filed into the courthouse from the long line.

Richard Bantam has been Kilborn's primary target from the onset but he can't risk losing his ultimate target to novice mistakes. He's made the deliberate decision to save Bantam until such a time that he has somewhat refined his murderous skill and technique. Why Bantam? Bantam is the arrogant attorney who represented Kilborn's wife during his divorce. He's hugely successful in his family law practice. It isn't so much that he possesses a great legal mind, or that he's a skilled trial lawyer or even a good negotiator. What makes Bantam successful is the fact that he has few morals and absolutely no regard for the long-term, even multi-generational consequences of his actions.

Ultimately, following his earlier, disastrous appearance in that courtroom with Bantam as his opponent, Kilborn found himself sitting on the bottom half of a bunk bed in the rented room of an elderly widow's house. At a time in life when many begin to contemplate the emerging signpost of retirement, Kilborn started work as an hourly employee with a near minimum wage job. All he had to show for his life were three suitcases of clothing and a half-dozen cardboard boxes. Bantam had effectively ruined his life and his future. His credit was in shambles and the false charges of child abuse made against him remained attached to his legal history. Any potential employer or licensing agency conducting a background check had access to this public information. It didn't matter that Kilborn led an exemplary life for forty-eight years or that he built a solid credit history during his thirty years as a tax-paying adult. It also didn't matter that all the charges against him were not only unfounded, but had been dismissed. The charges remained within the public domain for all to see. School districts and other potential employers refused to consider hiring him based upon who he was at the moment, not the stellar citizen he was before becoming entangled in a quagmire of fabricated legal issues. By the time Bantam was done with him, Kilborn could not so much as qualify to rent a modest apartment. If not for the gracious widow who did not require a credit report, Kilborn would have joined the growing ranks of homeless Americans whose only crime was having been divested of all their assets by greedy attorneys and a broken legal system. For Kilborn, there were only a couple of options; rebuilding or retribution. Rebuilding requires opportunity and that door appeared to be nailed and bolted shut.

Kilborn's trip down that twenty-four month old memory lane, is interrupted by the barking command of the Bailiff for the courtroom to come to order. Kilborn sits comfortably near the back as Judge Raven tramps out of a side door and assumes his position on what appears to be an elevated throne. A great medallion of the Golden State is positioned directly behind his seat, effectively producing an aura around his head. The courtroom view of the arbiter positioned in front of the circular metal cast provides an illusion of making him appear as a haloed saint posing in a Renaissance painting. If it were not for the muted finish on the giant seal, one might think they were in the presence of a deity.

Bracketed between the Stars and Stripes and the flag of the State of California, Judge Raven peers out at the courtroom almost as though agitated by all present. He is agitated. As with most family law officials, Judge Raven perceives himself to be the caliber of talent utilized for high profile criminal cases and thinks his ability is wasted in divorce court. This misconstrued self-perception is fed by years of unaccountability and rarely being challenged or proven wrong on any subject. The word on Raven is that he intentionally badgers both sides into a settlement because nearly all his appealed cases are overturned.

As the judge scans his files and caseload, the Bailiff scolds the overflow crowd into auditory obedience. The noise level drops but for a few whispers, then ratchets up again as the lawyers on the front row begin to disregard the process. Sensing that he will not be able to obtain the cooperation of the lower cast, Deputy Grimm politely approaches the attorneys, requesting they take their conversations outside. All cooperate except Bantam who appears oblivious to anything except what is happening in his own world. With a pointed stare, the Bailiff finally enlists his collaboration. Only a minute later the restless Bantam, motions to his client to meet him outside and they walk out together. Sensing an opportunity, Kilborn excuses himself, relinquishes his seat and follows after Bantam. Once in the hallway, Kilborn spots Bantam sitting on a bench with a female he presumes to be his client and sits across from them while pretending to review his notes. Bantam looks up at Kilborn, looks away, then looks at him a second time with an extended gaze. Although slightly skittish, Kilborn is hiding behind a week's growth of beard and a disguise he has complete confidence in. The only way for him to be discovered is to act out of character. He has practiced his newly discovered accent and invested several hours into learning a few Albanian phrases.

Within minutes Bantam's puppy, Ms. Strix, springs out from the courtroom and upon discovering Bantam's location, flashes a smile in his direction. From Kilborn's personal experience and while observing the pair, it's apparent from the dynamic between them that Bantam has no interest in Strix aside from what she's able to do for him. As a sociopath, Bantam is discerning enough to recognize Strix's emotional needs and is cunning enough to keep her firmly in his pocket. Bantam is a user and Strix is simply a tool to him. Strix, on the other hand, was the not-so-popular girl in school who lacked the attention she thought she deserved from the in-group. Bantam made her feel like she was valued. Some things never change.

Prior to this, Strix was briefly in court with Kilborn on only three occasions, a period that was in excess of twelve months ago. Even without his disguise, it's doubtful that Strix would recognize or remember Kilborn. As the two huddle, Bantam leans over and says something to Strix in a low voice. She responds by looking over her shoulder, back in Kilborn's direction, then tentatively nodding to Bantam. Bantam whispers something to her and she immediately turns around and approaches Kilborn.

"Dr. Klaudios? Is that you?"

"Hello young lady. It's been a little vhile."

Strix seems relieved that the imposter remembers her at all and with a slight smile she continues, "Yes, at least six months or more. You look different, I hardly recognized you."

"Vell I have been on a diet and trying to live more healthy."

Strix leans back, eyeing the doctor as he stands to his feet, and with flattery in her voice asserts, "I can see that. You look good! I like the facial hair."

Kilborn, not wanting to risk overexposure, looks at his watch and immediately attempts to remove himself from the situation. "I am on my vay to an appointment but it vas nice to see you."

Strix quickly interjects, "I have a case I'd like to discuss with you sometime."

"Very good," says Kilborn as he begins to walk away, remembering to do so with a slight slouch in his posture. "My number is the same. Call me and ve can discuss it." Kilborn exits the Orange County Family Law Court with an odd feeling of satisfaction. It's the first time he has left the facility without feeling completely devastated. He was successful in planting a new image of Dr. Klaudios into the minds of Bantam and Strix, and they bought it. The next time they see him, the old image they may have had of Dr. Klaudios has now been reprogramed. His new image will never be questioned by Bantam or Strix and to add to his scheme, he will use them to verify who he is to others. It's been a good day.

Part II
Forte

VII

The Interview

For Justin, early afternoon walks to the neighborhood park quickly became a daily routine. He isn't ready to admit to himself that he's interested in seeing Lucy again but each of his visits to the park includes an inspection of the bench where they sat and talked. More often than not, when he notices Lucy isn't there, he turns around and goes home. It's been a week since he and Lucy shared a fleeting sixty minute conversation. Although their time together was brief, Justin finds himself uniquely attracted to Lucy. She is entirely confident in herself, obviously intelligent and seems to possess a vast inner strength. Her laugh is natural and she appears to be completely transparent and genuine. Lucy is like a new variety of flower, one Justin has never been exposed to before. She is the single brightly colored blossom that dares to bloom among the omnipresent greenery of a forest; strong and determined to occupy its space yet delicate and beautiful at the same time.

As Justin reaches the bottom of the walkway, his eyes climb the knoll to the familiar bench where they first met. His heart jumps as he realizes someone is sitting there. Within a score of steps he recognizes the familiar position; eyes closed, hair pulled back and her head slightly tilted so as to allow the sunlight to drape her face. It's Lucy. Approaching her, Justin realizes he's somewhat clueless as to what to say. Although he's normally outgoing and at ease when engaging almost anyone in conversation, Justin suddenly feels like a middle school boy talking to a member of the opposite sex for the first time. He feels like the awkward kid who wants to ask the girl to the dance but all he can do is look down at his shuffling feet and mumble something that makes no sense. Within a few feet of reaching her, Justin realizes he's without a cunning statement or introduction. He panics, allowing his shadow to cross Lucy's face as he walks by in silence. A short distance away, he turns around and heads back toward Lucy with the thought that he's just going to be natural and say "Hi." By the time he gets within a few feet of her, Justin overthinks the situation. He convinces himself that showing up at the park the very day she happens to be there makes it appear way too much like he's stalking her. He passes her a second time without uttering a word, this time walking all the way down to the bottom of the knoll. Completely disgusted, Justin mutters to himself, "Okay, you did check the park every day to see if she was here, but she doesn't know that! Just walk up and say 'Hi'."

With renewed determination, Justin trudges up the knoll with his plan firmly in mind. Within a dozen paces of the bench, Lucy stirs, lifts her head upright and shakes her shoulder length hair so as to restore its fullness, then begins to finger comb her deep brown locks. The movement catches Justin off guard and leaves him not only captivated by her beauty but uncertain as to whether she's leaving. Justin, standing only a step away, panics and freezes in silence once again.

Lucy turns her head toward Justin and speaks to him with a smile in her voice. "Are you going to say hello to me Justin or are you just going to stand there?"

Shocked by the question, Justin pauses momentarily then responds, "I thought I'd stand here for a while and bask in the embarrassment. How did you know it was me?"

"I'm blind, Justin, I'm not stupid. I heard you walk by twice before and could see your shadow and feel it on my face as you passed in front of the sun."

"That could be anyone walking by. Do you have some super power you're not telling me about?"

Lucy continues to smile. "Sit down, Justin, before I beat you with a stick. I'm only going to tell you this once. It has nothing to do with special or enhanced powers or abilities. It's just a matter of paying attention."

Justin remains slightly perplexed. "You were paying attention to shadows?"

"Do you see me reaching for that stick to beat you with?" Lucy warns with a laugh. "Joggers, bicyclist, skaters and speed walkers all have their own pattern and unique sound. There's very little foot traffic here on a workday afternoon and hardly anyone on a casual stroll would walk by me three times in two minutes. Besides, I talked to you exactly this time and day last week. Since you didn't ask me for my phone number, I thought if you were interested in getting to know me better, you'd show up about the same time today, one week later. And here you are."

With a schoolboy innocence Justin responds, "So, you think I like you now?"

"Pretty sure, cowboy! You walked by three times and you're wearing cologne. Most men don't put on cologne to take a walk in the park."

Justin rocks back on his heels. "I'm feeling pretty exposed."

"If it makes you feel better, I wouldn't have come here today if I didn't like you too. Life is too short and unpredictable to play games, so here we are." Lucy was confident in her response but not cocky or rude. She knew she had embarrassed Justin but it was done in an endearingly flirtatious manner that made him appreciate not having to guess what she was thinking or feeling.

"Since we're being brutally honest, I came by the park every day. I didn't want to come across as a stalker, but I did want to see you again," explains Justin.

Lucy laughs as if she may have guessed that was the case but inside she was glad to know that Justin had made the effort and was willing to be vulnerable and admit to it. As Lucy stands, she folds her collapsible cane and puts it into her purse. "Give me your arm, Justin, and I'll let you take me to lunch."

"Is this a date?" says Justin, surprised, but eager to comply. "I had no idea we were going out or I would have worn my favorite blue shirt."

Lucy warns Justin with a mischievous smile, "That may be funny in another universe but keep it up and I will make sure you live to regret it. Remember, you're walking for both of us so pay attention and don't walk me into anything—and don't forget to tell me when there's an obstacle or a step. By the way, this is *not* a date. Think of it more in terms of an interview that you get to pay for. Also, do you see the young man playing basketball? He's my brother and he'll be coming with us. I had to bribe him with a free lunch but I'll pay for his meal. He won't sit with us but he'll be there just in case you walk me into a parked car or the side of a building." Lucy waves and the young man answers back with a short whistle in response.

"There's a little deli with outdoor seating only a few blocks from here. What do you think?" says Lucy with a big smile, turning toward Justin while awaiting his response.

"Yes, of course. I'd be happy to go on an interview with you. How could a person decline an escorted, family gathering like this..." Before Justin is able to finish his sentence he feels a sharp, almost painful pressure between his ribs. Looking down, a smiling Lucy has taken the knuckle of her index finger and playfully ground it into his side.

"Ow! Okay, okay," he acknowledges, laughing.

The first few steps are silent, each happy in the moment but tentative in the process. Lucy feels like a schoolgirl on Justin's arm but also realizes how easy it is for a seeing person to forget they are escorting someone blind. Justin, on the other hand, is like a young father holding a newborn for the first time, and is almost overly conscious of his new responsibility. It wouldn't have taken but half the time for Lucy to walk to the deli by herself but she gracefully allows Justin to be her guide and protector. She feels fortunate Justin didn't attempt to stop traffic or have a broom in his possession to sweep away pebbles in her path, but he was charmingly cautious. Once at the deli, the restless younger brother, a bare chested, beach-looking high school kid, accepts his sandwich and rides off on his bike. Pedaling away, he assures big sister he has his phone with him and he'll be around if needed. Lucy waves in his direction and in an elevated voice, tells him that she'll call mom later. "Got it," returns the voice as he disappears.

Lucy selects a seat at a square metal table in an outside seating area. Justin does his best to negotiate the line between being polite but not assuming Lucy needs assistance. After pulling her chair out, he takes the seat to her immediate right rather than sitting across from her. A tattered green umbrella moves above them in rhythm to the light breeze while dull, brown colored wrens dart between tables, snatching up crumbs. The ambiance is dominated more by their conversation than the slight rumble of automobile traffic or the rolling and clicking of an occasional skateboard as it glides over cracks in the sidewalk. Lucy turns her attention to Justin and, pretending to have his resume in front of her, speaks in an official sounding voice. "Well, Mr. Justin…"

"Manus," he provides.

"Yes, Mr. Justin Manus," continues Lucy, while attempting to be as serious as possible. "What qualities do you bring to this position?"

Justin plays along, "Parents love me, kids adore me and pets always try to get frisky with me. Actually, I'm only joking about the parents and kids."

"So you're an animal lover?" quips Lucy.

Jason laughs. "I just put that on my resume in order to get the interview. Seriously, I do like dogs but I prefer the medium or large ones over the purse decorations and dust mops."

The couple exchanges a few additional bantering remarks, followed by a brief silence. Justin, in a more serious and sensitive tone asks, "Do you mind telling me about your blindness?"

Lucy removes her sunglasses, exposing her dark brown eyes and lightly tanned face. "Not at all. It's a topic that's obviously going to come up and I don't mind responding to it now. There was a guy in Redondo Beach who invited my girlfriends and me to a party. I was twenty-one years old at the time and only a handful of classes away from graduating from college. My dream was to become a broadcast journalist. I remember arriving at what I thought was a nice house but can't remember anything after that. From the stories I was told afterward, it was close to midnight and a couple of the guys were in the next room looking at a small derringer pistol—one of those little guns that don't look like a real gun. The guys were drunk and one of them was convinced it was a toy and grabbed at it. In the ensuing scuffle, the gun was fired and the bullet went through the wall and into the next room which was filled with maybe a hundred people. It hit me in the back of the head and I collapsed. No one knew what happened at first. My girlfriends thought

I fainted until they saw the blood. I'm really lucky to be alive. That was over a decade ago and since then I've completed college, have my own apartment and co-teach third grade part-time at a private school. It's not the life I planned but it's a life I'm happy with."

Justin is slightly awed by the story and deeply respectful of Lucy. "That's an amazing story. What does it mean to co-teach?"

"I have my teaching credential but because of potential liability issues, I need to have an assistant in the class with me."

"So you gave up on the idea of being a broadcast journalist?"

With a slight frown Lucy explains, "It's not that I gave up. I think a more accurate statement would be that I was a little naïve at the time. I was convinced my obligation to the public was to uncover the truth or at the very least, report the facts of a story. I was an intern with a major station and had every intention to pursue that dream. I was told I had all the personal attributes and qualities they wanted but my downfall was resisting the trend to sell my soul for the sake of my career. It didn't take long to realize that on-air personalities are required to simply parrot the political views and agenda of those who write their checks, regardless of the truth. Maybe someday that will change but it forced me to rethink my direction and I really love what I do now. I can't imagine doing anything besides teaching. I love my kids."

"I'm sure the feeling is mutual," said Justin thinking any kid would instantly fall in love with her. "What about a social life and…"

Lucy interrupts. "Are you asking me if I've been on a date in all these years? I usually just troll the parks and beaches for lonely men on my days off," she says, a laugh in her voice. "Surprisingly, I get asked out more than you might think. Some of my kids have single dads but I won't date my kid's parents and it seems everyone wants to set me up but that's always awkward. Dating hasn't been that fulfilling for me yet, but I do have great friends and my family lives nearby so it's not as horrible as you imagine. What about you? Do you date a lot?"

Justin doesn't hesitate. "I'm divorced." He's hopeful that Lucy will move on to another topic but her silence indicates she's expecting more detail.

"I met my ex in college and we were married for ten years. We were separated about two years ago." Lucy remains silent, her hands now folded on top of the table. All of her attention is directed to Justin. After a slight pause and a rising level of discomfort, Justin continues, "We married young. I worked hard to provide a good life but messed up my priorities, convincing myself that it was beneficial for us in the long run. I wasn't sensitive enough to her issues and she became a little restless in the relationship. We ran into a tough patch in life and the marriage fell apart. She met a guy who satisfied some repressed adolescent needs in her life and decided to leave. She married this guy a week after our divorce was final. He turned out to be a chronically unemployed mamma's boy and wannabe rock star, but I guess it works for them. So, to answer your question, I'm kind of a dating virgin since my divorce. The closest I've been is an interview."

Lucy's straight laced exterior quickly dissolves into playfulness and she reverts back to her consultation mode. "I was afraid for a moment that you weren't going to pass the interview, Mr. Manus. I was starting to think you were going to hold out on the answers and we require full disclosure at this establishment. As you may be aware, the law prohibits us from discriminating against dating virgins so it appears once we check your references, you may qualify for an opportunity here."

Justin reaches for Lucy's hand. "You love playing the antagonist, don't you?" At first he intends to lightly, casually touch her hand but once he feels her flesh on his, he cannot resist the temptation to hold it. Lucy is initially uncertain as to Justin's motives but when his hand lingers, she gently and affectionately squeezes it to demonstrate her approval.

The afternoon quickly passes as the couple comfortably converse together in the shade of an old green umbrella. The glamor of the surroundings isn't of significance at the moment. The topics range from the comical and superficial to heartfelt experiences and dreams. Lucy continues to amaze Justin with her fearless attitude toward life. She wants to scuba dive, travel to new places and ride on a zip line through a jungle. She maintains pictures of the world in her mind and envisions standing atop the Eiffel Tower someday. It doesn't have to make sense to anyone else, she wants to feel the steel beams for herself, breathe the air of Paris and have the view described to her. Even though not spoken, it's easy to imply she desires to share these experiences with someone she cares deeply for.

Justin's world is much smaller at the moment. His mind isn't filled with dreams and fantasies, only survival. As Lucy becomes more animated in her enthusiasm, Justin retreats into himself, wondering if he's doing the right thing. He has to keep his secret about the killer to himself. It would be entirely selfish and uncaring to drag Lucy into his nightmare. Although tempted to excuse himself and run away, Justin finds Lucy's charm to be almost intoxicating. He has never met anyone so full of courage and life

"Yes, I'm heading back to my apartment now," Lucy states as she answers her phone. "Justin is walking me home. Yes, Justin Manus is his name. I'll be fine but thanks for calling."

Disconnecting from the call, Lucy smiles as she refocuses her attention back to Justin. "My little brother loves me."

The late afternoon walk to Lucy's apartment on the opposite end of the park is entirely different from their walk to the deli. Lucy's right hand is firmly nestled within Justin's while she holds to his arm with her left hand. While waiting on a corner for a car to pass, Lucy squeezes Justin's hand and briefly leans her head against his arm. The demonstration of affection floods his heart and mind with emotions he thought he had nearly forgotten about. He can only think of what a prize she is and how fortunate he is to have merited her attention, but thoughts of the killer continue to lurk in the back of his mind.

Lucy directs Justin through the small park and out on the other side where her apartment complex is located. It's an older building, fitting with the neighborhood and designed like a big square with a cement common area. It wasn't a structure of beauty but it appeared well maintained and clean.

"You live a block to the east of the park, don't you?" inquires Lucy.

"Yes, and it appears you live about the same distance on the west side," responds Justin.

"The only thing separating us are a few hundred yards of grass and a zip code."

That surprises him. "We have different zip codes?"

"Yes, the park is the boundary and yours is one digit different from mine."

Standing outside the apartment entrance in a small alcove that allows for marginal privacy, Lucy turns to face Justin and reaches toward him.

"Your hair is shorter than I thought it might be." Lucy's softly states while her hands glide down Justin's face. "You haven't shaved in a couple of days." Lucy smiles with Justin as she feels the contour of his face form into his own smile.

"The unshaved look is trendy right now," explains Justin. "I can't figure out if it looks good on me or whether it makes me look homeless."

Lucy laughs, commenting, "I think you're handsome and you probably look good either way." Her fingers trace the curve of Justin's lips again and he responds by gently pulling her into him. Feeling the contour of her body pressed against him, Justin leans into Lucy and kisses her. It's a soft but magical kiss; one that screams with the potential for a future together, even love.

It was a good first kiss, not overly lustful but tender and still passionate. They hold one another in silence for a few moments until Justin asks, "So, I guess I passed the interview?"

"Not just yet!" Lucy proclaims as she gives him another quick kiss and informs him he must call her tomorrow evening in order to get the final results.

As Justin enters the digits of Lucy's number onto his cell phone, a small voice speaks out from behind the entrance, "Hello Miss Lucy." Lucy turns and responds, "I know that voice. Hello Sam!" The unseen child giggles from his hiding place, and then runs away into the courtyard.

"I see you have a little boyfriend," teases Justin.

"He's my favorite," explains Lucy with a wide smile. "Little Sam Kim. Sometimes I call him Sammy."

"Did you say his last name is Kim?"

"Yes, why do you ask?"

"He's Korean then?" continues Justin.

"Yes," responds Lucy, now slightly puzzled. Almost everyone who lives here is Korean except for me and a young couple on the second floor... and there's also Miss Mavis who has been here forever. I don't know the young couple very well but I do sit at the bench near the mailbox and talk to Miss Mavis on occasion. The Koreans are really sweet people and have always been good to me."

"I'm glad you're happy here. Would you like me to walk you to your door?" invites Justin.

"This is fine for now," Lucy states as she embraces Justin for the final time. "I had a good time."

Justin watches as Lucy retrieves her cane, and then walks from sight into the apartment complex. Confident he is alone, Justin examines the mailboxes. After excluding Lucy's name, the Korean names, and then eliminating the young Caucasian couple, only one name remains—Mavis Kilborn.

VIII

The First Date

Justin's rented recreational vehicle has taken on the appearance of a burglary scene as he prepares for his first official date with Lucy. He has several hours to organize but in his eagerness to make everything perfect, he has started three projects for each one he completes. Clothes, cleaning products, building materials and articles of personal hygiene are randomly scattered throughout the motorhome.

"Oh, dude... you really know how to impress a girl," Hugh chuckles as he enters the RV, his face revealing both surprise and amusement. Somewhat out of character, today he's wearing his prosthetic legs. Under normal conditions the former Marine wheels around the house and yard in a wheelchair that he refers to as his throne. He unabashedly displays his amputated appendages, openly referring to them as his 'nubs' and treating them at times as though they were pets. "Seriously, dude, I've seen battlefields less dangerous than this."

Unable to roust a comment in return, Hugh continues with another verbal jab, "Do you need some help or are you planning on injuring her all on your own?"

Justin, finally realizing the voice is coming from within the motorhome, peeks out from behind the bedroom wall, "Hey, you have your legs on. You look good for a jarhead."

Hugh laughs, "Yeah, I'm stylin' today. I have an appointment at noon to talk to someone about a part-time IT job so I thought I'd dress to impress."

"I like the suit but what's up with the yellow tie? I thought yellow was a power color that screams out a desire to be in charge?"

"I must have missed that article in the magazine," explains Hugh. "I guess it's because I was so preoccupied with the report on how to save money on manicures."

Justin bites on the line, "Manicures? How do you save money on a manicure?"

"You only get one nail done," says Hugh as he flaunts his middle finger at Justin.

Justin responds with a hearty laugh at the prank, "Okay, the yellow tie it is! I'm one to talk. I have no idea what to wear tonight."

Puzzled by the comment, Hugh's eyes widen and his brows arch. "Aren't you going out with Lucy? She's blind, right? How's she going to know what you're wearing?"

"She can only see bright lights and flashes but she knows stuff… it's scary sometimes. I can't get anything by her. She's like one of those dogs that can smell narcotics from outer space."

"Seriously? She sounds interesting. Do I get to meet her tonight or are you going to keep her all to yourself?"

"I told her all about you and she wants to meet you anyway," teases Justin.

"What did you tell her about me?"

"I told her you got blown up in Afghanistan."

"You already told her about my nubs?"

"Hell no. I told her you were burned into a crispy chunk of sausage so she wouldn't want to meet you."

Hugh chuckles. "That's cold dude. That's wrong on so many levels."

"I told her the truth man," Justin admits. "I told her you were a war hero and that you're one of the best guys I know. She's looking forward to meeting you."

There's a brief silence as Hugh sees the sincerity in Justin's face. He turns to leave to the RV. "I gotta run dog. I don't want to be late for my appointment."

"Lose the yellow tie!" shouts Justin as Hugh passes out the doorway.

"Hey!" Hugh extends only a single hand back into the RV, "I got the same manicure deal on the other hand. See?"

It's been a busy few days for Justin. He's been on the phone with Lucy several hours each evening and their conversations carry on well into the night. Although she did affectionately inform Justin that he passed the interview, she won't allow him to see her again until their official first date. Justin feels confident that Lucy isn't being a tease on any level; it appears to him that she's simply appraising his sincerity and response to her boundaries. He has little doubt that she is confident in his motives so the temporary barriers must simply serve as a confirmation to what she already knows to be true about him. Both Justin and Lucy are mindful of the primary reason for the failure of his marriage. Lucy's oft repeated phrase of "paying attention" must serve as both a warning and a guide if there is to be a relationship. She is not one whose needs can be neglected or ignored and she refuses to commit herself to anyone in an emotional bull rush before feeling secure with key details. Justin knows that early in the relationship, if there is to be one, that he must demonstrate that he is paying attention. Justin has been intently listening. He knows Lucy loves the sound of the rain, full moons and roses. She was born in July and her favorite color is Caribbean blue; she enjoys a gentle breeze, the sun on her face and the laughter of children. It doesn't take much to make her happy. She's not materialistic and desires little more than to be loved and valued for the person she is. She's affectionate and enjoys the touch of someone she cares for. Justin knows he doesn't need to be perfect. He simply has to get a few things right while displaying an ongoing effort to demonstrate that her needs are important to him. He's confident Lucy isn't looking for a caretaker; she wants a man who views her desires and dreams on an equal level with his own. Justin wants to demonstrate to her that he can be that kind of man.

Over the course of the next few hours, Justin manages to nearly complete all his projects and reassemble the RV so it's presentable for Lucy. He's normally not nervous around women but anything to do with Lucy gets him a little on edge.

Hugh has warned Justin that women like this are dangerous. Although Hugh has never been in love, it doesn't inhibit him from dispensing relationship advice like a newspaper columnist. He thinks Lucy is going to pounce on Justin's heart like a feline on catnip. He's witnessed several of his buddies in the Marine Corp fall under the spell and they seem to possess a certain "look" in common. According to Hugh, Justin has the look. Every time Lucy's name is brought up, it's as though his eyes glaze over and he transcends to some ethereal happy place.

Justin and Hugh have shared many late night conversations. He knows Hugh has had a lot of girlfriends but has yet to succumb to "the look." This is largely due to the internal conflict he faces with his parents and their traditional values. According to what Hugh has told Justin, his parents would prefer him to find someone who can fully appreciate Japanese culture. But their image of Japan was established thirty years ago, before they moved to America. In their absence, Japan has changed. Justin thinks Hugh's situation is nearly impossible. In order to accommodate his parents, Hugh would have to find what his parents perceive as a traditional Japanese woman. Even in modern Japan, this may prove to be a difficult task in itself. To further add to Hugh's dilemma, he needs a woman who can appreciate his culture while being able to relate to his Western upbringing. Until he discovers this unique combination, he is content sharing the company of several female friends.

Justin, finishing up his housekeeping chores, hauls all of his dirty clothes and gym shoes to the laundry shed located outdoors. As a final touch he attempts to neutralize the musty man cave by dousing the entire interior of the RV with a rose scented spray. The last thing he wants is to open the door and have Lucy think she's entering a locker room. He knows Lucy likes roses so the idea is pretty simple; he's going to close all the windows, and then empty an entire can of spray into the mobile home. After shutting the door behind him, he will return with Lucy in couple of hours to the fabulous smell of a home-cooked meal and "spring sunshine," just like it reads on the label. With the task completed Justin checks the position of the lawn sprinkler one last time, and then heads off for his final errand at the florist. The flower shop is a short walk away, very close to where he and Lucy ate lunch together under the umbrella.

The lady who owns the small shop, a short, pudgy woman with a welcoming face, greets Justin as he enters. "How can I help you?"

"I have a first date... roses, she likes roses." Justin's eyes dart around the shop, "I don't know much about flowers."

The flower lady continues to smile, looking amused by Justin's awkwardness. "Do you know what kind of rose you want, the color or how many?"

"I only know she likes roses, so whatever it takes to make her happy." He gazes into the refrigerated display.

The flower lady patiently stands behind Justin. He knows she's studying his face in the reflection of the glass. "The roses aren't going to make her happy, young man. You paying attention to her and showing that you care will make her happy. The rose is only a symbol of your intentions."

Justin turns, facing the woman. "This sounds way more complicated than I originally thought."

"Okay, let me simplify it for you." The lady points out a few selections. "First dates can be tricky. If you don't know her well but you want to display something that says you're interested in her, a single yellow or pink rose is fine. Yellow would be my first choice but if she's very young and trendy, pink. What is her favorite color?"

"Purple."

"Oh, well that won't do. If you love her, red is a strong, passionate color and would be very appropriate... but as a first date, no. Hmmm...I think maybe your color is white."

"White? Why?"

"White is for purity. I'm sensing you already have feelings for this girl and white displays your honest intentions. White is like a blank slate and a new start. It represents a new love."

"That sounds like it works... give me a dozen of those."

"Why do you want a dozen?"

"I thought they came as a package deal that way."

"Maybe you're thinking of doughnuts," she says with a laugh.

After a brief pause the flower lady touches Justin's arm and confesses, "We do sell a lot of roses in quantities of a dozen. Twelve roses represent the hours in the day and the months in the year that you'll be thinking about her. Some even apply the number to religious meanings. But in your case, one is sufficient for a first date."

Justin pauses, thinks for a moment and then explains, "It's more than a first date because we actually spent time talking in the park the first day, then spent an entire afternoon together on what she referred to as an interview. From then on, we've talked on the phone every night—"

"Okay," interrupts the flower lady, eyes twinkling with amusement. "I think I have a solution for you. Believe it or not, there are no laws that govern this so you can do what you want without worry of being arrested by the flower police. I'm going to give you seven white roses. Give her six for the remaining months of this year to keep in her home and one to take with her on your date. If nothing else, it will display originality and thought. Without saying it, it implies that you will replace them with red roses when the time comes. What do you think?"

Justin impulsively puts his arms around the flower lady and gives her a hug. For the first time since he's entered the shop, she seems to have nothing to say. She continues to smile as she prepares and completes Justin's order, calling out to him on his exit from the shop, "I expect to see you back in here for red roses."

Justin acknowledges her statement with a smile and an affirming nod.

With the final errand completed, Justin continues his walk to the other side of the park to pick up Lucy for their date. The early summer evening will allow for another hour of daylight and keep the temperatures warm well into the night. Turning a corner, Justin is forced to pass a thuggish looking man on a narrow sidewalk. He's a large, overly muscular man with a shaved head. His arms and chest display a number of obscene tattoos. Justin is not easily intimidated but this man is scary and his thoughts immediately transition to a status of high alert. Within a dozen steps of passing him, the thuggish man looks up, smiles and in a bass voice that could crack concrete, says "Nice flowers man."

Justin smiles in return as relief washes over him. Continuing his walk, he's nearly at the middle of the park when he meets up with another threatening character. Everything about this man screams gang banger. Although not as big as his previous encounter, his aggressive walk combined with tattoos encircling his neck and wife-beater T-shirt make him appear dangerous. He boldly displays the top six inches of his underwear above his low-hanging jeans and maintains a facial expression that dares anyone to cross him. As with the first encounter, once within speaking distance, the gangster's scowl turns into a big smile and he makes some kind of sign with his hand. To Justin's amazement, it appears to be an obvious gesture of approval. It's as though Justin has stumbled upon a magical secret of some sort. A man carrying flowers is invincible. It seems no matter where someone's life takes them, everyone can relate to flowers and the hope of love that they represent.

Not many steps later, Justin arrives at Lucy's door and knocks. Lucy calls out his name and when he affirms it's him, she cracks open the door. Justin's heart is already racing. He hasn't seen Lucy since sharing their first kiss earlier in the week. The few days that have followed have left him craving her.

"I'm glad you're here," says Lucy as she reaches out for him. Unlike their first encounters, Lucy has departed from her professional wardrobe and is wearing a more casual and trendy outfit. Her snug designer jeans are accented with a form-fitting turquoise top that exposes her bronzed, bare shoulders while tastefully revealing a slight amount of cleavage. The bright color accentuates her dark features and the end result registers in Justin's mind as simply breathtaking. He immediately pulls her into him and they share a warm and welcoming kiss. Unlike their first moment of intimacy, this kiss possesses a slight increase of security and passion. There is no longer a question of motives or interest, it's now a matter of how far the relationship will go. Judging by their response to one another, the flower lady could be receiving an order for red roses sooner than she expects.

"What do you have in your hand?" asks Lucy after a long embrace following their kiss.

"Magic flowers!" Justin blurts out. He tells her the story of his encounter with the flower lady and the response of the thuggish men he passed. Lucy giggles with amusement as she searches for a vase to put them in.

"They smell wonderful. Are they white?"

"I'm not even going to ask how you knew that. I could have saved a ton of time just by asking you ahead of time. Who knew there were so many choices? By the way, the flower lady says to take one with you on the date. Besides, we can use it to fend off monsters and thugs in the park."

Lucy laughs, tosses a white sweater across her arm and latches onto Justin. "Shall we go?"

"You look amazing!" Justin says as they head into the park.

Lucy smiles and turns toward Justin. "So do you."

He's not going to ask. It doesn't matter what she sees or how she sees it. As long as she thinks he's amazing and whatever level that's on, Justin is happy. Hugh's house and his rented abode are only a few minutes away and he feels as if his feet aren't really touching the ground along the way.

Approaching the house, Justin sees that Hugh has left all the windows open. The summer nights, comfortable evening temperatures and mild breezes off the ocean allow many residents to forego any form of air conditioning. It provides a wonderful level of comfort but does little for one's privacy.

Once at the door to the RV, Justin turns to Lucy and states with a certain degree of pride, "I have some special things lined up for you. I'm not much of a cook but I know one Italian dish that I can do fairly well and I made dinner for you. Ready to go in?"

Lucy radiates an approving smile but as the door to the RV is opened, rather than the pleasant aroma of a nice meal and the "spring sunshine" he expected, Justin feels Lucy recoil as the couple is bowled over by an explosive blend of what smells like cheap perfume and rotten fish. The summer heat, scorched food, and lack of ventilation have combined to produce a gaseous fume so vile it had neighbors cursing and slamming their windows shut.

Lucy quickly backs away from the entrance. "Justin, I'm sorry, but I can't go in there." He can see she's trying not to laugh. "That's not the special dish you learned to cook is it?"

Justin cringes with humiliation. "It's the air freshener. It's supposed to smell like roses."

Lucy is unable to contain her laughter. "Justin, I realize you wanted to make this very special for me." Though she's speaking through laughter, there's nothing mean spirited in her voice. "I know you went to a lot of trouble to make a nice evening for me. But listen... everything is fine, we just can't eat anything in there. Why don't we order some Korean Barbeque and sit out here and eat it?"

"I thought you liked Italian."

"I do like Italian," Lucy says.

"I made fish with an Italian recipe."

"I also like Korean Barbeque." Lucy's laughing so hard she has to hold onto Justin. "I may never eat Italian again."

Justin laughs at himself, then takes Lucy's arm and guides her a safe distance away. With Lucy left standing along the side of the house, he bravely re-enters the motor home, opens up all the windows, attempting not to gag in the process.

As Justin works to contain the situation, Lucy hears a voice coming from the direction of the house.

"Pssstttt...Lucy! Lucy!"

Lucy turns her head in the direction of the voice and responds, "Yes?... Hugh?"

"How did you... never mind! I want to tell you what Justin is wearing so we can pull something on him."

Lucy is mindful of Justin's comment in the park about wearing his favorite blue shirt so she makes an educated guess in order to turn the table on Hugh. "I already know he's wearing a blue shirt."

"Hey, are you sure you're blind?" Hugh demands. Lucy has to smile at his tone of voice, a combination of amazement and frustration. "You're starting to freak me out. How did you know that?"

Lucy hides her smirk behind one hand. "Okay, if it makes you feel better, tell me what he's wearing. I might be persuaded to play along with whatever you're up to.

"A dark brown blazer with jeans and a blue shirt, but somehow I imagine you knew that. This is the gag—tell him his outfit would look so much better with a yellow tie. Can you do it?"

"I'll see what I can do. Nice meeting you, Hugh," Lucy says with a mischievous smile.

"Remember... yellow tie... you look really nice, by the way," says the voice as it disappears back into the recess of the house beyond the screened window.

Within minutes Justin emerges from the motorhome. Although Lucy can't see his face, she can hear disappointment in his voice. "I feel like an idiot," he says. "I worked all afternoon cleaning up the place. As you've probably guessed, things didn't turn out as I planned. It still stinks in there. We can go out somewhere. Do you have a good restaurant you'd like to go to?"

"I do know of one but it's a coat and tie kind of place. Do you know what would look great with your brown blazer and blue shirt?"

Justin, distracted by the ruined dinner and series of setbacks, responds to Lucy without thinking. "No, what do you think would go with my shirt and blazer?"

Lucy almost has to bite her lip while saying, "A yellow tie."

Justin stares silently into Lucy's face for a few moments, his mind racing to catch up with her statement and the situation at hand. "Hugh! Do you see my manicure Hugh?"

Lucy has no idea what the manicure crack is about but judging from Justin's reaction, it was a really good gag. She laughs in delight, and before the situation gets too far out of hand, she reaches for Justin and finding him, pulls herself toward him by using his lapels. Face to face she kisses him. "Thank you for making me feel special!"

"Really?" says Justin. "We're lucky to be alive and we're still in the first thirty minutes of the date."

"Yes!" responds Lucy. "I'm having a wonderful time so why don't you put on some different clothes, we'll order some take-out and find a place around here to eat."

"Different clothes? You don't like what I'm wearing?"

"I don't mean to hurt your feelings Justin, but your clothes smell a little fishy."

"She's trying to tell you that you stink, buddy," Hugh says as he exits the house holding a pair of sweat pants and a T-shirt. "These are baggy on me so they should fit you. If you don't get out of those clothes soon, your grandchildren will probably stink too."

Justin chuckles, thanks Hugh for the clothes and begins to make his way into the house to change. As he reaches the rear door of the house he abruptly stops and turns to Hugh, "I was going to introduce you to my date but it's obvious you've already met."

Lucy sits with Hugh on the back steps to the house while placing an order for the delivery of their dinner.

"Justin really likes you," says Hugh.

"How do you know that?" Lucy asks, as though she doesn't already know.

"He spent all day preparing for your date. He was even up in the fruit trees attaching lights and a garden hose to something. Has he used the hose yet?"

"No."

"Well, you're not out of danger, then.

Lucy laughs. "I like him too."

Justin soon reappears wearing an old pair of gray sweat pants and a tattered red T-shirt with the white block letters "Boston University" emblazoned on the front. It wasn't his best look but at least he didn't smell bad. Hugh, apparently satisfied with the success of his practical joke, returns indoors.

Justin utilizes the time waiting for the arrival of their food to guide Lucy into a tree swing hanging from one of the large branches and invites her to sit. After she's comfortable, Justin excuses himself. "I have to set up my next surprise." Lucy has no idea what's up but soon hears what sounds like running water, but before she can wonder long, Justin returns to sit next to her and gathers her in his arms. With the sun now below the horizon and in the twilight of the warm summer evening, the desired mood is set.

"I heard you turn on water somewhere," Lucy says with some degree of apprehension. "Are we going to be okay? Are we going to get wet?"

"Just wait for it. It takes a couple of minutes for it to work."

"Is this going to work better than the rose scent in the motor home?" Lucy asks with a nervous chuckle.

"You said you liked the sound of the rain, right?"

She nods. "Listen," says Justin.

First Lucy hears a single ping, then another, followed by a pong and a plink.

"What is it?"

"Artificial rain, just for you. I hooked a sprinkler up in a tree and turned it on low. The slow running water is dripping through the leaves and onto tin cans and pieces of metal I hung from the branches."

"Justin! That's so cool," Lucy says, wonder in her voice, "You made a rain chime. You've created a symphony of sound. You did this for me?"

Justin remains silent, basking in the glory of at least one thing that went according to plan. Lucy continues to squeeze him tighter, finally reaching for his face and whispering, "Best date ever!"

By the time their dinner arrives, along with full darkness, Lucy is quite comfortable with Justin's touch and displays of affection. Justin seats her at a table he had arranged earlier in the day and places a small object, about the size of a key chain, in her hand. It's a remote control with only a single button; the kind many use to activate Christmas tree lights. Lucy feels the surface of the small remote device in her hand and asks, "What is this?"

Before Justin is able to answer, she triggers the switch, powering on a canopy of small white decorative lights that Justin draped over a swath of the backyard. "I can tell that it's lighter but I can't see anything, Justin. What did you do?"

"We're having dinner under the stars," Justin explains, and as a final touch, he triggers a second remote that activates an old study lamp held firmly in a tree between a couple of branches. "We now have a full moon too."

"I can see the moon, Justin!" Lucy exclaims, excited.

"No you can't... Really, can you?"

"Well, not like you see it, but I can see what looks like a small, fuzzy ball of cotton. That's how the brightest full moon looks to me. It's perfect!"

A soft and romantic exchange of conversation and smiles accompanies their dinner. Justin is learning to fight the impulse to leap into action each time Lucy attempts something. He waits for her to ask for help but she rarely does. Justin's initial thoughts were to strap Lucy into a bib and provide her with only a fork. It became obvious by the end of dinner that she has a greater mastery of chopsticks and made less of a mess than he. Justin is beginning to relax more and worry less about Lucy's moment-to-moment activities. As the evening progresses, he spends more time focused on enjoying her company while admiring her beauty, intelligence and remarkable charm.

Lucy finds herself dazzled by Justin's care and concern for her. His efforts display more depth to his character and serve to enhance what she perceives as his good looks and masculine allure. Justin's actions display that he's listening and responding to her needs and Lucy is reacting by swinging open the door to her heart. There is always the reservation of moving too fast and being swept away in the excitement of something new, but it seems genuine to her. It seems right.

After dinner, they return to the tree swing, sitting comfortably in the warm evening under the manufactured stars and full moon. Lucy hears and feels Justin's sigh. "I suppose I should get you back soon," he says.

"Oh, okay," she responds, not trying to disguise her disappointment. Their time together has passed much too quickly.

"Do you smell roses, or is that just me?" asks Justin. "I think the motorhome may actually be habitable by now."

Lucy takes in a breath and responds with a smile. "You can tell me tomorrow if you survive the night."

"Is that your way of saying you want to hear from me tomorrow?"

"Of course I want to hear from you tomorrow. I'm looking forward to seeing you again."

With her hand tucked warmly in his arm, her other clutching the single white rose, Justin walks Lucy home through the park and the warm summer night.

IX

Following the Scent

Detectives Barnes and Fuentes pull to the side of the rural road and park their police cruiser well in front of the yellow crime scene tape. Normally Barnes would attempt to get as close to the investigation as possible but word from her cohorts in the Riverside County Sheriff's Department is that the victim is pretty ripe, having been dead about three days. Homicide detectives joke that their jobs wouldn't be that difficult if it weren't for the dead bodies. The sometimes gruesome murder scenes are situations detectives grow accustomed to but the smell of human decay burns its way into one's brain and leaves a scar that can never be removed. Rotting flesh has a cloying odor that is immediately repulsive and stimulates an abrupt gag reflex response. No one looks forward to this type of crime scene. Once exposed to the odor, there are times when the mere thought of the stench can reproduce the sensation and subsequent urge to vomit. The unique smell is initiated shortly after death as ravenous microorganisms devour the intestinal lining and seep into the body cavity, unleashing powerful enzymes that feed off of other organs. Methane and other gases are produced as these cells begin to rupture and liquefy before finding an orifice or wound to escape from. Unlike most gaseous odors, a decomposing body produces fat-based particles that cling to anything in its proximity. It's nearly impossible to remove the scent of death from any fabric or porous material that it comes in contact with. Even a moderate exposure to the vicinity of a rotting corpse can result in an aftermath of consequences. Those who become affected can carry the smell of the deceased in their hair and clothing for days. Almost any seasoned detective will admit that it's easier to deal with a fresh crime scene than one that has been flavored with time and the elements.

Barnes looks at Fuentes as though they're initiating a first attempt at sky diving. "Are you ready for this?"

"Oh yeah." Fuentes speaks with confidence. "Just give me a few minutes to get my kit out of the back and get situated."

Barnes smirks at Fuentes with amusement, "Kit? What kit? I have vapor rub for your nose if that's what you're referring to."

"I have kids. I can't afford to replace my wardrobe every time I come in contact with a fermented body. My wife won't even let me inside the house. I buy disposable paint overalls from the hardware store and combine it with a hairnet, gloves, a mask and shoe covers."

Barnes looks at Fuentes with her eyes widened and brows lifted, "You serious? You're going to go out there with the boys from Riverside dressed up like an extraterrestrial?"

Fuentes doesn't respond. He's made his point and obviously places a higher priority on the practicality of his position. He'd rather preserve his clothing and minimize the lingering odor as opposed to impressing fellow detectives as to how long he can tolerate the ungodly stench, pretending it doesn't bother him. Barnes, on the other hand, has built her career on the fact that she's as tough as any man. She jokes she would take a bite out of a rotting cadaver to prove it.

Barnes leaves Fuentes to dress on his own while she reacquaints herself with the detectives from Riverside County. She didn't have to venture too far beyond the yellow crime scene tape before being accosted by the smell. The mangled, nude body of a male victim lies only a few yards away from a popular jogging and hiking trail. It appears to have been dumped in the scrub brush and just out of view. The remains would have been overlooked for an indeterminate period of time had it not been for the distinct foul odor and the curiosity of a couple joggers. The killer made no attempt to bury the body or conceal it in any manner. It baked in the summer sun for a few days until the stench gave away its position. Only a minute behind, Fuentes appears on the scene, dressed like someone emerging from an operating room.

"Don't shoot!" Barnes speaks in a loud voice. "He's human and he's with me."

The Riverside detectives chuckle at the prank but Fuentes isn't about to let Barnes have the last word. "Okay guys, you laugh now, but when you still reek of zombie in two days, my kids will be cuddled up to me telling me how good I smell."

The detectives laugh. Barnes sidles up to Fuentes, smiling and speaking quietly, "Remember the Manus interview and all the comments about the bridge and the cows? I told you I was going to get you back for that."

"Oh, that's how you are? Okay, I see how it is… I can do that too," says Fuentes as his eyebrows lift to the bottom edge of his shower cap.

Barnes continues to laugh. It's not what Fuentes is saying that is so funny, it's his appearance and the fact that each time he speaks, the resulting puff of air causes his surgical mask to bounce like a woofer on an old audio speaker.

"Okay partner," Fuentes says, "I'm glad I amuse you but I still don't know why you dragged me out to Riverside County in this miserable heat to see this particular victim."

"I'm sorry." Barnes places an affectionate hand on his shoulder. "I'm not trying to be mean, but you have to admit… you do look a little like someone cleaning up a toxic waste spill."

"I can live with that… no worries. But this heat is worse than *Mijami* and if I stay out here too long it's going to kill me. So why are we here?"

Barnes drops her smile and clicks back into detective mode. "If you recall, after Art Conner's murder we interviewed both Justin Manus and Manus's ex-wife. A couple of days ago the former Ms. Manus pulled out the business cards we left with her and called me to report her current husband was missing. Per protocol, I arranged for a deputy to take the report but I kept the notes on our conversation. I didn't think much of it at the time but this morning I read few lines in the blotter describing a pudgy male victim, five-foot-six, with long hair and tattoos. I think this could be our guy. The lab boys have already been here so we're clear to look around."

With tweezers in hand, Barnes walks toward the corpse, taking short, shallow breaths through her nose as she approaches from thirty feet away. Fuentes and the two Riverside Detectives follow close behind. It appears the male victim was dragged from the nearby road, then lifted up and dropped into the thick shrubbery. No footprints or tire tracks were discovered but broken plant limbs formed a definitive path from the road to the dump site. The upper body strength needed to accomplish this task points to a male perpetrator. Large, thick shrubs cradle the body which lies face up. The upper body and legs are elevated by stronger branches while the limbs of the corpse dangle to each side like a discarded string-puppet. The only part of the body actually on the ground is the buttocks, now as dark as an overripe plum; a result of gravity and the accumulation of blood. Much of the interior musculature has dissolved and separated from the outer layer of skin, producing an illusion that the corpse is wearing a thin, loose-fitting plastic coating. Maggots hatch from every orifice and wound within the first 24 hours; other insects and animals join the human buffet thereafter. As alarming as the sight and smell is, the most appalling spectacle for Barnes is the thin, tight nylon rope tied around the victim's genitalia. Judging from the ripping of the surrounding muscles and the severity of the wound, it appears the victim was either pushed from an elevated platform or hung by his testicles. Barnes, using tweezers, pulls away the colorful bandana which is displayed on his forehead and tied behind the back of his neck. With the forehead exposed, she inserts the tweezers under the hairline and gently pulls it up. It's a wig and the flowing hair that extends beyond the victim's shoulders is exposed as being nothing more than a hairpiece.

"It's him!" proclaims Barnes as she quickly covers her mouth and scurries with the others to a place of safety.

"Who is it?" demands one of the Riverside detectives.

Barnes, with her hands on her knees and head down, briefly shakes her head as a desperate means to rid herself of the odor. "I don't know his name off the top of my head but based on his wife's description, I know who he is. A family law attorney was murdered a few weeks ago in Orange County, probably by the same guy. The method of operation and nylon rope look the same. It's obviously sexual, retaliatory, and the killer appears to enjoy torturing his victims before he kills them."

Looking toward one another, the Riverside detectives nod, and then one regurgitates what he understands of the situation, "You have a suspect from San Bernardino County who possibly murdered two people in Orange County and dumped one of the bodies in Riverside County?"

Barnes shrugs. "Is that a problem?"

"Not at all," continues the Riverside Detective. "But since you're handling the first case, why don't you take the lead on this and we'll provide whatever support we can on our end. We'll send the medical examiner's report and whatever data or forensic evidence we uncover."

Barnes and Fuentes agree to accept the responsibility but are quiet as they drive away from the crime scene. Fuentes speaks first, "There's something not right about this, partner."

Barnes looks in Fuentes direction but doesn't speak. She wants to let Fuentes air his take on the situation. "I know this all points to Manus and judging by what we know today, he's the obvious culprit... but it doesn't feel right. No, there's something jiggy about all this."

Contrary to her calm exterior, Barnes's mind and emotions are in turmoil. That gut feeling that produces red flags and alarms is on high alert. There's definitely something not right about this case but for now her training demands that she follow protocol. "I can't say you're wrong but we have to follow the evidence. Let's pick him up."

It's been a few weeks since the detectives conducted their initial interview with Manus at his apartment, and when they arrive, he's gone. Over the next few weeks their search for him proves unfruitful. They regret not monitoring his activities more closely. He appears to have left the area, deliberately cutting off all obvious trails to his whereabouts. He could be anywhere by now but Barnes and Fuentes suspect he's still in Southern California. There's no record of him leaving the country through normal modes of transport and without a vehicle his travel options are limited. Car rental agencies and most public modes of transportation require identification and his name hasn't popped up in their data bases. Interviews with friends, neighbors and relatives produce nothing. No one claims to know of his location; even his ex-wife is of little assistance in providing clues to his whereabouts. There's no cell phone to track and no credit card to monitor. He could have crossed over into Mexico but that wouldn't make a lot of sense. Manus doesn't speak Spanish and would find it difficult to blend in there. Regardless of the fact, the Mexican and even Canadian authorities are notified as a precaution.

The two detectives organize their search back at the office. "Okay Barnes," says Fuentes as he sets a chair just inside the entrance to her cubical, "Where are we on the Manus case? We both have the same impression of the guy. He's either the best liar either of us have ever come across or there's something we're missing."

Barnes looks away from her computer screen to play devil's advocate. With a challenging tone of voice she comments, "If he's smart enough to graduate from college and work his way into an executive position in only a decade, he certainly has the smarts to track down, stalk and kill his victims. Then too, he was arrested for domestic violence and fired for cause so we have to consider that, as well. He obviously has a mean streak."

Fuentes leans back in his chair, his lips gather tightly together while his eyes are riveted on an indiscernible spot on the wall. He's displeased with the comment. "Yeah, we both know how that routine works. Family law attorneys automatically file domestic violence charges as a means to give their client control of the residence. Besides, Manus finished his community service and that charge isn't even supposed to appear on his record as part of the plea bargain."

"When did that ever stop the DA from using it to demonstrate a suspect's violent nature in court?" asks Barnes.

"I don't disagree with you there but getting back to my point, almost everyone liked the guy and a lot of people from his company who tried to hang onto their jobs were fired. That can't be it. Besides, if he's that smart, he wouldn't have made himself such an obvious suspect by leaving his victims out in the open... and that rope was like attaching his name on a sticky note and placing it on the penis. I'm surprised there weren't helium-filled balloons, too."

Barnes laughs at the thought but continues to challenge her partner, "Who else has motive to kill the two victims besides Manus?"

Fuentes puts his hand to his face, nearly covering the chin and squeezing his lower lip as he thinks, "The attorney is easy," he says after an extended pause. "Who wouldn't have motive to kill a family law attorney? Judging from the interviews, I don't even think Art Conner's mother likes him and the widow has a boyfriend. She and her boyfriend were in Cabo San Lucas when all that went down."

Barnes takes a deep breath and looks up at Fuentes with widened eyes, "So, we're back to Manus?"

"What about this?" Fuentes proposes as he puts on his salesman face and becomes an instant pitchman, "I've gone over our visit to Manus's apartment in my mind a hundred times. In every response he comes across as being pretty believable so that leads me to only one of two conclusions. He is either schizophrenic, which I doubt… or something happened on that bridge that we have yet to figure out."

"The bridge?" Barnes replies with a laugh. "You mean the one he was going to jump off of?"

"Yes, yes… listen," Fuentes says, making a plea for his theory. "Both victims were murdered after the night on the bridge… he has no recall of the incident and he wakes up a few miles away with a handprint across his face."

Barnes leans back in her chair, folds her arms and says with a smile, "Is this where he gets abducted by aliens? Are you trying to scam me, partner?"

With a look of childlike innocence, Fuentes, makes an impassioned plea for his position. "No, no… I promise, this is real. I think he ran into someone on the bridge that night and he must have really pissed him off. The two fought and the other guy dumped him off a few miles away."

Barnes looks at Fuentes and shakes her head in disapproval. "You had me going until the fight. Men don't get into slap fights and if the other guy were really pissed off, he would have thrown Manus off the bridge himself."

"Good point," Fuentes admits. "I see what you're saying but it doesn't explain how someone that drunk ends up on the side of a wet road three miles away."

"Fuentes!" Barnes snorts. "My twelve year-old daughter can easily walk that distance in under sixty minutes."

Fuentes pauses, takes a deep breath and continues to assert his theory, "I know the distance isn't a deterrent for a sober person but it would have been nearly impossible for a very drunk person. Besides, when we asked him about cuts and bruises, he never mentioned his feet. If he walked all that way without shoes, his unconditioned feet would have been sore or even raw."

Barnes nods "That could be true," she concedes. "But how did he get back home from Chino after he woke up?"

Fuentes clasps his hands together, "Damn, we didn't ask him that."

Barnes smirks. "Well, when you find him, let that be your first question."

Fuentes's scowl and tension display his irritation with Barnes for challenging everything he presented. He pondered the evidence on the case for hours only to have Barnes dismiss everything he said. Making a final plea, Fuentes asserts, "I realize the bulk of police work is deductive logic… we follow the evidence to an obvious conclusion. But there are times when we need to look at things from a different angle and I think this may be one of those times. What if we use inductive logic? Let's assume Manus's story is true, and then either prove or disprove the theory."

Barnes blankly stares ahead without saying a word, either disengaged from the conversation or lost in deep thought. Feeling a little dejected Fuentes stands, grabbing the chair he brought into her cubical and begins to leave.

Barnes looks up at Fuentes. "Hey, partner."

As Fuentes looks around to acknowledge her, Barnes continues in a calm tone, "I think you're on to something. I appreciate the insight and the work you've put into this. I'm just trying to help you think it through, but you could be right."

Fuentes's responds with a smile, "Yeah, I already know what a pain in the ass you are. I'll let you know if I find anything at the bridge."

The following morning Fuentes navigates his way through a backwash of commuters, making his way into San Bernardino County and the Virgil Bridge. The Old Bridge is nothing spectacular in the daylight sun. Even during the busy morning rush, traffic on the structure is infrequent at best. Fuentes spends nearly an hour walking up and down the pedestrian walkway, examining the aged structure from every angle. His only discovery is a cap to a wine bottle that may or may not have been the top of the bottle Manus was drinking from. Even if the cap is from the same bottle, it only confirms what he already knows; Manus was drinking on the bridge. He takes a few photos of the area and bags the bottle cap as evidence, thinking it will only become useful if the bottle is ever discovered.

Entering his vehicle, Fuentes zeroes out the trip meter on his odometer and drives east towards Chino. He drives slowly, scanning the roadside for anything that may be useful, especially a discarded wine bottle. If he can find the bottle, he may be able to recover a multiple set of prints, perhaps identifying another person and validating his theory. By the time he reaches the three mile point, Fuentes level of frustration rises. He's found nothing and there doesn't appear to be a location where a cow may have appeared over a fence. He continues driving east over a small knoll until the trip meter reaches three point three miles. A barbed wire fence appears on the south side of the road as the countryside opens up into a large enclosed pasture. Scores of dairy cattle dot the landscape. At that point skid marks appear on the asphalt road and lead off onto the unpaved dirt shoulder. Fuentes drives a couple miles in the same direction before circling back to the skid marks. This is the only section of roadway that displays evidence of a vehicle being driven off of the shoulder and onto dirt. Although several weeks have lapsed, tire impressions are still visible. Marginal traffic on the rural route combined with mild weather both contribute to preserving the automobile's tread marks. Fuentes initiates a call to the lab to have evidence techs complete a cast of the tire impressions. Meanwhile, he photographs them, using a paper rule for scale. Searching the immediate vicinity, he discovers two additional items of interest—a couple of thick plastic cable ties. Although initially uncertain as to how they may fit into the overall scheme, he bags the evidence and heads back to Orange County.

The beginning of the following week is no different for Barnes and Fuente, until early Monday afternoon when Barnes stops in mid-bite of her sandwich, having heard Fuentes chuckling on the other side of her cubical. She stands, peers over the top of her workspace wall only to see Fuentes eagerly engaged with a report he is reading. She hastily swallows her food. "What do you have that's so interesting over there?"

Fuentes spins around, grabbing the report and evidence he had just received back from the lab, and nearly leaps the distance to Barnes cubical, "I wanted to wait until I got the lab report back before I showed everything to you. Look at this!"

Barnes in her typical skeptical, challenging and difficult to impress mode, has yet to share Fuentes's enthusiasm. "Okay, I see a bottle cap. How is that special?"

"It's from the Manus case. I found it on the Virgil Bridge." Fuentes looks up hoping to see a flare of excitement registered on Barnes's face but sees nothing. "It's the top to a wine bottle," he continues to explain.

With sarcasm pouring from her every word, "Yes, I can read the words right there on the cap. It's a wine bottle cap alright. I'm thinking that since we're both touching it that there are no prints on this and I don't see a bottle so I'm not even mildly excited yet."

"I know that but this is not the big item… I have more. Check this out," Fuentes says as he displays photos of the tire tracks. These were found at the end of a set of skid marks three point three miles from the bridge. As you can see from the picture, there's a barbed wire fence only a few yards away… and do you know what's on the other side of the fence?"

Barnes looks at Fuentes with her jaw slightly ajar and her forehead crinkled, "Cows? Are you seriously asking me to guess that there are cows on the other side of the fence?"

"No, no, no… well, yes but that's not the point," Fuentes states defensively as he scrambles with his report and the accompanying photographs. "It all fits Manus's story. He was on the bridge drinking as he said—"

Barnes interjects. "But there are no prints on the cap and no bottle so we don't know that yet."

Ignoring her, Fuentes continues as he points to a photograph., "Manus meets a man on the bridge and they drive three and three-tenths miles, at which point the driver skids to a halt on the side of the road... right here, a few yards from the fence."

"Those could be skid marks from practically any vehicle in North America," Barnes states as she challenges the information.

Filtering out her objections Fuentes continues. "The tracks are from fourteen inch tires that are commonly used as replacements on a few varieties of Japanese cars. So, the man who abducted Manus likely drives an older model Japanese automobile."

"Abducted? Okay, how do you make the leap from a bottle cap and tire tracks to an abduction? I'm not taking you with me on any more body dumps, 'cause I think that nasty stuff got in your head."

Fuentes arches his shoulders and puts his chin up, "You want to listen or not? I saved the best for last."

"All right, all right... I'll look at it. What you got?"

Fuentes reaches into his evidence bag and retrieves the two cable ties and extending his arms, holds them up to eye level for Barnes to examine. "Trash bag ties? She says. This is your big *coup de grace*? Please tell me you have more in that file than trash bag ties."

"Very funny," Fuentes replies with a sinister smirk, "I know you know what these are, and that they have nothing to do with trash bags. Even you've used electrical cable ties as make-shift handcuffs. Both of them have been cut but if you piece them together in the position before they were cut, what do you have?"

"One is bigger than the other. What are you getting at?"

Fuentes looks down at Barnes legs, "Do you mind if I touch your legs?"

Barnes stares at Fuentes as though he were out of his mind. "Do you mind being bloodied and unconscious?" she snaps.

Fuentes takes a quick step back, "You are such a mean person. I have no idea why I like you or why I put up with your evil attitude. Just pay attention then."

Fuentes takes the larger of the two cable ties and wraps it around his legs above his knees, reconnecting the thick plastic bindings by holding them in place, "See? It's almost a perfect fit."

Taking the smaller of the two cable ties, Fuentes repeats the illustration by wrapping the tie around his ankles, "Another perfect fit. Like I said partner, someone abducted Manus on the bridge and dumped him off on the side of this road. I know all of this is circumstantial evidence and none of it would fly in court... except for this."

Fuentes hands Barnes a photo of the murder scene of Art Conner. In the photo, his knees and ankles are bound in a similar manner and the cable ties appear to be the same variety. After Barnes has a moment to digest the information, Fuentes hands her the lab report and the conclusion is that the cable ties used in both crimes are identical.

"This is what I was laughing about when you peeked over at me. It's not enough for a conviction but it proves to me that whoever killed Art Conner is the same person who abducted Manus. We need to start looking for this other guy."

Barnes goes quiet for the first time. Fuentes can almost see the wheels turning in her head. After a brief silence, her voice soft but full of curiosity, she says, "Why didn't this guy kill Manus?"

"That's the big mystery to me too, along with why Manus ran when he knew he was innocent."

"Partner..." replies Barnes, "Did I ever tell you that you were a genius?"

Fuentes rolls his eyes, "No, I think you've been way too busy being critical of my work so I wasn't really feeling it."

"Can I have a hug," Barnes demands as she approaches Fuentes with her arms outstretched.

"Not unless you want to be bloodied and unconscious," snaps Fuentes.

Barnes places one arm around Fuentes from the side and squeezes him with determination, "I'm going to risk it anyway."

Fuentes graciously accepts the hug and begins to strut away when Barnes calls out to him again, "Hey, Fuentes!"

Fuentes turns to see Barnes with a radiant smile plastered across her face. She stops smiling only long enough to silently mouth the word, "Genius."

X

The Research Project

Kilborn positions himself at a rear table in a more dim and secluded section of the courtyard café. A small stack of file folders, in combination with his suit and tie, serve as a camouflage of sorts. Together they effectively allow him to blend into the lunchtime horde of attorneys and legal workers. With his back to the wall, he sips on a mediocre cup of coffee while staring aimlessly into the throng of restaurant patrons. His mind races with potential plots and schemes but in the end, he realizes there are few options. The most obvious is immediately dismissed. The easiest choice would be to simply use public records and online resources to locate the residence of each of his remaining targets. Buying a gun from an out-of-state source would be a relatively easy task. Assassinating his target would require little more effort than approaching the person and pulling a trigger.

Kilborn clenches his teeth. *No. It's not enough! Not near enough!* He continues to stare into the faceless crowd... With no one within his immediate vicinity, he speaks in a voice scarcely audible to himself, "I want them to experience the humiliation I experienced. I want to see the expression of utter despair and helplessness on their faces as they die. I want them to die in disgrace and know that I'm the one who killed them, and why I killed them."

Kilborn's mind races with various scenarios, searching for an opportunity to slither into their lives. His best option at the moment is Ms. Strix. He met with her two weeks ago to discuss a case and baited her by presenting himself in the role of a compassionate grandfather. He paid for her lunch, listened to her seemingly endless tales of woe and propped up her frail self-esteem with flattery and words of encouragement. Kilborn invited her to meet with him again the following day, then again the next. They have been meeting during lunch nearly every day for two weeks. In addition to a free meal, he provides what appears to Strix as a parental disposition and genuine concern for her. Kilborn listens, most often much more than he cares to. As with each of their afternoon meetings, the oblivious Ms. Strix rambles on with her daily minutia. All the while, the grandfatherly image sitting across the table from her is merely fitting the pieces together as a means to murder her.

Within moments of thinking of her, Kilborn looks up from his files only to take note of a pair of overly eager, yet almost sad, puppy dog eyes looking in his direction. He makes no effort to get Strix's attention or extend an invitation to her. She's been conditioned over the recent couple of weeks to seek out the welcoming doctor, near the same time and place each day.

"Hello Dr. Klaudios," says Strix with a school girl expression of glee. "Have you been here long?"

Kilborn closes his file, then responds with a welcoming smile. "Not long at all. I'm glad to see you." With a few weeks of language and acting classes under his belt, Kilborn has a much better mastery of his accent. He isn't stuck in the harsh sounding mode he once was. Although he still retains the capacity to bark out coarse statements, he has added a more delicate feature that is more fitting to his paternal role with Strix.

"I didn't think lunchtime was ever going to come," Strix says as her expression and tone changes from enthusiasm to concern. Standing directly across from Kilborn at the square table, she sets her purse on the chair at right angles. "Do you mind watching my purse for a minute while I visit the lady's room?"

"Not at all, young lady," Kilborn says with a smile, "I'll make sure no one runs off with it."

Kilborn continues to watch Strix as she navigates between the jumble of tables. Strix is a leggy brunette whose walk is more akin to a newborn giraffe than a runway model. On days when she makes an attempt to dress up, she can be quite pleasant looking. Most often, however, she simply lumps her long, light brown hair on top of her head. Her choice of attire is usually confined to a boxy pantsuit and low-heeled shoes. The combination only serves to accentuate her shoulders, giving her the appearance of a marshmallow held up by toothpicks. If one were to attempt to surmise her sense of fashion, or lack thereof, it might be said that she dresses for comfort and not for style.

Strix is approaching thirty and has never been married. At times she feels overwhelmed having to juggle work with being partially responsible for the care of a chemically dependent parent. Her mother has had substance abuse issues since Strix's childhood and now the long-term abuse of her body is having a devastating effect on her health. To complicate her life further, Strix herself, is a Type 1 Diabetic. Her condition is controlled with daily injections of insulin but there are occasions when she is exhausted for little reason. Socially, she appears to be completely inept. Due to her low self-esteem and insecurities, she gives herself completely to her friends and allows nearly everyone to take unfair advantage of her. When her relationships become overly one-sided and abusive, she retreats in self-hatred and despair, only to seek out someone else to pour herself into. The cycle then continues with the next person, and the next.

Subconsciously, Strix believes she has little to offer as a friend, a lover, or even as a human being for that matter. She frequently attempts to merit the relationship, purchasing small gifts and writing cards to people she scarcely knows. The sad reality is she wants to find someone who will value her and treat her with the same demonstration of appreciation. Her last relationship was with the Bailiff, Frank Grimm, a man about her age. It was a brief affair, spanning a period of only a few months. Presently, it appears Grimm is only interested in Strix as a sexual convenience.

As Strix disappears into the restroom, Kilborn makes use of the opportunity to examine the contents of her purse. Using his feet, he discretely slides the chair closer to his side of the table, positioning the open end of the seat toward himself. By placing files upright against the back of the chair, he effectively blocks the view of the seat from anyone positioned at nearby tables. Kilborn freely rummages through Strix's purse without attracting attention or drawing suspicion to himself. He quickly makes note of the items inside that may be of use. Seeing Strix's cell phone on top of the jumbled contents, he jots down a description of her cell phone along with the manufacturer's name and model number. Turning it on, he notes that it's password protected which is only an obstacle, not a dead end. The insulin medication he discovers is the newer "dial-a-dose" or travel variety that requires no refrigeration. The physician's information and prescription number are listed on the container. Her driver's license is easy to access as Kilborn pulls it from one of the credit card slots in her wallet. He makes note of her address and identification number, and then quickly returns it to its original location. Sensing that time is running out, Kilborn risks a final plunge into a zipped side compartment where he discovers a bottle of perfume and two unused insulin syringes. This suggests to him that Strix maintains a larger supply of the medication at home, probably in the refrigerator. He jots down the name of the perfume while taking one of the empty syringes, placing it in his lapel pocket and refastening the purse. After removing his files from the back of the seat, Kilborn discretely pushes the chair back to its original location with his feet. As if on cue, Strix reappears on the other side of the cafeteria and begins to make her way back toward the table. In a calm and deliberate manner, Kilborn finishes making final entries to his list of notes, then folds the page and secures it in his pocket. As Strix approaches, Kilborn stands to greet her.

"What can I get for you for lunch?" he offers.

"Oh, Dr. Klaudios, you've paid for my lunch almost every day this week. Let me pay for lunch today."

"No, I insist! Without you, I'd be forced to eat here all alone. The usual?"

"You're so sweet. Thank you so much."

With the meal ordered, Kilborn listens to Strix ramble on as to her litany of problems and responds in a heavy accent with the simple expression, "How does that make you feel?"

Once the topic is nearly exhausted, Kilborn follows up with, "What are you going to do about that?"

The same two questions and a few considering nods effectively transform Kilborn into the brilliant psychologist he's pretending to be. Little does Strix realize, she has exhausted Kilborn's recall of his own sessions with a marriage counselor from several years prior. He wisely withholds advice beyond this, thinking the only thing he might be able to say would mimic a line in a movie. When the conversation becomes too intense or it appears that Strix is seeking specific direction on an issue, Kilborn diverts her with another question.

Strix also reveals that Ms. Harpy, the woman Kilborn refers to as the "media whore," is also interested in dating Frank Grimm. Having eclipsed her forty-fifth birthday, she's twelve years older than Grimm and is on a self-improvement kick so as to look younger and become more attractive to him. Although very toned and physically fit, Harpy has hired a personal trainer and recently started self-injecting with a prescription steroid comprised of human growth hormone. She seems confident the drug therapy will increase her energy level and shave several years off of her appearance. Strix acts as though Harpy's interest in Grimm doesn't bother her but again, she smiles her way through the situation while secretly loathing the thought of Harpy becoming intimate with Frank Grimm. Strix appears so needy in friendships that she allows her insensitive friend, Ms. Harpy, to openly state her attraction to Deputy Grimm. Considering the fact that Strix sporadically sleeps with Grimm and maintains hope of a permanent relationship with him, the situation strikes Kilborn as being odd on many levels. As he listens to Strix endlessly drone on about her issues, at times he almost regrets having to kill her.

Kilborn realizes it's only a matter of time before Harpy makes an appearance. Similar to Strix, Harpy has few friends but for an entirely different set of circumstances. On the surface, Harpy appears to be a reasonably intelligent and attractive woman but her life is a contradiction in terms and values. Although she is the executive director of a local shelter for women, she is constantly at odds with the leadership of women's rights groups. Harpy's opinions are considered damaging to the image and long-term goals of these organizations. The other community based organizations focus their efforts on promoting women's rights whereas Harpy seems intent on inciting a free-for-all gender war. These groups do everything possible to distance themselves from Harpy as she is viewed as an extremist by them. Unfortunately, whenever there is a media occurrence that involves an opinion on women's rights, the always assertive Harpy is more than happy to sliver herself in front of the media interviewers. The leadership of the other organizations cringe when they see Harpy posed in front of the camera. Harpy's gender bashing rants are largely based on manufactured or highly exaggerated data, and she is adamant in her view that any societal failure is the direct result of men. One local community leader used a quote from Dr. Martin Luther King Jr. in reference to her, "Nothing in the world is more dangerous than sincere ignorance and conscientious stupidity."

Another factor that contributes to Harpy's disfavor is her choice of wardrobe and style, neither of which compliment her professional appearance. Her dress is more consistent with a call girl than the status she holds as a public figure. She rarely goes unnoticed. If not for the big blonde hair, one certainly notices her short skirts and large, overly exposed breasts. Harpy appears to be constantly performing. Her expressions are overly animated and she exercises little control over the volume of her speech. When speaking in a public environment, she frequently scans the horizon to take note of who is paying attention to her. Not by coincidence, she accomplishes little to advance the issues of her gender and seems more content using the subject as a soapbox for her own self-gratification. In her mind she envisions herself as a crusader for women's rights, while in reality her actions serve only to exacerbate tensions and generate controversy. Perhaps due to her extreme views or the uninhibited display of her large breasts, she is certainly a media favorite.

It was Bantam who leaked Kilborn's case information to Harpy over twenty-four months ago. He enticed her with the notion that a distinguished male educator was accused of child abuse and embezzlement. Bantam informed the press through an anonymous source and before Harpy possessed so much as a marginal grasp of the situation, she eagerly perched herself in front of the cameras. She provided the public with a scalding opinion of Kilborn without ever taking the time to meet him or review the evidence. Understandably, the public has virtually no tolerance for those who use positions of trust as a means to sexually abuse children or swindle community funds. In the eyes of the public, Kilborn had become both a sexual predator and thief. Even long-term friends and co-workers who believed him to be innocent found it difficult to stand in support of him. The public outcry and parental response was so quick that school officials felt compelled to immediately act or risk losing their own jobs. Kilborn, depleted of resources, lacked the ability to hire legal representation or wage battle on another front. School officials had no desire for prolonged public exposure and wanted to have the matter disappear as quickly as possible. Since neither the sexual abuse accusation nor the missing funds were reported as crimes, it merely became a human resources problem. The school district responded by offering Kilborn a way out. They offered not to press criminal charges or demand repayment of the funds taken by the court in exchange for a couple of concessions; Kilborn would have to resign and agree to hold the school district harmless for any type of legal action against them. It was a horrible deal but Kilborn took it. His personal finances were so strained at this point that he was only a few hundred dollars away from becoming homeless. By the time the charges against him were declared unfounded, it was no longer newsworthy and the story of Kilborn's plight was buried. The destruction of his life was of little concern to the public and it seemed in everyone's best interest for Kilborn to quietly go away. In the end, Harpy received her face time in front of the camera and the news media got a story; school district officials kept their jobs and the devious Bantam walked away with not only a paycheck but another huge stroke to his highly inflated ego. For Harpy's participation in the fiasco, Kilborn has determined that she too, must die.

As Kilborn sits across the table from Strix during their lunchtime meeting, his mind races between scattered schemes and the data he's been able to gather from her. If his plans concluded solely with the murder of Strix, he could formulate a strategy to dispose of her with little effort. But not only is Strix his least important target, she's also the facilitator in gaining access to Ms. Harpy and Judge Raven. Kilborn needs her. As far as Richard Bantam, Kilborn has been plotting his murder in his imagination for years, even before he killed Dr. Klaudios. It's unlikely he would have ever followed through on his plot had it not been for the fateful day he spent adrift at sea. Bantam made it easy. His public persona was such that his arrogant and self-promoting ramblings provided anyone with ears the opportunity to kill him. For now, Kilborn must confine his focus to the three birds before him that he hopes to ensnare. He must advance his scheme and use Harpy to draw the others in. It's time to cast the net. When Harpy pauses to take a breath, Kilborn interjects into her monolog, "I have a project in mind and I want to know what you think of it," says Kilborn as Strix looks up at him, eager for the details.

"I am going to conduct a study that involves the long-term consequences of divorce on the economy. I want to supplement and illustrate my research with recent case studies as well as interviewing various professionals who work in the field. What do you think?"

Strix, in typical manner, rushes to appease a friend, "That's a wonderful idea! If there's anything I can do to help, let me know."

"Well, there may be something," Kilborn says wryly. "Your input and experiences will certainly be valuable but I also need to interview someone who works outside of the court system. I want to be able to examine the topic from several different points of view. I can find someone on my own but it helps to have a personal connection. Do you know anyone who works in the area of women's issues and domestic violence?"

Strix pauses, reflecting on an appropriate response. Harpy immediately comes to her mind but Strix is reluctant to endorse her. Dr. Klaudios has become the image of the nurturing father she never had. On an emotional level, she doesn't want to share him with Harpy or risk losing him as with her part-time boyfriend, Frank Grimm. "I do have a friend who works for a community based organization but I'm not sure she's what you're looking for."

Kilborn senses her reluctance. "The project would only involve a few meetings a week over a period of three weeks. That would be the extent of it."

"Okay... okay, I do have a friend who is actually the director of a center for abused women. I wasn't sure if I should mention her because she's the one I was telling you about that likes Frank."

Strix takes the bait and Kilborn begins to reel her in. "So, do you think we can trust her?"

With a continued show of reluctance, she says, "Oh, I suppose…
yes, to some degree. I think she's a fairly honest person but like anyone,
she has some peculiar ways."

"Is she comfortable in front of a camera? I may need to document
her experiences and stories on film so that could be a consideration."

Strix rolls her eyes and bobs her head, "She is really good at that."

"Well, maybe we can use her for some small things. That would be
fine. What do you think?"

Strix manages a smile, but Kilborn sees the hesitation behind it. "Yes,
I think she might add something," she allows, "as long as you don't let
her push herself into taking over everything."

Kilborn, knowing that Strix is in regular communication with Harpy,
is confident she will relay the information to Harpy within a brief time.
The trap has been set for Harpy but he must also continue to tighten
the noose around Strix's neck. Kilborn enjoys the paternal role he has
developed with Strix, paying for her meals and consistently displaying
concern for her. It is, however, a double-edged sword. On one hand
he's possessed with a spirit of hatred and revenge, knowing he must kill
her to quench his thirst for retaliation. On the other hand, the details
of Strix's life pulls at a very fragile string of compassion in his heart.
Strix is a lost soul… aimless, and has obviously been victimized by
nearly everyone she has opened her heart to. She appears trapped in an
emotional death spiral for which she has no answer. With neither direction nor insight, and beaten down to a place where she doesn't expect
her life to change, Strix may as well have the word, "*victim*" tattooed in
bold letters to her forehead. She reminds Kilborn of an adult version
of some of the students he's had in his former years as a teacher. Strix
would likely be the female who sat near the back of the class, often
keeping to herself. She may have been the one singled out because of
her clothes, the way she spoke, or merely because she didn't stand up
for herself. As an adult, perhaps Strix sought to break away from her
childhood ensnarement and gain respect by making something of her
life. She obviously desires to be a person people like, take note of…
even admire. Lacking the scholastic aptitude to become a physician,
scientist or engineer, and perhaps in a desperate act for recognition,

she may have responded to the Army's recruitment of legal officers as a way to advance her life. Kilborn can only speculate. He knows that Strix graduated from an under acclaimed law school in Massachusetts and that the greater part of her education was paid for by the military. But even the Army released her when she failed to be promoted to the next grade and her military career ended after only a couple of years. Working now as the *Guardian ad litem* provides her with a job, but that's all it is to her. She lacks passion for what she does. There's no sense of commitment, drive or eagerness to make a difference in helping people. Strix shuffles paper, passes her caseload through the system and attempts to take the path of least resistance. Kilborn realizes that Strix's actions against him in his case were not premeditated, nor were they deliberately malicious. Strix's crime against Kilborn was apathy. She didn't care enough to uncover the truth. She's like an irresponsible drunk driver who gets behind the wheel of a vehicle. There's rarely a situation when a drunk intends to kill innocent people, ruin fortunes and cause multigenerational consequences, but they do. The victims of intoxicated motor vehicle operators do not spring back to life and innocent families are not immediately restored to health due to mislaid intentions. The dead remain dead and shattered lives remain broken, regardless of intent. In spite of the growing pity Kilborn has developed for Strix, she must be punished for the carnage she leaves in the wake of her negligence.

Not too many days later in the same week, a busty blonde with dark sunglasses enters the courtyard café where Strix and Kilborn are having lunch together. She immediately captures the attention of most men as well as the silent disdain of many female patrons. The volume of conversation becomes notably more subdued as she saunters between the tables in search of her friend. Finally locating Strix and Kilborn at their usual table in the rear, she walks with determination to where they are seated. Without acknowledging Strix, the blonde woman removes her sunglasses and extends her hand in Kilborn's direction, "Hello, I'm Ms. Harpy from the Women's Center. You must be Dr. Klaudios."

"Yes, Ms. Strix has told me about you. How nice to meet you," responds Kilborn as he pretends to struggle a little to rise to his feet and shake her hand. By this time, Kilborn has taken several acting classes and has weeks of experience practicing his accent and living as Dr. Klaudios. The role has become second nature.

Harpy places her hand on Strix's shoulder, belatedly acknowledging her presence. She offers her a quick smile and sits at the table without waiting for an invitation. Everything about Harpy screams for attention. Her artificially plump lips are accented with brightly colored lipstick while her low cut top and push-up bra make it appear as though she's offering her breasts on a serving tray. Perhaps having a pulse is the only quality that distinguishes her from an inflatable sex toy.

"I understand that you're involved in a research project," says Harpy, eager to hear the details."

Although Kilborn is not the psychologist he pretends to be, he instinctively knows that in order to gain Harpy's trust, he has to keep his eyes focused on her face and not succumb to the temptation of glancing at her ample cleavage. He realizes Harpy is an odd bird, one that he must approach with caution and discernment if he hopes to trap her.

"Yes, I have an anonymous foundation that is willing to provide a nice stipend for any community based organization willing to participate in the research I am conducting. It's regarding the long-term economic consequences of divorce. Ms. Strix immediately thought of you when I asked her if she knew of an expert. She said you were very knowledgeable and comfortable in front of a camera. What do you think of the project?"

Kilborn continues to hold his eye contact with Harpy as she contemplates the proposition. He was careful to acknowledge Harpy's skill and intelligence as opposed to anything to do with her appearance or physical attributes. The slight moment of silence seems much longer in real time but within a few seconds a smile burst from Harpy's face.

"Tell me more about everything! It sounds very interesting! And, yes, I've worked in this field for several years and I'm very good with interviews. I can—"

"Excuse me." Strix glances at her watch. "I'm sorry but I have to be back in court in fifteen minutes."

Kilborn rises to his feet and insists on escorting Strix outside. "Please, Ms. Harpy, order lunch for yourself as my guest. I will be back in a couple of minutes so we can discuss this more in detail."

Once outside and away from Harpy's view, Kilborn turns to Strix, "Don't you worry about a thing. I think I know how to deal with her. Everything will be fine."

Strix remains silent but looks at Kilborn as though she's relieved and grateful for him being sensitive to her needs.

"Oh, one more thing. I have something for you," Kilborn says as he gently places his hand on the back of Strix's arm. Reaching into his lapel pocket, he pulls out a plain white envelope and hands it to her. "There are twelve hundred dollars in the envelope."

"I can't take that from you Dr. Klaudios…"

"Yes, you can and you will," insists Kilborn. "I have already had someone check the laws and there is no violation or conflict of interest as long as it is a gift from one private party to another." In reality, Kilborn had not checked with anyone regarding the issue but was confident his bluff would work.

"I have only three conditions," continues Kilborn as Strix looks on smiling. "This is a personal matter just between me and you so no one else needs to know, especially your friend, Ms. Harpy. Also, you must not deposit the money in the bank and you must use it for something special for yourself like new clothes, a day at the spa or anything else that pleases you. Agreed?"

"Well, yes, okay… that's so generous and nice of you."

"Think nothing of it. If things go as planned with the foundation, I may receive $120,000 for my research project and I want to share the funds with those who assist me. So, there may be more to come."

"I don't know how to thank you, Dr. Klaudios."

"I feel the same way."

"Can I give you a hug?" Strix replies as she is obviously touched on an emotional level, both by the generosity of the gift and the implication that she is deemed of value and needed by someone.

"In my country we never hug young single women. It is considered very inappropriate, so how about I shake your hand?" Again, Kilborn is bluffing but he can't risk Strix coming into contact with his padded midsection and discovering his disguise.

Strix offers both her hands, clasping Kilborn's tightly. There is no handshake, only a deep smile of appreciation as she allows her touch to momentarily linger.

Kilborn watches for a moment as Strix walks away, then returns to the table where the flamboyant Ms. Harpy sits waiting for him.

"I'm sorry to have kept you waiting, Ms. Harpy. I have something for you that I did not want to give to you in front of Ms. Strix." Reaching into his pocket, he retrieves another white envelope containing twelve hundred dollars and slides it across the table. Kilborn provides Harpy with the same three conditions he gave to Strix. He also informs Harpy that the foundation is prepared to donate several thousand dollars more to her and the Women's Center general fund in exchange for her participation and expertise with the project.

"How much time is involved in the project and how long will it last?"

"It shouldn't be more than a few weeks and the work is part-time, mostly working with the time you have available. The only restrictions are due to the confidential nature of the subject; we want to protect our clients and we do not want anyone stealing our intellectual property. As such, we will keep everything just among us until the end of the project. Is that agreeable?"

Harpy nods to affirm her agreement but she doesn't appear to be as enthusiastic as Kilborn had hoped. He sweetens the offer without making the situation seem unrealistic.

"We will use actual case studies to produce the statistical data. I will do most of that myself. What I need you for is to narrate the results of the data on film and possibly act in a few scenes. Once the project is complete, the results could be viewed nationwide by educational institutions and government training facilities. You may end up being quite famous after this."

Harpy's expression immediately changes. "It would be viewed nationwide?" she repeats with a big smile.

With that enticement, the deal is set. Harpy takes the bait and now it's simply a matter of getting her to follow the trail of breadcrumbs.

"One more matter, Ms. Harpy." Kilborn fabricates another story. "Ms. Strix told me you know Judge Raven and I'd love to be able to include an interview with him in the project. How well do you know him?"

With a puzzled look, "Well, I don't know him on an intimate level. Over the years I've testified in almost every courtroom and know all the judges by name but I don't know a lot about their personal lives. I do happen to know a lot about Judge Raven, but that's only because I spend a lot of time talking to Deputy Grimm."

"Is that the handsome Bailiff in his courtroom?" inquires Kilborn, all the while knowing exactly who he is.

"Yes, it is!" Harpy's smile is broad and happy, as though she is receiving some sort of confirmation in her taste of men. "I know that the judge is an avid hiker and the courtroom will be dark in a few weeks when he goes to hike in the Sierra Nevada Mountains. Frank is taking that week off too. We're supposed to go out that Friday. Anyway, the judge is taking off the weekend immediately before and after the normal work week so he'll be off for nine days. That might be a good time to approach him."

"That's beautiful country. I've been in that area many times. Do you know where he hikes to?"

Harpy shakes her head. "I can't say that I do. All I can remember is Frank saying he complains that he can never get anyone to go with him because he's a judge. Everything is a potential conflict of interest and the hiking clubs never plan trips when he can go. He ends up driving up to Bishop the day before and stays in a motel there, then goes to the head of something... South. South River? South Falls? Something like that. Do you hike Dr. Klaudios? Maybe you could hike with him?"

"No, my hiking days are long gone," explains Kilborn with a deceptively sad smile. Apart from the somewhat frail image of his disguise, he's well aware of the fact that he's fully capable of a long hike, and he's somewhat familiar with the area as well. Without giving Harpy the idea that he is able to decipher even a portion of her information, Kilborn is confident of the judge's destination. There's a popular trailhead outside of Bishop that leads to South Lake. That has to be it. If not, Bishop is a small community with only a handful of motels. Kilborn has three weeks to prepare.

In the interim, Kilborn distracts Harpy with a list of questions and sample cases for her to review on her own time. It amounts to nothing more than busywork, designed to keep her mind filled with meaningless details and to occupy her attention from the blindside that awaits her.

XI

A Walk in the Park

The first meeting between Kilborn, Strix and Harpy is set for Tuesday morning of the following week. Kilborn arrives at the courtyard café half an hour early and secures his usual table in the back. The amount of files he stacks on the table in front of him is significantly larger than normal. The props served as a nonverbal visual ploy to reinforce the idea that the research project is a complex review and examination of several cases. As expected, Strix arrives fifteen minutes early. As a people pleaser, notwithstanding an apocalyptic event, Strix will always be on time. Harpy is just as predictable but on the opposite end of the spectrum. The world waits for Harpy to arrive.

"Good morning Dr. Klaudios, nice to see you," greets Strix with her usual wide-eyed, puppy dog look. "You look busy."

"Yes, yes… there's so much to do in such a brief time," feigns Kilborn. "I know you're a busy person too. I hope I'm not taking you away from your job." Kilborn isn't as concerned about Strix's job as he is wanting to know if she has an official record of an appointment with him.

"Oh, it's not distracting me from my job. I checked in this morning before coming here. I spend a lot of time at the courthouse so I won't be missed."

"That's very good," says Kilborn with manufactured concern, "I have something for you to act on right away. Court is in session in

Department F-6 in just a few minutes and I need for you to record as much information as possible using this data input form I've prepared."

"I thought we were having a meeting this morning to explain the process because I'm not really prepared for anything…"

"Oh, don't you worry about a thing," Kilborn assures her. "You don't need advanced preparation for this task. You are a very bright young woman and I have all the confidence in the world in you. It's a simple document. All you have to do is write notes on each case presented, filling in the blanks on the form I've prepared. If there's something unclear, just make note of it on the back."

"That's easy enough but I didn't realize I'd be going into the court-room today so I have my purse and cell phone with me."

"Is that a problem?" Kilborn asks, looking at her with concerned innocence.

"I know you don't use a cell phone, Dr. Klaudios, but almost all the new ones have a camera feature and this court doesn't allow cameras of any type inside the courthouse. I usually leave my phone in my car or office when I come to court. Do you mind if I leave it here with you?"

"Of course I don't mind." says Kilborn, assuring Strix that it won't be an imposition or problem. "You'll only be in court for about an hour so I'll be happy to keep it for you. As a matter of fact, since I don't have a cell phone it would be nice to be able to call Harpy if she doesn't show up this morning. Do you mind if I use it to call her?"

"Not at all… you just have to push this button and enter the numerical password," says Strix as she quickly jots down the code on a piece of paper. "Do you know how to use it from this point?"

As a former teacher, Kilborn has confiscated several varieties of phones from students who have misused them in the classroom. Although technically savvy, he purposely acts a little confused, looking up at Strix with a smile, "Maybe you'd better show me."

"I'm going to have to introduce you to the 21st century, Dr. Klaudios," Strix doesn't even try to hide her surprised amusement. "Once I show you how easy this is, you'll probably get all the new gadgets and wonder how you managed your life without them. She offers a quick tutorial on cell phone usage then says, "I have to run. I only have twelve minutes to get up to the sixth floor."

Strix quickly gives Kilborn a parting smile and an affectionate tap on the shoulder before she scuttles out the door. Kilborn puts the cell phone out of sight and then patiently waits for Harpy to make her appearance. There is no need to hurry or panic as it will be another fifteen minutes before Harpy arrives, undoubtedly reciting some excuse she has used countless times before.

As Harpy arrives late for their meeting Kilborn interrupts her in mid-excuse, "It's nice to see you, Ms. Harpy but we have to rush a little to complete the task we have this morning." Handing her a single sheet of paper, "It's pretty simple... just fill out the form as the cases are presented during the first call. Ms. Strix is in Department F-6 and I'd like for you to go to F-18. We'll meet back here for a few minutes to discuss our plan afterwards. I'm sorry to rush you off like this."

"It's not a problem, Dr. Klaudios." Harpy offers an obligatory smile and begins to walk toward the door.

After only a few steps Kilborn calls to her, "You don't have your cell phone with you, do you? I understand from Ms. Strix that they don't allow the ones with a camera feature inside the courthouse."

"Actually I do have it with me but I know most of the guys at the security entrance and I'm sure they'll let me get away with it this one time."

"I'll be happy to hold on to it for you if you run into any problems," Kilborn offers. Harpy acknowledges his statement with a hurried wave goodbye but doesn't relinquish her phone.

Only seconds after Harpy disappears out the door, Kilborn retrieves Strix's phone and taking a number he had already tracked down, initiates a call to the court security desk. A female with a serious tone to her voice picks up the line, "This is Deputy Eliot."

"Good morning deputy. I was required to return my cell phone to my car this morning because it has a camera feature..."

"That's our policy," interrupts the deputy.

"I do understand that," continues Kilborn, "but as I was walking back to the parking structure to put my phone in my car, I overheard a woman make a comment to her friend. As this woman was walking toward the courthouse entrance, she bragged to her friend that she sneaks her phone past security nearly every day. I don't mean to complain but I don't agree with the selective enforcement of a policy either."

"What did the woman look like?" inquires the deputy in a monotone voice.

"She's blonde, green top… has kind of a 'Barbie' look, if you know what I mean?"

"I see her walking toward the door now. I'll take care of it."

Only a few minutes pass as Harpy stomps back into the café, "That bitch!" she proclaims to Kilborn. "She purposely picked me out and announced to everyone in line to pay attention to the signs posted about cell phones with cameras. She must be on some power trip or be jealous of me. Anyway, Dr. Klaudios, will you hang on to my phone for me?"

"Actually, this may turn out to be a good thing," Kilborn says. I was going to use this time to make a quick trip back to my office but if you would allow me to use your phone to check my messages, it would save me a trip."

"I usually don't let people use my phone, but I'll make an exception for you, Dr. Klaudios." Harpy takes the phone and out of Kilborn's view, enters her password to activate it and hands it to him. "Just disconnect the call when you're finished and I'll pick it up when I return."

Kilborn raises the phone and waves goodbye to her with the device still in his hand. "Thank you very much."

With both of the women's phones now in his possession, Kilborn begins to review the language and style of their previous text messages, and then fabricates a text message dialog between the two of them.

"Strix > Harpy: Re our chat this a.m. - been dating Frank for 3 mths. Stay the hell away from my bf!"

"Harpy > Strix: Boyfriend? You're nothing but a friend with benefits."

"Strix > Harpy: & U? Cougar?"

"Harpy > Strix: He must like what he sees. We're spending the weekend together in a couple of weeks."

"Strix > Harpy: UB dead by then bitch."

After Kilborn finishes the last text message, he uses Strix's phone to call Harpy but allows the call to rollover into voicemail. He holds the phone pressed against his chest in silence for a brief time, and then disconnects. With everything completed to his satisfaction, Kilborn erases the text messages and the call generated from Strix's phone log. Neither Strix nor Harpy will ever be aware of their manufactured argument. It will only become an issue when the police investigate Harpy's murder and recover the erased data as part of their forensic search.

The second meeting on Thursday follows a similar pattern. Strix arrives early while Harpy is simply less late than the first meeting. Although convenient that the two women's paths do not cross, it is not a concern for Kilborn. They are oblivious to the danger that runs below the surface and neither is aware of the clandestine battle that rages between them. Both women leave their phones with the man they view as Dr. Klaudios. If asked, Strix would likely give the good doctor her bank account information as well as her personal identification numbers. Harpy, on the other hand, is slightly resistant to relinquishing her cell phone to Kilborn. He assures her it will only be another day or two. It is convenient for them and they have come to trust him. Perhaps it's due to the paternal image they see in him; perhaps it's the perception of opportunity or simply the easy money. Regardless, each day they are sent off to conduct their business in the courtroom, Kilborn uses their cell phones to add another layer of deceit to his scheme. The counterfeit text messages are becoming increasingly angry and violent between Strix and Harpy. Strix continues to warn Harpy to stay away from her boyfriend, Frank Grimm. She makes it clear in her messages that if Harpy intends to go through with their overnight date next weekend, she will kill her.

By Tuesday of the following week, the women have completed the three courtroom tasks and deposited their data intake forms with Kilborn. At the same time, Dr. Klaudios continues to meet with Strix each day during lunch at the courtyard café. The daily appointments serve as a means for Kilborn to stay abreast of her moods and monitor her activities. Little is discussed regarding the project. Both Strix and Harpy know that tomorrow night, Wednesday, they are scheduled to complete their video interviews. After that, there may or may not be a need for one additional video session. Kilborn has left the situation purposely undefined but has promised to pay each woman an additional twelve hundred dollars after the completion of their separate meetings with him tomorrow evening. There are only a few minor details remaining with regard to Strix and Harpy, but Kilborn has yet to secure vital information in order to advance his scheme against Judge Raven.

"You look distracted today, Dr. Klaudios," Strix says with concern as she bends her head and raises her eyebrows. "Are you feeling okay?"

"Oh, I'm sorry. I suppose I do have a lot on my mind." Kilborn represses a smile as he thinks of the irony of the situation. *Yes, Ms. Strix, I'm busy plotting the demise of several lives, including your own, but I do appreciate your concern for my well-being.* "Actually, I do have a lot on my mind," Kilborn says aloud "It's not only the project but I'm a little concerned about you. I notice each day at lunch you have coffee but I never see you drink water. Is there a reason for that?"

"I know I should but..."

"No matter," interrupts Kilborn. "I have something for you and I want you to drink the whole bottle. It's flavored water with vitamins, antioxidants and no calories. It's good for you!"

Kilborn pulls out a clear plastic bottle containing a raspberry colored liquid and offers it to Strix. She accepts the bottle with a welcoming smile, cracks open the seal and downs almost all of it in a single attempt. "How's that for you?" She sports a proud smile while dabbing the corners of her mouth dry with a napkin.

"Very impressive!" exclaims Kilborn as they both laugh. "I'm not going to ask where you learned to do that."

Strix reaches out and briefly touches Kilborn's hand. "Thank you for being concerned about me, Dr. Klaudios."

"Think nothing of it. If you like it, I'll buy a case of it for you and you can take it home."

Strix glances up at him and offers a smile in response.

At the conclusion of their meal, Strix excuses herself and walks with determination toward the women's restroom. The bottle of water has done its job, guaranteeing Kilborn an extra minute rummaging through her handbag. Although no other café patrons are seated near their table in the back of the café, Kilborn remains cautious. He discreetly moves Strix's purse onto his lap, below the lip of the table, and out of view from anyone who may wander by. Strix is a diabetic. Kilborn is confident she would never venture far from her source of insulin. Releasing the clasp to the handbag, he discovers, as expected, the medication in the same location as before. Using the plastic bottle cap from the container he offered Strix during lunch, he quickly discharges a significant volume of the clear liquid medication into it. As a precaution, Kilborn looks up to survey his surroundings. Seeing that he hasn't attracted anyone's attention, he stealthily removes the syringe from his lapel pocket that he had stolen from Strix's purse a couple of weeks prior. Uncapping the end, he places the needle into the pool of insulin, successfully drawing the medication into his stolen syringe. After replacing the cap over the needle, Kilborn carefully wipes the device clean of his fingerprints. As a final touch, he uses a corner of his handkerchief to wipe around the rim of Strix's perfume bottle, and then applies a fine veneer of her scent onto the clear plastic exterior. After closing up the purse and placing it in its original location, he puts the wrapped syringe on his lap while patiently waiting for Strix to return from the restroom.

"I hope I didn't keep you waiting long, Dr. Klaudios. There was a line."

"I was relaxing so it's no bother at all. While you were away I remembered something I wanted to ask you."

"What is it?"

Kilborn takes the wrapped syringe and places it in front of Strix as though he's handling a venomous snake. "Someone left this in my office and I have no idea what it is. I'm embarrassed to admit I'm afraid of needles and I don't know enough about drugs to be able to identify it. Do you know?"

Strix laughs, "There's no need to be afraid, Dr. Klaudios. It has a cap over the needle so you can pick it up without worry of being pricked." Strix removes the syringe from the handkerchief and brings it closer to her face to examine it. "It's a clear solution, probably someone's prescription medication. That's my guess. I know it's not insulin... that's all I can say about it."

"Why would it not be insulin?" inquires Kilborn.

"Oh, if it were insulin, this would be more than a lethal dose. The syringe is really common. I use these all the time. What are you going to do with it?" asks Strix as she places the item back on the handkerchief.

"I'll keep it in my office for a few days to see if anyone calls to claim it, then probably dispose of it." Kilborn reaches for the wrapped syringe from Strix as though she's handing him a soiled diaper

"You're funny, Dr. Klaudios," says Strix with a friendly chuckle. "I had no idea a highly intelligent man like you would express such dread over a little needle."

"Not to change the subject and deprive you of your laughs at my expense, young lady, but you mentioned that I need to make an appointment to speak with Judge Raven before he leaves on his hiking trip. Who should I contact to schedule that?"

"You certainly are changing the subject but I'll let you get away with it," teases Strix. "All you have to do is call his clerk and see if she can fit you in. He's leaving this Friday but he may give you a few minutes of his time. I can give you the phone number if you need it."

Kilborn nods and smiles in response but his fist tightens under the table as his mind is redirected, contemplating the notion of being in the presence of Judge Raven again. Aside from his ex-wife's attorney, Richard Bantam, no one has contributed more turmoil to his life than the inept judge. Kilborn's mind races to review a mental checklist of activities he has made in preparation to dispose of the black robed bully. The previous week he purchased a small white truck with a camper shell from a private owner. The vehicle is a few years old and completely unremarkable. There are no bumper stickers, sports emblems or even a license plate frame to attract the attention of anyone. It blends in perfectly with the local environment of the Sierra Nevada range. Over the past weekend, Kilborn made an exploratory trip to Bishop as a means to scout the terrain and calculate when the judge will be at his most vulnerable moment. He knows Raven will be driving a red truck. Using public records, it took little effort to locate Judge Raven's small residence located on the confined peninsular community referred to as Balboa Island. He parks his high-priced image automobile in the one-car garage, while situating the truck on the side of the house...

"Dr. Klaudios... Dr. Klaudios! Where did you drift off to?" asks Strix. "I've never seen you so distracted."

"Oh, I'm sorry... I suppose I am distracted today. I have a lot on my mind trying to wrap up the project by the end of the week. Do you mind if I borrow your phone again? Thanks to you, I can see the value of owning one so I promise I will look for one this weekend."

Strix immediately removes her phone from her purse, appearing to be both delighted and amused. She enters the code and without speaking a word, hands her cell phone to the man she can only see as the good doctor. Strix has come to care for the man she believes is Dr. Klaudios. Abandoned by her father at a very young age, she was raised alone by a single mother. Dr. Klaudios is the image of the father Strix never had. He appears caring, compassionate, generous, sensitive to her needs and willing to invest his time with her. She has come to a place where she would do almost anything for him.

Kilborn, still in character, displays a burdensome effort as he walks outside to make his call. Positioned away from the earshot of passersby, "Hello, Ms. Harpy... this is Dr. Klaudios. I wanted to briefly discuss our plans for the video tomorrow evening. Do you have a minute?"

"Well, of course, Dr. Klaudios... I do have a meeting in about fifteen minutes but if it's something we can wrap up in that time frame..."

"Absolutely. I'll be very brief," assures Kilborn. "I realize from speaking with you that there are several contributing factors to domestic violence but there are couple things that I can use your help with in filming tomorrow... substance abuse and infidelity."

"Okay, how can I help you with that?"

"I would like to film something dramatic such as a heroin addict taking a needle in the arm but I don't have contacts with people like that and I don't want to be exposed to an illegal drug. But I can duplicate a shot of the same process with a legal medication... does that make sense?"

"Yes, sort of..." Harpy replies with uncertainty as to how this might apply to her in particular.

"I understand that you are taking injections of human growth hormone—"

Defensively, Harpy interrupts. "Did Ms. Strix tell you that?" She huffs out an audible breath. "I knew I should have never mentioned it to her."

"Actually she mentioned it as a compliment as to how well you take care of yourself. She certainly meant no harm by it."

Harpy's tone softens. "I understand, but are you asking to film me injecting myself?"

Kilborn quickly dismisses what he perceives is her concern, "No, my dear, it's not a video of you in particular, it's a close up of an anonymous drug user. The audience would only see the entry point of the needle into the flesh."

"You're aware that Ms. Strix is a diabetic, right? Have you considered using her for this part?"

"I did consider her briefly but the reality is that the dosage she uses is so small it wouldn't have the same impact, and she's not as composed as you on camera. I'm afraid she would get nervous and inject herself at the wrong time and we would have to wait an entire day to schedule another attempt."

After a brief silence, Harpy, in a more receptive tone of voice, "If I understand you then, the final product will only display the syringe with an unknown individual's hand and arm or whatever, right?"

"Yes, that's exactly right."

"Okay... all right, I have to inject everyday anyway so as long as it's a close up it shouldn't be a problem," Harpy's manner denotes more of a concession than enthusiasm. "I have to keep it refrigerated so I'll just bring it in a cup of ice."

"Very good," Kilborn replies immediately. "But just to be certain, you use the standard insulin syringe, don't you? The thin, clear type? We have to be able to see the fluid exiting the syringe." Kilborn is aware of the fact that all syringes used for medical purposes are clear so as to allow the medical professional or end user to determine the correct dosage. He has previously made calls to various physicians who are known to prescribe the drug Harpy uses. They all utilize the same type of small, disposable insulin syringes. His query is simply a ploy to avoid a last minute gaffe that would ruin his entire plan.

"Yes," confirms Harpy, "I use the same type as Ms. Strix."

"Good, good, good… that is fine then. One last matter. Before we shoot your professional interviews, I'd like to set up the topic of infidelity by getting some shots of you in something you may wear to a cocktail party. Again, there will not be any facial shots… just a few images to portray an attractive female. I will capture some images of a male counterpart and edit the material later."

"Are you asking me to wear something slinky?" Harpy asks as though entertained by the notion.

"No, not at all… just something you feel pretty in. If you don't feel comfortable with it, I'm sure I can get Ms. Strix to do it."

The mere mention of Strix being considered for the part to replace her evokes an immediate reaction, "No, I'll do it. I have no problem dressing nice and playing a part for you. I'll bring something to wear over my dress for the professional shots."

"Yes, that's exactly what I had in mind. I'll see you near the fountain at Barabbas Park tomorrow evening at six. We will only have a couple of hours of daylight so please be on time. Oh, I forgot to mention… I will be dressed as a street person for a role I am playing. If you don't recognize me, look for a man my size wearing a purple knit cap on."

Harpy laughs, "I'll see you tomorrow Dr. Klaudios."

It is an onerous struggle for Kilborn to sleep that night. Rolling over in bed with the details of his schemes continuing to churn in his mind, he notes the time approaching 3:00 a.m. Everything should go as planned. Even if his arrangements fail, Kilborn hadn't painted himself into a corner. He can pull the plug at the last minute, even the final second, and make an attempt on another day. The door remains open for additional work on the project. But in the end, any delay appears to complicate matters and expose him to an increased number of risks. No, it must be done as soon as possible. With that thought in mind, he sleeps.

Kilborn is up a little later than normal the following morning. In spite of a restless night, he manages to check in at the office for a couple of hours before meeting Strix for lunch. The files that he normally displays on his table at the courtyard café are absent today. All of the dominoes are in position and it's simply a matter of initiating the action and watching the series of events unfold. Strix looks different today. She's smiling but not in her usual puppy dog manner through a veneer of sadness. She seems genuinely happy for no apparent reason. She has new clothes on, abandoning her boxy pant suit for a dress that makes her appear much more attractive and feminine. She's wearing her hair down and as she walks into the café she looks confident, even drawing the attention of several men.

"Hello, Dr. Klaudios!" Strix states with a boldness he had never seen displayed before.

"Wow, look at you!" Kilborn exclaims with sincere enthusiasm. Are you in love or what has gotten into you?"

Strix takes her usual seat across the table and declares, "This is the new me and I owe it all to you, Dr. Klaudios!"

Confusion covers Kilborn's face and he almost stutters in his response, "Me? How did... how did I have anything to do with this?"

Without hesitating, Strix reenergizes her smile. "I think you're the first man who has ever believed in me and genuinely looked at me as being intelligent and pretty. You were so patient listening to all my problems... I think I just wanted to be heard and understood. Recently I decided I don't want to be that person with all the problems. I want to be happy. I've only known you for six weeks but you've become like a father to me. You're my anchor, Dr. Klaudios. I realized I was wandering through life, shuffling through the days of my existence without direction or purpose. Thank you, Dr. Klaudios."

Desperately Kilborn seeks an appropriate response but has none. He lifts his head, looking into Strix's moistened eyes and chokes out, "I-I don't know what to say. I'm completely underserving."

Strix reaches across the table, gently clasping Kilborn's hand for a moment, then after a final squeeze she bolts to her feet. "Dr. Klaudios, I have an appointment to get a manicure, pedicure and some things I'm not even going to tell you about! I want to look good for my video interview so I'll finish my errands and meet you at the park later."

With a forced expression of happiness Kilborn looks toward Strix one last time as she returns his smile and darts toward the door. He watches her steps as she disappears from view, and then sits motionless in his darkened corner of the café.

Returning to his home, Kilborn labors over his decision the entire afternoon. Strix has inadvertently pierced the only remaining vulnerability of his heart. As a career educator, it was Kilborn's natural inclination to encourage and mentor unguided lives. Little did he realize, as he was purposely manipulating Strix, he had allowed himself to become attached to her in the process. In an impulse of anger he pitches an exotic vase across the room, shattering it against the opposite wall.

"Am I to throw away all my plans for one life?" Kilborn asks himself. "One single, misguided little girl? I can't!" he shouts, "I can't do it!"

With the 6:00 p.m. meeting with Harpy only thirty minutes away, he's not sure if he can go through with it. He needs more time, but there is none. He has come so far, plotting his retribution with near perfection up to this point. But he had lost all contact with his daughters and their lives mattered too. If he fails to act to reclaim his reputation, his rightful station in life, they will grow up thinking their father a monster and not knowing how much they were loved and missed by him.

With the veins of his neck engorged, Kilborn, in a maniacal rage screams, "They deserve to die for what they did to me… to my girls! How can I overlook that? How can I possibly throw it all away and give into the cowardly temptation to quit now?"

With self-loathing and despair, he reluctantly changes into his disguise and prepares to meet with Harpy. Kilborn positions his white truck on the third level of a public parking structure located a block away from the park. The spaces are primarily utilized during business hours and the few remaining vehicles in the garage are clustered deep into the interior of the building near the elevators. The elevation from this vantage point provides one with a view of most of the area.

Barabbas Park is a small patch of greenery located in an older part of town. In the sixty years since its inception, the business community has grown up around it and although visually appealing, it's rarely visited. At the park's center are a series of walkways and small hedges that lead to an old but functional fountain covered in a mosaic tile. There are three large arbors situated around the decorative pond, each covering a bench and displaying a vined curtain of greenery and flowers. The artistically designed fountain is beautiful if one takes the time to examine the craftsmanship, but it is too small and unremarkable to entice many visitors.

Kilborn, in disguise as a homeless person, has a small, wheeled cart in tow which serves to hide his camera equipment. By the time of his appointment with Harpy, Kilborn is ready. He sits on a nearby bench, push cart at his side, while displaying the signature purple knit cap on his head. Of the benches near the fountain, this one offers an almost hidden location. The mature foliage and flowering shrubs encase the seating area, providing almost perfect privacy. By 6:00 p.m. the park is empty. Most businesses have shut down for the day and almost all the local workforce have begun their commutes home. Harpy is late, but not by much. The clomping of her high heels on the concrete walkway announces her arrival long before Kilborn sees her walking toward him from another side of the park.

Harpy walks within a few feet of Kilborn, bends down and looks directly into his face. Almost squinting, "Dr. Klaudios?" Harpy stares. "Oh my god. Is that you?" She flashes a big grin. "You have to remind me to invite you to my next Halloween party. You look great!"

"Well thank you. You look pretty terrific yourself."

Harpy's near flawless physique is tightly wrapped in a very short red dress while the upper portion of her body is covered with a thin, light shawl. The wrap seems out of place for a warm summer evening, but it's apparent Harpy is covering a plunging neckline that she only intends to reveal at the appropriate time. Kilborn immediately takes charge so as not to allow Harpy's assertive side to become a hindering factor.

"I see you have your cup of ice and medication with you. Let me take that so it's not in the scene while we shoot the video." Kilborn takes the plastic cup from Harpy and immediately removes the lid in front of her. Lifting the syringe from the ice by the corners of the stem, he nods his approval. "Yes, this will be fine for what we need."

To Kilborn's relief, it is in fact the standard insulin syringe she had described. The dosage of human growth hormone is slightly less than the amount of insulin in the other syringe but the excess of insulin can easily be disposed of, still providing a lethal result.

"If you take a seat here on this bench, I'll put your cup in the shade next to my cart. I'm going to shoot the first scene from this side and the second scene with you over here by the water."

Kilborn pulls a tripod and video camera from the interior of his cart and sets it up while Harpy fidgets on the bench he's directed her to. He deliberately positions the video equipment so as to encumber Harpy's view of his activities and more importantly, the cup with the syringe. Each time he returns to the cart, Kilborn drops to his knees in front it. The move effectively blocks Harpy's view of both the cart and the cup. On the first trip he retrieves the insulin-filled syringe he had pilfered from Strix and places it alongside Harpy's in the cup of ice. Being careful to touch the vial only with his handkerchief, he disposes of a small amount of insulin so as to duplicate the dosage in Harpy's syringe. Moments later, when Harpy becomes absorbed with her reflection in a small make up mirror, Kilborn uses the opportunity to return to the cart a second and final time to switch the syringes.

"Are you almost ready, Dr. Klaudios? We're going to lose the sunlight soon," Harpy advises as she places the mirror back in her small purse.

"Not to worry, Ms. Harpy. It's 6:18 and the sunlight is perfect right now. Are you ready?"

Harpy nods in the affirmative while Kilborn turns and retrieves the cup. "I get a little nervous around needles so I'll let you handle it."

Harpy looks down her nose at Kilborn, almost in a chastising way for his act of timidity. She removes the syringe from the ice, and then quickly uncaps the end. Holding the exposed needle out to the side with one hand, she utilizes her unoccupied hand to remove the remaining unnecessary items from the scene. She pushes away her small purse, places the cap to the syringe on top of it, and finally removes her wrap, draping it carefully over her purse.

Kilborn returns to the camera, positioning it for a close up. For the first time, he has an opportunity to absorb Harpy's carnal allure. Using the necessity of focus, position and light as his vehicle, he virtually inhales her lusty appeal. Harpy's short, tight, red dress exposes her long, elegant legs, revealing a small portion of the buttocks as she crosses her limbs. The top of the vibrant red dress is connected to the bottom by only a decorative strand of material in the front. The narrow causeway of fabric covers nothing more than a slice of her toned midsection, revealing the top of her hips and almost all of her back. The upper portion of the skimpy outfit pushes and invites attention to all but the most intimate parts of her augmented breasts. Her blonde hair lacks its usual wild flair and is styled in chic and sophisticated abandon. In a darkened room, at first glance, she would appear to be a vision of ultimate beauty. If she were made into a poster, her toned and tanned physique would occupy the walls of millions of adolescents around the world. It is not until one attempts a closer inspection does it become obvious that Harpy is not really that pretty. Aside from all the trappings that scream sexual desire, her facial features are quite ordinary. Without all the enticing, lustful trappings; her face framed in luxuriant blonde tresses begging to be touched, the artificially plumped red lips pouting in kissable temptation, and the wrinkle disguising makeup, she's rather unremarkable.

In a moment of reflection Kilborn ponders why someone would go to such lengths to be attractive to men, yet hold them in such disdain. What hurt or trauma did this woman experience that brought her to this place? What mental, emotional or physical abuse was she forced to endure in her lifetime? The teacher and mentor that resides so strongly within Kilborn's core instinctively looks beyond the glam and glimmer of her exterior and into the wounded heart. Like so many of his students, they need only to be pointed in the right direction. Each pupil requires only to realize their own unique value and be shown the guideposts to escape or improve their lives. Many only need a purpose and a pat on the back.

"I can't do this!" Kilborn unintentionally shouts aloud as he becomes engrossed in his thoughts.

"You can't do what, Dr. Klaudios?" responds Harpy, clearly taken back by his vehement statement.

"Oh… okay, I have it now. I wasn't able to adjust the focus and everything was fuzzy… but I have it now. Are you ready?"

"I was born ready, Dr. Klaudios," says Harpy with a seductive tone and a sexy pooch of her lips.

Harpy's flippant response grates on Kilborn's last remaining reserve of compassion. "I'm happy for that," he manages to say, then adds, "You look ravishing, by the way. There's one last detail and then we're ready."

He retrieves his voice recorder from the cart, sets it at position two, and places it on the bench near Harpy. Turning the camera on, he positions the focus on Harpy's taut abdominal section where she normally injects her prescribed dosage of human growth hormone. She squeezes together a pinch of flesh with her index finger and thumb while bringing the syringe close to her skin. Harpy looks up at Kilborn one final time. Kilborn hesitates but concedes and provides an affirming nod. She looks down, then gently plunges the small, hair-like needle into her flesh and empties the content of the vial into her body. There's no turning back now. In about thirty minutes she will be dead.

Unlike the murder of Dr. Klaudios, Kilborn does not feel a sense of ecstasy over Harpy's impending death. To the contrary, he fights off an immediate sense of remorse. The doctor's death seemed necessary. He deliberately sold out Kilborn's parental rights for a mere paycheck and an easy lifestyle. His death provided Kilborn with a safe environment from which to rebuild his own life. Harpy, on the other hand, was obviously a misguided victim of another person's abuse. She never discovered a way out of her childhood dysfunction and that experience became her state of normalcy. Determined to save others from a similar grief, she attempted to liberate those like herself. Unfortunately, in the absence of a moral compass and direction from which to build, she became as abusive as her tormentors. She continued to feed her frail ego by attracting more and more attention to her herself, never feeling satisfied because she wasn't solving the real problem.

As Kilborn sets up the second scene with Harpy sitting on the lip of the fountain, he knows it's only a matter of minutes before she begins to display symptoms. Although reactions to an overdose of insulin vary from one person to another, he knows to look for the obvious signs of hunger, thirst, headaches and nausea; perhaps all at the same time. Harpy sits on the edge of the mosaic fountain with the soft, waning sunlight of the day draping the outline of her body. Her red dress looks magnificent posed against the multicolored background of the tile fountain. It would have made a beautiful picture if not for the persistent frown that now emerges on Harpy's face.

"I have a headache and I'm not feeling good Dr. Klaudios. We're going to have to wrap this up very soon."

"I'm sorry you're not feeling well. Give me just another minute and we'll be done."

Harpy doesn't respond. She bends over with her hands clasped in front of her knees. She lowers her head, almost touching her arms. Kilborn approaches, gently touching her shoulder, "How are you feeling?"

"I'm so dizzy," Harpy responds without lifting her head.

"Let me help you over to the bench," he consoles. "You can lie down there for a minute."

Kilborn assists Harpy as she struggles to her feet and staggers to the bench with Kilborn's assistance. This is the time Kilborn has been waiting for. For the next several minutes, Harpy will remain coherent but begin to feel a wide range of emotions. She could begin to exhibit erratic behavior ranging from what appears to be drunkenness or even mental illness. Not long thereafter, Harpy will lapse into a coma from which she will never wake.

Kilborn retrieves his voice recorder from the end of the bench, and then sits very close to Harpy's midsection. Leaning close to her ear he asks, "Ms. Harpy, can you hear me?"

Harpy, with her head resting on the shawl and her eyes closed, "Yes, I just feel sick all of a sudden. I'm very tired and dizzy."

Kilborn is face-to-face with Harpy, so close he could kiss her if that were his intention. He activates the recorder, placing it near her head. "Do you remember your TV interview regarding a teacher who was accused of sexually abusing his children and stealing funds?"

"What? Do I remember what? Dr. Klaudios, you're not making sense!"

"It was about two years ago. Perhaps your biggest interview. The teacher was a man named Travis Kilborn. Do you remember?"

Harpy's eyes seem to dart back-and-forth under the closed lids of her eyes and with some effort she responds, "Yes… yes of course I remember that. It was a big story at the time."

"Did you know that he was proven innocent but he never saw his children again?" Kilborn looks for signs of remorse but none is displayed. Although Harpy is well on her way to a coma and certain death, her life could still be saved with a timely call to emergency services. Kilborn presses her for even the slightest display of guilt or remorse.

"Innocent? They're never innocent! They're all liars and abusers but you can't prove it every time. They're all liars! All of them!"

Kilborn presses on, "Ms. Harpy, I'm Travis Kilborn."

Harpy's blue eyes burst open as she stares into Kilborn's face. At first her expression is tentative, revealing little emotion, but finally she gushes with an unrestrained laugh. "That's so funny, Dr. Klaudios!"

Time is escaping. Harpy could be slipping into a state of mind where she isn't able to process the information. Kilborn holds her by the chin and looking into her eyes he states with firmness, "My name is Travis Kilborn. I am the innocent teacher you pronounced guilty in the media. I have just given you a lethal injection and you are dying. Do you understand? I've murdered you!"

Harpy's eyes widen and she opens her mouth, attempting to scream. She lacks the strength and her only sound is a mournful cry, as though she were grieving the passing of her own life. She reaches up and grabs onto Kilborn, not in an attempt to injure him but to draw him into her as she weeps. She begins to fade in and out of delirium and with her last semblance of coherence, she doesn't want to be alone. Uncharacteristic of her life, this is the way Harpy's life ends, not with a bang but with a whimper.

Harpy is a stunning vision in death. Her face, now serene, as she lies on display on the bench and under the arbor's beautiful canopy of flowers. Kilborn's trancelike fixation is interrupted only minutes later as Harpy's cell phone rings. Predictably, the always reliable Strix calls slightly before the top of the hour to confirm the location as instructed. Kilborn uses his handkerchief to answer the call made to Harpy's phone. He intends to smother the device near his chest without responding, and then disconnect. Instinctively Kilborn knows Strix's will show up anyway. It was a nearly flawless scheme that had all gone according to plan until Kilborn, acting on pure emotion and impulse, answers the call, passion flooding from his voice. "Hello... Strix? Run sweetheart... stay away from here!"

"Dr. Klaudios? What's going on? You sound like you're sobbing! Dr. Klaudios! Talk to me!"

"Please don't come near this place... I'll explain later," his voice broken with distress, and then abruptly he disconnects the call.

Quickly and deliberately, Kilborn packs up his video equipment, voice recorder and the plastic cup Harpy used to transport the syringe. Confident the area is clean of his presence, he checks Harpy one final time. She looks like a goddess in death but it becomes painful for Kilborn to look at her any longer. He moves his cart out of the sound range of her phone, enters 9-1-1, and leaves the device in Harpy's hand. With the final hour of daylight escaping, Kilborn walks away in silence. He trudges back to his truck, climbs inside and begins to watch as the events unfold.

The quiet of the early summer evening is disrupted by a myriad of lights, sounds and fast moving silhouettes. Kilborn, perched in a place of safety, numbly stares into the throng of chaos. One of the shadows in the vicinity of the fountain appears to be Strix. Additional emergency vehicles arrive on the scene moments later, transforming the once tranquil park into sea of flashing lights. The local newscasters have already gotten wind of the story and quickly set up their broadcast system so as to pitch their story to the public. This will be the biggest story of Harpy's career. Kilborn should be elated. His plan appeared to have been executed to near perfection yet he feels empty inside, even remorseful. He expected to experience the ecstasy of satisfied vengeance. Instead, Kilborn feels only disappointment and loss. Harpy was a victim herself. She learned to use the tools at her disposal to fight back and punish those who either abused her or were like those that abused her. Kilborn inwardly ponders the notion, *"How much different is she... from me?"*

Strix will likely be prosecuted and convicted of Harpy's murder. Her text messages establish a clear motive and she possessed the means and opportunity to carry out the crime. She is the last known person to have been with Harpy; her cell phone record will display she was in the immediate vicinity at the time of Harpy's death. The insulin syringe will match the lot number Strix uses and the syringe itself may have her finger prints on it. If not, the residual chemicals left on the syringe will match the perfume in her purse. Harpy's body will be discovered unmolested, her handbag will be found with her cash and credit cards accounted for. There will be no evidence to indicate a struggle and no defensive wounds. Her murderer had to be a trusted friend, or at least someone she knew. There is only one person that the evidence points to and that's Strix. She will likely receive a prison sentence of twenty-five years to life.

Kilborn is mesmerized by the lights and immersed in thought as he continues to fixate on the distant scene. He cares for Strix, much more than he initially realized. Thoughts of his last meeting with her flood his mind. Unlike Harpy, Strix seemed to have experienced a personal revelation of sorts. She was different; she desired to change and wanted a better life for herself. She was just beginning to emerge from her cocoon of despair when Kilborn crushed her. She will spend the rest of her life immersed in a cloud of self-loathing and hopelessness. It's more than she deserved. Kilborn breaks his fixation with the lights and activity of the crime scene, casting his view downward and inward. *What have I done? What have I become?*

A tear streaks down his face as he looks back at the location where he last saw Strix's silhouette, "I'm sorry Strix... I'm so sorry."

XII

The Raven

The desert heat in the foothills outside of Bishop rapidly dissipates after the sun goes down. Kilborn wakes from a nap in the cab of the truck with a slight chill and in near total darkness. The only source of light is the radiant star-lit sky which is most often obscured in metropolitan communities. It's not until one makes the effort to step away from the hamster wheel of modernity and looks upward that a person is reminded of the wonderment of the cosmos. Kilborn retreats to the open tailgate of his truck; lying face-up, arms raised from behind, and using the palms of his hands to form a cushion for his head. Staring into the vast and brilliant night he experiences an immediate sense of smallness and an overwhelming urge to dialog with the universe. There is little consciousness of time and in the moment he feels like a wayward parishioner in a celestial confessional. Reeling with remorse from his betrayal of Strix and the unfulfilling murder of Harpy, Kilborn is compelled to empty his soul before heaven. If there is a god, he possesses a need to plead his case before the divine entity and declare his justification. Although alone and scarcely no chance of being heard by another person, he limits his communication to a jumble of thoughts and softly spoken words. In a nearly remorseful tone, "God, if you're there… if you're listening… I didn't plan for things to turn out this way. I planned a much different life."

After a brief pause, he flips into a different mindset; his comments become much more defensive. "This situation was forced on me. What could I do? Should I have resigned myself to a quiet, lonely and meaningless death, void of any attempt at redemption? Only those victorious in battle and survivors are afforded the luxury of recording their view of history. Most often the only factor that distinguishes a traitor from a hero is being on the side that wins. My legacy would have me being known as the failed teacher who absconded with money from the school fund and who abused his children. You know that's not true! Why didn't you help me? I did nothing to deserve being stripped of everything that was important to me in life! Why God? Why did things turn out this way?"

Aside from a soft breeze and the rhythmic chirping of crickets from places of obscurity, the universe is silent. The celestial parade continues to march on and stars appear to pulsate with life, all oblivious to Kilborn's presence. Is it that God is unable to act or does the divine lack interest in humanity? Perhaps it's the blood on his hands and the murderous intentions in his heart that prevent him from hearing a response. The only voice he hears in this moment is the rumble of rage that continues to simmer in his soul. Feeling shunned, ignored... rejected by God, Kilborn rises to his feet, spreads pleading hands wide and in an agonizing voice, shouts heavenward—"Why?"

His voice echoes back to him in the darkness, almost as though it has taken a life of its own; taunting him while whispering the same question as it dances away into the night, *Why?* Kilborn pauses, and then softly mutters the answer to himself. "Because I can't forgive what they've done to me. I have nothing left to live for except to satisfy my need for vengeance. I can't see anything beyond that."

Kilborn takes in a deep, cleansing breath and stands motionless in the near-silent darkness. Addressing the crickets he asks, "Should I kill Judge Raven?" The rhythmic pulse from his hidden audience continues in cadence without impact. Suddenly, in a rush of rage, Kilborn erupts with an agonizing scream, "Yes!" The crickets become abruptly quiet and the hillside resonates with what sounds like a cascade of voices; a score of demons hiss with assurance—*Yes. Yes. Yes...*

Becoming slowly conscious of time, Kilborn retreats to his vehicle. Although discouraged by his attempt to find resolve in his soul, he is now more committed and focused in his mission to kill the judge. Before he starts back into town, he double checks the enclosed camper shell of his small white truck to insure himself he brought everything to Bishop with him.

There are a few large metal containers filled with gasoline, a couple of wooden pallets, an ax, shovel, lantern and a rolled up section of carpet. Next to the metal containers is a covered cardboard box. Inside there's a roll of duct tape, nylon rope, cable ties, flip knife, eyed tent stakes, handcuffs, a pair of socks, sledge hammer and a stun gun. Situated in the cab of the truck is a sleeping bag, a change of clothes and a small cooler with enough food and drink for the entire weekend. Kilborn is well aware of the fact that it takes only a single blunder to expose all of his schemes. His plans do not include a stop for food or gas and he does not expect to have a single conversation along the way. As an added precaution, he has abandoned his disguise as Dr. Klaudios in favor of a more natural look. He removed the artificial girth, slicked the kinky side portion of his hair back and masks himself under a baseball cap and glasses. Although Raven has seen Kilborn a half dozen times, he has never seen him as Dr. Klaudios, nor has he seen him with a six-week growth of beard and disguised. In spite of his planning, Kilborn's anxiety level is high. Unlike his previous murder, he had little time to plan and knows nearly nothing about the judge aside from his courtroom persona. This time there is no room for error and no backup plan; unless of course, running away and hoping to avoid capture is considered a legitimate Plan B.

Although somewhat familiar with the vicinity, Kilborn carefully scrutinized the area a few weeks prior during a scouting expedition. Bishop is a small town. To the west are fabulous views of the Sierra Nevada Mountains and some of the best hiking trails in the country. The east is comprised primarily of desert and the unique White Mountains. Visual stimulation and natural beauty can be discovered in every direction. Mixed within the natural allure of the region is a potentially dangerous terrain and a quirky weather system. Careless visitors can easily get lost and die here. It's a perfect spot for someone to disappear.

Driving into town Kilborn notes that even on a Friday evening there is little activity. His research of the community revealed that there are only a few thousand residents and a couple of dozen hotels in Bishop. Of that number, about half are rated by travel websites as being above average or better. Among these, there are a few that consistently receive glowing reviews. Kilborn thinks his chances are pretty good that he will find Judge Raven's red truck holed up in one of them. The drive from Orange County to Bishop is about six hours. As the hour approaches midnight, Kilborn calculates the judge has had plenty of time to complete his drive and be settled into his room. All the hotels and motels are congregated within a few miles of one another, simplifying his search. It doesn't take long and with a marginal effort, he discovers the judge's vehicle in the parking lot of one of the higher end establishments. Kilborn parks on a public road near the outer perimeter of the hotel, carefully positioning himself with a clear view of the red truck. He will set the alarm on his watch to wake him an hour before sunrise.

Stretching out over the truck's front seat and resting his head against the window, Kilborn attempts to rest. The bed he has made is absent of comfort and the few hours of sleep he manages, seem to pass in only minutes. He wakes to a high pitched beeping noise emanating from his wrist. Temporarily disoriented and uncertain as to where he is, he jolts awake in panic. As the fog clears from his mind, he immediately draws his attention to the judge's truck. It's still there. He wastes little time attending to personal needs before bringing the cardboard box into the cab of the truck with him. Now it's simply a matter of waiting for the judge to appear. Although the sun has yet to rise, most hikers are conscious of maximizing the daylight hours and are eager to be on the trail at first light. Kilborn doesn't expect his wait to be long.

Night continues to dominate the early morning sky as a figure emerges from under the lights of the hotel parking lot. With backpack in tow the male figure walks directly toward the red truck and opens the tailgate, sliding his gear in the back. It's obviously Raven. Kilborn is surprised the egotistical bastard isn't wearing his robe or rigged a halo to his head. Without his judicial regalia the judge looks taller, probably a little over six feet. He looks strong and fit too. Although it's apparent the man isn't a body builder, he has a lean and wiry composition; the kind of man who could do several sets of push-ups and pull-ups.

It could pose a problem. To date Kilborn has only been successful in overcoming a senior citizen and a middle-aged woman. This will be a much tougher challenge. Hidden behind the tinted windows of his truck, Kilborn stares down the unsuspecting target of his hatred. As his rage mounts, he tightens his grip on the steering wheel; squeezing harder and harder, finally shaking it violently he screams, "I'm going to kill you, you son-of-a-bitch!"

As the judge enters his truck, Kilborn regains his composure and sets out ahead of him. His intention is to monitor Raven while driving in front of him. Once on the highway heading south from Bishop, there is only one route to the trailhead. The judge will not be suspicious of a vehicle preceding him up the mountain. Kilborn's lead is only a few hundred yards but he must slowly creep along the road to be certain the judge will turn in his direction. Although the wait is less than a minute, Kilborn rants in agitation. "I've made too many mistakes already! I only made an educated guess he's going to South Lake… he may go somewhere else or stop for breakfast. There are too many variables and I can't rely on guessing my way through this!"

A glance into the side mirror reveals the red truck swinging into view. Confident the judge is following behind him, Kilborn picks up speed and attempts to maintain the same distance between the vehicles while making the drive to the trailhead. The judge seems content to follow. As the vehicles make their turn off the highway, a subtle glow emerges on the desert horizon. The topography of the area is unique in that parts of the nearby desert terrain are below sea level while Bishop itself is 4,149' in elevation. After taking the turn from the main highway outside of town, the road climbs to 9,801' where there's a small paved area that allows for overnight parking near the trailhead. One has to arrive before the sun rises to expect to find an open space.

Kilborn parks his truck, immediately aware that he has to act quickly or miss the opportunity. After the sun rises, within minutes the busy camping area will experience a regular flow of potential witnesses. He stuffs the stun gun into the top pocket of his cargo shorts, cable ties in another, a sock, handcuffs and duct tape in one of the lower pockets. Looking in his mirror Kilborn sees that the judge has taken one of the few remaining parking spaces across from him on the other side of the small lot. He was hoping for a better arrangement but it's not a deal-breaker. Kilborn continues to make mental notes of his lack of planning. He should have insured that South Lake was in fact the judge's destination and figured out a way to arrange the vehicles next to one another. There's no time to lament his decisions or beat himself up over possible consequences. The judge is exiting his vehicle and Kilborn has to move now. Kilborn swallows hard and approaches the judge with a "Hiker Bob" persona he has developed in his mind, "Hey neighbor. You ever been up here before?"

Raven, who has reached the back of his truck and is in the process of lowering the tailgate, turns to face the friendly stranger. Responding with little enthusiasm and no apparent interest in an ongoing conversation, "Yeah, I've been here several times. It's a good place to hike."

Kilborn plays on the judge's huge ego in an attempt to engage him by displaying a need for information and instruction. "This is my first time here. You wouldn't happen to have a map would you?"

If the judge has a map, Kilborn can divert his attention to the map, allowing him the opportunity to get close enough to use the stun gun on him. As it is, Raven is only minutes from the trail and has no desire to continue placating an uninvited stranger. "I don't have a map but you can get one at the campground when it opens in a couple of hours."

The judge has his hand on his backpack and in one swift motion he could be on his way. Thinking quickly, Kilborn makes a final plea, "I understand the route to Bishop Pass Trail is clearly marked. Can you show me where the starting point is?"

The judge is a little befuddled by the request because it's within a stone's throw of where they're standing and there are clearly marked signs. Eager to rid himself of the pesky intruder, he points in the direction of the sign. Kilborn looks intently where the judge is pointing, crinkles his face and removes his glasses. After wiping his eyes, he places his glasses back in position, "There's not enough light yet. I can't see it."

Raven shakes his finger while pointing, as if to add more clarity. "It's right there! You have to be able to see it!"

Kilborn can almost hear the judge's unspoken *Idiot!* and senses this will be his final chance. He stares at the end of the judge's finger while siding up next to him. While Raven points and says, "Do you see the large tree behind the boulder?" Kilborn positions himself slightly behind him and reaches into his pocket to retrieve the stun gun.

Kilborn extends his left hand with his index finger pointed in the same direction, "Is that it right there… ?"

With the judge's attention intently focused at the landmark, Kilborn places the stun gun firmly into Raven's back and presses the button. There's a buzzing and clicking sound and the judge immediately falls to the ground. He's not unconscious as Kilborn thought he'd be but simply on the ground and moving about as though under the influence of a strong drug. Kilborn immediately looks around and spots a duo of hikers walking toward the trailhead but the dim light and wall of parked cars prevent them from seeing anything. He rolls the judge onto his stomach while fumbling for the handcuffs in the pocket of his shorts. By this time the judge is becoming vocal and attempting to call for help but he's unable to formulate words. The sound he makes is something akin to a human making a very poor imitation of a bloodhound. Anyone hearing the noise would immediately dismiss it as a prank but Kilborn knows his time is limited. With some effort he is finally able to secure the handcuffs from behind but now the judge is regaining his faculties and resisting. He attempts a wobbly kick in Kilborn's direction but the effort falls far short of causing him injury. Kilborn reaches for the stun gun and zaps the judge a second time. With the judge at the maximum level of passivity, he stuffs a sock in his mouth and secures it with several circuits of duct tape around his head. It leaves the judge covered in something resembling a football helmet but it serves its purpose. With his hands and mouth restrained, Kilborn utilizes a cable tie to bind the judge's ankles and places a second tie slightly above his knees.

With his victim tightly bound, Kilborn rolls Raven face down under the open tailgate of the red truck while he surveys the area. Headlights approach from the distance, perhaps ninety seconds away. Their likely destination is the overnight parking area, exactly where he's standing. He has only moments to decide what to do and attempting to drag and lift the judge into the back of his own truck without being seen is impossible. Only one option comes to his mind. It's not a great idea but one that may buy him some time. Kilborn darts back to his truck and retrieves the roll of carpet. Although this is not its intended purpose, it would have to do. His plan is to roll the judge up in the carpet, trapping him inside like a piece of meat in a burrito. As he lifts the tailgate to Raven's truck, the judge has a surprise of his own waiting for him. The small stun gun only incapacitates its target for a little more than thirty seconds and Kilborn has given the judge too much time to recover. Raven has rolled onto his back and drawn his knees to his chest. As Kilborn lifts the tailgate, the judge delivers a stout kick to Kilborn's upper thighs, knocking him backward off of his feet. If the judge had connected a few inches higher, Kilborn would have been incapacitated for several minutes and his scheme exposed. Kilborn is in pain but knows he has only about thirty seconds to do something. He reaches for his stun gun and dives toward Raven's upper body to keep from being kicked again. Climbing near his head, he rolls apart from him and applies a jolt to his neck. The judge begins to gasp for air as the muscles in his neck constrict his breathing. Kilborn isn't worried about him dying prematurely if that's what ends up happening. His major concern at the moment is being discovered by those approaching in the oncoming vehicle. There's no time to roll the judge in the carpet. He pushes him back under the tailgate and drapes the carpet over the end. The judge's lanky legs and feet protrude from the other end but Kilborn quickly snatches the judge's backpack from his truck and positions it to hide the appendages from view.

An older model van approaches and slowly drives by. The occupants display no indication of interest or suspicion. Kilborn keeps his back to the vehicle as it settles into what is likely the only remaining parking space. He watches the driver and his female passenger from his peripheral vision as they exit their vehicle and prepare their gear. As a precaution, Kilborn has slightly raised the tailgate and has his foot squarely on the judge's neck. He will not hesitate to put his entire weight down if the judge begins to emit a sound or resist. Raven remains compliant, still straining to breathe. The couple from the van seems eager to get on the trail and within a few agonizing minutes, they depart without exhibiting even a slight concern regarding Kilborn. Everything appears to be quiet again as Kilborn takes advantage of the lull of activity in the parking lot. He spreads the carpet flat on the asphalt surface while attempting to roll Raven onto it. At first the judge resists but Kilborn squeezes the judge's throat and he quickly becomes cooperative. Rolling the initial wrap of carpet around the judge was the most taxing, but once he's completely encircled the subsequent rolls are easy. Dragging his prisoner across the small parking lot and to the back of his truck was relatively uncompli- cated as well. The difficulty is lifting Raven. Unable to carry the judge's entire weight, Kilborn lifts the front of the rolled carpet first, leans it onto the tailgate with the intention of elevating the rear separately and then sliding the judge into the back of the camper shell. Raven resists again, intentionally leaning to the side and allowing himself to slide back to the ground. Kilborn cannot afford further delay. The sun is moments away from breaking above the horizon and he is too close to pulling this off to be discovered now. Kilborn tries again. This time he manipulates Raven's body higher on the edge of the tailgate, balancing him with one hand and clutching his throat with the other. As the judge begins to gurgle from a lack of oxygen, Kilborn releases him, and then in a swift motion pushes his weight onto the tailgate while lifting his feet. The car- pet slides easily into the bed of the truck and Kilborn hurriedly secures the tailgate. With a sock covering his hand, Kilborn returns to the judge's red truck, locks the vehicle and wipes the tailgate in the event he left fin- gerprints. Only Raven's backpack remains. Kilborn stores it on the front passenger seat of his own truck and looks around one last time to survey the scene. As the sun breaches the horizon, a strand of hikers emerge from the camping area only minutes away. Kilborn is satisfied that he has left nothing behind. Raven isn't expected back for nine days. By then his truck will be covered in a layer of dust and he will have long been dead.

Kilborn begins a nervous retreat from the mountain, sweat still rolling down his back and off his forehead. Capturing the judge was only the first part of this adventure. Now he will have to drive thirty miles away to an abandoned mine to complete the next step of his scheme. He is nearly halfway down the mountain when his senses are suddenly jolted into high alert...*Bam! Bam! Bam!* His eyes widen and he jerks his head up. Quickly reducing his speed, he checks the side mirrors to see if he has run over something. The road is clear. *Bam, bam, bam!* This time he sees the cause. Raven has somehow partially wiggled himself free of his cage of carpet and is using his powerful legs in an attempt to kick out the rear window of the camper shell. Kilborn swerves from side-to-side to keep Raven off balance, and then skids to a complete stop. Before Raven has an opportunity to regain his balance or completely free himself from the carpet, Kilborn rushes to the back with stun gun in hand. The judge attempts to defend himself but has only loosened the wool binding enough to lift his legs and isn't free of its grasp. Enraged, Kilborn leaps on top of the carpet, lying on the judge, face-to-face. With his hand on the judge's throat and stun gun in hand, he activates the weapon; it buzzes and clicks dangerously close to Raven's face. "If you move again," he warns in a soft, gritty voice filled with malice, "I will use this on one of your eyes until it melts out of the socket. Do you understand?"

For the first time, Raven appears to be genuinely afraid. His eyes are awash with fear and uncertainty. He nods in compliance but Kilborn lingers, staring into the judge's eyes until he's certain his threat has broken the judge's resolve. He's the one in control now. He has the power! At this moment he owns Raven's soul! This is the emotional rush he was waiting for! This is how it felt when he rolled Dr. Klaudios from the stern of the boat and watched sharks tearing into his flesh!

"I decide your fate now," Kilborn says as he slowly lifts himself apart from the judge, "as you once took it upon yourself to decide mine." His eyes continue to stare into those of his victim with a simmering rage. After several lingering moments the trance is broken by Kilborn's low, malevolent laugh. The judge, his eyes filled with terror, offers no resistance as his captor tightens the roll of carpet, securing the ends with several strands of duct tape.

The obscure, abandoned mine is only a couple of twisted turns and a few miles off of the highway. Kilborn drives as close as possible to the entrance, dumping off Raven who remains imprisoned in the coil of carpet, and then parks his truck within a cluster of nearby oak trees. The entry to the mine is an old boarded blockade, in disrepair and partially torn down. Kilborn has been here before. During his exploratory visit of the area a few weeks ago, this is the site he settled on. He knows one has to step through the wooden planks and into an interior space approximately the size of a maintenance elevator. Once inside, the ground is littered with shattered beer bottles; in the middle there's a remnant of an old fire circle. It's apparent that aside from Kilborn's recent visit, no one has been here for years. The small area in the immediate entrance is the only place where one is able to stand up. There's another barrier deeper inside the mine. This too, has been pushed aside. It once covered a tunnel with an opening about the size of a doghouse. From there, the shaft slopes downward for a few feet before it reaches the edge of an eighteen foot drop. Without having crawled to the bottom, Kilborn believes it to be the extent of the dig.

He trudges back to the mine entrance with all his gear in hand; setting up a battery-powered lantern inside before bringing in the remainder of his equipment. Using the sledge hammer, he drives four tent stakes with eye loops on the end, deep into one of the walls; two at the top and two at the bottom. It's now time for the judge to make his grand entrance. After cutting the duct tape from the coil of carpet, Kilborn kneels on the open end while pushing the roll down the slight elevation. The judge spills out of the roll on the other end, sopping wet in his own sweat and urine. Wrapped in several layers of wool for nearly an hour has left him in a dangerous state of heat exhaustion. Had it not been for the coolness of the early morning hour, he would likely already be dead. Summer temperatures in this part of the country commonly approach triple digits and Kilborn is eager to complete his mission before the heat becomes unbearable.

Standing over his victim, Kilborn spills a partial bottle of water over the top of his head. Raven, with his eyes closed, jumps when he feels the liquid on his skin. Amused by the response, Kilborn laughs. There is no response from the judge. He lies in a weakened state, motionless apart from trying to push the sock from his mouth, breathing stertorously through his nose. Kilborn drags Raven into the shade of the mine and sits him against a wall, quickly returning outside to retrieve the carpet and the rest of his gear. Once inside, Kilborn tacks the carpet over the mine entrance so as to buffer any sound. With the mine entrance secure to his satisfaction, Kilborn cuts the tape away from Raven's head and removes the sock from his mouth. The judge needs water but Kilborn will keep him in his weakened state until after he ties him to the wall. He places Raven face down with his feet near the wall, removes his hiking boots and tightly ties nylon ropes around both of his wrists, then his ankles. Then, he threads the loose ends of rope through the eyes in the tent pegs. After one ankle is secured, Kilborn cuts the cable ties on Raven's legs and fastens the other ankle in place. Wordlessly, he tugs on the cords attached to Raven's handcuffed wrists. The tension causes the judge to rise to his knees, instinctively knowing if he doesn't comply, Kilborn will haul on them until his arms break out of their sockets. With the judge in a kneeling position, head hanging, Kilborn removes a bottle of water from his supply and trickles it over Raven's head. The moment Raven raises his head to drink, Kilborn cuts off the flow in a baiting, tormenting manner. "Stand up!" Kilborn demands.

Raven struggles and fails in an attempt, "I can't... I need help."

Kilborn wraps his arms around Raven's waist and lifts until the judge is standing erect. When he's on his feet, Kilborn ties his wrists individually to his belt with a separate strand of rope. With his hands secure, Kilborn removes the handcuffs and then drags each hand separately until Raven is finally tied against the wall, limbs apart, resembling Leonardo da Vinci's drawing of Vitruvian Man.

Again, he douses Raven with water but this time allows him to drink freely. Kilborn's motivation is not one of mercy but of necessity. He wants to be able to have a conversation with the judge and then kill him slowly. With Raven helplessly tied to the wall, Kilborn approaches him with the open blade of his knife. Looking deeply into the judge's eyes, he tauntingly slides the blunt end of the blade over his forehead before using the razor sharp edge to cut into his clothing. Within minutes, Raven is stripped of his clothing and stands naked in the dim light of the lantern.

Reinvigorated by the water but enraged for being exposed, Raven screams, "What are you? Some type of pervert? Is that what this is all about?"

Kilborn chuckles, coldly, softly, sardonically. "Is that what you think? You think I have a sexual interest in you?" He snorts in disgust. "You can put that huge ego away because you're not my type, Mr. Raven."

With his identity acknowledged, Raven reverts to his authoritarian mode. "If you know who I am, then you know I'm a California Superior Court Judge. Every state and federal officer will be looking for me and they will hunt you down!"

The small space accentuates not only Raven's pronouncement but Kilborn's laughter. "Shall we take a gander outside?" Kilborn mocks. Lifting the side edge of the carpet from the wall of the entry, he reveals the empty, rural terrain. "Hmmm, they must be busy saving other judges today."

"Who the hell are you and what do you want with me?" Raven demands.

Kilborn cocks his head to the side. "You have no idea who I am, do you?"

"Of course not!" Raven's tone belittles Kilborn.

"I'm the teacher who was in the news for stealing funds from his school. Do you remember the non-profit funds you illegally authorized to be taken from the school fund I administered? No?"

Despite the reality of being tied to the wall of a mine in the middle of nowhere, Raven slips into his judicial mindset of arrogance and insensitivity. "I handle hundreds of cases every year. Why would yours be memorable?"

"Why would mine be memorable?" Kilborn asks softly, turning his back to the judge and reaching for the sledge hammer. "The loss of my children, my reputation, career and everything I owned may not have been memorable to you," he says, then swiftly spinning back to the judge, fully enraged by his callousness. "But it was everything to me!" he shouts while slamming the hammer down on Raven's right foot.

Raven screams in instant agony! It was not only the immediate and horrific pain but the surprise and realization of his predicament. Many, if not most of the bones in the judge's foot and toes are broken. The judge shifts his weight to the other foot and clinches onto the nylon cords with his hands, still writhing in distress.

"Does that help your memory?" Kilborn snarls.

"I'm sorry, I'm sorry… it's not me, it's the system," wails Raven. His body quivers with pain as he attempts to speak without whimpering.

"The system?" questions Kilborn. "Did you forget that I walked the halls of the Orange County Family Law Court for over a year? I sat through scores of proceedings. I was there when you granted custody of a soldier's children to his unfaithful spouse. While the ex was sleeping with the neighborhood, the soldier was risking his life in a foreign land, fighting to protect our Constitution and Bill of Rights while pompous asses like you, who have never served a day in the military, are throwing our guaranteed freedoms away. That's the system?"

"Someone has to decide… that's what I do," Raven whimpers.

"You have to decide?" says Kilborn gritting his teeth. "It's you who decides to violate a person's civil rights? Aren't Constitutional issues above your pay grade? How is it that the fourth and fourteenth Amendments to the Constitution are so easily tossed aside? In case you don't remember, that's the part that specifically guarantees that no State is to deprive any person of life, liberty or property without due process of law. How is it that I was restrained from entering my own home as a result of bogus charges, and without a trial? How is it that once the charges were proven to be unfounded that I was still barred from returning to my home? How is it that my accounts were frozen and I was denied access to my own funds to survive? You also authorized the seizure of funds from a non-profit organization that I administered and I faced criminal charges for the disappearance of this money. Ring a bell yet?"

Raven, with his head slumped to his chest, meekly responds. "I regret your situation but I am not responsible for the way the system works. If there is no clear solution to an issue, we decide in favor of what is best for the children."

"You're saying it's best for children to grow up in a fatherless home? This is a gender issue?" replies Kilborn in an astonished voice. "I don't see gender as being an issue in the Constitution! You allowed my wife control of the community assets and she was able to use them to hire legal representation. I had no one to represent me and you knew that, you son-of-a-bitch! Why was I denied my Constitutional right to equal protection under the law?"

"It's not like that!" Raven's quavering tone indicates his extreme pain, "I decided that the children needed to have the resources to begin a new life without being dependent on the State for assistance. It's easier for a single man to start over than a woman with children."

Kilborn's laugh, though soft, shows his disbelief. "And what about a man with children and my best interest? What about a man falsely accused of being violent and a child abuser? When they're proven innocent, do they get a chance to start over?"

The small room is eerily quiet for several moments. Raven doesn't have an appropriate answer, not one that will satisfy Kilborn's blood thirst. Kilborn stands in silence for a moment, looking... waiting. Still there's only silence. He retreats to the cardboard box, removes the voice recorder and checks to see that it is set on position three. He gently sets it on the ground beside the judge.

"The happiest moments of my life," Kilborn states with a sad smile, "were the days I'd come home from teaching to be greeted at the door by my kids. They loved their daddy... and they thought he was a pretty great guy. They looked up to me and thought I was the best at everything. I was the best dad in the world to them. When I tucked them into their beds, there were moments I never wanted to look away from their angelic faces as they slept. Have you ever experienced that joy, Mr. Raven? Have you, Mr. Raven?"

The judge remains silent, his chin nearly resting on his chest. With the sledge hammer in full view, Kilborn approaches Raven using his fingertips to lift his face. Looking straight into his eyes, "Your pain will be over soon, mine will be with me forever. What government consents to the heartless theft of children and the raping of private property while it fights wars for freedom and the protection of democracy? Is this what our ancestors and our present day warriors fight for... the illusion of freedom and the pretense of opportunity?"

Kilborn removes his fingers from under Raven's chin, allowing it to once again, rest on his chest. Bending to the ground, he activates the recorder, and then returns to his original position directly in front of Raven. Face-to-face with the judge, speaking in a soft and mournful voice, "Do you know how many times I've seen my girls in three years? Three times... the answer is three times. The last visit was over two years ago. On my last visit they said I was a bad person and that they hated me. Do you know what that feels like, Mr. Raven? Have you ever known the pain of losing your child's love? Your discomfort is nothing in comparison." He crashes the sledge hammer on Raven's left foot.

There is a beginning of a yelp, broken off, followed by silence. The judge has passed out from the pain. Kilborn grabs up the recorder, switches it off and then sits a few feet away and waits. Nearly all of Raven's upper body weight hangs on his outstretched arms and by now they are entirely inflamed and quivering. Within a minute Raven regains consciousness, inhaling a large gasp of air, then screams in anguish, "Oh god! Oh god... Help me!"

Raven leans with his back against the wall, placing his weight on his heels in a desperate attempt to reduce his suffering. Kilborn approaches his victim slowly, waiting for Raven to calm down. When the judge has downgraded his outburst to a mere whimpering, he asks, "Do you remember Dr. Klaudios? He's the court appointed psychologist who recommended my wife have full custody."

Raven doesn't respond but it seems apparent that he's listening. "I killed him by cutting his Achilles Tendon and then fed him to sharks. Here, listen..."

Kilborn plays the track, smiling as though the judge is enjoying the experience with him. At the end of the first setting, he says, "What about Ms. Harpy? You have to remember her. Everyone remembers Ms. Harpy. She's the media whore who broke the big story about an honored educator who absconded with money from the school and abused his children. Before you left on your trip you may have heard the news that she was murdered. Would you like to hear her last words?"

The judge remains silent as Kilborn plays the second track. "I didn't care as much for that one. It lacked a certain demonstration of suffering, if you know what I mean. Look here! This is setting three, reserved specifically for you, Judge Raven."

Kilborn activates the recorder and sets it on the ground. Returning his attention to Raven he lifts his head and looks into his eyes. The manifestation of hopelessness and despair has returned to his face. "We'll make your edition special," Kilborn promises.

Kilborn drops to his knees, hammer in hand, tauntingly tapping the ground around Raven's feet. The judge can only respond with an expression of torment, terrified by the horror of where this door leads. At first, there's a gentle rapping, and then much more. The hammer falls lightly on the broken and swollen feet of his captive, plunging the judge into a painful fit. His screams begin to fill the voice recorder with the treasure Kilborn seeks. Standing up, Kilborn steps back to admire his work. The judge's body is burning in agony but it's time to finish his work. Kilborn takes the sledge hammer in both hands, winds up and swings with all his might, slamming the blunt instrument into Raven's side. The impact hits the judge as a train ramming a stalled vehicle on the railroad tracks; the accompanying sound is like a plastic watermelon being crushed and cracking open from the force. A few of Raven's ribs have detached from the skeletal frame; the floating ribs will restrict his breathing, ultimately leading to his slow and tormenting demise. Kilborn sits holding his voice recorder as the final minutes of the judge's life ebb. There's no hatred in Raven's expression, only desperation and pain. Each new breath produces a rush of agony. If he could choose to stop breathing, he would, but the body's involuntary hunger for oxygen trumps his pain. Raven's eyes are wide with panic; his mouth forms a type of oval as though he's gulping air and his mind cannot focus beyond his immediate misery. Sitting in the dim light across the small enclosure, Kilborn remarks, "There's only a single question left to ask... a single response to hear. Judge Raven! Will you ever rob a man of the love of his children again?"

The judge is still alive and though the words may rattle through his consciousness, there is no attention given to it. Kilborn, aware of this, answers his own question, "Never again... nevermore."

Kilborn watches as several minutes pass. Suffering with each agonizing breath, Raven takes a final and violent gasp, and dies.

Kilborn, continues to sit, staring at the judge. It was a good kill, even spectacular at moments. It would have been even better if he wasn't forced to remember the loss of his children. Raven's dead, dangling body at the end of a nylon rope didn't fix that part of his life. Kilborn cuts

Raven's lifeless body down and drags it near the narrow portion of the mineshaft. After removing all the gear from the mine, he returns, gutting Raven and tossing his soft innards into the shaft. Utilizing a plank that was once used as a cover for the opening, the pile of human organs is pushed into the eighteen foot pit. After loading most of the gear into the truck he returns with an ax to cut up the body and roll the pieces into the carpet. What little blood remains will be absorbed by the layers of wool surrounding it. He removes the tent stakes from the wall with a crowbar and rakes the soil to redistribute and cover the pools of blood. It's not a perfect clean up, and certainly there will remain some traces of DNA, but someone would have to know exactly what they were looking for and where to find it.

Kilborn emerges from the mine and is almost surprised to discover that it's not yet 9:00 a.m. The day seemed longer; much longer. He loads the roll of carpet into the truck, places his clothing in a plastic bag, refuels the truck and then sponge bathes himself under the oak trees. The only task remaining is to dispose of what is left of Raven's body.

Kilborn grew up in San Diego's East County, in a community named Lakeside. One local politician referred to the East County as the anus of San Diego. Those who grew up in the town and remember the uniqueness of the community likely hold to an entirely different opinion. The quaint, small lake for which Lakeside derives its name is Lindo Lake. Its shallow waters are separated into two parts by a causeway. Other than locals such as Kilborn, not too many people know the greater part of the east side of the lake is only a few inches deep. The murky bottom makes the veneer of water on the surface appear much deeper than it is. During the hot summer months, the shallows along the fringe of the lake evaporate, leaving only a layer of thick mud exposed. Within the lake there are several pockets of large, thick growths of willows and cattails, many reaching heights of twelve feet or more.

Kilborn drives most of the day, stopping only once for a nap. By the time he reaches the rural town the sun has set and the park's visitors have left for the day. Aside from the causeway, there are only a few lights along the lake's perimeter. The grocery store and string of apartment buildings across the street provide the only substantial source of light. There's always a stranded shopping cart to be found between the store and the multiunit rentals. Kilborn has little trouble finding one. He settles his truck into a dimly lit space of an elementary school and wheels the shopping cart to the back of his truck. Loading Raven's dismembered remains into the bottom of the cart is relatively easy. With his body cut into pieces and absent of internal organs and blood, the judge is much lighter and folds easily. As quickly and quietly as possible, Kilborn throws a shovel and the two wooden pallets into the cart and wheels his load into the park. Although his path forces him to walk near a string of modest homes, the flash of television screens and the smell of dinner indicate the residents are preoccupied with other matters. He passes by unnoticed.

Kilborn pushes the cart into the deepest and darkest section of the lake, positioning it close to a large cluster of willows and cattails. He sets down the two wooden pallets, one in front of the other; placing the shovel and the carpet with Raven's remains on the front pallet. After stepping onto the front pallet, he lifts the pallet in the rear and positions it in front. The process is repeated, allowing Kilborn to walk over the mud and shallow water and into the middle of a large vegetative growth. Within the knot of foliage, Kilborn digs three shallow graves about three feet deep. He intends to dig deeper but the weight of the mud and the trickle of water into his holes make the process more difficult than he anticipates. He buries the limbs and torso first, leaving the head for last. Sitting beside the final burial spot, lifting Raven's head by his hair, Kilborn brings it to eye level and speaks to it softly and with sincerity. "Do you see the elementary school across the street? I went there as a child. I used to walk home from school through this park. Decades ago, before this side of the park became an extension of the lake, I played in a youth baseball league and hit my first home run very close to where we are now. You will spend your eternity listening to the laughter of children all around you and never know one of them. You will forever be reminded of the joy they bring to others, but never again to you. You will forever be reminded of the freedom and civil rights you denied others, but you will never be free again. Nevermore!"

Kilborn removes a typewritten note from his pocket and reads it softly to Raven's head. It's a written decree and final judgment of Raven's soul; a pronouncement of his assignment to the afterlife.

"All of Hell bemoans with excitement at your arrival. Liars, cowards and the greedy step back from their fresh mounds of feces to allow your passage into the depths reserved for you. The rotting limbs of thieves and the flesh of child abusers entwines with a millennia of decaying corpses, permeating the air with a stench known only to those forced to inhabit this depth of despair. Tears of blood rain eternal, each drop burns its way through your naked and exposed flesh. Your pathway is a cascade of murderous heads, each one a gaping mouth to bite at your bare feet as you pass. This is simply the doorway, the place where even the imps and demons dare not enter. Beyond the door lies the final place of pain and darkness. This is your eternal home… a place exclusively reserved for abusers of authority."

Part III
Finale

XIII

Coming Full Circle

The following summer...

Moisture gathers on the windshield from an intermittent evening mist that some refer to as rain in Southern California. Tiny droplets merge until their combined weight pulls them into a downward stream that streak from view. Inside the older model vehicle sits Travis Kilborn, tightening his wig and pressing down the corners of his fake moustache. For most Southern Californians, this is a night of inconvenience; for Kilborn, it's a summer evening he's eagerly longed for. A bright yellow raincoat with the words, "Tire Repair," lies in the back seat along with a high voltage stun gun that looks and works like a flashlight. Gathered on the floorboard are handcuffs, leg ties, a flip knife, six feet of thin nylon rope and a roll of duct tape. He doesn't plan to use the duct tape, but it makes him feel more confident having it with him.

Kilborn's target is a tall, arrogant attorney named Richard Bantam. Bantam is one of a group of individuals whose combined efforts stripped Kilborn of his home, career, wealth, reputation and family. All of the others are dead; the exception is serving a long-term prison sentence for a crime she did not commit. It has taken Kilborn all of three years to extract his revenge; nearly a year since his last murder. This is the final, and most prized piece of the puzzle. Kilborn has been plotting this malevolent scheme for months, determined not to repeat the mistakes made in his previous slayings.

No one knows for sure if Richard Bantam is a fan of big league baseball or if he simply uses the subject of baseball to brag about his VIP diamond box seats at Angel Stadium. On the days his wife stays home, he certainly seems to pay less attention to the game and more to the young, attractive woman who services his seats. Bantam's wife, a faithful and devout woman, attends a Bible study on Wednesday nights and it's a sure bet that she will not be with her husband this evening. Tonight's contest is against the perpetually underperforming Royals of Kansas City. Considering the weather, visiting team and day of week, it is almost certain that attendance is going to be light.

Kilborn picked up a discarded VIP parking pass from the previous night's game, even though it is unlikely he will need it tonight. He knows the VIP parking guards leave their posts after the third inning, especially if the weather is less than perfect. The entire lot is monitored by a roving vehicular patrol and a couple of long-range security cameras. When the yellow, flashing lights of the roving patrol ventures to another section, Kilborn calmly moves his car into the nearly empty VIP Section and backs into the space next to Bantam's expensive German automobile. Bantam always parks in the space closest to the stadium and next to the slot designated for handicapped persons. He frequently infringes well on the side of the handicapped parking in order to allow himself more room.

The very worn but reliable vehicle Kilborn is driving was purchased with cash from an elderly couple only two weeks prior. Although he has the signed title of ownership in his possession, it was never registered with the Department of Motor Vehicles. Once he's finished with the car, he plans to park it in front of their house with the keys and a note that simply informs the senior citizens that the car wasn't what he wanted. As a reward for the inconvenience, they are able to keep the money he paid them.

Stolen license plates further mask the identity of the car so in the event the stadium cameras record anything, it would take weeks of police work to narrow down their search to similar vehicles. Even then, all the police would have is an odd tale from an elderly couple; a man bought their car and gave it back to them. The description of their buyer would be quite different than what is depicted on the stadium security film, and quite different than his real appearance. Kilborn has had three years to refine his skills and has become quite adept at the art of disguise.

The baseball game wears on at an agonizing pace for Kilborn. He sinks low in the seat so as to avoid detection while listening to the progress of the game on a hand-held radio. Kilborn is not a baseball fan and doesn't care anything for the sport. Becoming bored, his eyes drift over to the small voice recorder siting on the front seat next to him. He knows he should leave it alone, especially tonight.

Kilborn tells himself, "Don't touch it! Don't!"

As his eyes remain fixated on the recorder, he shouts aloud, "Not tonight! Not now! It's too important to screw up!"

His hand impulsively slides over to the other seat and in a much calmer voice he asserts, "I'll just keep it next to me, close to me… that won't hurt anything."

Gently cuddling the device as would a three year-old holding a favorite doll, he nervously turns it on, then off. Kilborn reassures himself, "All I really want to do is check the settings to see if they're all still there." After firmly securing the ear pieces, he sets the device to the playback setting for the first saved recording and turns the volume up. He gently rubs the play button, knowing he is only one motion of his thumb away from listening to the content. A slight sheen appears over his face as he begins to perspire. His heart rate increases. His jaw drops. His hands begin to twitch. His eyes close. His legs jerk spasmodically. He reaches a point of no return. With a nervous swallow and full anticipation, he slides the button into the play position. The replay of the murderous recording produces a state of near ecstasy. Audible moans rise from his throat. His hands flail recklessly above his head and he lurches violently forward from the waist, then back again. Dropping his arms, he beats on the seats with open palms; first with a sort of rhythm, then without restraint. If an outsider were watching, Kilborn may have resembled a recently decapitated chicken. The jerking becomes more pronounced, violent. "Yes! Yes! Oh god… oh god… oh god!" he cries out, oblivious to his surroundings… and suddenly he stops.

Soaked in sweat and out of breath, Kilborn sinks back down in the seat. Panicked at the realization he might have been observed in his orgasmic lack of inhibition, he cautiously looks in all directions, then in the rear view mirror. As waves of faint mist continue to spritz the blackened parking lot, he sees no indication of movement. It appears he was lucky. Kilborn looks down at his recorder to note that it has stopped at the second saved position. He quickly tosses it into the glove box to get it out of his sight.

The baseball game lingers, reminiscent of a waiting room in an old fashioned dentist's office. Each inning seems to take longer with lengths of silence broken up only by an occasional cheer. Finally, it's the ninth inning and time to go to work. Kilborn tightens his latex gloves, pulling each finger snug to the end. Looking in the rearview mirror, he adjusts his glasses, and then checks his wig one last time before exiting the car. With his disguise secure, he picks up the knife and steps from the vehicle, wearing jeans and a black hoodie. It's not time for the yellow rain jacket yet. He takes one last look around, secures his hood snugly around his head and with knife in hand, he calmly walks to Bantam's left rear tire and plunges it into the rubber sidewall. Although Kilborn practiced this maneuver once on another tire, the anticipation of the escaping air still manages to startle him a little. He initially jolts backward before realizing there is no significant burst of air or sound generated by penetrating the tire. He does, however, have the presence of mind to keep his head down and not draw attention to himself. Kilborn repeats the action on the other rear tire before returning to his car. Having secured his trap, there is nothing left to do but sit and wait for his prey to appear.

With the game finally over, the crowd begins to disperse from the stadium, back into the summer night and in search of their automobiles. Although damp, the entire evening's precipitation can be removed from a windshield with a single stroke of a wiper blade. Amusingly, there are those who bundle up in a manner more consistent with a winter trek through the Rocky Mountains. Others run toward their cars or cover their heads with programs so as to prevent that single drop of moisture from reaching the surface of their body.

Kilborn keeps a watchful eye on the exit but knows Bantam loves to dawdle. The self-promoting, fifty-four-year-old Bantam will stand around discussing golf or his latest business venture with anyone who gives an ear. It also gives him more of an opportunity to gaze at the young body of the woman he's attracted to. Bantam is clueless in thinking he'll get anything more than a smile from the adolescent female, even with a sixty dollar tip.

With the crowd nearly emptied from the stadium, Kilborn reaches in the back seat for his flashlight and yellow raincoat. Exiting the car, he opens the trunk and pulls out a flattened tire that he prominently displays near the rear of Bantam's car. Seeing Bantam at a distance as he casually strolls from the exit, Kilborn quickly dons his raincoat and bends over as though inspecting the tire he's using as a prop. His back is to Bantam as he approaches; the only view Bantam has of him are the words, "Tire Repair" prominently displayed on the back of his yellow raincoat.

Obviously upset, Bantam rushes toward his new car. "Hey! What's going on here?"

"Oh, hello." Kilborn casually glances upward toward the irate Bantam. "This must be your car." He continues to tighten the stem cap to the flat tire. Standing, and turning to face Bantam, he explains, "Yeah, I see yours are flat too. Both rear tires." He shakes his head in wonderment. "We had a half dozen of them tonight. Who knows why they pick this car or that one."

"Don't you have security to prevent things like this?" demands Bantam, looking disgruntled.

Kilborn shrugs, lifting his hands palms up, "Oh, I don't work security, I just fix tires. You have to take that up with them."

"Well what kind of racket do you have going on here?" Bantam is now both suspicious and sarcastic.

"No racket at all, sir. If I had a racket, I'd charge you $399 a piece for new tires on your car. I only charge twelve bucks per tire for a short-term fix."

"How short of a term?" asks an unconvinced Bantam.

Kilborn pulls a canister from one of the pockets of his raincoat, "I fill each tire with a can of foam and it hardens as it expands, filling up any holes in your tire. It's only a forty-eight-hour fix but it'll save you a $180 tow bill."

Bantam, becoming suddenly conscious of the time, looks at his watch, "How long does it take?"

"I can set you up in just a few minutes. All I need is the stem number" Kilborn picks up his flat tire and walks toward the space between the two cars.

Bantam raises his eyebrows, looking bewildered. "Stem number? What the hell is a stem number?"

"It's the number on the tire that's displayed right after the air pressure. Come over here and I'll show you." Kilborn strategically sets the flat tire upright and perpendicular between the two cars. Although few people remain in the area, the position of the tire intentionally obscures the view of any stray passersby. "Let me get my flashlight out and I'll show you where it is on your tire."

"I'm not getting down on that slimy asphalt! It'll put wet spots on my knees."

"You're going to have to," Kilborn says. "I don't have my reading glasses so I can't see it." Removing his raincoat, he states, "Here, you can kneel on this."

"Damn!" complains Bantam as he bends down and puts his face close enough to the tire to be able to kiss it. "Can you at least hold the light steady and show me where to look?"

Kilborn scans the immediate area a final time, and then reaching down, places the stun gun, turned to full power, directly on the back of Bantam's neck, disabling him within a second. His limp body, lying between the two cars, is obscured from the sight of anyone remaining in the area. It takes less than a minute for Kilborn to apply handcuffs, leg restraints, rope and even a strip or two of duct tape to his victim. He has to move quickly. Putting Bantam in the trunk is not an option as the risk of exposure is too great. Kilborn elects, instead, to put Bantam into the back seat of the car. He struggles with Bantam's long legs but finally situates him face down, in a relaxed U-shape, on the rear floorboard of the car. The disabled overhead light and recently tinted windows reduce visibility inside the vehicle.

With the arrogant attorney secure and inside the car, Kilborn grabs the spare tire and raincoat left outside and places them in the trunk. He throws a blanket over Bantam and he's ready to set out. With his back to the security cameras, Kilborn takes a final look around to see if anything is missing or if he's attracted anyone's attention. Satisfied that all has gone according to plan, he drives toward the exit gate, mingling in with the few remaining automobiles leaving the stadium, and disappears into the misty night.

With one hand on the steering wheel, Kilborn reaches into the glove box to retrieve the voice recorder he placed there earlier in the evening. With a quick glance he sets the device to a new save position to be used at a later time. Muffled groans are emitted from the rear seat of the small car as Kilborn's hapless victim regains control of his faculties. Kilborn smiles. He knows, as Bantam regains his full strength, the lawyer will suffer immediate pain and despair. Lying on his stomach, his legs are tightly tied together from behind, the nylon cord stretching from his ankles up the length of his back and secured by a loop around his mouth. Any attempt to straighten his legs will tighten the rope and cut into the flesh surrounding his jaws. Bridled like horse, Bantam's only recourse is to fight off surging leg cramps and attempt to remain as still as possible.

"Did you find that stem number, you dumb ass?" mocks Kilborn with a sarcastic laugh in his voice. "Ha... stem number!" Kilborn taunts as he continues to ridicule Bantam. "You do know now, that there's no stem number on a tire, don't you?"

Bantam lets out a series of unintelligible grunts. Kilborn fills in the blanks and determines that Bantam is threatening him with the degree of his personal power and demanding to be released at once. Kilborn laughs louder.

Bantam, desperation rising, assaults the nylon rope but his attempt to bite through it is unsuccessful. The taut cord is wedged tightly to the rear of his mouth and even turning his head gives him only slight access to the rope with his molars. He realizes the tactic is futile. After only a few minutes, Bantam is exhausted. With each spasm of his legs, he bleeds more profusely from the corners of his mouth. The taste of his own blood is repulsive but it does make the surface of the duct tape moist and slick enough to allow an attempt to slide the nylon harness over the front of his face. All Bantam needs is one good surge, and if he can pull his feet up from behind, getting his heels close enough to his head, he can turn his neck upward and slip free of the cord.

Bantam struggles through waves of leg cramps, forcing his long limbs forward toward his head, but fails. The cord jolts back into his jaws like a punch in the face, cutting even more deeply into the corners of his mouth. As disconcerting as the thought of losing half his face is, Bantam realizes he must free himself from the agony of the rope. With the nylon cord saturated in his own blood, Bantam bends himself like a contortionist, bringing his feet as near to his head as his body will bear before his middle-aged frame cracks. With a large grunt, he lunges forward with all the determination he is able to muster, leans his head back and pushes the loosened cord from his mouth with his tongue. The rope snaps backward, catching only his upper lip and the tip of his nose as it recoils at his feet. Immediately, he rolls to his back and stretches his lanky limbs over the top of the back seat. There are no thoughts of escape at the moment, only relief from the horrible pain.

Kilborn reaches for the stun gun. "Feeling better, are we?"

Bantam, still handcuffed and legs tied, knows he's not going anywhere and can only respond with a muffled grunt.

"I'll keep the rope off as long as you follow directions. Got it?"

After a slight pause, Bantam responds. "Uh huh."

Kilborn activates the stun gun, allowing Bantam to hear the threatening buzzing and clicking noise, sending a clear message to Bantam that he has it near him. After turning the device off, Kilborn reaches into the back seat and rips off the remaining loose strands of duct tape on Bantam's face, allowing him to speak.

"We're almost there," Kilborn says.

With his mouth now free Bantam screams, "Almost where, you crazy bastard?"

"Careful now," warns Kilborn as he lifts up the stun gun. "You don't want Dr. Sparky to answer that question, do you?"

Bantam wisely remains quiet, allowing Kilborn to provide more information. "We're going to an abandoned dairy farm I bought a 90-Day Option on in Chino. I negotiated a deal with the owner that gives me access to the property. Most people are surprised to know that a large swath of land near L.A. was once prime dairy land. It's real private and I even brought a few of my pets for you to meet. I think you'll like it." Kilborn turns his head just far enough so Bantam can see his smirk.

Bantam, uncertain of his captor's motives, says, "Who the hell are you and what do you want with me? Exactly how much money are you attempting to extort from me?"

Kilborn continues to drive, unwilling at the moment to show his hand. "You'll see soon enough."

He rolls the front window down The odors wafting in make it obvious they've entered into dairy farm country. "A lot of people may consider the smell a little offensive, but not me," Kilborn comments. "To me it smells like home."

"Isn't it bad enough you're holding me hostage? Do I have to smell cow shit too?" complains the haughty Bantam, his normal arrogance apparently unfazed by being hog-tied.

Kilborn makes a sharp turn onto a dark dirt road, drives a short distance then stops, unlocks a gate, drives through, stops again and locks it behind him. There are no lights around except the distant flicker of a residential tract development located over a mile away. A brief drive brings them to the large doors of a rustic barn. Kilborn drives inside, then closes the barn doors. "We're here!" exclaims Kilborn, his tone revealing his excitement. He takes a deep breath of air and exhales. "Ahhhh, country!"

After stepping out of the car, Kilborn opens the rear door only to have Bantam feverishly kick at him while screaming out for help. Kilborn steps back and smiles at the helpless man. "Scream all you want. No one will hear you. But you can either cooperate or I'll let Dr. Sparky handle that for me," he warns.

Bantam is suddenly much more compliant. "Fine. All right. What do you want?"

"Put your feet out the door!" Kilborn orders.

Bantam cooperates and places his feet, still bound together, out of the car. Kilborn grabs each leg by the ankle and with a series of jerks, successfully extracts Bantam from the vehicle, ultimately landing him on his ass.

Bantam scrapes off the edge of the floorboard and lands with a thud. "Am I sitting in cow shit? What is that horrible smell? I'm sitting in cow shit, aren't I?"

Kilborn looks back to answer his question, "No, you're not sitting in cow shit. On this side of the barn, I'd say it's more likely to be dog shit."

Bantam makes a gagging sound. "What kind of dog produces a stench like this?"

"I'm glad you asked." Kilborn smiles. "You stay put and I'll turn on a few lamps and show you around the place. Don't try to wander off because there's more than one thing to worry about in here."

With only the automobile's front beams for lights, Bantam sits obediently next to the car door from which he slid out. Although uncomfortable, he prefers it to the unknown horror of attempting to hop away into the darkness and falling headfirst into something equally unpleasant. Within minutes, several lamps begin to illuminate the big, dank and empty shell of the barn's interior. At the distant end of the barn there's a rustling noise and the excited barking of a dog. Within seconds, a beastly looking animal is inches from Bantam's face. He can't see it clearly yet but he knows it's a rather large dog and it's nearly nose to nose with him. Bantam is petrified with fear as the animal sniffs at his every orifice.

"He's probably just wondering why you smell like him," assures Kilborn from the other end of the barn. "He doesn't bite but he may get friendly with you."

As the glow from the lamps begin to provide more light, the terrifying beast turns out to be a rather young but large black canine of mixed origin. He has an overly friendly face and appears ready to cause mischief at a moment's notice.

"That's my dog, Stink," says Kilborn as he approaches from the other side of the barn.

"You named your dog, Stink?"

"Yeah, it fits him. He eats anything but his gas can melt iron and cause a saint to curse."

"How impressive." Bantam responds, sounding patronizing.

"I also have three hogs," explains Kilborn as he walks to the side of the barn, releasing a small door that connects from outside into an interior pen. As the hogs stroll into the barn from their exterior cages, he adds, "See the big black and white hog? His name is Six."

"How extraordinary." Bantam is snide. "Does that have anything to do with the owner's IQ or hourly wage?"

Pretending to ignore the comment, Kilborn continues, "The hog next to it is also named Six... as is the third."

Kilborn grabs the blanket from the car, places it next to Bantam and smashes the toe of his boot into the side of Bantam's head. The stunned Bantam is immediately disoriented. Kilborn pushes his arrogant victim onto the blanket and drags him to a large wooden support beam in center of the barn. Once there, he straps and locks Bantam into a harness, hoists him into an upright position and chains him to the wooden beam, encircling links around his hands and feet. A studded leather strap anchors his head to the post. With his flip knife in hand, Kilborn savagely cuts into Bantam's clothing until his attire is reduced to a pile rags and Bantam stands before Kilborn completely exposed. As Bantam begins to recover from the shock, the direness of his situation begins to sink in.

"What are you doing?" he shrieks. "What the hell are you doing to me?"

"Shhhhh... wait." Kilborn sprints to the car. Reaching inside the vehicle, he removes the voice recorder and on his walk back, checks to insure the setting for the next recording is on position four. He insures himself that the device is on pause, and then clips it on his belt.

As Kilborn walks toward Bantam, he removes his disguise and after rolling it together with his black hoodie, tosses it onto a nearby table. "You don't recognize me, do you?"

Bantam tilts up his chin and looks down his nose at Kilborn. "I have no idea who you are. All I want to know is how much money you want to release me so I can get out of here."

"Money? You think this is all about money? You have no idea what your actions have cost me, Mr. Bantam. I've walked the halls and occupied the seats of the Orange County Family Law Center for over three years. Do you think the suffering people you pass in the halls are immune to your haughty conversations and they can't hear you? Or is it that they are so small and ant-like to you that nothing they feel or think matters?"

"I have no idea what you're talking about!" proclaims Bantam with as much innocence as he's able to express.

Kilborn steps closer to Bantam, looking him in the eye. "I know quite a bit about you, Mr. Bantam and it required almost no effort but to sit and listen to your arrogant ramblings. You own a boat that you keep moored at Dana Point Harbor. You're a member of the Laguna Springs Country Club. You have a beautiful home in the gated community of Pointer's Crest and have diamond box seats at Angel's Stadium. You're a wealthy man. Not bad for a guy who graduated from a state college with average grades and a law degree from an unaccredited school. How many attempts did it take you to pass the bar? Three? You're not the only attorney that talks too much in public."

"It's not about the grades," protests Bantam. "Success is what matters. I get results and that's what clients pay me for."

"Yes, I know," says Kilborn in a much softer voice. "I know what you do for your clients, Mr. Bantam. I know that unlike any other profession, your industry has virtually no regulations and you can charge whatever fees you can extort from your clients. In addition to an hourly rate that exceeds what a surgeon would charge to save someone's life, you egotistical asses pass on the cost of doing business as well. Isn't that true? You bill your clients for copies and even the time it takes for a receptionist to answer the phone. And then the public has to trust that the time you bill is the actual time you spend on the case. What makes your time so valuable? In essence, you're just an overcompensated clerk who fills out the same mindless forms and makes the same mundane and repetitive arguments every day."

Bantam stands in silence, still hoping there is an escape; thinking he may still be able to negotiate his way out.

Approaching his captive, standing inches from his face, Kilborn, maintaining his own control, growls, "I'm the teacher you accused of molesting his own daughters. I'm the one you deliberately lied about and humiliated in the media. I'm that defenseless man whom you dangled before the court like a chew toy, then gloated as you ripped my heart out. I'm the one you stripped of everything I loved."

In nearly a whisper, Kilborn touches nose-to-nose with his victim and then leans in even closer to speak in his ear, "Do you remember me now?"

Bantam's eyes widen. He jerks his head away. An expression of terror exposes his memories of the events. "Why are you after me? Why don't you go after your ex and her new husband? I'm just the hireling!"

Kilborn looks into Bantam's vacant eyes with disdain. "She's the mother of my children. As much as I despise what she did to me, I know she loves our children. She's all they have now."

Changing his voice pattern and accent Kilborn continues, "Vell, surely you must remember your associate, Dr. Klaudios? I fed him to the sharks and have been using him to stalk you for three years. And do you remember Judge Raven? He vent missing a year ago? Rest assured, I didn't miss him!"

Kilborn fixes a long, silent, penetrating stare directly into Bantam's eyes, then his smirk grows into a Cheshire Cat's smile. "This is the fun part," he says in his normal voice as he lifts his knife. "This is where I see your eyes change."

In a final burst of courage, Bantam demands, "Don't put that damn knife near my eyes!"

"I wouldn't think of it," assures Kilborn as he explains further. "I need to see your eyes in their fullness. I wouldn't think of damaging them."

He pauses for a moment. "Do you remember my three hogs, Six, Six and Six, Mr. Bantam? These hogs are going to eat your flesh until there's nothing left but the bones. Do you remember my dog, Stink? He likes bones."

Kilborn reaches down to his belt and activates the record function on his voice recorder. Looking up at the naked Bantam, Kilborn smiles. "You're a greedy and heartless man, Mr. Bantam." He pushes his knife about a half inch deep into Bantam's midsection, beginning at a point approximately three inches below the umbilicus and using a downward, jerking motion, opens the cut a few inches.

"My god, my god, why are you doing this? Stop! Stop! Please stop!"

There's surprisingly little blood as Kilborn proudly explains, "The Huron Indians used this method to test the bravery of the enemy warriors they captured. As usual, you wouldn't get high marks, Mr. Bantam."

Bantam screeches in pain and agony! "Please, no more!" he begs. "I'll do anything!"

"Oh, this is nothing, Bantam," boasts Kilborn. "Here Stink! Where are you boy?"

With the dog at his feet, Kilborn reaches into the open wound with his forefinger and while pushing aside the yellowish omentum, pulls out a loop of Bantam's small intestine. He cuts into the pale pink loop, releasing a thick, dark green ooze, slightly less viscous than honey. Pulling slowly at the slippery, tubular flesh while cutting away small blood vessels, Kilborn dislodges a length of six feet from Bantam's open cavity. Bantam's screams serve only to push additional loops of intestine through the small incision. Grabbing the separated end, Kilborn reaches down to the eager dog and speaks in an animated voice, "Want a treat, Stink?" Stink, of course, is ready to consume anything offered to him.

The intense humidity of the abdomen and the cool air of the evening combine to form a small cloud of steam which rises up from the fist-sized mound of intestine now balled up near the open wound. For Bantam, each scream produces the sensation of escaping intestines which in turn produces pain akin to being kicked in the groin, over and over again. Bantam wants to scream, must scream! But he must also contain his screams to avoid additional waves of torment. The resulting sound is a series of short, powerful bursts like a woman giving birth while attempting to control her breathing, "Heh! Heh! Heh! Heh!"

Turning quickly toward the fully conscious Bantam, Kilborn forces Bantam's head firmly against the wooden plank, and then places his hand on his forehead while staring deeply into his eyes. "There it is! That's what I wanted to see! The look of complete despair! You know you're dead but you're not dead yet. How does it feel to be completely exposed, cut open and helpless to do anything about it? How does it feel, you arrogant bastard? And I'm not done with you yet!"

Reaching for a small blow torch that he has planted nearby, Kilborn ignites it and begins to brush it across Bantam's body. Each pass of the torch adds a whiff of burned flesh to the air and produces screeches of pain few outside of a mental institution have heard. Kilborn must be careful and quick. He knows he has only about eighteen minutes before Bantam bleeds to death and he can't afford to put him in so much pain that he becomes unconscious. This is Kilborn's moment of glory as he bathes himself in the insanity of Bantam's screams. Bantam cannot beg for mercy. He is unable to produce even a single, intelligible word. His only language is a series of blathering wails and screams as enormous waves of suffering engulf his conscious mind.

Kilborn momentarily stands back to admire his work of art. Bantam's legs gave out long ago but the harness continues to hold his body firmly against the support beam and the head restraint keeps Bantam's face focused upward. Thick green chyme oozes from the intestinal appendage that Stink chewed through, and then abandoned. The arterial veins supporting the blood flow of the intestines continue to squirt in rhythm to Bantam's fading heart, emitting pulses of blood. Bantam is pale, gasping as though he can't breathe, his lips turning from bluish purple to gray, then silence. Bantam is dead.

Kilborn pokes and prods at Bantam's lifeless body, desperately hoping for one more minute of life and one last scream. He stares in silence for a moment at Bantam's lifeless body then switches off his voice recorder and announces to the animals, "It's time to clean up boys and girls!"

Kilborn removes all restraints and lets Bantam's lifeless body fall to the ground. Within moments he guts his victim and begins to chop the naked remains into pieces with a large ax. When satisfied the pieces are of manageable size, Kilborn metes out near equal shares to each of the hogs as he tosses pieces of Bantam's body into the pen. Stink seems to prefer the softer organs so he's given portions of the heart and liver as his reward.

Retreating to the far corner of the barn, Kilborn uses a hose to clean himself off and change from the blood soaked clothes he was wearing. "All in all, it's been a good night."

After packing all his gear back into the car, Kilborn allows himself one last pleasure. Placing his earphones firmly into his ears, he sets the replay button on his voice recorder to saved position four and activates the recording. As Kilborn walks the length of the barn, his steps become increasingly more dramatic and out of control. With hands in the air, Kilborn relives Bantam's recorded screams, drinking them in as if they were a sort of liquid, bathing himself in the sound. As the volume increases Kilborn walks a few steps, then leaps into the air and turns, his body jerking violently from the waist in one direction, and then back again. It's a victory dance of sorts, almost sexual and most assuredly, insane.

Kilborn exits the barn in the early morning hour, stepping out into a light mist. As a precaution, rather than immediately accessing the freeway, he takes an alternative road back to his home in Orange County. It's not that he expects to encounter difficulties; it has more to do with the direction of his life. The ecstasy he felt earlier in the evening after successfully avenging himself has turned inward. What does he do now?

Kilborn's route takes him to an older part of town and across the Virgil Overpass. Locals refer to it as the Old Bridge or the Virgil. Approaching the bridge Kilborn sees a man without shoes sitting on the pedestrian walkway. Kilborn stops and observes the man for a few moments, and then drives up next to him. Rolling down his window, he calls, "Hey, are you okay?"

The man is obviously intoxicated and has difficulty tracking the direction of Kilborn's voice. Finally making eye contact with him, the man on the bridge responds, "I'm a great matador!"

XIV

The Magic Coin

It's an irritating noise unlike anything Justin had ever heard before; immediately unpleasant to the ear and equally annoying. *Screech... grind... tap tap.*

He was up most of the night, moving and organizing the last of his belongings into a small storage shed located in the rear of Hugh's property. Having collapsed on Lucy's couch only a few hours earlier, Justin's mind pulsates with a kind of road buzz that one gets from driving too many miles late at night and consuming too much caffeine. It's a condition one arrives at when the body reaches exhaustion but the brain is still behind the steering wheel and moving to the motion of the road. Justin is fatigued. He tries to ignore it. *Screech... grind... tap tap.*

Closer this time, the eerie and repetitive sound is difficult to get out of his head. It's a grating, scraping... metal on concrete, reverberating and echoing throughout the cement fishbowl that serves as an apartment courtyard. But the racket isn't confined to a single abusive clamor of sound. The pattern begins with an elongated screeching followed by a pause, then a muffled rubbing of two elements that are obviously incompatible, similar to flesh on carpet. Curiously, the sequence concludes with a simple, soft double tap. *Screech... grind... tap tap.*

Justin bolts up to a sitting position, "What is that awful noise?"

Lucy chuckles in the background, "Good morning, honey. I made breakfast for us."

Justin attempts to open his eyes and focus for the first time. "Breakfast? Why so early?"

"It's after nine. I let you sleep in."

"Isn't today a holiday or something? Shouldn't I be able to sleep until noon today?" he suggests with a sleepy smile.

"It's Saturday, if you consider that a holiday." Moving to sit next to Justin on the couch, Lucy continues, "Maybe the holiday you were thinking of is our third month anniversary today. Did you forget?"

Justin turns quickly toward Lucy, rubbing his eyes and suppressing a groan, "Did I forget... umm, no, of course not!" He pauses, then reaches into his pocket and retrieves a coin. Placing the coin in Lucy's hand Justin boldly proclaims, "I got you this!"

Lucy, knowing she's being conned, but not sure how the situation is going to pan out, responds with a smile, "Justin... it's a quarter."

More awake and animated Justin continues with his act, "Yes, but it's no ordinary quarter! This is a magical coin it will allow you passage on an adventure you will never forget."

Lucy laughs. "It doesn't involve you cooking anything for me does it?"

Justin pulls Lucy into his embrace. "There's no cooking involved and I'm pretty sure you'll enjoy what the magic coin does."

Lucy pretends to be perturbed, looking for assurance, "You didn't forget?"

He kisses her forehead and teasingly whispers, "You'll just have to wait." Standing, Lucy plants her fists on her hips. "Well, while I'm waiting, you need to brush your teeth so I can kiss you... then come to the table for breakfast."

"You won't let me wait until after breakfast to brush my teeth?"

Lucy laughs. "No, and you sound like a twelve year-old boy, attempting to negotiate the terms of basic hygiene.

Upon his return from the bathroom, Justin finds Lucy at the table, smiling. The promised meal is artfully displayed and a decorated greeting card stands near his plate. Opening the card activates a musical jingle whose lyrics are both humorous and endearing. Lucy's message is clear.

In her straightforward manner, she reveals how much Justin has come to mean to her in three months. They've almost been inseparable.

Lucy comes close to telling Justin that she loves him without actually mentioning the word "love" in her message. If her instincts about Justin are correct, his magical coin ruse will result in another sincere display of his affection toward her. Justin thanks Lucy for the card and breakfast. He takes her hand, gently pulling on it to indicate he wants her to lean toward him. Lucy is eager to comply as the couple share a kiss across the corner of the table.

Their moment of intamcy is interrupted by the awful noise. *Screech… grind… tap tap.*

With his eyes wide and clearly annoyed by having a special moment infringed upon, Justin complains, "What is that noise? The reverberation is so bad it almost hurts my teeth."

Lucy smiles. "That's Miss Mavis coming back from the mailbox. If you're curious, take a peek out the window."

Pushing aside the corner of the curtain, Justin peers into the court-yard only to see an elderly woman supporting her steps with a ragtag walker. She lifts the light-weight aluminum frame only to force the worn and bare metal front legs into the concrete. In order to propel her ongoing motion, she slides it forward, having replaced the rear wheels with tennis balls for added traction. The ensuing tapping is simply her modest steps as she catches up to the walker so as to repeat the process.

"She used to be a pageant queen of some sort in her younger days," Lucy informs him while still seated at the table. "The maintenance worker told me her apartment is filled with old trophies and newspaper clippings of her glory days. She doesn't go outside without dressing up like she's going to an elegant party."

Miss Mavis is unaware of Justin's ongoing scrutiny of her as he continues to stare at her from the corner of the window. She's tall and possesses remarkable posture for an eighty-one- year-old woman. By squinting one's eyes and using a considerable amount of imagination, he can see how the stately neighbor could have been a statuesque beauty at one point in time. "How well do you know her?"

"I used to sit with her on the bench near the mailbox and we talked all the time. About six months ago her Alzheimer's took a turn for the worse and she doesn't remember things as well. Over time she began to be more distant and to make matters worse, she became ill a few weeks ago. She hasn't been the same since."

"That's sad," says Justin as he continues to gaze out the window. "Does she have anyone to take care of her?"

"She has a grandson whom I met once, but she doesn't talk about him now. I don't know if he still has contact with her or not. Why all the questions about Miss Mavis?"

Justin pauses before responding, "I'm just curious about your friends."

Justin's mind begins to race with conflicting scenarios and possibilities. Could this woman be the killer's grandmother? Inside, his heart is churning with the reality that he likely made an educated guess and stumbled onto the killer's trail. Although he is oblivious to the killer's name, the clues certainly point to Miss Mavis. How many elderly Caucasian grandmothers live in a Torrance apartment building comprised primarily of Koreans? Of those, how many struggle with Alzheimer's and have a grandson who visits them? If Miss Mavis is the killer's grandmother, what now? Justin has been so absorbed in his relationships with Hugh and Lucy that he has done little else but live in the moment, enjoying his new life. He has virtually done nothing to advance his search or to take measures to protect himself from the killer's threats. If he doesn't find a solution soon, he could face a long prison sentence or even his own death. Additionally, if this is the killer's grandmother, how can he possibly protect Lucy from him? The killer has the advantage of being able to recognize Justin while he has no recollection whatsoever of the killer's appearance. Justin's mere presence with Lucy places her in danger.

Lucy approaches Justin as he stares out the window, absorbed deep in his thoughts. She places her hand gently on his shoulder but her touch startles him. Acting out of character, Justin panics and jerks away from her.

"Wow!" Lucy exclaims. "I was going to comment on how suddenly quiet you were but it's obvious that you have something much deeper on your mind. Do you want to talk about it?"

"I'm... I'm not sure that I can."

Lucy allows the silence to continue until she can formulate an appropriate response. She's worried. In her heart she knows she loves Justin and now there's something unknown, a threat of some kind that puts her heart in jeopardy. Lucy reaches for Justin's hand, and squeezes it, "Do you remember our first time together... at the deli? One of the things I stated was full disclosure is required. That hasn't changed. I need to know what's going on."

Justin pulls Lucy into a gentle but silent embrace. Lucy remains patient, waiting for him to speak but his hesitation and lack of communication becomes almost unbearable. After clearing his throat he says, "I'm in a dangerous situation and my mere presence puts your life at risk too."

Lucy's strength is challenged as the statement sends shock waves riveting through her soul. Tears begin to stream down her cheeks as she responds to what she perceives as tragedy and loss. The flood of emotion she's experiencing doesn't draw a line between the threat of losing Justin or her own life; at the moment, it all feels the same. Lucy pushes herself out of his hold, but grips his upper arms. "My life at risk? Justin! What have you done?"

"I'm so sorry Lucy. Sit down and I'll tell you everything."

Over the course of the next fifteen minutes, Justin discloses all the details of his contacts with the serial killer, including the night at the bridge, the police interview and the clues that led him to Torrance. Lucy quietly listens, shedding an occasion tear. When it appears Justin has divulged his entire story to her, Lucy asks "Who else knows about this?"

"I told Hugh about it the first night. He's been really supportive... even gave me a cell phone and a gun."

"You have a gun? Justin, you have a gun?"

Lucy leaps up, openly sobbing. "So, you and Hugh are going to play super hero together and do what... walk into Dodge and shoot up the town? There's a vicious murderer out there who knows who you are and the best plan you have is to wait around here for him to kill you?"

Justin feels the pain of Lucy's tears but has no defense for putting her life at risk. "Lucy, I'm so sorry. I was torn when we met." His voice cracks under the strain, "I almost ran away from you but I was so captivated that I made excuses to stay another day. It came to a point where I wanted you in my life so much I blocked out everything else. It almost seemed not to be real anymore until I saw Miss Mavis."

"Why didn't you tell me in the beginning, Justin?" The sorrow in her voice cuts into him.

"I was selfish. I'm sorry… but I haven't done anything wrong. I'm not a criminal! I was a victim on the bridge that night, just as you were when you were shot at the party."

Justin's choice of words and uncharacteristic insensitivity take a heavy toll on Lucy's patience. "I told you I was blind the instant I introduced myself to you and my blindness has never put your life in jeopardy. You need to leave, Justin."

Justin slowly stands and attempts to touch Lucy's arm. She steps away, an occasional unchecked tear flows down her face. "So, is this it?" he asks.

"I'm not saying that. I don't want to make an impulsive decision… I just need time to process the information and think about what I'm going to do. I'll come by tonight at six as we planned to let you know what I decide."

Justin shuffles out the door, making no attempt to touch Lucy. He looks back only once and in a soft voice replete with repentance, says again, "I'm sorry Lucy." The door closes slowly and with a final soft click, Justin is gone.

Justin's lonely walk back home across the park is devoid of the carefree and endearing strolls with Lucy. Each step is agonizing and breathing is nearly painful. There's no physical calamity to account for his discomfort, only the grip of emotion encircling the heart that men learn to contain.

Approaching the house, Justin discovers Hugh sitting in a flower bed near the front by the entryway. Hugh is shirtless, wearing only a pair of camouflage shorts and a soft, floppy boonie hat with a similar military pattern. His toil under the morning summer sun has already caused a fine sheen of sweat to envelop his body. With a tray of new flowers at his side, Hugh sits with his nubs crossed, preparing the next plant for its new space.

"Aren't you supposed to do that in spring?" Justin takes a seat on the front steps.

"They were on sale," Hugh defends himself with a grin.

When Justin remains silent, Hugh looks up at him a second time. "Dude, you got the uglies. Something happen between you and Lucy?"

"Yeah... I told her everything. She was hurt and I can't say I blame her."

Hugh flips up the rim of his hat and looks at Justin, "Well, it is a lot to unload on a woman... Oh, by the way honey, there's a maniac trying to kill me and he may kill you too."

Justin's weak laugh can't cover his hurt feelings.

"So, what's the plan now?" Hugh asks. The sympathy in his dark eyes tell Justin he'd like to help but is unsure how.

"I guess I should get busy doing what I intended to do when I first moved here. I think the killer's grandmother can only be in one of a dozen locations. I think we should eliminate all the other possibilities."

"Oh, this is a 'we' thing now?" says Hugh with a smile. "Well, 'we' better finish our gardening before we start checking out apartment complexes. You can grab the other tray and start working on the other side."

By late afternoon, they complete the gardening project and eliminate all but three of the other apartment complexes as possibilities. The few that remained were not strong candidates. It was becoming increasingly clear that Miss Mavis is in fact, the killer's grandmother. The effort to track down the information took up almost the entire afternoon, leaving Justin just enough time to shower and prepare for Lucy's visit. The busyness of the day's activities provided enough of a distraction to keep Justin's mind from dwelling on his situation with Lucy. Now, with only minutes before her arrival, the familiar tightness around his chest has returned. Unable to sit and wait in the RV for her, Justin walks to the middle of the small park and protectively watches for Lucy to appear at the opposite end. Within minutes, her familiar silhouette emerges from the shadows on the horizon. Justin waits quietly, standing on the grass several feet off the walkway. He stands facing the sun, confident that he will remain undetected by Lucy as he waits for her to pass his position. She walks past him but not by too many steps, then stops.

"Justin?" Lucy doesn't raise her voice beyond a conversational volume.

"I'm here, Lucy," as he approaches her from behind, wrapping his arms around her waist and kisses her neck.

Lucy leans into him, inviting his affection, and then turns toward him to kiss him again on the lips. "I was worried all day," confesses Justin. I thought I may have lost you."

"You almost did," Lucy responds in a soft voice. "But I knew in my heart that when I counted out the steps through the park that you'd be here near the middle, waiting for me."

"But how did you know I'd be here?"

Lucy reaches up, clasping her hands behind Justin's head and drawing him close to her face, "It's not about paying attention to sounds and shadows, it's about paying attention to a person's heart and character. I know you're protective of me and you'd never let anything happen to me that you could prevent. I think you let your heart rule out over your head and you made some poor choices but I can forgive you for that."

He holds her, rocking gently in silence for a moment then says, "I have something for you, Lucy. Can we walk up to the bench where we first met?"

"This isn't going to involve smushed bugs is it?

Justin laughs, "No bugs... I promise."

"Is this where I have to give my magic quarter back to you?"

"Not just yet, you can hold onto the magic coin for a little while longer."

The bench is a brief walk from where the couple is standing. Once seated, Justin carefully removes a piece of paper from his pocket, pulling Lucy close to him and handing her the note. Lucy graciously accepts the document with appreciation but after holding onto it for a few seconds, her mind races with options as to what to do with it. After smelling it and not detecting a scent, she turns to Justin with a smile and asks, "Is it a note? Are you going to read it to me?"

Justin laughs, gently taking the piece of paper and turning it over, "You have it on the wrong side… you just have to pay attention."

"Oh, I bet you lie awake at night thinking of the day when you would get to say that to me," Lucy retorts with a teasing smile.

Lucy's fingers first explore the edges of the note and then glide over the surface to discover a series of bumps. "It's Braille!" Lucy exclaims. "How did you do this?"

"I went online," Justin explains. I discovered a website that translates written letters to Braille. Then all you have to do it print it out and add drops of glue to the highlighted areas, creating the little bumps. I discovered it works better when the glue is dry, otherwise the only message it delivers is that you have something stuck to your fingers. It took a few attempts but I think I finally got it right. Read it."

Lucy's fingers gently course over the raised letters of the message, at times repeating the same spaces twice. "Is it a poem? Did you write a poem for me?"

"Yes. I don't know much about writing poetry and I make no claims as to the quality, but it is from the heart. Did I do it right? Read it to me!" Justin demands, making no attempt to hide the deep affection he feels.

The Moon

Last night I watched the moon
sitting perfect, silent sky.
Within the thoughtful darkness
that blanketed my eyes,
a shower of silver paleness,
a single shard upon the ground
lighting up the pathway
to the serenity I had found.
So I prayed beneath the stars
beyond the shadowed lined twilight
that you could love me half as much
as the moon does love the night.

As Lucy finished the final word of the final line, "It's beautiful Justin. What are you saying?"

"I was thinking about your world without sight, seeing only flashes of light. But as I reflected on the situation, I realized I was the one standing in darkness, seeing only a glimpse of light. Your life provided me with a beacon... a way to see the world from a different view. You bring light to my darkness."

"Justin." Lucy's radiant smile and the urgency in her tone tell him what he needs to know. "Less explanation," she says, "and more bottom line."

Justin, smiling but intentionally pausing, takes Lucy's hand, "I love you Lucy."

Lucy kisses Justin with a depth of passion he had yet to experience from her. With her lips still close to his face she says, "I love you, too, Justin. I wanted to tell you this morning."

Justin basks for several minutes in a comfortable silence, enjoying the twilight serenity of the park and the afterglow of his and Lucy's newly expressed love. With night and day flirting on the autumn horizon, the tranquility appears to suspend time until Lucy stirs, reaching in her pocket. Retrieving the coin that she had nearly forgotten about, she places it in Justin's hand and thanks him for the magical moment that he provided her with. "Hang onto it," instructs Justin, "you're going to need it later."

"There's more?" Lucy responds in a surprised but delighted voice.

Justin stands and draws her up with him. Without providing her with clues, an immensely annoying habit to Lucy, Justin merely tells her to put the coin in her pocket for now. "You'll need to come back with me to my place."

As the two begin their walk back toward his side of the park, Justin relays the story of his joint gardening experience with Hugh. Once in view of the house, it's apparent that Hugh has returned to the front yard, admiring his new flowers while hand watering the front lawn from his wheelchair. He smiles as they come toward him, hand-in-hand.

Hugh welcomes them. "Hey kids!"

Lucy looks in his direction and says, in an uncharacteristically firm tone, "Hugh, I need to talk to you!"

Justin responds to Hugh's questioning look with nothing more than a mystified shrug.

Hugh turns off the water. "Is Justin in trouble for something?" After a brief silence, with no response from Lucy, he asks sheepishly, "Am I in trouble for something?"

"I need to talk to the two of you together, please." Lucy sounds very much like a teacher who is prepared to dispense an after school punishment.

In Hugh's living room, Lucy occupies the large overstuffed chair while Justin takes a place on the couch. Hugh, in silent refusal to sit next to Justin on the sofa, remains in his wheelchair.

"I'm not angry..." Lucy begins. Hugh and Justin look at one another, nodding and rolling their eyes. Hugh makes a little heart sign with his hands, points to Lucy and then places his hands around his neck as though he's choking himself. He realizes there's something different about the dynamic between Lucy and Justin. Justin has resorted to biting his finger to keep from laughing at Hugh's antics.

Lucy hears their muffled snickers and senses they aren't taking her seriously. She leaps to her feet. "I'm not joking, you two!"

Her eyes now moist with unshed tears, she commands both of the men's attention. Tears are a language most men understand. "Our lives are in danger and all you can do is act like children?" Her lips quiver with pent up anger and hurt and a stray tear escapes to run down her cheek. "I can't bear the thought of losing either of you!"

Pausing for a moment to regain control of her emotions, Lucy resumes her seat. In a more restrained tone, she adds, "I understand why you've done the things you've done to this point, but we need to become more proactive in this situation. We can't just wait around for something to happen. We need to discreetly interrogate Miss Mavis about her grandson and get into her apartment to obtain a photo of him. Once we have his name, we can search public records and find out everything possible about him. If we can gather enough evidence, we can contact the police and not place ourselves at risk.

"There's one more thing," Lucy continues after a moment. She lowers her head as if she's ashamed to speak the words. "I want you to teach me how to use a gun."

Justin jerks his head toward Hugh, partially in astonishment, partially to ascertain Hugh's reaction. Hugh, now in deep thought, stares blankly in Lucy's direction. His emotionless expression doesn't reveal much. Slowly his head begins to nod up and down as though he's processing the information, filtering it though his military experience and training. When the nodding stops, his focus returns and in a confident voice, "We can do that."

Lucy lifts her head, her expression that of a novice boxer going into the ring for the first time—more determination and courage than aptitude. "Will you take me this week sometime?"

The two men look at one another and shake their heads in agreement. "Guys! I'm blind. I can't see what your heads might be doing."

"Yes!" Justin says, in unison with Hugh.

"So," continues Lucy, "the plan is to engage Miss Mavis and figure out a way to access her apartment. I think I know how we can do that. Otherwise, we need to stay out of sight until we obtain the evidence we need, then call the police as soon as we discover where her grandson is or when he appears."

Justin puts his arms around Lucy, pulling her hair away from her face and kissing her softly on the cheek, "I'm sorry to put you through this but we'll take care of everything."

"I was only teasing you earlier, Lucy," says Hugh in a more responsible tone. "I couldn't resist poking fun at Justin but I totally agree with what you said and you know I'll do whatever I can to help out. And just so you know, aside from my own mother, there's no woman I have greater respect for than you."

Lucy, obviously touched by his statement cautiously steps across the room, giving Hugh an appreciative embrace. "Thank you, Hugh. I just want for all of us to get through this so we can get on with our lives."

With her hand still on Hugh's shoulder, Lucy gives him an affectionate tap and then says, "If you will excuse us, Justin and I have some
third-month anniversary business to take care of."

Hugh smiles and gestures a thumbs up to Justin as he takes Lucy by
the arm. Together they walk to the back of the property where Justin has
a two-person hammock set up under one of the fruit trees.

Lucy reverts back to a more vulnerable side to her personality. "A
hammock, Justin? Is it safe? Why did you buy a hammock?"

"I didn't buy it... well, not recently anyway. This is one of the few
items my ex graciously allowed me to keep. Maybe she thought it would
make my homelessness more tolerable. Since I was already moving my
junk from storage, I thought I'd set it up here."

"How does this work? Am I getting in first?"

Without waiting for a response, Lucy leans forward, exploring the
contraption with her hands while Justin guides her into a sitting position. Before he can provide her with further instructions, she attempts to
place herself in a reclining position. At times, Lucy is like a broken dam.
One is unable to halt the forward motion so the best solution is simply to
guide the flow. Justin grabs her, gently directing her descent with one arm
around her back and the other under the bend of her knees. Once settled,
Lucy comically extends her limbs in each direction, resembling someone
attempting to make a snow angel. Initially she lies motionless, her face
tense with an expression of dread. After a few moments, she begins to
slightly relax, resuming the banter with Justin. "Okay, it's not as awful as I
first thought it would be. Here's my quarter... let me out now."

"Stay right there, I'll be right back."

"Justin! Don't you leave me here! Justin?"

Lucy hears Justin's quick steps as he races into the RV for an undis-
closed reason, repeating his annoying behavior of not providing her all
the details. Only moments later he returns, easily sliding into the hammock and pulling Lucy into him.

With an almost comical timidity Lucy asks, "Are we going to be okay
here?"

"Lucy, we're only twelve inches off the ground... it's not like we're
skydiving, explains Justin.

"Oh! I want to do that!" Lucy says, gushing with enthusiasm. Can we go skydiving sometime? We can take Hugh and I get to push him out!"

"Let's start out with a few minutes at twelve inches before we start making plans to go skydiving," Justin teases. Then eagerly, he asks "Are you ready for your adventure?"

"Yes! Of course! Should I get up?"

"No, this journey takes place with us right here under the trees and early evening sky. It's a story... a verbal adventure. All you need to take the trip is a magic coin."

Lucy laughs aloud while reaching in her pocket to retrieve the quarter Justin had given her earlier in the day, "I love stories! Where are we going?"

"We're going to Africa. Have you ever been to Africa before?" asks Justin.

"No, Lucy demurely responds as she snuggles tightly next to Justin, "This is my first time."

Over the course of the next thirty minutes, Justin escorts Lucy on a descriptive and interactive African adventure. Lucy prods for more details and includes her own animals and surprise elements along the way. She is set on the idea that their guide's name is Nobby and their trek is taking place in Kenya. The story concludes with the two of them standing on a bluff, overlooking a wide expanse of the African savanna at sunset. As the sky radiates with brilliant colors, all the animals are making their evening trek to the lake below for their evening watering.

Lucy reaches for Justin's face, gently directing it toward her until their lips meet. Their kiss was equal in scope to the adventure they had just completed together; sensual, beautiful... filled with imagination and promise. "Thank you for a most wonderful adventure," Lucy says with a loving tone.

After a lengthy silence, Lucy comments, "I think I kind of like this hammock a little now."

Justin laughs.

Lucy raises her head off of Justin's chest and sounding childlike, demands, "Tell me another story." Quickly, she adds, "Please."

"Do you have a magic coin?" inquires Justin.

Lucy reaches in her pocket. "I have a dime. What can I get for a dime?"

Justin reaches behind his back and produces the item he retrieved from the RV earlier in the evening, placing it in Lucy's hand.

"It's a rose. It's red isn't it?" Lucy says as she smiles. "I love you too."

XV

Release the Hounds

Fuentes sits at his desk, biting on the hard plastic barrel of an ink pen and staring at a string of clues pinned to the cubical wall in front of him. The diagrams, photos and potential leads appear as a complicated mathematical problem; there's a connection but he's not seeing it. He must solve for "X" but the data is insufficient. It's a perplexing riddle. Manus plus "X" has resulted in the deaths of his ex-wife's new husband and her attorney, Art Conner. But who is "X" and what is his relationship to Manus? Is the undetermined killer responsible for additional murders before meeting Manus on the bridge?

Barnes walks in from behind and teases him. "Hey, you trying to burn a hole in that wall? Any ideas yet?"

Fuentes turns slowly, almost reluctant to disengage from his examination of the display on his wall. "We need to be all over Manus or connect the killer to another crime." Turning to face Barnes, he continues, "This man is nasty! He doesn't just kill his victims, he likes to play with them first. Forensics sent up a photo of a flesh burn on the neck of our wannabe rock star... probably from a stun gun. It appears the perpetrator attacks his victims at an unsuspecting moment, disabling them with a stun gun and then binding them. Once the victim in his control, he takes them to another location where he plays amateur surgeon before he kills them."

Barnes takes a step closer to the photos, "What about the physical evidence? Anything there?"

Fuentes stands, shaking his head as he points to the photos, "Nada! The cable ties, duct tape, nylon rope... all can be purchased from almost anywhere. We can only use what we have to support our case if we find our suspect with the matching items in his possession... but we have to find him first."

Barnes, now staring at the wall of evidence, says, "Where did this guy come from? There must be some connection to Manus prior to this. Did you check the phone records?"

"Did I check the phone records?" Fuentes, sarcastic, snorts. Arms akimbo he tilts his head to one side as he glares at his partner. "You think I got my detective badge out of a cereal box? While you're over there reading old cases and blotter reports—and doing crossword puzzles I've been busy like a bee over here on this side of the wall."

"Okay, okay" Barnes responds with a smile, "I hear you... I know you work hard but we have to check all the possibilities."

Dropping his hands from his hips, Fuentes continues to explain, "I perused the phone records for both Manus and his ex-wife for the previous year, made at least a million or two phone calls and no one fits the profile. The guy on the bridge could be completely random."

"A million or two?" says Barnes with a smile. "And you got nothing from that?"

"I have one little thing but it didn't lead me very far."

"One little thing? How long were you going to hold out on me? Let's see what you got." Mischief flashes in Barnes's eyes.

Fuentes knows that expression of hers. She's going to tear his theory apart. "It's nothing... really," he says, "and I don't want you to start in on me. I really didn't want to show it to you until I had something more concrete."

Barnes raises her hand as though she's taking an oath, "I'll be good... I promise!" she assures him while restraining an unconvincing smirk.

Fuentes pauses, arms folded across his chest as he considers, then he accepts her word and reaches across his desk to retrieve a video disk. Before he plays it, he glances back at Barnes. She snaps her arm back into the oath position a second time while managing to display her best impression of an innocent smile. Fuentes cautiously continues, "The only thing I dug up from the phone records was a call made to Manus from the Rosewood Hotel about the same time and day we were at his apartment questioning him. I followed up on the call and it was made from a room whose sole female occupant had already checked out. Apparently the caller was able to slip into the vacant room as it was being cleaned. The hotel does have video surveillance so I was able to obtain an image of him walking down the hallway and another of him leaving the hotel. I ran the image through our facial recognition software but didn't get a hit. He keeps his head down most of the time and is wearing a hat, sunglasses… possibly even some sort of facial prosthetic."

"Play that back!" Barnes exclaims. She leans closer into the screen, reviewing the footage several times. "This could be our guy! He's obviously disguised and the video doesn't show much detail, but at least we have confirmation of your bogeyman on the bridge theory."

Fuentes leans back from Barnes with an inquisitive expression, "Wait! You're not going to question and critique every component of this like you usually do? What do you know that you're not telling me?"

Barnes flashes a smile. "I was waiting for a little more information too, but what you have here confirms what I have. Wait here!"

Barnes disappears for a moment, and then reappears with her laptop in hand. "I've been searching old cases, looking for something that matches our killer's MO. I didn't find anything so I checked missing persons. As it turns out, Anaheim PD was investigating a missing persons report which led them to review the stadium security video. What they discovered was an abduction. I received a copy of the video yesterday."

Fuentes turns his nose up to Barnes. "And you were waiting for what before you showed it to me? Angeles to descend from heaven?"

"You know I'm not like that, partner. I had to review it a few times to be certain it was relevant to our case. Like you, I attempted to get a hit from facial recognition software but it's dark and he's obviously disguised."

Barnes plays the video while commenting, "Here's an interesting view." Pointing at the computer screen, Barnes directs Fuentes attention to the action, "Look at this! When he punctures the victim's tires, watch him jerk back."

"He's a rookie!" exclaims Fuentes. "He's expecting the tire to pop. This isn't a streetwise career criminal... this is new for him."

"Watch the process," advises Barnes. "The MO is the same... he lures the victim out of view, uses the stun gun to subdue him, and then binds him with handcuffs, nylon rope and cable ties. It's the same process he's used on Art Conner, the wannabe rock star and now with Bantam. There was a slight variation in the process with Manus because he was so drunk, stunning him wasn't necessary."

Fuentes replays the hotel video and compares the two images side-by side. "Okay, let me play the devil this time and debunk your evidence."

Barnes corrects Fuentes. "Do you mean devil's advocate?"

"No, I mean diablo... the devil! You're like a devil when you tear into me," Fuentes snaps.

Barnes laughs. "Okay, you can be the devil this time."

Fuentes points to both images, "The only thing that's obvious is that they're both Caucasian males. I've determined by using markers in the lobby, the suspect at the hotel is about six feet tall and I'm guessing he weighs somewhere around one-sixty-five. But with the ball cap, sunglasses, facial hair and maybe even a facial prosthetic, there's not much detail you can glean from this video. Your suspect is disguised in a grey wig and a bushy moustache that covers most of his face. The thick glasses don't help us either but I can tell you how tall he is in just one second."

Fuentes freezes Barnes's video where the suspect is standing directly next to the open front door of the car. With a few keystrokes he accesses a website and enters a few details as to the subject automobile's make, model and year. "There it is. Do you see the bottom edge of the door-frame? That's twelve inches off the ground. If I take an index card, I can reproduce that length approximately six times on your suspect. But that only proves your perpetrator is about the same height, build and race. I admit he's similar and the MO is the same but none of this proves this is the guy we're looking for."

Barnes sits back, looking smug. "You have to consider that the guy in the stadium video is using an older model Japanese car. Look at this close up photo of the perpetrator's wheels. The tread pattern and the manufacturer matches the profile my brilliant partner set up from the tire impressions he found by the bridge."

"That's a very good point," Fuentes beams with pride.

Barnes pauses each of the two videos with both suspects walking in full stride. She looks at Fuentes and, with restrained enthusiasm says, "But another factor to consider comes from a trick I learned from the FBI. Look at his posture and gait as he walks. The federal agencies can identify suspects with this technique from drones and satellites. Although we don't have the same resources as the feds, we can still apply the concept."

Freezing each of the videos at key motions during a single stride, Barnes measures several points of the outer edge of each suspect's silhouette. Linking the measurements of each subject's outer perimeters and comparing their individual body shape and hip rotation, provides a general assessment of their gait. Although eyeballing it with this simple means is far from being scientifically verifiable, the subjects are certainly similar.

"Now watch this," says Barnes. Using a thin piece of paper placed on top of one of the video images, she outlines its shape and cuts it into a little figure. "Without the software this is far from being a perfect method, but we can get an idea."

Barnes holds the paper cutout in position on top of the other suspect's video image while instructing Fuentes, "We have to allow for a variation in size due to the distance of the cameras and the size of subject, but if we freeze the video at exactly the same position in his stride, the silhouettes should be the same."

After comparing the two videos, it's apparent the girth, shape and posture are very similar. Looking back at Fuentes with a smile, Barnes remarks, "It's almost like a fingerprint of how someone walks. It doesn't prove anything yet but it shows we're on the right path."

Fuentes reviews the two images together, squinting closely at each, "Okay, I admit, I'm impressed. I take back what I said about hating you."

"You never said you hated me," responds Barnes with a frown.

Fuentes turns to face Barnes with a grin, "I must have been thinking it."

Barnes maintains a straight face but says without rancor, "You must love the punishment I dish out because you know I'm going to get you back if you keep it up."

"Okay, seriously then, what do we know about the person abducted?" asks Fuentes in more of a business manner."

Barnes sits down in the chair across from her partner. "Here's where it gets interesting. The missing person is a guy named Richard Bantam. He's a family law attorney with a reputation for being ruthless."

"Ah, okay… that is interesting. Any connection between him and Art Conner?"

Barnes shakes her head. "No, the only connection is that they both lived in Orange County and both worked out of the same courthouse. So far, that's the only link. There's nothing to indicate they knew one another or even opposed one another in court."

Fuentes continues to stare at the paused video, "What about the car? Have you checked anything on that end?"

Barnes widens her eyes. "I was hoping you would do that while I found out more about Bantam."

"Yeah, sure, make me do the boring, tedious tasks." Fuentes says, then nods, begrudgingly accepting the challenge.

He invests the bulk of the next few days attempting to uncover whatever leads he's able to gather on the suspect vehicle. It's not his favorite part of the job; probably the part of police work that can be as exciting as sorting paperclips. The license plate used during the abduction was stolen from another vehicle. Fuentes tracks down and interviews the registered owner. He's a young, naïve man who parks his vehicle each night in a dark, unguarded space of a sprawling apartment building. He admits noticing his license plate was missing but made no effort to report it. Without cameras in the complex, any thought Fuentes has of a quick solution immediately vanishes.

Fuentes still has a few options. Once back at the office, he checks into the police database that links into the regional network of License Plate Readers (LPR) and another, separate system tied in with red light cameras. LPRs are cameras mounted either on police cars or are positioned in stationary locations along major highways whereas the red light cameras cover major intersections. By entering even a partial license plate number into the system, Fuentes has the capacity to retrieve a photo of the suspect vehicle along with a time stamp and location. Sometimes the photos even capture images of the occupants of the vehicle.

The search is negative. Fuentes uncovers a couple of shots of the young apartment dweller in his black automobile but none of the perpetrator in the gold sedan he's looking for. It's apparent to the detective that the man he's looking for either changed the plate in a remote location before entering the stadium or he switched it out once inside the parking lot. After the abduction he likely changed the plate back or navigated his way through a more rural route. In the near future, all new automobiles will come equipped with black boxes that will reveal not only the vehicle's current location but its entire travel history. The collected data will be able to produce a minute-by-minute report on the vehicle's instrument panel as well as record the length and duration of stops, speed and mileage. For now, all the detective can do is hope he can get a hit off of one of the other police data bases.

Fuentes is aware that finding the car is like panning for gold. He has to wade through and eliminate layers of undesirable material before reaching a glint of the desirable ore. He turns his attention to a local data base, bringing up a system named COP-Link. Although the volume of vehicles listed is relatively small in comparison to the others, it does include area reports of automobiles that are collected as a result of law enforcement contacts. The range of vehicles compiled can be for almost anything from those suspected of being used in a crime to automobiles parked for several days in the same location. Entering a specific description of his suspect vehicle results in only one hit matching the description of the older model Japanese car he's looking for. Fuentes reads the responding police officer's Field Investigation Report of the incident.

"...registered owner's state they sold the subject vehicle described above to an unknown buyer who paid in cash. Their automobile was returned to them a few days later with a typewritten note, allowing them to retain possession of both the subject vehicle and cash payment. Owner's state the automobile was returned under suspicious circumstances. Subject vehicle returned with rear windows tinted and dark, blood-like stains on the carpet of the rear floorboard. A brief inspection of the vehicle confirmed

owner's claims and uncovered a wine bottle lodged under the rear portion of the pas-
senger front seat. Evidence techs were requested to recover samples of the substance on
the carpet as well as the wine bottle and typewritten note."

The words "wine bottle" blare from the report. Fuentes reviews the video of the abduction of Bantam to make sure everything is there—vehicle make, model, color and year; consistency of the dates, tinted windows, the victim placed face-down on the rear floorboard. Everything fits. Fuentes immediately calls Anaheim PD to request the vehicle be impounded and tire impressions to be made. Once the vehicle is in police custody, the crime scene unit will take prints from the wine bottle and confirm whether or not the substance on the rear carpet is blood. The DNA evidence they gather will be instrumental in separating and identifying all the characters in the crime.

Barnes sits on the other side of the cubical wall, mulling over missing persons reports and wondering if she didn't give away the easier task to Fuentes. Although the list of missing persons is trifling in comparison to a vehicular search, the connections are more difficult to match. The great majority of individuals reported "missing" originate from parental abductions of their own children by a non-custodial parent. Another large group is comprised of teenage runaways. With children and juveniles eliminated from the search, the resulting list becomes very small. Only a handful of possibilities remain, including a single listing with what may be a remote connection to Richard Bantam. It's a twelve-month old case involving a missing judge.

Barnes doesn't recall ever meeting Judge Raven, a superior court judge who worked in family law while Barnes's cases were conducted in the criminal division in an entirely different courthouse. According to the report, Raven never returned home from a hike in the Sierra Nevada Mountains. Hotel security video records him safely leaving their facility early in the morning before sunrise. His truck was discovered in an overnight parking lot near South Lake but he seems to have disappeared after that. Although his backpack was missing from the truck, not a single witness could confirm seeing him on the trail. Search and Rescue dispatched teams of hikers. Helicopters conducted a grid search and dogs were brought in to track him. Nothing. The canine units didn't pick up a detectable scent of Raven anywhere along the route. There are bears in the area but bear attacks are not common and none had been reported. If a bear had attacked, there normally would be evidence of such and there was none. The grid was expanded but after two weeks, the search was called off. It was officially determined to be a recovery matter at that time and no longer a rescue. Due to the suspicious circumstances and the fact that the missing person is a judge, the case remains open. But without evidence of a crime, little can be done to further the investigation. The judge is presumed dead and many think his bones will be discovered at the bottom of a remote ravine someday. Others suspect Raven's life came to a more nefarious end but without evidence, one can only speculate.

Barnes doesn't see an immediate connection between Richard Bantam and Judge Raven but continues to dig for more information. Over the course of his eighteen years of legal practice, Bantam has presented a dozen cases before Raven. Of these, only half have been processed in the most recent six years and none of the parties associated with the cases have criminal histories. Three of the Respondents to Bantam's Petitions for Dissolution of Marriage currently reside out of state, the other three are local. The detective highlights the names, makes notes and writes a brief bio on each of the six suspects before turning her attention in another direction.

Barnes impatiently taps her pen on the desk, "There has to be another link," she mutters, and continues digging. She scours the list of Orange County murders from the past few years. After eliminating gang related deaths, domestic violence incidents and murders committed during the commission of a crime, she is left with only a handful of cases. She reads the details of a few files but discards them when the names or facts have no obvious connection to either Bantam or Raven. Nearing the end of her search, her eyes focus on an unusual case involving a female community worker named Harpy who was allegedly killed by an Orange County attorney. The case is twelve months old and has yet to go to trail but the suspect, a woman with the last name of Strix, is incarcerated in the Orange County Women's Detention Center. Working as the Guardian *ad litem* in the Orange County Family Law Court, Strix undoubtedly had contact with both Judge Raven and Richard Bantam. But what's the connection? Barnes is perplexed. Strix was nowhere near Raven when he went missing and she was in jail when Bantam was abducted. There has to be a connection but nothing is obvious.

Focusing on the Harpy murder, Barnes peruses every file and every report, looking for a link between one of the six names on her list and Bantam's cases assigned to Judge Raven. She's hopeful that one of the six suspects she has compiled will be named in the files. The detective's level of frustration rises as none of the names match. She places her face in her hands, breathes slowly and ponders her next move. As she uncovers her eyes, she redirects her efforts to a new approach.

Rather than attempting to link the list of six suspects to the Harpy murder, perhaps there's a direct connection to Strix or Harpy. During Strix tenure as Guardian *ad litem*, she made scores of appearances on behalf of children. By entering a name search into the data base containing Strix's cases, Barnes is able to retrieve any of the six names from her list of suspects from within the Strix files. With only a few strokes on her keyboard, a single name appears as a match from her list of six potential suspects; Travis Kilborn. It's a good lead but not conclusive. Considering the number of cases in which Strix appeared, it's reasonable to assume she might be involved with one of the six suspects. There's nothing profound about this piece of information quite yet. It will only become significant if the case was assigned to Judge Raven or Richard Bantam is one of the attorneys of record. Since divorce documents are public information, Barnes needs only to enter Kilborn's name and case number into the system in order to have access to all the data of his case. If the screen pops up with the case assigned to Judge Raven or the opposing counsel is listed as Richard Bantam, Barnes will push the case near to the finish line. She moves the cursor to the appropriate box, clicks on the space, and then closes her eyes while taking a deep cleansing breath. As a large lungful of air slowly dissipates from her lungs, Barnes opens her eyes and focuses on the two names she was hoping to see.

Yes! The case was assigned to Judge Raven and Richard Bantam was the attorney for the Petitioner. In an expression of glee Barnes shouts aloud, "I got you now you son-of-a-bitch! I got you now!"

Heads begin to pop up above cubical tops like meerkats in an African savanna. As Barnes leaps to her feet in a sort of victory celebration, she unabashedly looks around the office, almost singing the line, "I got you now!"

The meerkat heads begin to disappear below the cubical line as they sense there is no danger. Fuentes strolls by the scene moments later holding a fresh cup of coffee in hand, "What did I miss guy? What was the commotion in here?"

"Well partner," explains Barnes, "while you were empting your bladder and refreshing your coffee, I discovered our murderer!"

Fuentes is slow to respond, taking the time to take another sip of his coffee.

Barnes stares at his calm expression, her own one of surprise "You don't seem too excited."

Fuentes attempts to restrain an impish smile. "I'm afraid you're going to tell me it's Travis Kilborn. According to the records, he's been dead for three years."

"How could he be dead? He's a perfect fit to all the pieces!"

"I know," Fuentes responds, disappointedly shaking his head, "I know. I got the results from forensics this morning and Travis Kilborn's prints were on the wine bottle under the seat. He has really nice fingerprints for a ghost. We know that the vehicle was definitely the one used to abduct Bantam and it was Bantam's blood on the rear carpet. Also, the tires on the car are a perfect match to the tire impressions taken at the scene. There were two major problems though. Aside from Kilborn being dead, I questioned the people who originally owned the car and the person that bought their car was a shorter, older, and heavier man. The sellers described him as walking slightly hunched over and speaking with a foreign accent. Although the DMV records for Kilborn show he's a perfect physical match to the person we have on video, the guy is officially listed as being deceased."

"Well, he's obviously not dead," snaps Barnes, irritated.

"Yes, obviously… and he can't leave fingerprints behind if he's dead, but he did rent a small fishing boat from King's Harbor in the South Bay and it sank during a surprise storm. I already verified it. They don't normally rent boats if there's even a hint of a storm. There's no way he could have predicted that storm."

"So, they never discovered a body?

"Okay guy, I thought the same thing. In Mijami we have people who try to collect insurance claims by faking their deaths. They always show up. But I researched his records and there wasn't a life insurance policy or single hit on his credit cards, cell phone… no one has seen him. He had a small amount of money in the bank that hasn't been touched and he never returned to his car or apartment."

"So, no one discovered a body?"

"The Coast Guard searched for him for a few days… found the wreckage. The currents are strong and there are a lot of sharks between here and Catalina Island."

"So, what you're saying then is no one ever found a body?"

Fuentes takes a sip from his coffee and looks into the increasingly impatient eyes of his partner. "Yeah, I guess you could say that. If he's still alive he's figured out a way to completely vanish."

Barnes throws her hands in the air, making a plea to Fuentes. "You've got to work with me here partner, give me some ideas. What are our options?"

Fuentes, enjoying the torment he's putting Barnes through, shrugs his shoulders and explains, "I only have two possible theories right now."

"What's the first one?" Barnes snaps.

Straight-faced Fuentes says, "You believe in zombies… the walking dead? They're real popular in the movies these days."

Barnes spins around, splays her palms on the wall and makes a pretense of banging her forehead on the surface between them. "Okay partner, what's your second theory?"

"You don't want to hear about the zombies? Hey, I'm from Mijami… I've seen things."

Barnes laughs, turns and makes a mock threat to choke Fuentes. "I keep reminding you that we're not in 'Mi-Yahmi' as you say it. We don't arrest zombies in Southern California… they have civil rights just like everyone else."

Still holding to Fuentes collar, Barnes states firmly, "Tell me what you really have before I inflict you with bodily pain."

Fuentes drops the jokster facade and provides her with an accurate assessment. "The person that bought the Japanese car from the elderly couple has to be his accomplice. He's the one hiding Travis Kilborn. There's no forensic evidence of the second person from the car but he has to be hiding him and providing for his needs. I did attempt to track down all of Travis Kilborn's known friends and associates but after his divorce he isolated himself. No one has seen or heard of him for years and his only living relative is a grandmother named Mavis Kilborn."

"Is she local?" interjects Barnes.

Fuentes reaches into his shirt pocket and retrieves a folded note with Mavis Kilborn's name and address on it, handing it to Barnes, "Apparently she doesn't have a phone but she's local… here in Torrance."

"You had this in your pocket the whole time and didn't tell me?" complains Barnes. "Why didn't you just tell me?"

Fuentes takes another sip from his coffee and looks up with a smile, "Because I knew you wouldn't listen to my zombie theory."

"There's something seriously wrong with you." responds Barnes, miffed as well as entertained. "You ready to take a ride to Torrance?"

XVI

The Trap

Justin slides his finger between the vinyl slats of the window covering, peering out into the courtyard of Lucy's apartment complex. Aside from the three small, unremarkable deciduous trees planted in the center of a quadrangle of concrete, no one would suspect that autumn had arrived. Clear skies and warm temperatures create the illusion of an extended summer. Perhaps the most noticeable difference is the reduction of traffic noise and the absence of children playing in the nearby park. Students have returned to their academic routines and most of the tourists have gone home; allowing locals greater access to beaches and the amenities of their community. Winter rudely interrupts the process with shorter days and cooler temperatures.

Lucy approaches her boyfriend from behind, placing her hand softly on his back, "Justin, are you still gawking out the window? Miss Mavis isn't going to come out until it's time for the mail to be delivered. You already know how much noise she makes and how slow moving she is so there's no reason for you to stand guard."

"I know, Lucy, I know." Justin responds as he releases his finger from between the blinds and turns to face her. "I feel a little edgy, like I need to be doing something. Besides, I have to call Hugh the minute Miss Mavis shows up."

"Why call Hugh?"

Justin sparks with animation. "You know how excited he gets about this. He's like a big kid on a secret mission. He wants to see Miss Mavis and inspect the layout... just to have an image in his mind."

Lucy laughs, "Yeah, he's the only big kid I have to worry about."

Justin turns, grabbing Lucy by the waist, and teasingly responds, "What about you Ms. Lucy? What happened to the innocent teacher I know? You took to the firearms training better than most military recruits I know. If I didn't know any better, I'd say you have a commando side that's begging to come out."

Lucy pushes away from Justin. "Yeah, right! I secretly dream of parachuting out of an airplane loaded down with guns and explosives in order to complete a secret mission." After a slight pause, Lucy wraps her arms around Justin's neck. "Come to think of it, that does sound like a lot of fun. Do you think after we finish this gig I could sign up to become the first blind woman in special forces?"

Justin chuckles. "That would push the boundaries of political correctness and equal access, don't you think? But, if anyone could figure out a way to make it happen, it would be you. That reminds me, where did you put my gun?"

"It's in the drawer of the end table, next to the sofa."

A few doors down, toward the middle of the apartment complex, Miss Mavis stands peering at herself in a mirror. She's carefully applying a final layer of lipstick before making her trek across the concrete common to the mailboxes near the front of the complex. She doesn't leave her apartment without making herself "presentable" as she often says. In her time, a lady never appeared in public without making every effort to look her best. She's wearing one of her favorite dresses today. It's an elegant white gown with long sleeves and a high neck collar that covers the length of her body from the bottom of her chin to the top of her feet. Her thinning hair is covered with a stylish silver wig. From a distance, she appears to possess beauty that surpasses her years. In closer proximity, however, one may be tempted to describe her heavy makeup as being more suitable for a corpse in funeral home.

Mail delivery is normally about noon. On days when the postal worker is running behind schedule, Miss Mavis sits patiently on a nearby bench, enjoying the warm sun on her face. Months ago, before she began to display symptoms of Alzheimer's, relaxing for a few minutes in the sunshine was a pleasure she frequently shared with Lucy.

When Lucy first met her elderly neighbor, their initial social exchanges were cordial and filled with small talk. As time passed Lucy became captivated by Miss Mavis's stories and her wealth of life experiences. As a child, the elderly neighbor lived through the Great Depression. In her teens she competed in several beauty pageants and won many of them. In order to avoid becoming an "Old Maid" at the grand age of eighteen, Miss Mavis married the only man she has ever loved. She had a child with him and lived what she describes as a happy and fulfilled life. During her marriage, she and her husband gained and lost a couple of fortunes but they were always content. Their only son died in the Viet Nam War, only eighteen months before he was to retire. It was a crushing blow, nearly equal to the devastating loss she felt when her husband succumbed to lung cancer fifteen years ago. By the time of his death, they had been married forty-eight years. Miss Mavis has no interest in being with anyone else. She has only a single living relative; a grandson named Travis.

Her facial expression changes when she speaks of him. "He's a good boy. People say he looks a lot like his grandma," she frequently says with a proud smile. That was before her symptoms of Alzheimer's became obvious. Now it's a daily toss up as to where her mind is. Some days are nearly normal; other days are like being introduced to someone for the first time.

Screech… grind… tap tap.

"Justin! Justin! I hear Miss Mavis!" Lucy exclaims.

Justin, in the kitchen, responds. "I hear her, baby. No worries. I'll call Hugh and once she's settled, we can approach her."

Screech… grind… tap tap.

"Hugh is on his way after he finishes up with an errand. I think we should go ahead without him and fill him in on the details when he gets here."

Lucy takes Justin's arm and the two walk the short distance to where Miss Mavis sits perched on one end of the bench, staring at the arched entry to the apartment complex. After Justin's steps come to an end, Lucy instinctively reaches for the edge of the wooden plank and guides herself into the open seat on the opposite end of the bench. Miss Mavis continues to stare ahead, seemingly disinterested or unaware of anyone around her.

"Hello Miss Mavis. It's Lucy, your neighbor."

Miss Mavis is slow to respond, almost as though she has to process the information before turning her head to face Lucy with a friendly smile. "Yes, you're that nice girl. I'm happy to see you again."

As she completes the turn of her head, she notices Justin standing near Lucy. "I've been waiting and on the lookout for you," the old lady says.

Justin is taken aback by the comment. "Wha—" he bites off the question as he stares back into the steely blue eyes that somehow seem familiar. Was the comment intended for Lucy or does the elderly grandmother of his nemeses know something about him? Justin doesn't offer a reply as Miss Mavis turns away, redirecting her stare back toward the arched entry.

Lucy, missing the visual clues, responds directly to the elderly woman's words. "I've been here every day Miss Mavis. I check around for you when I get the mail, but I haven't noticed you around as much. I know you were sick with a cough and sore throat for a while."

There's a prolonged silence before the elderly neighbor speaks again. "Yes, my voice is still a little hoarse from it. I was named after a song thrush that appears in spring. My mother immediately took to the name after reading it in a book that was popular during her day. Oddly, I was never much of a vocalist, and now I sound more like a crow choking on sandpaper."

Lucy is quick to offer a word of encouragement. She momentarily places her hand on the sleeved arm of her neighbor commenting, "You've had such a great life with so many wonderful experiences. I've enjoyed all of your stories."

Without waiting for the elderly woman to respond, Lucy says, "Miss Mavis, I'd like for you to meet my boyfriend, Justin."

Justin offers a courteous smile but stands motionless as the elderly woman continues to stare forward. "Boyfriend?" she remarks. "You have a boyfriend? Do you love him?"

Lucy blushes but immediately responds, "Yes, I do. I love him very much."

Before anyone speaks again, the postal worker arrives and greets everyone with a smile before beginning to fill the resident's mailboxes.

While the day's delivery is separated and parceled, Lucy says, "Miss Mavis, you've told me stories of your days as a pageant queen and that you have a collection of newspaper clippings and trophies in your home. Since Justin is with me today, would you mind if he reads a few of the stories to me and describes some of your awards? I'd love to know more about them."

Justin hopes this will allow him access to the elderly neighbor's apartment. Once inside, he'll have the opportunity to view her photographs and possibly discover information regarding her grandson.

Miss Mavis sits in silence for a moment, and then slowly nods her agreement. Softly she replies, "Yes, I suppose that would be alright. I don't think Travis would mind."

After a brief pause she continues, "Did I tell you I was named after a bird? My mother read a story of a woman named Mavis Clare whose voice was like a song thrush. If mother knew how poorly I sing, I wonder if she would have named me something else?"

On the laborious walk back to Miss Mavis's apartment, Lucy reduces the elderly neighbor's effort as she takes her arm, supporting the aged frame while Miss Mavis provides a line of sight across the courtyard and to the door of her apartment. Justin walks on Lucy's other side, his hand on her shoulder to remind her he's there watching her steps while carrying the battered walker in his other hand.

The door opens, allowing the only source of natural light into the room. Once inside, Justin closes the door behind him and is immediately greeted with a dank, musty smell, a combination of elevated room temperature and a lack of ventilation. All of the doors and windows appear to be bolted shut. A quick scan of the apartment reveals that Miss Mavis limits her housecleaning chores to what she is able to see at eye level. Books, some in neatly stacked piles, others in stacks that obviously fell over long ago, are scattered throughout the room. There is no television, only a boxy radio about the size of a loaf of bread resting on top of a small antique table. Several old, ornate mirrors surround the living room and an elegant but dusty chandelier hangs oddly out of place in the center of the small dining area. The decorative cluster of multifaceted prisms that hang from it are much too large for the low ceiling of the apartment; it nearly overwhelms the presence of a splendid dining room table set beneath it. Antique lamps with dangling teardrop crystals accent the room but only a single light is turned on.

Once Justin's eyes adjust from the outside light, the room becomes an offbeat mixture of mundane earth tones and dull, drab and dusty colors. Amid the collection of antiques, one piece of furniture stands apart from the others. In the space where most would likely place an entertainment center or large television, sits a make-up table pressed against the wall. It resembles the type of furnishing one would see backstage for the use of models and entertainers. Several high intensity light bulbs are clustered around the outer perimeter of a large mirror hung behind a flat, horizontal desktop covered with cosmetics.

Justin offers Lucy his arm as he guides her into the room, grateful for her temporary silence. He would be at a loss in describing the room to her without offending Miss Mavis.

"Would you like to see my fairies?" asks Miss Mavis. Her eyes dance with excitement.

Justin looks to Lucy for some sort of affirmation but immediately realizes his mistake, "Yes, Miss Mavis... I'd love to see them."

The elderly neighbor slowly creeps toward a light switch on the wall, first activating a ceiling fan which slowly stirs the air, and then another switch to turn on a small strand of track lights. At the flip of a switch, the room immediately transforms into a circus of color and activity. As the light reflects from one mirror to the next; it penetrates the dangling, multifaceted crystals of the lamps and chandelier resulting in a myriad of small rainbows across the room. The slight stir in the air from the ceiling fan causes just enough motion to create the illusion of a miniature army of brilliantly colored images darting about the room.

"Do you see them?" asks Miss Mavis as she looks upward, captivated by the view. Without waiting for an answer, she adds with a childlike awe, "Aren't they beautiful?"

Even with a pressing ulterior motive, Justin is momentarily enchanted by Miss Mavis's fairies and how easily they transformed an otherwise gloomy room into a gathering of colorful fairies. But the added light reveals more than just splashes of brilliant color and light to the apartment's interior. Attached to the walls near the make-up table are a dozen or more aged newspaper articles and on the floor below, a pile of scrapbooks. Pushed into a straight line against the wall are several trophies; some reaching a height of three feet. These are obviously the tokens of Miss Mavis's beauty pageant success. In the process of escorting Lucy to the other side of the room, Justin describes the vivid colors and the "fairies" as Miss Mavis labels them. Closer to the make-up table, photos and memorabilia become clearly visible. Justin provides Lucy with a summary of the array of pictures and newspaper articles that attest to Miss Mavis's youthful beauty. A large black and white photo of a young woman sporting a victor's crown is prominently displayed at eye level. Justin describes Miss Mavis's beauty to Lucy, much to the elderly neighbor's delight. A few articles are read aloud for Lucy's benefit and then he notices a photo of a man on the other side of the mirror.

Justin leans toward the wall to examine it more carefully. The face on the headshot appears to share the same steely blue eyes as Miss Mavis. Could this be the elderly neighbor's grandson, the one she lovingly refers to as Travis? It has to be him! This must be the murderer that haunts his life and poses such a threat to his future! Justin retains his composure but acts quickly to verify the identity of the photo, "Is this your husband?"

Miss Mavis looks intently at the photo as thought she had forgotten it was there or who the person was. "No, no… that's my grandson. I have pictures of my husband over here."

As the elderly neighbor turns her back to retrieve a photo album from a stack across the room, Justin quickly detaches the picture and places it in his rear pocket. He looks toward Miss Mavis only to see her back as she stands in silence next to a stack of books. Initially it appears as though capturing the evidence was successful. Turning his head in the other direction to face Lucy reveals a different conclusion. The position of the numerous mirrors stationed around the room had exposed his theft. For only a fraction of a second, he sees someone lurking in the shadows, their steel blue eyes staring back at him in the reflections of the ornate mirrors. Miss Mavis, or someone, had seen him take the picture! As much as Justin scrambles to form an excuse or rationale, none comes to mind. His only thought is to exit the apartment as quickly as possible. He firmly holds onto Lucy's arm and nudges her in the direction of the door. Lucy, is in midsentence, asking a trivial detail regarding the deceased husband's life when she feels Justin's urgent tug on her arm. It was time to go and Lucy was discerning enough not to ask why.

"We have to go now Miss Mavis," Justin says. "Thank you for showing your photos to us."

Miss Mavis doesn't respond. Only steps from the door, Justin takes a final glance back in her direction. She still has her back to them but in one of the numerous reflections he sees a flash of something metallic, perhaps a letter opener, maybe a knife. Although he cannot be certain, it appears Miss Mavis has grasped onto a pointed metal object and is slowly turning around. There's no time to ask questions.

As Justin reaches for the door knob, the bright lights go out, leaving only the pale light from the single lamp. Before Justin's eyes adjust to the dim light and before he's able to open the door, Miss Mavis speaks in an odd, almost growling tone, "Did I tell you I was named after a bird? It was a song thrush… but I can't sing."

The voice becomes louder, closer, but the door appears to be stuck. The high room temperature combined with the moisture in the apartment causes the wood to swell and form a seal against the doorframe. Any other time a slight tug would free the door but under these conditions time seems to stand still. Lucy stands helplessly behind while Justin wrestles with the door.

Lucy's breathing changes as if she senses his tension but he knows she is unaware of the potential danger or that there is an unknown threat. Justin's heart races. With a final tug, he dislodges the door, and it opens to the daylight and air from outside. Quickly, he pulls Lucy to him and slams the door closed behind them. Neither speaks until they have retreated and secured themselves inside Lucy's apartment.

"What was that all about?" Lucy asks.

Now well away from the inexplicable sense of danger he'd experienced in the old lady's apartment, Justin feels sheepish. "Miss Mavis saw me take the picture of her grandson. After I put it in my pocket I looked up and she was staring at me. I panicked and just wanted to get out of there."

"She saw you?!" Lucy said with almost a giggle.

"Yeah, I looked back and it appeared like she was reaching for a knife, the lights went out and the door got stuck. I was a little nervous for a minute."

Lucy laughs, "So you thought the mean, old eighty-one-year-old lady and her army of fairies was going to get you? Was my big, strong man scared?"

Justin smiles with amusement. "Didn't you hear her chanting the line about being named after a bird? When then the lights went out, all I wanted to do was get out of there. I had images of being attacked by thousands of evil fairies."

They share a laugh until Lucy finally speaks, "But you have the picture?"

"I have it here." Justin removes the photo from his back pocket and studies it. "It's remarkable how similar their eyes are. These are the eyes I saw staring at me in the shadows"

"Well, they do share the same gene pool so that's to be expected."

Justin takes a final look at the picture before placing it on the countertop for Hugh to view when he arrives. He's surprised Hugh's errand is taking so long and now he may not have an opportunity to see Miss Mavis. Turning to Lucy Justin asks, "So how should we handle the situation with Miss Mavis?"

Lucy takes a deep breath and shrugs her shoulders, "Chances are she'll forget all about it in a couple of days so just avoid contact with her for a little while."

—∿—

Across the courtyard in the elderly neighbor's apartment, bathing in the lights of the brightly lit makeup table, sits Travis Kilborn. As he adjusts his grandmother's wig and applies a final touch to his makeup, he pauses a moment to admire himself. He has been practicing the art of disguise and taking acting classes for nearly three years; almost immediately after killing Dr. Klaudios. This is just another role, another performance, another murder. Uncertain of Justin Manus's memories of his drunken night on the bridge, it was Kilborn who placed the photo of himself on the mirror. When Justin snatched the picture, he confirmed Kilborn's suspicions.

He had underestimated the inebriated man who sat shoeless and soaking wet on the pedestrian walkway that evening. He erred in becoming overly interested and overly personal with his passenger's pathetic life. In the process he slipped up by providing a tidbit of information that led his formerly pardoned victim to the doorstep of his grandmother's house. He cannot be allowed a second chance. Kilborn stuffs his handbag with his tools of murder and then stands to admire himself in the mirror one last time.

—⁊⁊⁊—

Screech... grind... tap tap.

"Justin! Do you hear that?!" exclaims Lucy, even more tickled.

"What should I do?" asks Justin.

Despite Justin's discomfort, Lucy finds the situation irresistibly humorous. Speaking through a laugh she says, "You're the thief, baby! The evil fairies are coming for you, not me!"

Sensing Justin's lack of amusement, Lucy advises, "Okay, seriously, just take a picture of the photo and return the original to her with an apology. That should do it."

Screech... grind... tap tap.

Moments after Justin finishes snapping a photo of the print, there's a faint knock. He opens the door, greeting whom he perceives as the elderly neighbor, and offers an immediate apology.

The counterfeit version of Miss Mavis nods with an appreciative smile and with a gravelly voice, asks to come inside for a moment. Justin eagerly accommodates her. Leaving the walker outside on the doorstep, Kilborn hobbles into the room clutching onto a small handbag, obviously weighted with something inside.

Hearing the sound of the door closing behind the imposter, Lucy speaks, "Miss Mavis, we're so sorry. Justin thought he recognized the person in the photo and he wanted to borrow it for a closer look."

Kilborn responds with a strange smile. "It's not a problem dear. You seemed to have an interest in my grandson so I brought some of his things by to show you."

Lucy immediately senses something is off but is reluctant to risk offending her neighbor twice in the same day. The neighbor's voice isn't right, even with a sore throat... and she smells distinctly different. It's similar, perhaps even the same perfume, but something isn't right.

Kilborn lifts the handbag to eye level to show Justin he brought something along but before opening the purse, he turns and speaks directly to Justin, "Will you be so kind as to get my walker outside on the doorstep for me? I've been on my feet too long."

Justin, eager to appease Miss Mavis for his earlier offense, turns toward the door, exposing his back to Kilborn as he attempts to exit the apartment. With the skill and choreography of a magician, Kilborn removes a stun gun from the purse. Before Justin's hand reaches the door knob, there's a buzzing and clicking sound, followed by a moan and a thud as his body slides from the door and onto the floor. Justin lies temporarily incapacitated at Kilborn's feet.

"Justin?" Lucy asks.

There's no response. The room is nearly silent.

"Justin! What just happened?" Lucy demands as she hears the clasp of metal followed by what sounds like plastic zippers.

"Miss Mavis? What is going on!" Lucy edges toward the door.

A strange voice comes from the other end of the room. "Stay where you are and don't say a word!"

Lucy's mind races with possibilities but for the moment she chooses to stand in quiet obedience near the end of the sofa. Silent tears roll down her cheeks. She's mindful of the handgun only a few feet away from her in the end table drawer but it's not an option at the moment. She doesn't know Justin's condition or his location and firing helter-skelter into the unknown is not a choice she's willing to make. There's a distinct and familiar sound—some type of tape being unwound from its roll, followed by a muffled voice.

"Justin?! Justin?! Is that you?! Are you okay?" Lucy struggles to keep her voice steady and clear of the fear that courses through her.

"If you scream, I'll kill him." The voice, clearly masculine, advises.

Lucy remains motionless as she listens to what is obviously Justin being dragged away from the door and across the small living room. He lies only a few feet to her side. Justin, recovering from the shock of the stun gun, attempts communication but with a sock taped inside his mouth, he's unable to form words. Although Lucy can't hear or understand Justin's muffled tones, in her mind she can see exactly where he is.

"Would you like to sit down, Lucy?" asks the voice with obviously false consideration.

"I'm fine standing! Who the hell are you and what do you want with us?" demands Lucy, her voice now steeped with agitation.

"I'm so glad you asked. My name, as you may have guessed by now, is Travis Kilborn."

Reaching into the sleeve of the dress, Kilborn retrieves a knife and steps within inches of Lucy's face, like a dog sniffing a perimeter. Lucy feels his presence on her as a cloak of evil and trembles as his breath brushes across the back of her neck. She feels trapped, helpless, and jumps when he places the flat side of his knife on her bare shoulder.

The seemingly eternal silence is broken by Kilborn's menacing explanation, "I spared Justin's life when we met on the bridge. Did he tell you that? I offered him a new life, protection, and all the money he would need to start over. My graciousness was rewarded by the two of you meddling into my personal life. Instead of accepting my generous offer, you elected to violate me by bringing this issue to my grandmother's doorstep!"

Justin is fully conscious and can only watch as he lies helplessly, handcuffed and with his legs bound. His muffled screams scarcely escape the sock taped inside his mouth. All he can do is witness each tormenting moment with widened eyes. He assaults the bindings with all his strength but the results are completely futile. Kilborn begins to slowly circle Lucy, pressing himself against her from behind while holding the knife to her throat. In a gritty snarl he asks, "Did violating my grandmother's and my privacy provide the two of you with some sort of satisfaction? Did it?"

Kilborn clutches Lucy's throat with one hand while positioning the blade of his knife near her ear. In a splenetic voice dripping with revenge he asks, "How does being a victim feel now?"

Kilborn slowly drags the blunt end of his knife across the side of Lucy's face and down to her neck. He glances down at Justin to insure he has his undivided attention. Justin's widen and furry-filled eyes provide him with the answer. The blade slowly continues to flow down the contour of Lucy's firm, young body, over the top of her breast, pausing to circle her nipples. Justin continues to struggle against his bindings, nearly working himself to a point of exhaustion. He is only able to witness the act while perspiration drips down his rage-inflamed face.

Kilborn responds with a smirk as the blade continues on its course over Lucy's abdomen and continuing down to her vagina. Kilborn's sexual arousal doesn't stem from the close proximity to the beautiful woman in his arms, it's in Justin's response. It's the feeling of power, control and the orgasmic tingle he's beginning to achieve as he senses the imminent kill. Kilborn turns Lucy to face him, with Justin lying on the floor behind him. He inserts one hand into Lucy's thick, brown hair; clutching the back of her neck as he pulls her close to him. Lucy leans away but Kilborn has a firm clasp of her mane and forces her compliance. Face to face with her, he continues to torment her by placing the pointed tip of his dagger on her face and neck. "You're genuinely beautiful and I truly regret having to kill you."

Unable to break free of his bindings and sensing the horrific outcome, Justin can only manage to roll to the back of Kilborn's legs, bumping into him while emitting muffled screams. Kilborn looks down at him with mock sympathetic eyes and explains in a patronizing voice, "You brought this on yourself my friend. I spared your life once and even attempted to resurrect your miserable existence. And what is the reward for my patience?"

Justin screams become repetitive. "You want me to kill you and spare her, is that what you're saying?" asks Kilborn, slightly amused. "I don't think so." He shakes his head, never losing the mocking smile. "I think I'll make you watch while I kill her... then I'll kill you."

Kilborn returns his attention toward Lucy as Justin's muffled cries become more frantic and he drums his heels on the floor. Lucy senses Kilborn's escalating rage. His breathing deepens, becomes more rapid. Discerning her imminent demise, in an act of pure desperation, she swings her fist around with as much force as she's able, striking Kilborn in the side of his face. Her petite hand is too frail to deliver a decisive blow; it serves only to surprise Kilborn and force the release of his grasp. Lucy stumbles back into the small end table, intentionally knocking it onto its side before she herself falls to the floor. With her hand outstretched, Lucy is able to touch the bottom rim of the drawer but isn't successful in opening it before Kilborn is on top of her. Kilborn's steel blue eyes radiate rage as he takes a final look back at Justin, places his hand over Lucy's mouth, and then plunges the knife deep into Lucy's abdomen. Lucy deeply gasps, perhaps not as much from pain but the shock of being stabbed. She instinctively applies pressure on the wound with her hand after the blade is removed. The wound is deep, penetrating into her intestines. Surprisingly, only a slight amount of blood trickles through into the fabric of her clothing and onto her fingers

"No! No! No!" Justin screams. Despite the sock in his mouth, his volume increases.

Lucy is breathing deeply and is apparently in a slight state of shock or unable to scream. Kilborn stands to his feet, examining his elegant white dress for evidence of blood. He is not one to hurry at a time like this. Murder has become very personal to him; an act of intimacy. He spots the purse he carried in with him across the room and knows he cannot complete the slaughter of his victims without recording the victory. Lucy, still dazed by the horror, cannot sense where he is in the room. She's uncertain as to her condition but has come to realize that this will likely be her only opportunity to defend herself. Keeping pressure on her wound with one hand, she fingers open the drawer of the end table with the other. The small piece of furniture sits resting on its side. As the drawer is edged out, the open end faces the wall, keeping the contents out of view. Kilborn announces his return, proudly displaying his voice recorder while boasting of his six previous kills. Lucy continues to fumble inside the drawer, attempting to locate the gun. Justin's only option is a feeble attempt to buy Lucy a few additional seconds of time. In an act of desperation and defiance he rolls into Kilborn's path, attempting to kick at him as a means to prevent him from reaching her. The motion is only slightly successful as Kilborn circles around to his head, clutches onto Justin's upper body and drags him to the side. With all obstacles removed, the killer takes a step toward Lucy, standing over her while glancing back at Justin to insure he's an audience to the looming mutilation. As Justin eagerly looks in Lucy's direction, her facial expression displays a slight change as her fingers tickle the edge of the handle of the 9MM handgun. All Justin can think to do is emit a muffled scream, "Now! Now!" as loud as he is able. Kilborn snaps his head around to face Lucy but by this time she has a secure grasp on the weapon. Lucy removes the pistol from hiding, using her thumb to release the safety, and fires two rounds immediately in front of her and above where Justin lies on the floor. Gunfire cracks the air with two loud pops. Kilborn jumps to the side but not before the second shot hits its target and is confirmed with resounding groan. Justin flips to his side to locate Kilborn as he runs away, screaming

"Door! Door!" Justin tries to tell Lucy with the same volume as one would have with a pillow over their face.

Lucy fires a single, final shot in the direction of the door and then allows her arm to collapse back onto the carpet. Although the third shot misses its target, it serves as enough of a deterrent to keep Kilborn from returning. Kilborn escapes, clutching onto both his knife and the voice recorder; his legs tangle in the long, white dress and he stumbles out the door. Lucy weakly holds her hand over her wound while Justin locates Kilborn's purse across the room. Rolling to the purse, Justin manages to take hold of it from behind his back and fumbles through the contents until he finds the key to unlock his handcuffs. Within a few determined moments, he frees himself and removes his bindings, including the duct tape and awful sock which has left his mouth coarse and dry. He screams for help and then returns to Lucy's side. Pushing the gun aside, he takes hold of her hand and painfully pleas, "Lucy... Lucy, please hold on baby."

Lucy squeezes his hand but doesn't speak. Her eyes are closed as she lies motionless on the carpeted floor. Justin feels helpless. His mind fills with thoughts of remorse, guilt and shame. He shouldn't have involved her in his nightmare. He shouldn't have had such a cavalier attitude toward the danger it represented to her. He should have protected her and now all he can do is call 9-1-1 and turn himself into the police. He initiates the call as he holds to her, engulfed with remorse and repentant silence.

XVII

All Roads Lead to Torrance

Midday street parking in front of Lucy's apartment is readily available as Hugh pulls into a spot only a few car lengths from the entrance. Standing on the sidewalk, he looks back, noting the proximity of the complex in relationship to the nearby park and his own home on the other side. Although he can't see his house, Hugh's familiarity with the area allows him to draw a straight line to it in his mind. Approaching the arched entry, he notes the building looks much like Justin described it to him. There's nothing exotic about the structure but it does appear to be clean and functional. The neighborhood is quiet except for the faint sound of distant sirens which Hugh didn't notice until he reached the entrance to units. Immediately after passing the mailboxes and entering through the arched entry, he comes upon a distressful sight. There's an elderly women in a white dress, standing hunched over, holding her left hand over an injury on her right arm. She's obviously hurt! The blood of her wound stands out against the white of her dress like neon in a darkened sky. Hugh's mind races with an appropriate response but based on his conversations with Justin, he surmises that this can only be one person. "Miss Mavis?" Hugh asks.

Kilborn's head snaps up and his steel blue eyes immediately lock onto Hugh as a Bengal Tiger onto prey. Without being able to identify the inquisitive face standing before him, Kilborn can only assume Hugh is a threat. He exposes the hidden flip knife held in the palm of his idle hand and lunges toward Hugh. The former Marine, although trained in hand-to-hand combat, is caught completely by surprise. He is only successful in blocking the bloody blade from cutting him before he falls backward onto the ground. His artificial limbs were designed for walking and offer little benefit as far as agility or making quick lateral movements. In a seated position, Hugh can only scoot backwards and away from Kilborn while pulling his jeans-clad legs in front of him. Kilborn slowly walks in Hugh's direction, oblivious to Hugh's prosthetic legs. His focus is placed entirely on trapping his victim, backing him against the string of mailboxes that will block any further retreat. With a complete disregard for potential consequences, the hubristic murderer is determined to kill this unknown intruder before completing his escape.

Kilborn removes his hand from his blood soaked arm wound and activates the voice recorder that he managed to hold onto in his retreat from Lucy's apartment. Stepping closer to his seated target, his mind flashes on memories of debilitating Dr. Klaudios by slicing into his legs. Rather than risk being struck by this stranger on the ground, Kilborn has determined he will cut into the hapless man's legs while he is defenseless and then finish him off as he thrashes in pain. Hugh's back reaches the mailboxes. He has nowhere else to go and his prosthetic legs do not provide him the ability to spring up like a cat and run away. Hugh appears to be massaging one of his legs as though he has a cramp, carefully watching Kilborn as he inches ever closer. Kilborn lunges toward Hugh once again.

Hugh, from his seated position is not as helpless as the knife-wielding man believes. He feints a feeble kick toward the attacker, distracting him for the brief time he needs to detach his opposite leg. Kilborn captures the bottom of the shoe kicked toward him, cupping it in one hand as he reaches from below and slices into the location of where his Achilles tendon should be. Hugh wily feigns injury, screaming "My leg! My leg!"

By the time it registers in Kilborn's mind that he's been duped and is attempting to cut into the titanium of an artificial limb, Hugh has successfully removed the other prosthetic and is now swinging it with the force of a baseball bat into Kilborn's face. By design, the socket of the limb is lightweight and hallow; it doesn't possess the necessary weight and substance to knock Kilborn out, but the force of the impact stuns him, and is successful in propelling him backwards onto the ground. The knife drops from Kilborn's hand, falling closer to Hugh. Still clutching the artificial limb as a bat, the two opponent's eyes meet. Hugh's nonverbal stare dares Kilborn to make a move for the knife but Kilborn is not in a position to challenge him. He has a bullet wound to his arm and is sprawled out on the ground in a long, leg-binding dress. His only option is to gather himself and flee. Kilborn picks up his voice recorder, pulls the dress to his knees and retreats into the street while Hugh continues to guard his position over the knife. With the sound of sirens growing closer, Hugh scoots to the entry wall and then stands up, resting his weight on the single limb. He is reluctant to reattach the other limb in the event he needs something to protect himself with.

Pulling up to the apartment complex in an unmarked police car are Detectives Fuentes and Barnes. They have arrived on scene in an effort to interview Mavis Kilborn but are not scanning local police channels and have no knowledge of the shots fired or the 9-1-1 calls initiated by Justin and several neighbors. They bring the cruiser to a stop in the middle of the road as they check to confirm the address. Darting out in front of their vehicle and sprinting down the street is an elderly woman with corpse-like makeup and what appears to be a blood-stained white dress pulled up to her knees. Under the arched entry stands a one-legged man holding a leg like a baseball bat. Fuentes looks at Barnes with his eyebrows raised, "Now do you wish you would have listened to my zombie story?"

Barnes smirks. "You want Olympic granny or the one-legged guy?

"The guy with one leg looks easier to catch—"

Barnes interrupts, "Okay you take granny and I'll take the guy with one leg."

Fuentes rolls his eyes at Barnes, exits the cruiser and begins to pursue the geriatric sprinter. About the same time local police officers arrive on the scene. Without knowing the details of the situation, the two detectives pause to confer with local police before proceeding.

Hugh, upon seeing the commotion, reattaches his leg and begins to search for Lucy's apartment on the first level. Although there are a number of units, only one has an old walker pushed to the side and the door wide open. Hugh slowly peeks into the room, "Lucy?"

"Over here Hugh! Hurry, she's hurt!" Justin yells out. Hugh hears the pain in his voice.

As Justin kneels over Lucy holding onto her wound, Hugh drops into a seated position beside him. "What kind of wound is it?"

"He stabbed her! In the gut. I couldn't do anything to protect her," Justin sobs... "He was going to kill her and she shot him. There was nothing I could do!"

Hugh places a compassionate hand on Justin's shoulder. "Dude, I know how you feel but the place is crawling with cops. You have got to get out of here! I got this!"

"How can I leave her?"

Hugh squeezes his grip on Justin's shoulder, "Focus! Stay on task. Complete the mission. You're the only one that knows who this guy is and you can't find him if they arrest you for murder. I got this! Move out!"

Without speaking a word, Justin takes a tearful glance back toward Lucy, removes his hand from her wound and Hugh quickly covers it with his own. Justin darts out the front door and retreats downstairs to the subterranean parking area, escaping through the back gate and into the park.

Barnes takes a few steps in the direction of the arched entry to the apartments when the Torrance Police began to swarm to the scene. Rather than chase down the curious individual with one leg, she opts to wait for Fuentes who is breathing heavy as he completes his sprint toward her. "Shots fired!" warns Fuentes, weapon already drawn.

Barnes pulls out her sidearm. They cautiously enter the apartment compound, seeing several Korean faces appear in their doorways, some speaking English and others a mixture of both their native and an adopted American dialect. Their excited voices and gestures make their message clear as they point to Unit 21; the door is open and a raggedy walker rest on its side near the entrance. Barnes approaches the door, risking a quick peek into the room before entering and shouting, "Police! Hands where I can see them!"

Fuentes follows her into the apartment, scanning the room for others who may be there.

A man, seated on the floor, holds a bloodied hand over an inert woman's abdomen, immediately places his free hand in the air with his fingers spread "I want to see both hands in the air!" shouts Barnes.

The man glares defiance at her. "You can shoot me if you want but I'm not letting go of this wound until someone takes my place."

The two lock eyes in a momentary silence. Barnes speaks to him with a very clear and firm voice. "If you even flinch, I'm going to shoot you. Do you understand?"

Hugh nods his head to affirm his cooperation but as Barnes circles around to Hugh's backside she discovers the gun near Lucy's other hand. "Gun!" shouts Barnes as Fuentes rushes to her side and two police officers hurry in from outside.

Three guns menacingly point at the couple on the floor while Fuentes checks the rest of the apartment. "The rest of the unit is clear," reports Fuentes.

Barnes continues with her instructions, "After you are face-down on the carpet, my partner is going to handcuff your free hand, and then you are going to relinquish your hold on the wound while this officer takes your place. Understand?"

The suspect nods again in agreement and is quickly handcuffed. An officer drags him away from the injured woman while Fuentes secures the weapon near her hand. Another officer attends to the injured woman for a brief time until paramedics arrive and take over, eventually sliding her onto a gurney and wheeling her out. Fuentes follows them out in order to obtain a test swab of the woman's hand for gunshot residue.

Hugh, who is now bound and seated on the other side of the room, doesn't display a thread of emotion until Lucy disappears out of his sight. He's uncertain as to Lucy's condition and can only imagine the turmoil Justin is in. After Fuentes returns to the room, Barnes identifies herself and Fuentes to him, then sends two uniformed officers to Miss Mavis's apartment to assess the situation there. She presses Hugh for information. "How do you know the injured woman and what is your part in all of this?"

Hugh is cautious in his response. He has no idea the detectives have identified Travis Kilborn as their primary suspect. His only thoughts are of protecting Justin from being captured while the real murderer is free. Having come face-to-face with Kilborn himself, he realizes the danger Kilborn poses. "Her name is Lucy, she's my friend. I came by to visit and I was attacked by someone in a white dress I thought I recognized ... but I don't know who or what it was."

"The person in the white dress attacked you? Do you have any idea who it was?" asks Barnes.

Hugh shrugs with uncertainty, "Initially I thought it was Lucy's neighbor, Miss Mavis, but after the way I was attacked... that was no old lady."

Barnes and Fuentes eyes meet when Miss Mavis's name is mentioned, a silent but obvious communication between the two of them that confirms Hugh's suspicions. He continues to explain, "She came at me with a knife and I hit her full force with my prosthesis. It only knocked her backwards. And she had a predatory look about her that I've seen before."

"Is that when you shot her?" Barnes asks.

Hugh looks at Barnes, surprised by the question, "No, she had her hand over the wound until she attacked me. I only got a quick look, but she appeared to have a gunshot wound through her arm."

Barnes continues to press the issue. "Have you shot people before? You know what that looks like?"

Hugh, indignant says. I served two tours in Iraq, so yes, I know what gunshot wounds look like." Then more humbly, adds, "I've never been in trouble."

Hugh offers no further information or clarification and the detectives don't ask. His identification was checked and came back clean. He's clearly not the suspect in this crime but his involvement mandated that they spend more time questioning him. To permit the crime scene investigators to continue processing the evidence, Hugh is taken away by one uniformed officers and retained in custody at the station.

With Hugh out of the room the detectives begin to more closely examine the scene. There's no evidence of a forced entry so the attacker must have been someone she knew, or thought that she knew. Based on the raggedy walker at the door and the wounded person fleeing the scene, it appears the perpetrator gained access to the apartment by means of a disguise. Handcuffs, two cable ties, a wad of duct tape, a sock and a stun gun are sprawled about the floor. It's apparent there was a third person in the room. The cable ties were obviously used and the roll of duct tape will contain hair samples and DNA from the other victim. Fuentes, after a quick examination of the room injects, "How much you want to bet the person he tied up was her boyfriend?"

Barnes snorts a brief laugh. "How much you want to bet the boyfriend is Justin Manus?"

"I was thinking the same thing, but how did you come to that conclusion?" Fuentes asks.

Barnes smiles. "English is my primary language and I can read. Look who this card is addressed to."

"Fuentes examines the attached envelope. "Aside from the addressee's name," he says, "there's nothing on here but bumps. What is this? Braille? The woman is blind?"

"Yeah, the collapsible white cane with the red tip on the kitchen countertop is a pretty good indicator."

"Okay," says Fuentes, irritated, "You're doing that devil thing to me again."

Barnes laughs, "All right, I'll stop being the devil if you stop with the zombie stories."

"Hey," Fuentes displays the toothy grin of a used car salesman, "there's a big difference between the two because my stories are true. I told you... I've seen things."

Fuentes continues with his summation of the evidence, "Here's how I see this. The two officers we sent to Mavis Kilborn's apartment report that the elderly woman is alive and well but somewhat incoherent. They suspect her grandson, Travis Kilborn, had recently visited there. I think Travis Kilborn is the 'woman' in the white dress who attacked the Iraqi vet. Kilborn has to have known Justin Manus was here otherwise he wouldn't have needed a disguise to fool a blind woman. So, Manus lets Kilborn in; Kilborn follows the MO he's familiar with... stuns the victim, handcuffs him, binds his legs with cable ties and then secures a sock in their mouth with duct tape. With Manus helpless on the floor, Kilborn intended to make him watch while he dissected his girlfriend.

What Kilborn didn't know was the blind girl is a Kung Fu master and she—"

"Wait, wait, wait!" Barnes interrupts, laughing at Fuentes obvious theatrics. "You had me until the Kung Fu part. Obviously she either had a weapon on her or she was able to retrieve one during the altercation. I suspect she was stabbed before she shot back at him. What I can't figure out how a blind woman can hit a target and someone like you barely qualifies on the firing range every year."

Fuentes looks down, shaking his head and smiling, "I see how you are. I knew the devil was going to pop up and say hello again."

Barnes looks at Fuentes with snake eyes. "Somebody's got to keep you in line, otherwise you'll be off claiming Kung Fu zombies are on the loose in L.A.. Back to business Fuentes. Do we have Manus's DNA on file?"

Refocusing on the matter at hand, Fuentes nods. "His DNA sample was taken after his domestic violence arrest."

"But that's a misdemeanor. I thought DNA was taken only after felony arrests."

Fuentes shrugs while replying, "It's common to pad domestic violence cases with a felony charge, knowing it has no chance of conviction. Once the DNA is taken, it's in the system for good. Even when the person is proven innocent and all charges are dropped, their sample stays on file. People have sued to get it removed but with no success."

Barnes focusing on the photo on the counter, "This must be Kilborn. His picture is very similar to the one we have from his driver's license."

Fuentes agrees. "Yeah, I noticed that. Why would a blind woman have a photo of Kilborn? Manus had to have used the blind woman to gain access to it which means he's probably been tracking Kilborn since after we questioned him at his apartment."

"You think he's been out here that long?"

Fuentes nods, "I'm the one that checked all the phone records. I know for certain he wasn't making calls to her before he disappeared. He has a few items of clothing in her closet and the extra toothbrush in the bathroom is probably his, but I don't think he lives here."

Barnes, bites on her lower lip, staring into the distance, deep in thought. "Hmmm, she finally says, "he probably lives right here in the neighborhood. We need to find the man before he gets himself killed trying to do our job."

—⟋⟍—

Kilborn, after escaping from the man with the artificial limb, streaks across the street as the sounds of sirens grow nearer him. He risks a backward glance as he runs and observes the man defiantly staring at him; still clinging to his other prosthesis as a weapon. As the sound of sirens becomes more pronounced, Kilborn seeks refuge in a neighboring apartment complex. Inside the structure he lowers his dress, composes himself and reassumes his role as an elderly woman. Passing by the list of residents on the directory, he makes note of the name Scott in Unit 75. Scott would become his temporary identity until he escapes to his white truck, parked a few blocks away.

Almost all the apartments in the area have a community laundry room and Kilborn waste little time finding it. Residents rarely, if ever, stand guard over their clothing while it's being cleaned. The washers and dryers are nearly always located in a dank and uninviting place, positioned in the rear or downstairs and away from the normal pedestrian traffic. In a basement room located within the subterranean parking structure, Kilborn finds what he's looking for. Within minutes he's able to locate a pair of jeans and a plain, dark T-shirt that comes close enough to fitting him. He snatches them out, quickly slams the dryer door closed and pushes the start button so as to reactivate the tumbling cycle.

The generic clothing he has selected is absent of unique features or designs that would alert the real owner should he encounter him. He changes clothes, using pieces of the white dress to bandage his arm, others to remove his makeup. The remainder of the blood-stained garment is deposited into the covered trash receptacle. There's little concern about leaving evidence at this juncture. His real identity is now exposed by the evidence left behind at the apartment. He can never return to his life as Travis Kilborn.

The wound in his arm is painful but his need to escape and the subsequent adrenaline rush temporarily serves as a deterrent to his pain. It's apparent the bullet entered under his raised right arm as Lucy fired at him from below. There's a small hole on the underside and an exit wound the size of a large coin on the exterior. For now, all he can do is clean it and keep pressure on it with a tourniquet. The dark colored T-shirt should adequately keep it from being discovered for a brief time.

Having just completed his change of clothing and disposing of evidence, Kilborn hears the unmistakable jingle of police gear rattling down the stairs. He glances outside the laundry room and around the corner but another officer stands only thirty feet away at the exit to the unit. There are a couple of chairs and old magazines littered about the laundry room. Kilborn sits, positioning his wounded arm away from door, placing his feet up on the other chair and begins to flip through the pages of the magazine. The officer cautiously rounds the corner and carefully examines Kilborn.

Kilborn, assumes his "Hiker Bob" persona, looks up at the officer, smiles and greets him with a friendly, "Hey."

The police officer, seeing both hands in plain view, stands back from the unknown white male with his hand positioned on top of his holstered weapon. As his eyes dart around the laundry room, the officer asks, "You live here?"

Kilborn displays a quizzical expression replying, "Yeah, my name is Scott. I'm in Unit 75. You down here lookin' for a car thief? Three months ago I had my car broken into..."

"Excuse me, sir!" interrupts the officer as he speaks into his shoulder radio to another officer who must be positioned on the first floor near the mailboxes. "Scott's" identity checks out but as a precaution, the police officer instructs him to return to his apartment while the buildings in the area are searched. Kilborn complies with his instructions and walks upstairs while the police continue checking the parking structure. Walking past the evacuated pool area, Kilborn spots a pair of flip flops and a baseball hat. He adds the items to his wardrobe and continues to walk out the side exit. At the end of the breezeway he has only a couple of options. The police have blocked off the area leading back toward the garage, leaving him only the street exit where two vehicles are parked. One is a utility truck and the other a bottled water delivery truck.

His only choice is to boldly walk toward the street and hope one of the vehicles is empty. Out of his peripheral view, he can see the utility truck and immediately to its side is an individual with a hard hat and brightly colored vest. Only the bottled water carrier remains. Although the street is speckled with police cars and a helicopter flies above, the police officers have retreated to the interiors of the buildings. If any remain on the street, Kilborn doesn't bother to look for them. His attention is entirely focused on the brightly colored truck in front of him. As he approaches the vehicle he can see the driver's side window is down and it's likely the door is unlocked. It makes perfect sense to him as he briefly reflects on the subject. In the history of motor vehicles, he has never heard of a water truck reported stolen.

Rationalizing the situation further, Kilborn thinks of the many stops demanded of the driver combined with his requirement to stay on schedule. It would be an easy and convenient habit to keep the keys in the ignition. His hand touches the handle and with confidence he pulls the door open and slides inside the cab. Everything is as he hoped—except the keys are missing. He looks in the obvious places; on top of the sun visor, inside the glove box and even under floor mats—nothing! He's discovered the only responsible bottled water truck driver in Southern California.

A police officer exits one of the buildings and eyes Kilborn from across the street. Kilborn cannot afford to panic. The loose papers and clipboard on the seat provide a perfect prop for Kilborn's ruse. He gathers them together, flipping through the pages as the officer approaches with her hand on her holstered sidearm. Kilborn entirely ignores her until she is right in the window. Standing close she orders, "Sir, place both your hands outside the window so I can see them!"

Kilborn reverts back to his "Hiker Bob" persona and looks at the officer with an expression of complete surprise. As the role of his halfwit character demands, he sticks his arms out to each side like a scarecrow, exposing only his left hand to the officer while extending his right hand toward the passenger side. "Both hands out the window, sir!" demands the officer.

Kilborn looks at the policewoman with desperation, "I can't reach the window on the other side, ma'am."

The officer's mouth twitches as she restrains a smile, "Put both your hands out this window sir."

Kilborn complies and after seeing he has no weapon in his hands, she instructs him to hold the top of the steering wheel while she opens the door and inspects the interior of cab. Seeing no evidence of weapons or anyone resembling the initial description of the suspect, she closes the cab explaining, "We had a shooting in the neighborhood earlier and we're making sure everyone is safe. Have you seen anyone in a white dress while making your deliveries?"

Kilborn can feel the blood from his wound begin to drip down his side. If this conversation lasts longer than a couple more minutes, he may expose himself as the subject of their search. Slightly shaking his head he responds, "No, no… I can't say I remember anyone in a white dress."

The officer appears satisfied and no longer perceives Kilborn as a threat. She begins to scan the surrounding buildings, instructing Kilborn, "Well, you need to vacate the area as soon as possible."

Kilborn explains he has only a few more entries to make in his paperwork and he'll be ready to move out. The officer acknowledges his statement and retreats back into one of the buildings.

The street appears, once again, to be absent of uniformed police. The driver of the water truck will be out any minute. Kilborn realizes there's only one option now. Police officers respond to distress calls as quickly as possible. When they arrive on the scene, speed is of the essence and they do not concern themselves, nor are they cited for parking violations. They often drive their automobiles pointing toward the curb at haphazard angles and sometimes leave them in the middle of the street. The vehicle barely comes to a stop before the officer jumps from out of it, leaving the keys in the ignition. But all police vehicles are equipped with tracking devices and have a large number painted on the rooftop as a means of identification. Only an idiot would attempt to steal one. To borrow one for a three-block ride under the present conditions may not be a bad idea.

Kilborn wipes off the excess blood from his wound with the papers on the front seat, displaying little regard for the mess or evidence he leaves behind. To the contrary, the soiled dress left in the laundry room and the blood soaked papers in cab will serve to taunt the police officers who had him within their grasp and let him go. Kilborn uses the truck's mirrors to check the position of the helicopter and then calmly exits the cab, walks to nearest police car, and sits in the driver's seat. The keys are in the ignition as he suspected. Kilborn inspects his surroundings. An officer emerges onto the street from behind but he is too far away to recognize Kilborn and pays no attention to him as he drives away. Less than sixty seconds later, Kilborn parks the cruiser in plain view outside the police search perimeter, and then walks back to where his truck is parked. As he drives away, securing his escape, the pain returns to his arm. Kilborn laughs aloud as he fondly holds to his voice recorder. His only regret is not quenching the growing hunger of his beloved recorder as it feeds on the horror of his victims.

XVIII

Tested by Fire

L ucy awakes, trembling under a lightweight blanket. Her cold and dark world is accessorized with the pulsations, beeps and clicks of unfamiliar machinery. Immediately frightened, she resists the temptation to scream. Her mind swirls within a drug-induced fog; her weakened body fights being overwhelmed with helplessness. Retreating deeper into her soul, she summons the inner warrior of her personality; that part of her that became so viable after she lost her eyesight. Lucy clinches her fist under the blanket as another machine, much more demonstrative than the others, announces its presence with more urgency. Lucy attempts to move but the sharp pain in her abdomen immediately restrains her. Within moments, the offensive noise is eliminated and a hand is gently placed on top of hers. There's a soft, lilting and reassuring voice speaking through the fog... something about surgery... a hospital. The message darts around her mind, finally alighting at a place of rest in her consciousness that she's alive. She's safe.

In an isolated curbside parking space across from the hospital, Travis Kilborn, emerges from his white truck dressed with coat and tie and disguised as Dr. Klaudios. He has only murderous intentions on his mind; Justin must be punished and Lucy must die. In the few hours since his brazen escape from Lucy's apartment, he has successfully cleaned and patched his arm with an over-the-counter medical glue used for closing wounds. The medicine chest remedies do little to curb the pain but the bleeding has stopped. He can tolerate the sting long enough to complete this undertaking.

Kilborn's time invested in the hallways of the family law court taught him several viable lessons. One insight he quickly attached himself to is that one needs only to blend into the environment, observe and listen. Many have smugly stated the words, "If only these walls could talk." Kilborn's experience is that they do talk. They never stop talking. Even without sophisticated listening and recording devices one has only to be an ambiguous figure, perched in plain view while pretending to be oblivious to the many conversations bantered all around them. He simply has to blend into the recognizable environment of the hospital and become like a familiar piece of furniture that one sees everyday but gives little thought to. Once in position, the ambiguous voices emanating from careless conversations will provide a pathway to Lucy.

Approaching the hospital, Kilborn observes that much of the traffic streaming into the facility centers around two portals; the main entry and the Emergency Room. A conveniently displayed directory serves to map out his destination and escape route. To gain access to Lucy, he will work his way into the surgical section of the hospital and then into the Intensive Care Unit, both located on the third floor. Once he kills Lucy, he can escape through the basement morgue by accessing the area where bodies are picked up by funeral home transport.

Although the time of day may allow him access to Lucy's room with a visitor's pass, he has little intention of being scrutinized or tip off security as to his entry. The busyness of the ER makes it a more viable choice. Kilborn slips into the waiting area and blends in among the throng of inflicted and their companions without difficulty. Mild hysteria permeates the room like a vapor from a scented candle. There are the very loud and vocal; a baby incessantly cries at full-lung capacity while a drug addict sits handcuffed to a wheelchair, muttering nonsensical phrases until he can no longer contain his rage. He screams a cluster of profanities toward anyone or anything upon which he is able to focus. The sole security guard stands dutifully at his side; not so much to control his outburst but to assure others of their safety. Moaners contribute an underlying background noise to the atmosphere. Their slow paced, unrelenting guttural emissions provide the percussion section for this symphony of suffering. Several televisions are mounted to the walls with the volume turned off. Some mindlessly stare at the soundless screens as a way to detach themselves from the discomfort of their surroundings; others bury their noses in reading materials. It's difficult to gauge and separate the sane from those afflicted. A woman stands alone near a window nodding and whispering. She could be a devout religious person praying for another or simply a lunatic attempting to communicate with apparitions she sees within the glass. A young man is ushered in holding a blood soaked rag to his head. For a very brief moment, he captures the attention of the room and then all look away, either out of disinterest or to refocus on their own affliction. There's an odd, nearly hypnotic ebb and flow to the room. Only the scrub covered hospital workers seem immune to it. They remain unruffled and businesslike, methodically shuffling each patient from one point to the next. Their reality is that very few die and the vast majority get better. Those in discomfort, however, are submerged within a framework of pain and it's difficult for them to perceive of anything beyond their moment of suffering.

The double doors leading to the interior workings of the hospital are marked with a sign, "Authorized Personnel Only." It frequently swings open to allow hospital workers and patients access to the treatment and services they require. Positioned behind a large artificial plant, Kilborn waits for the next opportunity and then nonchalantly follows behind a hospital worker and into the clustered interior hallways that are lined with more patients. He has learned from his acting classes to keep his head up and act as though he possesses the deed to the facility. The scrub-cloaked hospital workers pay him little regard for the moment as most are preoccupied in their immediate tasks. After only a few steps into the hallway, signs provide directions to an elevator and he immediately enters the first door to open. The oversized entrance to the lift is clearly identified as a service elevator but once the doors close behind him, no one remains to question or correct him. The convenience offered by the hospital is that everything is clearly marked and identified. The informational tags next to the buttons for the matching floors confirm "Surgery" as being on the third floor.

The bulk of surgeries are performed during normal business hours so by this time in the late afternoon, the hallways are empty. Strolling casually down the corridor, Kilborn eyes a security camera posted at a walkway intersection ahead of him. He cannot aimlessly blunder through the hospital without a security badge and not expect to be questioned. Turning onto an unmonitored hallway, he stops by a room with what appears to be patient or administrative files attached to the door in angled slots. He removes the file jacket from one and a few interior pages from another. Neither item will be missed for the time he intends to use them. With his new prop in hand, Kilborn walks past the security camera seemingly preoccupied with the contents of the file. He uses the folder as a shield to cover his chest and prevent anyone from noticing his absence of security clearance. After a couple of turns, he finds what he's looking for. There's a small sign on a door labeled, "Doctor's Lounge" but it's secured with a numbered key pad. If he can get inside, he will have access to lab coats, security badges and scrubs. A nearby nurse's station and security monitor prohibit him from attempting to force the door open or jimmy the lock.

Standing in the unmonitored section of the hallway, Kilborn removes the jacket to his suit, folds it over his arm, turns the corner and walks directly toward the nurse's station. He is betting on the theory that if he gives the woman behind the counter only a moment to make a decision, she will decide in favor of caution. There is almost a military mindset in the operating room and the surgeon is the senior ranking officer in this scenario. Even outside of surgery, the unspoken rank that a surgeon possesses spills into the hallways. Nurses rarely challenge their authority and that is what Kilborn is relying on. Seeing a well-dressed man approaching her station while examining a file provides all the visual clues she should require. The nurse will be forced to assume the unknown man is a physician and that his security badge is attached to the coat folded over his arm. Kilborn has two objectives in mind. The first is to remove one of the lightweight chairs that are stringed along the wall and the other is simply to allow her to become acquainted with his appearance. Once he has the chair, he will reposition it around the corner in the unmonitored hallway and wait.

Kilborn continues to study the file in his hand as he approaches the station with a determined stride. He looks up only once about a dozen feet away, glancing at the name "Alex" prominently displayed on her scrubs. The petite, exotic-looking female nurse appears to be a woman of mixed ancestry, possibly Black and Asian. Her deep brown eyes are intently focused on Kilborn but he does not intend to engage her in even the slightest dialog. He provides her with only a forced smile and immediately turns his back to her as he reaches for a chair. It is at this moment that Kilborn is only able to wish for a video of her expression. The professional caregiver's eyes scan the backside of this unknown person but she cannot detect evidence of a security badge. He didn't request assistance, nor did he attempt entry into the ICU so in the two seconds she has to evaluate the situation, she chooses to remain silent. She risks only embarrassing herself and there are far too many other important matters for her to contend with at the moment than having to deal with a rogue physician intent on relocating furniture. After taking only a few steps back down the hallway, Kilborn smiles, knowing that his ploy was successful.

With the chair repositioned around the corner and out of view from the security monitors and nurse's station, it now becomes a waiting game. Kilborn restrains his anxiety while anticipating the development of his next opportunity. Several minutes elapse. Each time Kilborn hears footsteps or notices someone in his vicinity, he becomes absorbed in the medical file and by doing so, reduces his visual profile to near obscurity. He is hoping for a late surgery and an opportunity to follow a physician into the doctor's lounge. Several more minutes elapse until finally, a figure emerges in the hallway. This could be what Kilborn has been waiting for. She's nicely dressed, professional in appearance and wearing a white lab coat. Kilborn ignores her as she walks by but intently listens to her conversation with the nurse. There's an emergency surgery coming in from the ER and she's the surgeon on-call for the day. The exchange of information with the nurse is brief as the physician heads back toward the doctor's lounge. Kilborn stands but before he steps into the main hallway, the surgeon turns back in the direction of the nurse and seeing no one around asks, "What is the zip code here again?"

The nurse speaks in an elevated voice to insure that the doctor can hear her from the slight distance, "It's 90505."

Moments after, Kilborn hears the clicking of the numeric keypad and begins to initiate his original plan to follow the physician into the lounge. He takes a step and then stops. In an instant moment of clarity he realizes that the nurse did not offer the street or city information, but only the hospital's zip code. The digits she revealed must be the numerical combination to the lounge! Kilborn pauses, and then returns to his seat. After waiting a few minutes, he walks to the door of the doctor's lounge, enters the code and is more than relieved to hear the clicking reward of an open lock.

The doctor's lounge is unimpressive at best. It's a small room with a couple of couches arranged around a television set. There's a computer terminal set up in one corner and a coffee pot in the other. A single door with a small sign, "Lockers" directs one to a side room where the surgeons are able to change their clothing. Inside, the locker rooms are divided by gender but in the immediate common area there is a metal rack with stacks of unisex hospital scrubs assorted by size. The scrubs are all the same color and have the hospital name imprinted on them. Kilborn is surprised to see a couple of lab coats with security badges attached, carelessly abandoned by their owners. His first inclination is to take one but none of the surgeon's photo ID's look similar to him, and it's likely the nursing staff is familiar with their names. He can hear the female surgeon through the paper-thin wall and risks asking her a question. "There are a couple of lab coats over here. Should I turn them in or leave them here?"

Her voice comes through the wall, "You must be new or from out of town. Obviously you can't wear your ID into surgery, so we leave them on the lab coat. Since we're local, we wear scrubs home and sometimes forget the lab coat. I have one over here too. Just leave it and they'll pick it up tomorrow."

Kilborn is relieved there is no tone of suspicion in her voice. He risks asking an additional question, "How will they gain access to the hospital without their security badges?"

The helpful voice on the other side of the wall responds, "The staff knows us pretty well but you'll be okay as long as you're wearing the hospital imprinted scrubs. No one will ask anything."

Kilborn thanks the physician for the information and quickly changes into the appropriate attire. With scrubs on, he adds a hair net and loosely hangs a surgical mask below his chin. As an added prop, he steals a stethoscope from the pocket of one of the lab coats and dangles it around his neck. After putting his leather dress shoes back on, he stuffs his necktie into one of the hip pockets. In this environment, Lucy's death has to be silent. Given a choice, he would much rather bathe in her screams but considering the circumstances, Kilborn will have to be satisfied with choking her to death with his silk tie. Satisfied with his disguise, he grabs the file he's been using as a prop and walks into the ICU.

Alex, the same exotic-looking nurse sits behind the counter as he passes her station. They do not exchange words but from his peripheral vision, Kilborn can see that she has given him an extended look. He cannot afford to be distracted by her at this point. He has his escape plan mapped out in his mind and if something were to go awry, he will head for the nearby stairwell, descend one floor and then pick up the elevator to the basement morgue. Kilborn places himself near the center of ICU, pretending to examine his fake file while looking for Lucy. He spots her within seconds but by this time, the nurse stationed at the entrance is standing and looking in his direction. He's uncertain as to her issue but he's determined to kill Lucy and get out as quickly as possible.

Alex continues to stand, focusing her attention on the unfamiliar surgeon. She is the daughter of a career police officer and grew up hearing suspicious characters described as "hinky" by her father. There is something definitely hinky about this doctor. Unlike other physicians and techs in the hospital, surgeons do not wear their stethoscope around their necks but place them in a hip pocket. It's an idiosyncrasy they adhere to, perhaps as a way to set themselves apart from other medical professionals. All the nurses are aware of the practice. Another curious matter is this physician's street shoes. Surgeons don't wear street shoes into the operating room. They're usually expensive, not comfortable to stand in for several hours and they can easily become contaminated by body fluids and lingering smells. The third strike by this unidentified physician comes about as he enters Lucy's room. There's a security alert accompanied by photos of two men who may attempt access to Lucy's room. Although this mysterious surgeon does not match the description of either suspect, his actions prove sufficiently suspicious to the nurse. As Kilborn steps into Lucy's room, the diligent nurse picks up the phone and alerts security.

Kilborn, unaware of the nurse's call, calmly steps into the room and pulls the privacy curtain around the bed.

Lucy stirs. She's slightly medicated but is now completely conscious and aware of her surroundings. The distinct sound of the screen being tugged through the metal track above her bed can only mean she is about to receive medical attention. Lucy instinctively pulls the light blanket up to her chest and greets her visitor. "Hello," she says in a groggy but friendly voice.

There's no response to her greeting and Lucy's senses immediately go on high alert. She remains calm even though her anxiety level is quickly rising. "What are you here to do?" she says with as friendly a voice as possible under the circumstances.

Someone speaks softly, saying, "This will only take a minute," and gently lifts the back of her head and slips something—a bandage?—under her neck, and then crosses the opposite ends across the front of her throat and ties what feels to Lucy, like a simple knot. She draws in a deep breath and immediately recognizes the subtle but lingering scent of a woman's perfume, the voice, whatever this object is around her neck—it's not a bandage! It's Kilborn! She attempts to scream for help, but in that instant Kilborn closes the knot and chokes the word away from her.

Lucy gasps for air but the noose is too tight. She flails in the bed in an desperate effort to rid herself of the knot but Kilborn is kneeling above her, placing the entirety of his weight on the strangle hold. Lucy digs her fingers into the silk lasso but cannot relieve herself of its grip. Her beautiful brown eyes widen with fear and desperation.

A monitor alerting the medical staff to Lucy's vital signs is triggered and the persistent nurse who was suspicious of Kilborn, immediately rips open the curtain, "Can I help you, doctor?"

Kilborn, having been caught in the act of murder, sadistically looks back with a smirk, "I've got this nurse... I'm almost finished."

The petite woman raises her hand to signal another nurse who begins to broadcast, "Code Silver... ICU... Code Silver."

With a complete disregard for hospital protocol, the wily nurse attacks Kilborn from behind, jumping onto his back while attempting to force his release of the knot around Lucy's neck. In the process of the struggle, she opens Kilborn's arm wound and blood begins to trickle from the injury. She hits the wounded area with her clinched fist until Kilborn is forced to surrender his hold on the tie. Using his good arm, Kilborn swings wildly at the nurse, striking her across the upper body and sending her skidding across the floor. He returns to finish disposing of Lucy but the unrelenting nurse springs to her feet. Grabbing a food tray, she strikes Kilborn's wound with all the determination and force her small body is able to muster. The crushing blow sends him reeling in pain as he slams himself with his back against the wall. Kilborn looks back at the nurse, covering his injury with his opposite hand. "Get out of my way now or I'll slice you into little pieces!"

The nurse is crouched six feet away. Her eyes are aflame as she holds to the food tray with the determination of pinch hitter in a need of a game winning hit. With confidence that stems from a courageous gene pool she states with absolute confidence, "No way in hell!"

Kilborn is not going to win this battle and now too much time has elapsed. He must make his escape. He staggers past the obstinate nurse and out of the room but not before she gets one final lick in across his back.

No sooner does Kilborn step out of the room, the little nurse with the giant heart leaps toward the bed, removing the tie and reviving Lucy. "I've got you now sweetie... you're going to be okay!"

Lucy nods, unable to speak. She reaches up and wraps her arms around the nurse and tightly hugs her. The two warriors weep together. "I'm not going to let anyone get near you again, even if I have to work double shifts to make that happen."

Lucy can only express a distressed smile while squeaking, "Thank you... thank you so much."

Security rushes to the door only moments latter but by this time, Kilborn has left the ICU. Medical personnel point to the direction of his escape but he has a sixty-second lead and could be almost anywhere. The hospital is ordered on lockdown and the local police are called. Barnes and Fuentes are among the first to be notified and they arrive at the hospital near the same time as the first responders.

By the time the lockdown order is broadcast, Kilborn has already traversed his preplanned route down to the morgue. The details of the lockdown are not clear and cannot be communicated rapidly enough by hospital security. Most personnel know a lockdown has been ordered but few know the reason; fewer still have details as to the situation or a description of the suspect. The confusion works to Kilborn's advantage and provides him with a little more time. His original plan was to simply walk out of the morgue exit and return to his truck, but he can see the lights of emergency vehicles streaming in and converging onto the hospital parking lot.

The morgue has few visitors and a low volume of pedestrian traffic. Kilborn encounters only a single medical tech along the way. To the tech, Kilborn is a physician and an authority figure. He doesn't question his presence or even why he has his hand over his right arm. His only comment is to inform him of the lockdown and the necessity of exiting the building immediately in order to avoid being stuck in the hospital. Kilborn nods in appreciation and within a few steps, he has successfully exited the building. Outside, he realizes it would be too risky to attempt to walk across the parking lot under the increasing police presence and scrutiny. In the loading area sits a mortuary van and perhaps his easiest method of escape. Kilborn approaches the window only to discover the driver engaged in a text message exchange. He raps lightly on the window, standing slightly behind the driver's seat so as to keep his wounded arm out of view. The driver is slightly startled by Kilborn's presence but dutifully opens his window upon seeing what he perceives as a physician. "We're on lockdown." Kilborn states with a degree of authority. "Can I review your paperwork?"

The young driver appears a little frustrated, "I was told I could go. Is there a problem?"

He begrudgingly hands over the documents. Kilborn examines the mortuary driver's papers and then asks, "You're carrying two bodies?"

The driver nods to affirm the information. Kilborn continues with his ruse, "I'll need to check them. Is the back open?"

The young man nods again. Kilborn moves to the back of the van and opens the rear door. There are racks to hold as many as four bodies. The cargo section is separated from the passenger area with a divider and a small door that leads to the front of the vehicle. He jumps inside, noting by the clicking noise emanating from the front seat that the driver has returned to his text messages. With the driver distracted, Kilborn shifts his weight in a modified hop while still inside the van, simulating that he has exited the vehicle. He leans out the back door and shouts, "You're clear!" followed by two quick raps on the side panel. The door closes and in the driver's mind, everything checks out and he's free to go. He drives away completely oblivious to the fact he's carrying an extra passenger.

Back inside the hospital, Fuentes and Barnes have reached the security office and are reviewing the video footage while officers begin a floor-to-floor search. It takes only a few minutes to bring up the time and location of the incident in the ICU. From the point of origin the camera views are switched as they retrace Kilborn' route down the stairwell, into the elevator, and finally his exit from the morgue. A camera positioned in the loading area captures him entering the back of a van. Tracking the license plate to the vehicle's owner isn't necessary as the name of the funeral home is conveniently displayed on the side panel of the van. Judging from the time stamp on the video, the detectives determine Kilborn has a jump on them of approximately twelve minutes. An APB is issued for the mortuary van, officers sent to the site and a helicopter is dispatched to cover the area. Barnes and Fuentes rush to their vehicle in an attempt to catch up to the action.

The mortuary van pulls into a rear loading area at the funeral home. The structure resembles a large enclosed garage with parking space for three vehicles. The other two spaces are occupied by traditional-looking hearses that have been backed into their separate parking spaces. The enclosed structure allows for the discrete pickup and removal of the deceased while limiting the public's exposure to the dead. Generally speaking, people don't like to be confronted with the mortality of others or reminded of their own. Everyone is well aware of the reality but prefer it to happen out of plain view. During the fifteen minute ride from the hospital, Kilborn is tempted to exit the van during one its many traffic stops. In the end, he deems it a greater risk to expose himself and his bloody wound to a busy street filled with witnesses and potential captors. When he hears the garage doors open, he quickly nuzzles himself next to the door leading into the cab. The van comes to halt and he hears the driver's door as it opens and then closes behind him. Kilborn peeks into the front. Seeing the empty driver's seat, he scrambles into the passenger seat and pulls the van's inside door closed. He waits in the front seat to hear the back door open and times his exit from the van at the same moment to avoid detection.

Double doors lead into the interior of the facility. With the driver now safely preoccupied in the vehicle, Kilborn cautiously slips into the main hallway of the building. The offices, viewing areas and chapel are on one side of the structure and the services that process the dead on the other. The doors leading to the offices are locked and it appears the employees have gone home for the day. Kilborn is mindful he has only minutes to find an exit... one he can quietly escape through, one that doesn't signal an alarm. The first open room is the refrigeration unit with enough storage space to accommodate two dozen bodies. Judging from the exterior tags, only six of the shelves are being utilized. Gathered on one side of the room are three caskets. There is a narrow, horizontal strip of windows near the ceiling and no exit. Kilborn has to move on. This room is likely where the driver intends to put his new clients.

The next room over is obviously for embalming. The sign on the door labels it as the Prep Room, an area where most surfaces above the floor are stainless steel. Again, the windows are placed near the ceiling, designed more for privacy than a source of natural light. There's an exit door but it's clearly marked for emergencies and rigged with an alarm. He ducks into the room as he hears the clicking of gurney wheels and the driver approaching with the first body. Once Kilborn is confident the mortuary worker is busy with his task, he quickly moves down the hall. The next room is an office but its transparent, windowed door is locked. To his horror, the open curtain inside the office allows Kilborn a glimpse of a police car pulling into the parking lot! There remains only the break room and crematorium down the remainder of the hall. Escape is now going to be nearly impossible. He has to figure a way to either outwit or hide from his potential captors.

After the van driver exits through the double doors, Kilborn moves back to the cold storage unit. He doesn't have much time. The three caskets there are distinctly different; the first a richly polished wood, the second is an attractive but lower quality wood and the third is a very plain, reinforced cardboard. Only two of the caskets are occupied. A well-dressed elderly female has been placed in the ornate and expensive casket while a rather gaunt looking man lies in the other wooden casket. Only the least expensive unit is empty. Kilborn's first inclination is to attempt hiding inside a casket but it seems a little too obvious. He hesitates too long. The double doors open immediately down the hall to signal the near arrival of the van driver. Kilborn ducks under a table on the far side of the room. He can't see the funeral employee from his hiding place but he can hear him talking to himself. "Okay, sir, you're going into Unit Six. Unit Three goes into the casket and the lady goes on display in the viewing room for tomorrow morning. One casket goes in the hearse and the other goes to Pedro. After that, I'm outta here."

The driver wheels the embellished casket into the viewing area on the other side of the funeral home. As soon as Kilborn hears the unlocking click of the door that leads into that section of the building, he bolts from his hiding place and examines the remaining caskets. Both are now filled. After a slight struggle, he removes the gaunt man and returns him to a cold storage unit and then climbs inside, closing the lid on himself. If his strategy is successful, the driver will load his casket in the hearse and past the scrutiny of the police. Once they search the building and don't find him, they will have to conclude that he escaped from the van before it arrived at the funeral home.

Kilborn is nearly passed out from exhaustion as he feels the wheels to the gurney turning under him. It's been a very long day and he's lost a lot blood. He's weak. Near total darkness inside the casket and the gentle rolling sensation invite him to sleep. If not for the adrenaline rush surrounding his circumstances, he wouldn't be able to function. The rolling sensation stops. He overhears a brief conversation emanating from outside the casket but isn't able to decipher the exact words. He expects to hear the start-up of the hearse's engine and the motion of the vehicle but notes only the silence. *What is taking so long?*

Kilborn drifts in and out of consciousness, finally waking to a sensation of warmth. In a state of grogginess and in total darkness, Kilborn takes a moment to collect himself. His last thought was being in the back of a hearse but it seems so warm. "Is this black vehicle parked in the sun? I'm roasting back here!"

—ɯ—

Pedro runs the crematorium for the morgue. The bodies are most often taken from a refrigerated unit of forty-two degrees, placed in a casket and wheeled back to the retort which burns an average-sized corpse at eighteen hundred degrees for a little over three hours. The bodies are contained within a closed casket and both burn together. It's not Pedro's job to look inside the casket. He only checks the identifying tags on the exterior of the unit and matches them with his own roster. Once a corpse slides into the retort and the doors close, no human scream can be heard. The thick, heat retaining walls of the furnace and the all-consuming inferno nullify every noise except the gas fed whoosh of the flames.

Kilborn risks opening the lid of the casket and sees only a blinding light. The screams he emits equal any of those he preserved on his precious voice recorder. Only Pedro can save him from the flames that now lick the base of his coffin hiding place.

—ɯ—

Back at the hospital, Justin has been arrested while attempting to gain access to Lucy. Unaware of Kilborn's second attempt to kill her, he walked into the hospital under heightened security and was immediately identified and taken into custody. Alex, the nurse, was unable to convince security to bring him to the ICU but she did make a special trip to where he was being held. She let Justin know that Lucy was grateful that he came and that she loves him.

Fuentes and Barnes are notified of the arrest as they sit outside the funeral home contemplating their next move. Joining them are a half-dozen police units that have surrounded the facility and are currently awaiting orders. After a call to the owner of the mortuary, they discover there is one, possibly two employees that remain inside. Pedro manages the crematorium and the other person is a driver who may have checked out fifteen minutes ago. He has a couple of errands inside the building and then he has to deliver a casket to another facility in Long Beach. The owner provides the detectives with the cell phone numbers of both employees.

Detective Barnes calls Pedro's cell number and he immediately picks up. He's in the crematorium, finishing up his final cremation of the day. He states he's completely unaware of any other activity in the building. The detectives instruct him to lock the door and wait for them to come in. No sooner do they complete the call, when the garage doors open and a hearse begins to pull out from the garage. Police units are ordered to move in and the hearse is immediately surrounded by officers with their weapons drawn.

The astonished driver drops his phone in mid-text and displays his hands as ordered by the police. Once the driver is removed from the vehicle and handcuffed, the officers turn their attention to the rear of the hearse and the casket inside. When the lid is opened, several guns are pointed directly at a very dead corpse. Some of the officers smile in a release of tension; others continue to inspect additional areas of the vehicle. The hearse is clear but the young man is driving with a suspended license. They hold him until the funeral home manager or owner show up to claim the vehicle and the corpse. "Who else is in the building?" demands Barnes.

The nervous driver nearly stutters in his reply, "Only Pedro. He's the only one."

Barnes continues to grill the young man, "You didn't see a man dressed in surgical scrubs?"

"At the hospital… I saw a doctor at the hospital. He told me my papers were okay."

The young driver was clueless. An officer stands with him while the rest of the squad moves in to search the building. Each room is quickly cleared until they finally reach the back where the crematorium is located.

Fuentes instinctively stands to one side of the door while reaching for the doorknob. It's locked so he calls out, "Pedro! Open up! It's the police!"

The voice on the other side of the reeks of suspicion, "How do I know you're the police?"

"How else would we know your name?" offers Fuentes as an explanation.

The lock is opened and the police rush in but find no one but Pedro and a corpse burning in the retort. Pedro is a bearded man with a trim physique, wearing thick glasses, baggy pants and a wife beater T-shirt. He accessorizes his semi-gangster look with a dark purple bandana that is folded into a triangle and placed around his forehead, crossed over the top of his head and tied off in the back. A matching bandana is wrapped around his right arm. His hair is slicked back and sweat rolls from his face and body as a result of the heat generated in the room with the door closed. "Who's the person being cremated?" asks Fuentes.

Pedro shrugs, responding with a slight Hispanic accent, "He's from Unit Three but if you want to know the name I have to look it up."

"Did you see anyone in here tonight?" continues Fuentes.

"No, I'm pretty much alone back here," explains Pedro. "The driver dropped off a body to me not long ago but that's it."

"How many bodies do you have here?" injects Barnes.

Pedro directs his attention toward Barnes, "There were a total of six in the refrigerated area earlier today, four inside the units and two in caskets."

He begins to look at his fingers and count them out, "Let's see, the driver brought in a couple more and took out three. He put one in the viewing area, one in the hearse and one in the retort… that leaves a total of five in the refrigerators."

Barnes radios the officer standing outside with the young driver, "Ask him to describe Pedro, what he's wearing and how many bodies are in the facility."

There's an initial pause as the officer obtains the information. After the silence Barnes mutters, "Okay... yes, okay. Got it! No, that will do."

"Can you take me to the refrigerated units?" asks Barnes.

The detectives and a couple of the officers follow Pedro down the hall as he opens each of the twelve refrigerated units. To the detective's surprise, there's an extra body.

"Where did this body come from?" demands Barnes as she scowls at Pedro.

"I don't know, ma'am... I don't know. Let me look at the toe tag," he says, then, examining the information, continues. "Umm... this is the body that should be in the retort right now. I don't open the caskets, I just match the numbers and cremate everything together."

The detectives walk with Pedro back down the hall to the crematorium. Along the way, Fuentes spots a trail of blood drops. "Is it common to have blood spills on the floor like this?"

Pedro looks at the floor, "No... no... all the bodily fluids are taken care of in embalming. That looks pretty glossy still so it must be fairly fresh."

Fuentes orders the few remaining officers to stand clear of any blood and sends another to retrieve his kit so he can collect it as evidence. Standing back near the furnace, the two detectives look at one another, "What do you think?" says Barnes. "You think this could be our guy roasting in here?"

"I'm not sure," responds Fuentes. "I mean, it does make some sense because the ICU nurse reported she reopened a wound somewhere on the attacker. I wouldn't doubt that the blood is his but how did he end up in here? If he's been bleeding all day, he has to be weakened by it. Maybe he just passed out."

"Regardless," says Barnes as she turns toward Pedro, "I need for you to shut this down so we can retrieve the evidence."

Pedro shakes his head from side-to-side, "Ma'am I would love to help you but if I shut this down without a court order, I would be breaking the law. I could end up losing my job for exposing the business to all sorts of legal things. Even if I could shut it down, it would take at least forty-five minutes for the retort to cool enough to get you to the body. That corpse has been in there for an hour and if it takes another sixty minutes to get a court order, there's not going to be much evidence left."

Barnes and Fuentes look at one another and come up with nothing. In desperation she turns to Pedro, "Is there anything you can think of to help us out?"

Pedro thinks for a moment, "Well, I know you fine officers would never ask anyone to break the law… but we do have contingency plans in the event of an earthquake or power outage. I also know that if you saw a crime being committed, you'd have to make an arrest so maybe if you and your fellow officers were to busy yourself with police work, I may be able to go outside and check on a thing or two. You get what I'm saying?"

The two detectives nod in unison and Pedro disappears out of the building. Fuentes looks at his watch. Several minutes pass but finally there's a power outage and both the gas and electricity are shut down. The emergency lights come on right away as they wait for Pedro to return, but he's never seen again. A man matching Pedro's description and having a wound to his right arm is reported to have stolen a car only a few blocks away.

—m—

Pacific Daylight Savings Time has switched back to Standard Time and the days seem much shorter as Lucy ventures out for the first time in weeks. The daytime temperatures are still warm and it's refreshing for the young teacher to feel the sun on her face again. She follows a familiar path up to the bench where she first met Justin and sits. It's approaching noon when she hears a series of steps approaching.

"Do you mind if I sit on your bench or will you call the police?" speaks a familiar voice.

Lucy smiles, "Well, as long as you don't sit too close to me, it should be okay. I do have a boyfriend you know."

"I heard about him," responds Justin as he nuzzles up to Lucy. "I heard he's the criminal type. Didn't he get out of jail today?"

"He must have had a good lawyer to have all the charges dropped," Lucy teases as she pulls Justin in to kiss her.

"Hey Kids!" A voice rises from the bottom of the knoll, temporarily interrupting the couple's intimate moment.

"Oh my God!" Lucy shouts. "Was there a jail break? I have both of you back?"

Hugh wheels up the knoll and stops directly in front of their bench. "My other leg is still in the shop so I'm wheeling it for a while. They've advised me not to use it as a baseball bat in the future. I was thinking of getting a cane. I'd look cool with a cane, right?"

"Of course you would!" Lucy smiles. "Now do you mind turning your head so I can kiss my boyfriend?"

Hugh chuckles, "I don't mind you kissing, it's the noise you both make when you kiss that's disturbing."

"Push that man back down the hill, honey!" Lucy comments.

The trio laugh together in the shared comment. There's a moment of silence while all bask in the warmth of the sun and the pleasant atmosphere of the park. Lucy breaks the silence as she squeezes her boyfriend's hand, "I love you Justin."

Justin puts his arm around her, leans his head next to her, I love you too, Lucy"

"Okay, okay... that's enough! I'm leaving."

Lucy and Justin laugh as Hugh makes his departure. "I love you too, Hugh!" shouts Lucy before he gets too far away.

"He says he loves you back," explains Justin. "He used sign language."

"He's a good friend, isn't he Justin?"

At the bottom of the knoll and several steps toward the park's grassy outer perimeter, Hugh passes a man with frizzy hair and wearing a beret-styled cap. In spite of his odd manner of dress and the slight hunch to his posture, he would have gone unnoticed had he not turned and menacingly stared in Hugh's direction.

Humanity knows despair. Tenacious few claw through uncertainty and darkness, possessing the resolve to keep going; one more step, one more day, one more breath. In the absence of light and hope, motivation is fed from a level of the soul that screams for justice, survival, restitution or revenge. Most are crushed and silenced forever. Those whose hands breach the tomb of hopelessness, their plight continues with personalities ravaged by pain and contaminated by grief. It is only the rare soul who emerges from the depths of despair who dares to forgive, love, and dream again.

Made in the USA
Charleston, SC
28 April 2014